THE NUMBER OF LOVE

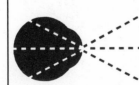 This Large Print Book carries the
Seal of Approval of N.A.V.H.

THE NUMBER OF LOVE

ROSEANNA M. WHITE

THORNDIKE PRESS
A part of Gale, a Cengage Company

GALE
A Cengage Company

Farmington Hills, Mich • San Francisco • New York • Waterville, Maine
Meriden, Conn • Mason, Ohio • Chicago

Copyright © 2019 by Roseanna M. White.
Unless otherwise indicated, Scripture quotations are from the King
James Version of the Bible.
Scripture quotations marked NKJV are from the New King James
Version®. Copyright © 1982 by Thomas Nelson, Inc. Used by permission.
All rights reserved.
Thorndike Press, a part of Gale, a Cengage Company.

ALL RIGHTS RESERVED
This is a work of historical reconstruction; the appearances of certain
historical figures are therefore inevitable. All other characters,
however, are products of the author's imagination, and any
resemblance to actual persons, living or dead, is coincidental.
Thorndike Press® Large Print Christian Historical Fiction.
The text of this Large Print edition is unabridged.
Other aspects of the book may vary from the original edition.
Set in 16 pt. Plantin.

LIBRARY OF CONGRESS CIP DATA ON FILE.
CATALOGUING IN PUBLICATION FOR THIS BOOK
IS AVAILABLE FROM THE LIBRARY OF CONGRESS

ISBN-13: 978-1-4328-6749-2 (hardcover alk. paper)

Published in 2019 by arrangement with Bethany House Publishers, a
division of Baker Publishing Group

Printed in the United States of America
1 2 3 4 5 6 7 23 22 21 20 19

To David,
who always knows the question to ask
to make me see my own heart
and who never lets me get away with
the easy answer.

In the day of my trouble I sought the Lord;
My hand was stretched out in the night
  without ceasing;
My soul refused to be comforted. . . .

And I said, "This is my anguish;
But I will remember the years of the right
  hand of the Most High."
Psalm 77:2,10 NKJV

There were others — a brilliant confeder-
acy — whose names even now are better
wrapt in mystery.
Winston Churchill
in *The World Crisis,* on Room 40

1

Old Admiralty Building
London, England
25 September 1917

The numbers marched across the page in a glory all their own. Margot De Wilde stared at them for a long moment, looked back at the German telegram sitting on her desk, and then scratched a new number onto the column. Almost there. Almost. She darted a glance out the window.

The sun grew mockingly brighter. When last she'd looked up, it had been only the slightest glimmer beyond the buildings of Whitehall. Now it had cleared them. Soon the day shift would arrive, and if those on night watch hadn't cracked the new codes, there'd be an insufferable amount of jeering.

Her lips twitched. She did her own share of jeering when it was another team that failed to crack the Germans' new codes

9

between midnight and eight in the morning. And her fair share of shoulder slapping and approving nods when she came in of a morning to find the night watch happily asleep at their desks, the new cyphers waiting.

"Come on, come on, come on." At the desk beside her, Nigel de Grey fisted his fingers in his hair. Months ago, he had been the star of the office, having been the one to hand the Director of the Intelligence Division the telegram from Zimmermann that had brought America into the war. The Germans had thought themselves quite clever, trying to strike a deal with Mexico to bring them into the war on their side. But the Americans hadn't taken too kindly to it when they were informed that *their* territory was to be Mexico's reward.

But that wouldn't matter today, not if their night shift failed to break the daily code for the second night in a row.

"We'll get it." Remington Culbreth indulged in a long stretch, squeezing his eyes shut. "We're too close not to." He'd grown more serious over the last three years, his smiles less frequent. He'd never said why, but Margot suspected it had something to do with the photograph in his wallet that he didn't take out to look at anymore.

10

She heaved a sigh and let her eyes slide shut. Let the intercepted telegram that had come zipping up the pneumatic tubes just after midnight play before her eyelids. Let the numbers she assigned to correspond to each word go from marching to jumping.

"That's what we said last time. I'll not go out hanging my head again. Dilly didn't stop mocking me about it all week. I —"

"Got it!" Margot surged forward as those beautiful digits settled at last into her mind in the proper order. Ignoring the rustling of her colleagues as they slid over to look at her work, she picked up her pen again and scratched the final numbers into the column on her paper. Checked it against the telegram. Breathed a laugh as she finally was able to scrawl the decrypt of the intercepted message onto the fresh sheet of paper.

"Ah." De Grey gave her shoulder a friendly *whack.* "Good man."

Were Maman in her usual spot at the desk by the door, her lips would have thinned at that compliment — as they always did every time the other cryptographers seemed to forget she was a young woman and not another of them. But Margot grinned. And took a moment to be grateful that the secretaries weren't obliged to take a night shift once a week like the cryptographers were.

Victory sang through her veins. *Three, nine, twenty-seven, eighty-one, two forty-three . . .*

"You have saved us infinite shame, De Wilde." Culbreth nodded, almost smiling, and then wilted onto his desk. "Have we time for a nap, do you think?"

"Doesn't sound like it." Margot could just make out the first of the morning's footfalls on the stairs and the *ding* of the lift. The Old Building, or OB as they often called it, was coming to life.

She took a moment to order her desk while her colleagues did the same. To obliterate, as much as possible, the evidence of a night hard at work — empty cups, the stale crust of what had been a sandwich, eraser leavings. They had no cleaning ladies in the hive of Room 40. No girls to wheel in tea carts and wheel out the dishes. What tidying got done, they did themselves. The decrypt she'd just managed in hand, she stood and turned to her mother's desk. Her eyes skimmed the message again. It was a list of ships, possible targets for the U-boats that day. *Boynton. City Of Swansea. Dinorah.*

Nothing out of the ordinary. She'd long ago given up wishing they could send a warning to each one. They couldn't — it would mean revealing to Germany that they intercepted their every message. It would compromise Room 40. It was a form of *yosu-miru,* as the terms of the game Go stated it — a move that might require sacrifice, but for a greater purpose.

Besides, all the ships in all the world knew the dangers, with unrestricted submarine warfare declared in January. They would be on their guard. They would travel in convoys.

But still, an average of fifteen per day would still sink. Margot dropped the list of U-boat targets into the basket and tried not to do that math. *Fifteen a day, average of thirty days in a month, four hundred fifty ships every month for the nine months since the declaration, equaled four thousand fifty ships lost.*

The door opened, and Margot looked over to see Admiral Blinker Hall stick his head in. "How did the night go, chaps?"

De Grey motioned to Margot and, presumably, the decrypt she'd just carried over. "De Wilde cracked the cypher. Haven't had time yet to apply it to whatever has come in since."

The Director of the Intelligence Division — fondly referred to as DID by everyone

13

under his command — sent her an approving smile. "Well done, Margot." He blinked a few times and moved his gaze to take in de Grey and Culbreth. "Will you be leaving, then? Knox was just behind me, and Adcock too."

Culbreth nodded and stood, placing his hat over his blond hair in the same motion. De Grey smoothed his tormented locks back down to hide the hours of frustration his fingers had left in them. "I need to speak to Dilly first, but then I shall, yes."

Hall arched his brows her way. "Margot?"

"I'll wait until my mother arrives before I go." Otherwise she might miss her on the walk to their flat, and then Maman would worry all day. No matter how many times she'd made the trek on her own, no matter how old she got, still her mother worried.

Her prerogative, Maman claimed.

A useless argument, Margot knew.

"Very good." Hall moved away a step, then pivoted back again. "I have an appointment first thing this morning with Lady Hambro and a new recruit. If by chance they arrive before the secretaries, could you direct them to my office?"

"Of course." Margot smiled at her superior and then kept it in place as her colleagues followed him out — Culbreth ap-

14

parently aimed at the stairs, de Grey turning the opposite direction, toward Room 53, which Dilly Knox had claimed as his domain. Among the first cryptographers to be recruited to Room 40, Knox had already been firmly established here when Margot arrived. Though absentminded about practical things, he had a head for mathematics. Margot had liked him from the start.

Silence fell. Crystalline, perfect, and soon gone as the pneumatic tubes delivered another passel of papers with a *thunk*. Pulling in a long breath, Margot took a moment to wish they'd finished the codebreaking an hour earlier. She would have let herself into Knox's chambers and made use of the bath he'd had installed. The very thought of gallons of warm water surrounding her was enough to make her shoulders sag. The flat she shared with her mother had a private bath, but the room was always frigid, and there was never sufficient hot water.

She fished the papers out of the tube and sent the holder back down to the basement, where a team was constantly at work typing up the intercepted telegrams from Germany and sending them wherever in the intelligence department they needed to go. A glance at the latest collection told her that if she sat down to get started on it, she'd still be at it come noon.

Tossing them instead onto another desk, Margot stood, stretching as she did so, and wandered to the window. She was more accustomed to this view than any other in London — the familiar rooflines of Whitehall's buildings, the street that led to Charing Cross Hospital with its banner demanding *Silence for the Wounded.* A twenty-minute walk would lead her to her flat, and another twenty would take her to where her brother Lukas lived with his wife and their little daughter. A short tube ride and she'd be in Hammersmith, where said wife's extended family always welcomed her, any time of day or night.

She leaned into the window frame and touched the tips of her fingers to the glass, still cool from the night. Sometimes it was hard to remember that this hadn't always been her world. Even harder to contemplate was that it wouldn't *always* be her world.

Not once this war was over. The war she spent her entire focus on trying to end.

She let her fingers fall from the glass. It *had* to end. The Central Powers must be stopped. And with the United States now fighting on the side of the Allies, with their fresh soldiers and virtually limitless resources, surely it would happen soon. The war would be over. And then . . .

And then . . .

What? Maman would want to go back to Belgium. The longer they were here, the more wistful she became about the house in Brussels that was no doubt currently occupied by some faceless German officer. Lukas and Willa had already decided to split their time between London, Brussels, and whatever cities wanted to host the two renowned violinists on tour.

But Margot? She drew in a long breath and held it while her mind churned out a prayer. *Nine, eighteen, twenty-seven, thirty-six, forty-five, fifty-four . . .* What would be left for her in Belgium? There was her childhood friend Claudette — assuming they would even still like each other, after living such different lives since the De Wildes sought refuge in England. Would a university welcome her there? As a student — or as a professor, eventually? Or would the world expect her to be a typical girl, too busy thinking about needlepoint and knitting and finding a husband to care about academic degrees?

The numbers came to a screeching halt in her head, as they always did when she contemplated a future like that. No, domestic "bliss" would be torture. She'd be a dunce of a housewife. What she needed was something intellectually stimulating with which to fill her days after the war was over. Something in academia, most likely. In mathematics.

Here. In London, if they would let her stay after the war was over. Here, where she'd first tasted the freedom of being who she was.

Muffled voices came from the hallway. One male, one female. Margot tilted her head to better hear them. Lady Hambro and DID? No, it wasn't Hall's voice that said, "Just *knock,* Dot."

Nor, for that matter, was the head of the secretaries called *Dot.* And she certainly never sounded as uncertain as the voice that replied, "But the sign says to ring the bell. . . ."

Margot's lips twitched up. Yes, each and every door along this hallway had a sign that said No ADMITTANCE. RING BELL. But not a single door actually *had* a bell. One of their little jokes, meant to dissuade anyone who didn't belong from interrupting them.

But it was probably Hall's appointment. Margot strode to the door and pulled it open, noting that it made the girl jump. The man did nothing but turn to look at her.

Siblings, she'd bet. They shared rich

brown hair and striking silver-blue eyes ringed by dark lashes. The man, probably mid-twenties, had a knot on his nose that all but shouted that he'd exchanged a few fisticuffs in his day. He wore a naval uniform. The girl, probably around nineteen, took a step back and cast her eyes down at the floor.

Given that she'd been up for twenty-four hours, the smile Margot managed to summon was small. "Are you here to see DID and Lady Hambro?"

The girl seemed to be trying to vanish into the polished wood floor. Her brother cleared his throat and nudged her forward. "Yes, she is. Miss Dorothea Elton. Applying for the position of secretary."

Three years ago, Maman had been the only secretary in the department, and she'd been hired more as a means of getting Margot here than because the then-boss wanted anyone from the outside coming in. Now there were nearly twenty other females employed by Room 40. They were full of giggling and gossip and tips for keeping one's dress fashionable even with the shortages.

Margot found the lot of them baffling — and new hires nearly intolerable. New ones always thought she was one of them, to be chatted with.

She despised chatting as much as she despised knitting.

She nodded to the man — Lieutenant Elton, if her guess on their relationship was correct and her glance at his uniform accurate. After stepping out into the hallway, she motioned the two to follow her to Admiral Hall's office. "Lady Hambro is not in yet, but the admiral asked me to show you to him." That news delivered, she set off at a brisk pace. Once she delivered them to Hall, she'd go downstairs. Maman should be here any moment. If they didn't pass in the halls, Margot would wait at the front door for her.

"Oh . . . well . . . thank you. I mean . . ." Miss Elton's voice shook. Nerves, no doubt. Though she'd better get a handle on them, or she'd never survive the interview.

For that matter, who had recommended this girl? The secretaries' names were all submitted by other Room 40 staff, and then they were vetted and interviewed by Lady Hambro. Perhaps someone here knew the brother, the lieutenant. It was as likely as anything.

And none of Margot's concern. Having reached the admiral's door, she rapped her knuckles on it twice. After Hall's "Enter" sounded, she opened it and motioned Miss Elton in.

The admiral offered a smile, but he aimed it at Margot rather than the new recruit. "Thank you, my dear."

"Certainly." Duty done, Margot spun away.

And nearly collided with Lieutenant Elton, who was, inexplicably, right behind her rather than where he'd been a moment before, two steps to the left. She sucked in a breath and sidestepped him. "Excuse me."

He slid in front of her again. "Belgian?"

She lifted her brows. Her accent was scarcely noticeable anymore, she'd thought. Not nearly so pronounced as Lukas's or Maman's. Her English was as fluent as her French had ever been. She even dreamed in it, most of the time.

And what business was it of his? "Antarctican." She prepared herself to stalk away . . . but there was something about the grin he gave her. Something that said he appreciated her answer.

Margot sighed. She'd always been drawn to anyone who actually enjoyed her sense of humor. She supposed she could stand to be friendly. For a minute, before her exhaustion fully caught up with her.

He held out a hand. "I'm Drake Elton.

Have you a name?"

She blinked. It was a question stupid enough that it should have made her itchy. But he'd smiled at her Antarctica quip, so she'd keep playing along. "No, my parents forgot to give me one. It's a great tragedy. I've been answering to 'you, girl' all my life." She extended her hand too, but not with a limp wrist, as women usually did. She held it out to shake.

He breathed a laugh and shook her hand. "All right, You Girl. I'll simply astound you with my powers of deduction." He made a show of concentration — pursed lips, narrowed eyes, and fingers pressed to his temples. "Given that lovely hint of an accent, I would guess Wallonia or Brussels."

Apparently Drake Elton wasn't a complete idiot. A corner of her mouth pulled up. *"And, actually. Not or."*

"Two homes, or did you move?"

She tilted her head to the side. A clever question. The answer would tell him quite a bit about her family's station. "Two."

Elton leaned against the wall, exaggerated concentration fading into an easy smile. "Which one did you prefer?"

Not the question she would have expected, exactly. But an easy one to answer. "The one in Louvain."

Being not-an-idiot, he would be familiar with the name *Louvain* — the place that had become synonymous with the German army's brutality. The place that was now more pile of rubble than actual town.

But his face didn't settle into lines of horror. Acknowledgment flickered through his eyes, and his smile lost a single degree of its ease, but he held it in place. "What do you miss most about it?"

She drew up straighter. Occasionally people asked her about her former home — what it had been like, how they escaped the destruction, whether the German occupation had been as cruel as the papers reported. But no one had ever asked her *that,* and she didn't have a ready answer — a strange state, for her.

Memories crowded, shouting to be recalled above the others.

The pastries from the bakery down the street. The library at Papa's university. The old schoolroom where tutor after tutor had fled in exasperation when she'd insisted — and proven — that she knew just as much already as they did. The mountain of books and newspapers and articles they'd lost in the fire when the soldiers invaded.

Strange. Just a few minutes ago, she was thinking of how she didn't want to go back.

Now, in her mind, she had done just that. And her lips curved up. "The tree in our back garden. There was a bench under it — the best place in the world to read."

His smile brightened again, went warm, invited her to say more.

Maybe she would have, had voices not been echoing down the corridor. But the last thing she wanted was the secretaries to see her talking with a smiling young man and mistake it for something inane, like flirtation. She'd be drilled by them for weeks. So she nodded and stepped away. "If you'll excuse me. It seems everyone is arriving for the day."

He pushed off the wall. "Aren't you going to tell me your name before you go?"

Perhaps her smile was a bit impish. And perhaps she took a bit too much joy from saying, "No." Perhaps she would if he actually ever asked her for it. . . . "But you're a clever man. You'll work it out."

If she'd been too impish, he apparently didn't mind. His laugh followed her down the corridor.

It took her only a moment to dart back into Room 40 and gather her things. By the time she exited again, though, the lift had opened and spilled out a veritable sea of codebreakers and secretaries, all chattering.

Margot aimed for the stairs, jogging down them with more of a bounce than she usually had after her once-weekly night shift. The energy would fade soon, but with a bit of luck she could ride it through the walk home.

Maman was just gliding through the doors, her beautiful face lighting in a smile upon spotting her. *"Bonjour, ma petite."*

Margot smiled. She returned the greeting in French, let her mother enclose her in a quick embrace, and then pulled her chin out of Maman's hand when she tried to examine her face far too closely.

"You have shadows under your eyes," Maman said, still in French.

Margot shook her head. "I'm tired," she answered in English. "But I am well. Do you need me to run any errands this afternoon?"

Maman shook her head too, but it looked far different than Margot's mechanical motion would have. All smooth elegance and grace, her every movement. Even dressed in a simple cotton blouse and grey wool skirt, Sophie De Wilde looked exactly like what she was — a gentlewoman, the beauty of her day, a lady to make heads turn wherever she went. One of refinement and elegance that war shortages and a menial job couldn't hide.

"I left a meal on the table for you. Eat it before you go to bed, *ma puce.*"

Margot pressed her lips against another smile. Her mother still seemed to think that she'd let herself starve if she didn't issue that command. As if Margot were not the one to prepare half the meals — sparse as they were. "I will." She leaned over to kiss her mother's satiny cheek. "Have a good day. I'll see what's to be found in the shops this afternoon."

Maman gave her a pointed look. "We both know you will be right back here by two o'clock. But we are dining at your brother's tonight, do not forget. We must leave at a decent hour."

"*Oui,* Maman." Her bed calling all the louder from down here, she stepped away. "I'll see you later."

"Rest well."

Margot slid her hand into her pocket to reassure herself that her key was still there and set off for their flat. A meal, some sleep, a chilly bath. Then she'd be back here, where she belonged.

2

Drake Elton stared down the hallway, half a grin on his face, long after he'd been left alone by the nameless girl with the impossibly dark eyes. It was the eyes that had done it — that had made the questions surge to life in his mind.

Who was she? What was her name? And the more important one — what thoughts raced through her mind to make those dark eyes so deep?

Questions were old friends. Questions kept him alive. And in this particular case, it shouldn't be *too* difficult to find the answers.

Of course, even if he didn't manage it on this visit, it wouldn't mean bullets whizzing at his head or cuffs threatening to encircle his wrists. But the questions were no less interesting for being a bit less urgent. He leaned a shoulder into the doorjamb and called those dark eyes to mind again.

She had a wit to match the eyes, the type he most preferred. Antarctican, indeed. His lips refused to lose their grin. Though her accent was so faint it was scarcely there, discernible only in a few vowels, he'd recognized the French Belgian in her. She'd probably been young when she came to England. Maybe at the start of the war, when the rest of the refugees flooded the country? Probably, given that she was from Louvain. If so, then she must be around Dot's age, or a little younger even. To look at her, he hadn't been able to peg that. Her skin was smooth, but those eyes . . .

She must be trusted implicitly to work here, that much he knew. And Hall had called her *my dear* — an endearment that some men might apply willy-nilly to any female they knew, but not DID. DID never did anything willy-nilly.

At the same moment, he heard the lift *ding* and Hall's door open and shut quietly. Drake pushed off from the wall and turned toward his superior. If the interview was over already . . . But when he turned to look, Hall's expression seemed pleasant enough. No scowl, no exasperation.

Please, Father in heaven, let Dot find favor here. Drake's fingers tightened around the hat he held.

Admiral Hall inclined his head, indicating something beyond Drake. He half turned even as female voices flooded the hall. Two women, both in their late forties or early fifties, were exiting the lift, laughing. The one on the left had dark hair, dark eyes — though not *so* dark — and a face of utter elegance.

The other he recognized as Lady Ebba Hambro. The woman who, if all went well, would soon be the one to demand his sister get up every day and get out of the house. Come here. *Do* something.

Not that Dot didn't *do* plenty — but nothing that would put food on her table while Drake was gone.

If Father were still alive, he would hate that it had come to this. That the shipping business once so prosperous now rested at the bottom of the Atlantic, victim to U-boats. That his daughter had to work to survive.

But it could be good for her. *Would* be. He'd have to cling to that.

The women paid him no particular mind. The pretty one just slid through the same doorway You Girl had first emerged from, and Lady Hambro charged right past him, her sights set on Hall. "Is Miss Elton here already?"

Hall nodded and indicated his office. He said something to the lady — too quiet for Drake's ears to pick up — and motioned her in.

Then he met Drake's gaze and jerked his head to the side.

Yes, sir. He followed the admiral into another room, still night-dim but for the light coming through the windows. Once Drake had shut the door behind him, his shoulders relaxed a degree. "I haven't had the chance to congratulate you on the promotion, sir."

Hall waved that off. "You leave again for Spain tomorrow?"

He had to force his fingers to remain loose and easy around the brim of his hat. He nodded. He *ought* to have left a week ago, but their aunt had been all aflutter about evacuating London, and he'd had to see to Dot. She'd refused to go with Aunt Millie. The war had already forced her from her haven once, she'd said. She'd not leave a second home for it. Which meant she had to find a way to support herself if she stayed. "Thank you for the extra time, sir."

"You earned it. Besides, you would be distracted in the field if you were worrying after your sister."

"I won't be now, I assure you." Assuming

Dot got the position here. *Please, God. Please.* Everything else they'd tried had been a bust. "She's a good worker. Trustworthy. I know she comes off as awkward, but with Lady Hambro's discipline giving her incentive —"

"Easy, Elton." Hall's lips settled into a smile that matched his instruction. "Your sister will be given a chance. What she does with it, of course, is up to her."

Thank you, Lord! Drake's shoulders sagged. "You have no idea how grateful I am."

"Of course I do. Now." He reached into his uniform jacket and pulled out a folded paper. "Our sources indicate that the huns will be trying to get their hands on some of the Spanish wolfram."

"Wolfram." Drake's brows furrowed. "That's a metal used in armoring, isn't it?"

"That's right. And as a neutral country, Spain shouldn't be selling its wolfram to anyone — Germany *or* England. But of course, that won't stop the Central Powers from trying to purchase it." Hall's eyes flashed. "And if by chance we can catch them taking it and intercept it . . . well then, we're within our rights to confiscate it for our own use."

Clever. Drake nodded. "If it's to be found

in Bilbao, I'll find it."

With a nod, Hall held out the paper he'd withdrawn. "Thoroton's reports on your work have all been glowing."

Drake tucked it into his own pocket. It would have what information he needed before meeting up with the head of operations in the Mediterranean, Charles Thoroton, but it would be sparse. Most of the information on the subject would be sent to Thoroton in code, and he'd see each agent had just what was needed, no more.

"Thank you, sir. I'm only glad my mother's family connections can be helpful." He'd been a bit surprised when he'd been ordered off the *Royal Oak* within a month of enlisting, but Thoroton, also known as Charles the Bold, had quickly explained himself. They needed men on the ground in Spain, gathering information, and Drake was a prime candidate. After attending university in Bilbao, he knew each alley and warehouse . . . and all the officials, thanks to his *abuelo*'s connections. It had been a simple matter of pretending to have changed his focus in university and enrolled in more classes. "I won't let you down, Admiral."

With a few rapid blinks, Hall chuckled and turned toward the door again. "You haven't yet." He paused with his hand on the door. "If your sister fits well in this position, then perhaps you can tell her in a few months that you are one of my agents. In the meantime, Lieutenant, it is best you simply claim that you're being sent back to your ship."

"Not a problem, sir." He would, in fact, stop on his way out of the city at one of the little closets of a room that Hall rented and exchange his naval uniform for his usual civilian clothes. Drake knew that Hall would continue to route any letters Dot wrote to him on to Spain via Thoroton. And any letter he wrote back would similarly be put in with the rest of the navy's post so it would work its way to her through the expected channels.

Frankly, he couldn't imagine *ever* telling Dot what he really did. She was anxious enough at the thought of his being in the navy. Even prior to that, she'd been worried by all the time he spent at their grandfather's in Spain. If she realized that their half-Spanish heritage had made him a prime recruit for the Admiralty's intelligence-gathering operations, she may never be able to breathe normally again.

As his superior exited the room, Drake took one more moment to be grateful. For now, at least, Dot would have a bit of income to support her and a position that would make her feel a part of something. There may even be new colleagues who, with a bit of luck, might become friends.

Maybe he'd return to England next time and find her actually willing to step outside her flat without his having to use a crowbar to accomplish it.

With that happy thought buoying him, Drake slipped out of the room too and found a corner in which he could wait for his sister without being in the way of the men now filing in. Most wore the "Wavy Navy" uniform of the Royal Naval Volunteer Reserves. The pattern of interlocking rings on their sleeves put one in mind of waves, hence the nickname.

But Drake knew very well these weren't navy men. They were professors and German experts and bankers and businessmen — anyone with a knack for finding patterns and turning them into words. These were the men making sense of all the German telegrams that were being intercepted. The decrypts from this signal intelligence — SIGINT — were passed not only up the chain of command to Jellicoe, the First Sea Lord, but also along to Thoroton in Spain. And the information Drake and his fellow agents found in the field — human intelligence, or HUMINT — was, in return, sent back here for Hall to use in conjunction with the SIGINT.

It was quite a system they'd built. Drake couldn't begin to fathom all that went into keeping it running smoothly, but this building gave him a peek. All these chambers with their signs proclaiming them off-limits. The basement below that he knew was filled to overflowing with incoming signals, dark rooms, and storage. Hundreds of people coming and going, men who had left their normal positions to help their country.

A number of women were coming in, too, in pairs or sets. Their heads more often than not were bent together, laughter on their lips.

But he didn't see *her* again. All of these women had the look of typical English lasses. Not like the dark-eyed girl at all.

He ought to have asked Hall who she was. Then he could have answered her challenge within minutes. Perhaps even found her again and greeted her by name before he left.

Ah well. It hardly mattered. He'd be leaving again tomorrow and would spend this evening with his sister, so he didn't have time to get to know her better anyway.

Still. He had a feeling those dark eyes

wouldn't leave his memory any time soon.

DID's office door opened again at last, and Lady Hambro led the way out. She was, praise God, smiling. And even clasping Dot's hand in her own. "That's no matter at all, Miss Elton," she was saying as they stepped into the bustle of the hall. "Many of our secretaries don't know the first thing about typing when they begin. But I'll turn you into an expert in no time. As long as you show up in the morning and determine to give your best while you're here, we'll get on well."

Poor Dot. Her smile wavered even as she nodded. "Thank you, my lady. I'll . . . I'll not disappoint you."

"Good." With a brisk motion, Lady Hambro patted Dot's arm and then released her. "I'll let you enjoy your day with your brother. Just come in tomorrow at eight-thirty. That room there." The lady indicated one along the corridor. "Ignore the sign and let yourself in. I'll be waiting, and we'll begin your training."

Dot nodded. "I'll be there." She clamped her lips shut, but Drake knew well what had nearly slipped out. *I promise.* The assurance she always felt she had to tack on whenever she was telling *him* she'd do something like this.

Worry nibbled away at his relief. What if she couldn't do it? He knew she'd manage it tomorrow . . . but the next day, and the next, and the next? What if instead of getting easier, it got harder?

Lady Hambro vanished into the room she'd pointed out, and for a moment, Dot just stood there, adrift in the sea of Wavy Navy men streaming by. He could see her struggling for control — her chest heaved with a few breaths, first uneven and then *too* even as she counted them in and out. In and out. Then, finally, she lifted her chin and looked around for him.

Drake waited until she spotted him before stepping forward. He wanted to help, to rush in to protect or shield as he'd always done when they were children. But he couldn't do that now. It wouldn't help her, ultimately. She had to learn to get along on her own.

Blast, but he wished Nelson hadn't gotten himself killed at the Marne. Wished he hadn't joined up at all. He should have just stayed at home, married Dot like they'd planned. Then his sister would have had a reason to remain in the house, matters to attend there. And Drake wouldn't have to worry about her each and every day while he was off in Spain.

She gave him a smile that very nearly covered the panic as she wove her way through the crowded hall toward him. "It went well! I begin tomorrow."

"Excellent. I knew you could do it." He took her hand, squeezed it, and tucked it into the crook of his arm as they turned. "This will be good for you, Dot. I bet you'll soon be writing to tell me about all the new friends you've made."

"Oh . . ." Her fingers dug into his arm. "I'll just pray for *one* friend, for now."

Drake bit back a sigh. Her prayer was not because she hadn't the faith that the Lord would send her more, but because she lacked the faith that she could *cope* with more. "I'm sure the Lord will provide." He always did. First a friend in their neighbor, Ada, when they were small. And then even an honorable young man who wanted to protect and cherish her in adulthood, in Ada's brother. Blasted war, taking that chance from her.

"And I should write to Ada when we get home. Tell her I found a position." She angled a teasing smile up at him. "Have you any message you'd like to include for her, brother dear?"

"Certainly. Ask her if the chauffeur at Ralin Castle ever got to drive a Renault."

"Drake."

"What?" He grinned down at her. "No telling the next time I'll make it to the Cotswolds, but if she's to be there for the duration of the war, she could well run into the chauffeur."

"You're hopeless."

"I believe the word you're looking for is *sane.* Glad as I am that you and Ada have always had each other" — at least until Ada and her parents had fled London soon after Nelson was killed — "you know very well I can't tolerate her for more than an hour at a clip."

"Well, you *could* if you just *tried.*"

Exactly what he was looking for in a wife — someone he had to *try* to like. Rolling his eyes, Drake led his sister toward the lift. "Let's not ruin a perfectly good day with talk of Ada. What would you like to do in my remaining hours of leave? Catch a show? A moving picture? Perhaps take a turn through the museum?"

"I think . . ." Dot pursed her lips as she considered, sending her eyes up to the ceiling. Drake braced himself, fully expecting her to say she'd prefer something at her flat: for him to read to her, or make a meal for themselves at home, or do a crossword puzzle. But instead she grinned. "A moving picture. I haven't been to one for ages."

Perhaps Drake's smile was as much relief as actual pleasure, but if so, his sister didn't point it out.

Maybe she *would* be all right in this new position. Maybe it would stretch her just enough. Maybe the firm but fair authority of Hall and Hambro would be just what she needed.

Maybe he'd have only simple things to worry about while he was away . . . like the German agents out to identify and eliminate him. Far more easily managed than a sister who was afraid to leave her flat.

Water. It closed in around him. Rushing, thundering, filling his vision and his lungs and his every sense. Black and turbulent and overpowering. He thrashed against it, trying to find his way to the surface. But the depths sucked at him as the ship went down. They reached greedy fingers toward him.

He could hear only the roar of the water, but he could imagine the rest. The screams of the other passengers. The shrill whistles. The hundreds of feet pounding toward the lifeboats.

He sucked in a breath and coughed. Coughed until the blackness cleared and

40

blinding white replaced it and he convulsed his way off the pillow. His hands found not the wood of the lifeboat's sides, nor the life vest he'd snatched, but rather the cot of the hospital bed he'd been in . . . how long now? A day? A week?

Boynton. He coughed again and cursed the very name in his mind. Cursed the blasted U-boat that had fired its torpedoes at it. Cursed the order that had told him to be on it.

Another cough came from the bed beside his. He peeled his eyes open to see his neighbor wiping at his mouth. Their eyes caught. The other fellow jerked his head toward the game board he'd set up on the rickety table between their beds and lifted his brows in question.

They hadn't told each other their names. What did it matter? They'd play a few rounds while they were both in hospital, then they'd go their separate ways. The end.

Anonymity. His best friend.

He nodded and, after convincing his diaphragm to relax, swung his legs over the side of the cot.

How long before he could get out of this place? He had to get back to his flat. Check for messages. Get word to the Continent that he would be delayed.

41

Try to determine if the High Command had purposefully tried to kill him.

"You take black today."

He nodded and accepted the little velvet bag of game pieces. He'd always preferred black. Something about making the first move made the whole game seem more conquerable.

"I usually prefer black," his neighbor said. With what might pass for a smile on his lips, he shoved a handful of disheveled hair out of his eyes. "But you seem a good bloke."

"Do I?" His voice sounded scratchy and hoarse to his own ears. And his lungs still burned.

The other chap laughed, until he too lapsed into coughing again for a moment. Pneumonia — that's why he was there. *Pneumonia.* The same word the doctor had muttered to *him* as the primary fear after his ordeal.

"You're right. Hard to say, isn't it? We're all good. We're all bad. The hero in our own stories. The villain in someone else's."

It sounded like something Heinrich would say — but his brother had always wanted to be the hero in *every* story, his own and every other. "I never pretend to be the hero."

The bloke lifted his water glass in salute. "Smart. Why bother? Sometimes . . ." His gaze went distant, cloudy. As troubled as the waters that sucked down the *Boynton.* "Sometimes I wonder if I'm even still alive. Maybe I drowned. Maybe I'm just a ghost. *Yūrei. Le fantôme. El fantasma. Das Gespenst.*"

His lips turned up. Heinrich could keep his heroic tales. "I always liked the ghost stories best."

His companion took a sip of the water. "They're the only stories based in reality these days. More men are dead than alive, it seems. Everyone is gone. *I'm* gone."

He wasn't. And yet he had been for years. He reached a shaky hand for his own water glass and lifted it. "The wisest way to be. Already dead. Just a ghost." He took a sip and then eased the cup back down. "I'll call you Yūrei."

Yūrei chuckled. "Suits me well enough. And you? The French or Spanish or German?"

He spoke them all fluently. "Your choice."

"Hmm." Yūrei shook the white stones from his own velvet bag into his hand and placed them on the intersections of the lines on his side of the game board. "Das Gespenst. In honor of the U-boats that landed us here."

Das Gespenst. "That'll do." He slipped

43

the last of his game pieces onto the board and made his first move. And tried not to curse the U-boat again. Or the High Command that had first ordered him on the *Boynton* and then ordered it sunk. Why? Had he lost their trust? Or were they simply incompetent, one department not communicating with another?

His fingers tightened around his black stone. He would have to assume the worst. And then prove to them that he was still useful.

They'd made no more than four moves each when the nurse came in, a clipboard in hand and a smile on her face. "Good news for Mr. Walsh and Mr. Williams. You both get to go home today."

So much for anonymity. But . . . no. He preferred Das Gespenst, really. He'd do well to remember that a ghost was all he could afford to be. He coughed again into his handkerchief and let all the tasks awaiting him fill his mind.

First and foremost, get in touch with Berlin.

His lungs burned. His chest ached. And his spine had no interest in straightening. He'd served them well all these years, hadn't he? Why would they have decided to take him out?

He nodded at Yūrei. "After the game?"

3

Margot put down her pen and stretched out her lower back, knowing well it wouldn't be so sore if she would listen to her mother and mind her posture. And she *tried.* But over the course of the day, she always ended up hunched over her desk.

The walk home would loosen all her tight muscles though. Not that it was time to go home yet. She checked the dainty little watch on a pendant that her brother had given her for Christmas last year and saw that it was only noon. She'd made good progress today.

Noon. *Blast.* She'd been planning on pausing to eat, but if she did so now, she'd find herself surrounded by all the secretaries on *their* lunch breaks.

"Ah, what good timing today, *oui?*" Maman slid Margot's latest decrypt off her desk and gave her a far-too-knowing smile. "You can eat with us."

She stifled a groan. Barely. "But I really ought to get through one more telegram —"

"Nonsense." Obviously not trusting her to do anything other than pick up her next assignment and get to work, her mother tugged Margot away from her desk. "Come."

"But Maman —"

"Do not make me say it again, Margot. No matter how brilliant, you are still a young lady. You need to associate with other young ladies now and then."

Margot made no reply to that. There would be no point, and she wasn't one to waste breath that could be better spent on other words.

"Here." Maman bustled to her own desk, slid Margot's decrypt into the In basket, and handed her the neatly typed stack of papers from the Out basket. "Hold these a moment, will you? I need to deliver them to the commander on our way out." She reached for the bags that contained what little food they'd been able to find on their last trip to the shops. Grains were getting far too scarce. And sugar . . . sugar was a luxury Margot missed like nothing else.

Margot jostled the stack of typed decrypts until their edges all aligned. "I can run them over now." There'd be little hope of slipping away at this point, and no real purpose to it. And it wouldn't be too bad, if she could just sit with her mother and perhaps Lady Hambro. It was only the younger women, the secretaries, she'd rather avoid.

Maman made no objections as Margot slipped out of Room 40 and into the room across the hall, where Commander Willie James was bent over his desk. Up until a few months ago, it had been Herbert Hope at this desk, and Margot hadn't yet grown accustomed to the style of their new head of day-to-day operations. But then, *he* hadn't quite grown accustomed to *them* either.

Now, for instance, he was staring rather blankly at Frank Adcock. "I haven't the foggiest notion what you just said, old boy."

Adcock huffed. "Well, I say, Bubbles, if you'd but pay attention, you'd have puzzled it out. It's a *poem,* I tell you." Adcock shook the telegram. "Not one of the standard codes at all, but a key of some sort."

Margot pressed her lips against a grin when the man scowled at the name *Bubbles.* The teasing had been merciless in the office ever since someone had realized that a painting of him as a child staring up at a bubble he'd just blown had been used in a soap advertisement years ago.

But despite the mutual bafflement between their new leader and the staff, Commander James *had* managed to organize them far more effectively over the course of the summer. Margot needn't ask which basket she was to put her decrypts in; she had only to slide the stack into the one marked *Intelligence* and slip back out.

Maman stood in the hallway waiting for her, their lunches in hand. "Outside, perhaps? The sun is shining again."

And they'd better enjoy it while it lasted because all too soon autumn's rains would be upon them. Margot nodded and accepted one of the brown paper bags. She tried not to ponder how little was in it. One would think that after three years at war — including a few months in Belgium, where food had been so scarce they'd been waiting in bread lines within the first several weeks — that she'd be used to the lack.

But one never really got used to it. Especially not with the newspapers full of images of newly arrived American troops. *Doughboys* indeed. To European eyes, all the Americans looked pudgy.

"I think I had better begin knitting that cardigan for little Zurie tonight. How big do you think she will be by Christmas?"

Maman asked as they started down the stairs.

Margot sent her mother an amused look. "Well, in my considerable experience with small children, I think they probably grow at a rate of —"

"Never mind." Maman laughed and bumped their shoulders together. "I forgot with whom I was speaking. Perhaps instead I should ask what *you* decided to make for your niece."

Margot shook her head. "I have decided that I love my niece enough that I will not make her anything."

Maman turned wide eyes on her. "Margot!"

As if she'd neglect Zurie altogether. "I *bought* her something instead. I found a beautiful collection of children's stories by a lady named Beatrix Potter. Far lovelier than anything I could create."

Maman faced forward and pressed her lips together. Whether in rebuke or to hold in a smile, Margot couldn't tell from this angle. "Those fingerless gloves you knit last year were not entirely horrible. You are getting better."

Margot laughed at the obvious lie. "No I'm not. One of these days you're going to stop trying to turn me into a knitter."

"It is an invaluable skill for a woman. Think how cold we would have been last winter without the clothing I made for us."

"Indeed, it's a wonderful skill for *you* to have. But I don't share it. If left to my own devices, I would simply have had to purchase a scarf."

"And then we would not have been able to put so much back in our savings." As they stepped outside, Maman drew in a long breath of the autumn air. "The war will surely be over soon. We will go home, and who knows how much money we will need to repair our house — if it is even still there in Brussels? Who knows if our accounts will be returned to us, or if the Germans will have somehow drained all the funds from our banks? We need every pence we can save, Margot."

Margot's fingers crinkled the paper bag. She opened her mouth, ready to defend the sum she'd spent on Zurie's gift as being for the purpose of education and therefore worthwhile, but before she could speak, movement caught her eye. And more, numbers filled her head.

The Pythagorean theorem. Then Euclid's proof of infinitely many prime numbers.

It was the Lord, calling her attention to something.

To what? She let her gaze shift over the scads of people milling around, trying to identify what had demanded her attention. She frowned when she spotted a feminine figure slinking around a corner.

Maman must have followed her gaze. She stopped in front of Margot, facing said corner, with her brows drawn. "I believe that is the newest secretary. Miss . . . Felton?"

"Elton." Miss Dorothea Elton. Margot hadn't seen her since she delivered her to the admiral a week ago, but she recalled the name easily enough.

"That is right, *oui.*" Maman nudged her arm. "You ought to go and introduce yourself, Margot. That young lady could use a friend, I think. She does not seem to fit in well with the other secretaries."

A mark in her favor. And the thought of following her around that corner made well-ordered numbers skip through her head, which was all the confirmation she needed. With a nod, she left her mother's side and hurried after the secretary.

Miss Elton didn't seem to be aiming anywhere in particular. She moved at an amble, not a stride, letting her fisted hand bump into the white blocks along the wall at her side with every other step. The rhythm of it spoke to something in Margot.

It took her only twelve steps to catch up. "Hello. Miss Elton, isn't it?"

Miss Elton startled and splayed a hand over her chest. "Oh! I beg your pardon. I didn't hear you come up. Yes." She held out that hand in greeting, but it was shaking. "Dorothea Elton. Dot, if you like."

Was the shaking from the surprise? Margot couldn't think so. Not given the suspiciously red rims to her eyes. She clasped her hand and offered a smile that she could only hope was friendly. "I'm called Margot. Margot De Wilde."

"How do you do?" Dot's smile was a bit faded, a bit strained.

Most people would expect such things to be politely ignored. Margot instead tilted her head. "Rough morning?"

The sigh Dot let out trembled. "The work isn't too hard. I've taken to typing rather well — Lady Hambro called me a natural at it this morning."

Dot's response didn't even pretend to answer Margot's question. She started forward at the same pace Dot had been going a moment earlier. Within a step, their gaits matched. "If only work were all we dealt with in a new position."

Dot's shoulders sagged. She wore rather

53

typical attire for a secretary — a simple blouse, a simple skirt, a simple jacket. Her hair was pulled up into a simple bun. But there was something not so simple about the way the muscles in her face moved, as if she were trying to force them into an expression they refused to take. "How long have you worked here, Margot? If you don't mind my asking."

"Three years." At the girl's quick glance, Margot renewed her smile. "I was among the first people hired, as was my mother. Before Lady Hambro, even."

Dot clasped her own elbows, creating a barrier across her middle. "I can't imagine."

"I love it here. You'll find the team to be an exceptional group of people. All so very different, all working in unique ways, but all toward a common goal. I do realize that we take a bit of getting used to, but —"

"It isn't that."

It wasn't? After Margot made such a valiant attempt to be personable? Apparently her skill at getting to the heart of a person came far short of Dot's brother's. She still couldn't quite fathom how he'd managed to plant her so firmly back in her childhood with one well-placed question.

Her lips twitched. No, she was no Drake Elton. So she would be herself, instead.

After a moment, when Dot didn't volunteer what *it* was, Margot nodded toward the building across the street at which Dot now stared. "Eight thousand seventy-eight."

"I beg your pardon?"

"Bricks. In that building."

A few of Dot's facial muscles smoothed out. "You counted?"

"Of course not. I calculated."

A bit of a smile snuck into the corners of her mouth. "What of that one?" She motioned to the next building down, which, much like the OB, was a combination of white blocks and red bricks — though much smaller.

"Two thousand bricks. Nine hundred twenty-two blocks. Thirty-four windows."

Now the smile even reached the young woman's blue-grey eyes. "What about . . . stitches in my blouse?"

"Hmm." Margot leaned close enough to see how small they were, approximated the length of seams and hems and cuffs. "Ten thousand, three hundred sixty."

"Really?" Dot lifted her sleeve and studied the cuff. "That many?"

"Give or take twenty, depending on how the seams are joined."

A droning sound filled the air. They both stopped and tilted their heads back. Margot's every muscle went stiff until the aircraft zoomed overhead.

Dot visibly relaxed. "Sopwith."

"One of the new Camels, I think." Hand up to shield the sun from her eyes, Margot watched it as far as she could. Definitely not a German Gotha, which was the important thing. Only a few of them had made it all the way to London, but when they did, hundreds died.

Not today though. Not here. *Thank you, Father. Eight, sixteen, twenty-four, thirty-six . . .*

"Would you like to sit and eat with me? I've been finding a bench facing the arch."

"That sounds lovely." She was a bit surprised at how true her statement felt. But thus far, Dot was certainly the least objectionable of all the young women around. Margot could even come up with what she assumed Maman would deem reasonable, friendly questions to ask. "Are you from London?"

"All my life, yes. Well, mostly." Wincing, Dot led the way around the corner. "I'm not much of one for travel. There was one time when I went to visit my mother's family in Spain. And another time when I went on holiday with my friend, Ada, to the Cotswolds. Perfectly pleasant journeys by all accounts, but . . . I prefer to stick close to home."

"Spain! How interesting." To look at the Elton siblings, she wouldn't have thought they were Spanish. But that was no doubt silly of her, to expect them to fit some sort of mold when it came to their coloring. "Given your surname though, I'm assuming your father is English?"

"Was." A few clouds shadowed her voice as she said it. Dot motioned to a bench. "He passed away just before the war began. Some sort of cancer. My mother — she died in a boating accident when I was only nine."

"I'm very sorry." Margot slid to a seat on the bench. "My father died not long before the war began as well. I still miss him. Every day." She missed him every time that she picked up pen or pencil, let the numbers flood her mind, and used it to turn an encoded message into plain script. Every time she drew out a notebook in their flat and set to work on a theorem. Every time she read a newspaper and looked for secrets hidden within, though she well knew there was no one to plant them for her now.

He'd be proud of her. Proud of what she did. Perhaps he was looking down on her from heaven and smiling . . . but it wasn't the same. She hated that she'd never get to show him all the discoveries she'd helped make, the codes she'd helped break. She didn't get to come to him in joy whenever a codebook was recovered from a sunken U-boat or German agent. He was so much a part of who she was. And yet he was gone.

She shook herself. "But I have Maman still. Sophie De Wilde — I think you've met her? And my brother, Lukas."

"Oh, yes, she's been very kind." Dot opened up her lunch sack. Then paused. "Wait. Lukas De Wilde? The violinist? I've a recording of him!"

Margot smiled and reached into her own bag. "Yes. He came to Wales with the orchestra in the first days of the war, to help raise money for the Belgian Relief Fund. Now he stays here in London to be close to us, rather than touring with the others. Well, and because his wife's family is here."

"He's so very talented. And how lovely that you're all together." Dot pinched a bit of crust from her sandwich and tossed it to a flock of pigeons.

A waste of precious grain, Maman would say.

But the pigeons needed to eat too. Margot tore off a small piece and sent it to them as well. "Does your Spanish family ever visit you here?"

The young woman's laugh didn't sound very amused. "Oh no. Never. Abuelo never leaves his house in Bilbao, and he is all the family my mother had. I have an aunt though, on my father's side. Aunt Millie. We lived together until just recently. That bombing in Poplar shook her far too much, and she finally fled for the countryside. So it's just me here now. Except for when Drake is on leave, of course."

His image sprang to mind — amused eyes, ready smile, knotted nose. The evidence suggested he hadn't discovered her name before he left, but he'd certainly have no difficulty now that she'd volunteered it to his sister. Margot tore off a bite of bread and cheese and grinned. "Your brother? The one who brought you here last week?" She popped the food into her mouth.

Dot nodded as she chewed a bite of her own. "It seems I've scarcely seen him since the war began. And before that, he was attending university in Spain. But he's always been attentive, as brothers go."

"I know just what you mean." Lukas, too, had spent much of Margot's childhood traveling on tour with the orchestra. Of course, he was quite a bit older than her too, already practically grown by the time she came along. Still. He was her brother.

He had always been one of the dearest people in the world to her, and she was glad they lived so near to each other now.

Silence fell for a moment as they both took another bite, interrupted only by the sounds of the busy street before them and the coo of the pigeons feasting on their crusts.

Then Dot drew in a long breath. "It isn't the work. It isn't even all the strangers I'm expected to remember. It's . . . I hate leaving the house. It *hurts.* No one understands that, no one can grasp how my chest gets so tight at the very thought of needing to go out. I can manage it one day a week without too much stress. Twice, if someone is with me. But every day? *Every day.*" Her hands shook again as she lowered her sandwich to her lap. "I don't expect you want to be burdened with such a friend, so I won't take it personally if you keep your distance. I'm a wreck. Aunt Millie declared it completely irrational of me to prefer to stay here in the flat I've made my home rather than flee to safety. I couldn't explain to her that it feels safer than somewhere new."

Margot kept her attention on a car sputtering its way along the street. "I get itchy. So itchy it hurts — not when I need to leave the house, but when something doesn't make sense, including people and their faulty reasoning, which means I'm itchy more often than not. Wanting to stay at home is a rather reasonable inclination, in my opinion. I'll never judge you for it." Now she looked over and found Dot looking at *her.* "I'm not a secretary — I'm one of the cryptographers. I hate fashion, I hate gossip, and I absolutely cannot *stand* girls who giggle over every man who sends a smile their way. So if *you* want to walk the other way, I won't begrudge it."

Peace in her eyes, Dot shook her head.

"Well then." Margot smiled and reached into her bag for the handful of almonds Maman had tucked in there after Margot had made both their sandwiches. She handed a few to Dot and popped the others into her mouth. "It looks as though we might as well be friends."

Dot munched on her nuts and didn't say a word. Just smiled a little and relaxed against the bench.

Margot did the same. This could work. Which she had pretty much known the moment the Pythagorean theorem spun through her head upon spotting her.

Mathematics never led her astray.

4

"Margot."

She looked up, numbers still clouding her eyes until she blinked. Admiral Hall came into focus. He stood at her side, irritation on his face and a paper in his hand, which he slid onto her desk. "Would you? It's from Thoroton. I've been called in to a meeting with the First Sea Lord."

He looked none too happy about it, that was for sure. But then, she knew he had not been pleased with how Jellicoe had been running things of late.

Her gaze dropped to the paper. With a glance, she saw that it was one of their own telegrams, not an intercepted one, encrypted in the code Hall used with his agents and operatives in the field. All it would take to decode it would be to pull out the book he'd slipped her a year ago for occasions such as this and perhaps twenty minutes of deciphering. "Of course. Shall I just put it on your desk when I'm finished?"

"Yes, that will do." He patted her shoulder. "How is the latest German codebook working for us?"

"Quite well." The cryptographers in Room 40 could break the new variations day by day — that was simply a matter of finding a new starting place in an existing pattern. But to unravel the pattern itself was a different story, and the Germans were constantly changing their codebooks. Oh, they could crack the codes by sheer mathematics — eventually. They'd done it with Code 13040. And while that might be more sporting, it also took more time. Months, *years* more time. And they hadn't that leisure.

Hence why DID offered prizes to divers who could recover German codebooks from U-boat wreckage. That was where this latest one had come from, which she was now using to render a message sent last night to UC-44, a German minelayer. Putting Thoroton's telegram aside for now, she tapped the page on which she was writing the translation. "I could be wrong, sir, but . . . but so far this reads rather knowledgeably. 'Sweeper to be in harbor at midnight on Tuesday. Postpone operations until Wednesday and then proceed. . . .' "

Hall grunted. "You're right. Our minelaying code must have been compromised — that's the only way they'd know when our sweepers would be out clearing the waters. Well." A mischievous twinkle entered his eyes — the very sort that had always been in Papa's whenever he had an idea for a new puzzle to hide for her. "If they have our minelaying code, let's use it against them. Would you mind encrypting something for me too?"

In answer, she pulled out a blank sheet of paper and handed him her pen. If it was something to be put into the minelaying code, which she suspected it was, she'd have to fetch the codebook from downstairs. But for the pleasure of getting to *en*crypt and not just *de*crypt, it would be well worth the exercise.

Hall leaned over and scratched a message onto the page. *In minelaying code. Harbor clear.* He drew a horizontal line under that quick message and then wrote *In personal code. To harbor master. Close harbor to all traffic. Do not — I repeat, do not — clear mines already laid.*

The light of mischief traveled from his eyes to the corner of his mouth, which turned up in a smile. "There we are. We'll send the all clear tomorrow, which the huns will intercept, letting them think all their mines are gone. Then, when they come to lay more, they'll come across the ones still there. How is *that* for turnabout?"

Margot chuckled and accepted the pen back from him. "Perfect, DID."

He patted her shoulder again and then turned away. "Just leave the encrypted telegram with the decrypt of the other on my desk, if you would. Thank you, Margot."

"Of course." She picked up her pen again and went back to the original U-boat message. It only took her a few minutes to work through the rest of it, given that she'd almost been finished already. There. She set the completed decrypt into the basket for a secretary to type up and deliver to Commander James. And then she turned to the work from Hall.

First, the fun bit. She rarely had the opportunity to encode anything, so she took the five minutes necessary to fetch the British minelaying codebook from downstairs, then pulled out Hall's personal code from her own desk drawer and got down to the pleasurable task of encrypting. Given the brevity of the messages, it didn't take long.

But it made the numbers hum in her mind. It made her shoulder warm where Hall had patted it — where Papa always had too, when she'd managed a task he'd thought would challenge her. Where sometimes she imagined God resting His hand.

She turned then to the message from Thoroton. With Hall's codebook still before her, she got down to work on the considerably longer message from their head of intelligence in the Med.

Briefing from Spain. Twenty-two agents currently in the field. From Madrid . . .

Hall often asked her to work out the messages sent to him. Just a month ago she had decoded a briefing from Thoroton in Gibraltar, but this was the first she'd done from Spain. Perhaps she would have ciphered it with less interest had she not a new friend who was half Spanish. But with Dot in mind, she tackled each line rather eagerly. She knew Spain was officially neutral, but she also knew both England and Germany had been working behind the scenes ever since the war began to win favor with the Spaniards — both the officials and those in positions that could prove useful.

From Corunna . . .

Her pen kept working as the numbers flipped along inside her mind. With the codebook before her, it was a simple task. Easy enough that her mind wandered as she wrote, and she remembered one of Hall's early bids for Spain's favor. He'd sent an agent into Spain on a private yacht to wine and dine whatever harbor officials he could find. The Germans had done the same at nearly the same time . . . but *they* had only brought beer. Hall's agent had requisitioned the best champagne to be found, and the officials had been friends ever since.

Not that Hall's superiors approved of the use of navy funds for champagne and private yachts, but they in Room 40 had thought it hilarious and had cheered on their intrepid leader.

From Bilbao . . .

Margot's pen stilled. Not because the name was familiar, thanks to the stories Dot had been telling her of her family that resided there, but because of the sudden silence of the numbers in her mind.

And then there was a quick succession of them that had nothing to do with the code before her. The Lord, all but shouting at her. *Pay attention!*

Her breath knotted up in her throat. There had been plenty of times over the years when those numbers instructed her to pray for someone. But never while at work, when she was decoding something.

Interesting.

Agent Eighteen has been searching dili-gently for any stores of wolfram within the city.

67

If we can find them here, we can track anyone else showing interest in it. Thus far nothing, but he has a lead he intends to pursue on Tuesday. Will update on outcome.

Tuesday — today. Margot's pen stilled. Was this what God wanted her to pray about? *Twelve, one hundred forty-four, one thousand seven hundred twenty-eight, twenty thousand seven hundred thirty-six . . .*

She would take that as a yes. *Eternal Father, whatever this Agent Eighteen is doing now, I ask that you protect him. Make a way for him, clear the path, ensure his safety. Eleven, twenty-two, thirty-three, forty-four . . .*

Not until the numbers tapered off did she breathe out again. Pick up her pen again. And focus again on the telegram.

From Cartagena . . .

Drake kept his gait smooth and casual as he walked along the street, even whistling a popular tune that anyone listening would recognize and dismiss. Just a normal Spanish man, out for a stroll before he retired to his home for an afternoon out of the heat.

The glance he sent upward took in the tall, narrow windows in the building. A warehouse, without question. But was it *the* warehouse? The one he'd been searching for this past fortnight? He couldn't be sure until he looked inside.

That, though, was proving a challenge. The windows were too high up for him to see into from the street and too dusty to give him a clear view from the building across the way — he'd tried that yesterday.

He was running out of time. If he loitered around this neighborhood much longer, people would begin to notice him and wonder who he was, why he'd suddenly appeared. They'd start asking questions.

No one knew better than he that questions could lead to answers — and he didn't much fancy anyone finding answers about *him.*

He had to get inside. There was no other option.

At the corner, he paused. A lorry was rattling by, giving him a good excuse not to cross the road. He leaned against the building instead. Into his pocket he reached for a slender cigar, a cutter, and a match. He didn't much care for them, to be perfectly honest, but they did provide handy cover when he wanted to stand in one place for minutes on end and not look suspicious while doing it. He sliced off the end of the cigar, slid the cutter back into his pocket, and struck the match.

How could he verify the contents of the

warehouse? He'd asked that question days ago and had made a list of the possibilities. He could look through the windows — *failed.* He could engage and weasel information out of a worker — *attempted but not successful.* He could try that tactic again. Go back to that dingy little bar and buy another glass of wine for the sweaty bloke he'd tried to strike up a conversation with last night. But the chap was more interested in his sangria than in talking and had only grunted his replies.

He could get inside. The trickiest but surest option. Drake drew on the cigar to get it to light, careful to keep his distaste from showing on his face. Abuelo loved these things, but for the life of him, Drake couldn't determine why.

Once the cigar was smoldering, he leaned against the building as if it were there solely to hold him up on a lazy afternoon.

Dark eyes filtered into his mind, full of intelligence that begged many a question. What was she called? No doubt he could discover that easily when next he went to London. His sister would be able to tell him. But more to the point — would she perhaps have dinner with him? Give him another taste of that wit of hers?

He sighed around the cigar. Even if she

did, what then? Unless the war was over by the time he reached London, he'd just be sent away again in a week. Hardly enough time to get to know someone.

Besides, compelling dark eyes and a quick tongue didn't make a girl someone he'd actually *like*. For all he knew, a longer conversation might prove her the type he couldn't stand — another Ada. Which, come to think of it, confirmation of such would convince his mind to stop throwing the memory of her eyes before him at all hours of day and night.

Yet another reason to try to meet her.

Cigars burned slowly enough that he could amble a few feet closer to the door without it looking odd. There was no one stationed outside the warehouse — *a good sign or bad?* — but he'd bet there'd be someone *inside* somewhere.

He catalogued all he'd been able to discover about the building from out here. There was a back door — *locked.* He'd tested it. A front door, which was near him now. And a loading bay with a large rolling door that moved upward. He'd spent a couple of hopeful minutes examining the few inches it had been up today, calculating whether he could slip underneath.

Perhaps, if he didn't breathe and could

71

angle his head correctly. But it was risky. He could get stuck, and it would likely take quite a bit of maneuvering, which could draw the attention of any workers inside the warehouse.

"Al pie. Al pie, Barto."

Drake's gaze flicked up, over. Across the street, an aged man walked, a cane in one hand and a dog straining at a leash in the other. Upon the command, the dog came to a halt. But it whimpered and looked back at its master, tail wagging. The old man paused, patted a pocket, and felt around the ground with his toe. "Where did it land, Barto? Eh?"

The dog whined a response, and the old man muttered a mild curse. "Come, dog, I heard the coin fall, and we need it if you're to have a bone tonight. Where is it? Coin? Eh?"

The dog wagged its tail again.

Pushing off from the building, Drake jogged across the street. "Can I help you find something?"

The man looked around, his gaze skimming over Drake. When his eyes rested not on Drake's face but on his shoulder, Drake realized he was blind.

"I believe I dropped a *peseta.*" His voice

72

was hesitant. "If you happen to see it, young man?"

Drake quickly took in the area around the old chap. Within a few seconds, the glint of sun on the coin drew his attention to a dirty crack where road met building. "There it is. Just a moment." He moved over to grab it. "Here you go, *señor.*"

The old man stretched out a hand, surprise lining the crags of his face when Drake pressed the coin into it. His fingers curled around it, feeling its contours. *"Gracias."*

"De nada. May I pet your dog?"

The old man chuckled and slid the peseta back into his pocket. "I would rather you didn't. I'm sorry, but he works best when he is not distracted. I promise you, he receives his reward for a job well done when he guides me safely home."

Drake was glad he'd asked, then, and not just reached out to ruffle the mutt's fur. "I understand. Is there anything else I can help you with, señor?"

The man grinned. *"No,* gracias. Are you new to the neighborhood, young man?"

"Just visiting, *sí.* Esteban Martín Caminante." It was the name Thoroton had provided for him to use when not in a part of the city where he was already known, or when in another part of Spain — that second surname literally meaning traveler. A little joke that no one would understand.

The old man smiled. "And I am Pietro Rodríguez Brasa. You have made my dog's day and done me a kindness, Esteban. Again, gracias." When the wind shifted, Señor Rodríguez turned his face a bit and sniffed the air, his eyes lighting at the whiff of cigar smoke that drifted by him.

Drake grinned too. "I don't suppose you would care to finish my cigar, señor? I probably shouldn't take the time to do so. My abuelo expects me home." He'd have offered the old man a fresh one, if he'd had one on him to offer.

Señor Rodríguez didn't appear to be put off by the thought of sharing. His eyes brightened still more. "I haven't enjoyed one in nearly two years. If you are certain you don't want it . . ."

He had no idea how happy Drake was to give it up. "I will have another tomorrow. Here. Enjoy." Drake slipped the smoldering cylinder into the man's outstretched fingers. *Buenas tardes.*

"Good afternoon to you as well, Esteban." Looking far happier than he had when he told his dog to heel a minute ago, the old chap gave a command to walk and sauntered down the street.

Drake watched him until he turned the corner, still smiling a bit. He'd have helped the old man regardless, but in this particular case, helping him could help Drake too. He angled a glance across the street to make sure their exchange had been out of sight of the tiny window in the warehouse's door and, satisfied, jogged over and pounded on it.

Within a few seconds, the creaking door swung open, revealing a man with a cap pulled low over his eyes. "Sí?"

"Sorry to bother you." Careful to keep an expression of mild concern on his face, Drake gestured to the street. "My uncle Pietro — his dog slipped away from him. Perhaps you heard him calling to him? Barto?"

There was enough shift in the bloke's eyes to prove he was familiar with Pietro and Barto. "Barto? But he's such a good dog!"

"He is." And Drake hated to malign him. "I don't know what has come over him. But he ran around the back of your building here, and then I lost him. I think he may have slipped under that door in the back. Could I check?"

"Of course!" The bloke opened the door and waved him in, searching the street behind him. "Where is your uncle? Does he

75

need to come in, to rest?"

"Ah." Drake motioned to the corner he'd turned. "I got him settled with a cigar. He will be all right until I return with Barto."

The guard chuckled. "I imagine. Go, go. Find the dog. I'm afraid I must stay here at my post, or I would help you."

"No matter, I'm sure I'll find him soon enough. Gracias." Victory singing through his veins, Drake hurried down the short corridor that blocked the warehouse proper from this door. He whistled and called for Barto as he went, darting one look over his shoulder to make sure the helpful guard really was staying at his post.

All clear. Drake muttered a prayer of thanksgiving and jogged into the cavernous, dim space.

Inside were crates of various sizes. Equipment. Shelves. The light coming in through the grimy windows was barely sufficient to show him anything, so he withdrew a small electric torch from his pocket and got down to business.

"Barto!" he called again for good measure as he moved along one row of wooden crates. He switched his light on and shined it on the black words stamped onto the wood. This stack, apparently, was grain. He shook his head at the sheer volume of it. All this grain sitting here, and yet Pietro would probably go to bed hungry tonight. The owners of these warehouses and shipping ventures were getting rich from the war, while the average worker was all but starving.

He couldn't worry about that right now though. Hall wasn't interested in grain — or at least that's not what he'd sent him here to investigate. He moved down another row, calling for the dog now and then, until the black words he sought filled his torch's circle of light.

Tungsteno.

Wolfram.

Yes! Drake flashed the light along the row, counting how many crates there were, making note of the weight stamped on them. He'd have to do the actual math later with paper and pencil, but a quick estimation was sufficient to confirm that this tonnage was enough to tempt the Germans to try to obtain it — and to tempt England to let them, so that they could then confiscate it.

Drake rounded the corner of the stack to make sure there were no more crates hidden behind what he could see. He'd done a bit of research on wolfram after Hall mentioned it — enough to know that it was crucial not only in armor plating but in weapons themselves. It was rather impressive, having the highest boiling and melting temperatures of any known metal, and had first been identified right here in Spain some hundred and thirty years before.

More importantly, it was here now, in this warehouse.

A scuffing sound made him pause. It was not coming from the front of the warehouse, where the guard presumably still stood sentinel, but from the rear. Another guard? He'd have thought the first would have mentioned if there were someone else who could help him search for the dog.

It almost sounded like a dog. Or some sort of animal, scraping and shuffling. Drake eased forward, switching off his torch and sliding it back into his pocket. Gripping the handle of his pistol instead, he pulled it out of his waistband. He'd never actually had to use it — but he would, if necessary.

It was probably just a big rat, scrounging for spilled grain. Or a cat. A dog. Nothing to warrant his alarm. He'd not assume so, though. He picked his foot up and set it silently back down, moving stealthily along until he could see the bar of afternoon light spilling through the scanty inches left open by the massive door at the rear.

Not an animal. A man, squeezing through

the space, as Drake had considered and then dismissed doing. Someone out to liberate a few pounds of grain?

No. As the bloke squeezed through and stood, Drake caught a glimpse of his face. A face he'd seen before, skulking about much like he himself tended to do. Thus far he hadn't found a name, but he was all but certain the man was a German agent — Drake's opposite number.

In the same instant, the man spotted him and apparently recognized him just as quickly. In a flash, he'd whipped something from his own waistband and squeezed the trigger.

Drake ducked behind the crate of wolfram as a bullet bit into it, and he swallowed back a curse. The shot wouldn't have drawn any attention. There'd been a Maxim Silencer on the pistol's barrel, something he didn't have on his.

And attention was the last thing he wanted. Attention would mean more guards and possibly the move of this supply of metal. The undoing of all his weeks of searching. No, he wouldn't go shooting at the man shooting at him.

Keeping his head down, he ran in a hunch along the crates. Another muffled shot sounded, another bullet bit into the floor an inch from his heel. The man must have come to the end of this aisle. Drake tossed himself over another stack of crates and rolled across it, dropping to his feet on the other side. "Barto! Get back here, you mutt!"

Footsteps sounded from the front. From his crouched position, Drake saw the shadow of the German freeze, then melt away as he sought cover.

The friendly guard must have come to the end of his corridor. "Is all well?"

Drake emerged from the rows of crates, putting himself in plain sight of the German, no doubt, but also of the guard. His gut told him that the agent wanted secrecy as much as he did, otherwise he wouldn't have that silencer on the end of his barrel. He wouldn't shoot him with anyone watching.

He hoped.

Pasting fond exasperation on his face, Drake jogged to the front. "Silly animal slid back out the rolling door. I'll get him." He moved into the stubby corridor, smiling despite the breath he held. *Please, God. Please.* A prayer not for his own safety at this point — the chap had had a clear shot of him as he'd moved and would have taken it already if that were his intent — but for the guard. He didn't *think* the opposite number would attack him. If he were here to scope out the wolfram, too, then he wouldn't want it moved any more than Drake did, and shooting a guard would pretty much guarantee that anything valuable in this warehouse would be shipped to another. But sometimes the Germans surprised him.

The guard chuckled and opened the front door for him, obviously blissful in his ignorance of the bullets that had just seared their way through his warehouse. "Better hurry. Best of luck!"

"Gracias!" Grateful he had an excuse to run, Drake kicked his speed from jog to sprint once he was on the street.

Even so, the hairs on the back of his neck stood up. Had the man gone out the same way he'd come in? Was he out here yet? Which direction would he go?

A muted shot answered that. Drake kicked up his speed as the bullet took a chunk out of the wall behind him. At least the bloke didn't seem to be a crack shot. Too close for comfort though.

Where, then, to run?

Spying an alley that would remove him from the gun's line of sight, Drake dove down it, sprinting to the end, a prayer pounding with every footfall that he'd reach the exit before the other bloke reached the entrance. His ears strained to hear anything over his own breathing, his own pulse, his own steps.

There. Other running steps — but Drake was even then turning out of the alley onto the street running parallel to the one on which the warehouse sat. A farm wagon loaded with hay — no doubt destined for another warehouse — creaked by. A lorry sputtered along opposite. His eyes darted this way and that, his mind darting just as quickly through the options.

He could toss himself into the hay wagon, burrow down.

No.

He could run into that open door of the next building down and then search for a back exit.

No.

His gaze latched onto another alley, not quite opposite. He'd scouted out this section of town enough to know it would deliver him to the river. If he could get out of the *Bilbao la Vieja* — the city's industrial left bank — and across the river, he'd be back in the *Casco Viejo,* the Old Quarter. And there, he'd be on his own turf, where he knew every street, every turn . . . and many of the people.

Go.

The lorry was rattling in the right direction. He dashed into the street and to the opposite side of the automobile, getting as close as he could to its side and matching its lumbering speed. His legs he kept aligned with its rear wheels, and his back he kept hunched enough that his head wouldn't clear the top of the lorry's frame. He grasped one of the cords holding a canvas top over the cargo to steady himself and glanced ahead to where that next alley drew slowly closer.

Ten more seconds. Five. *Now.* He peeled away from the lorry's side and into the narrow street while the lorry covered the entrance.

With any luck, his opposite number was following the hay wagon, poking into that for him. Or running down the street proper.

If so, all Drake had to do was be out of sight again by the time he crossed the mouth of the alley. It was a short little thing, improving his chances. He increased them more with another muttered prayer in Spanish.

The scent of the river washed over him in the seconds before he charged out of the alley's shadows and back into the golden afternoon light. He skidded out of the alley and to the side, out of view from the other end, and took stock of where he'd come out.

"Señor?"

Perhaps some would think it an outstanding coincidence that one of his grandfather's men stood on a barge not ten yards from where Drake had emerged. He knew, rather, that it would have been far stranger had any of the docks here on the Bilbao la Vieja *not* had one of Abuelo's barges at it.

The only thing particularly notable was that it was Eneko who stood there with his pole already in hand. His grandfather's most trusted employee. His mother's childhood friend. The man least likely to cause him any trouble by saying too much to Abuelo.

Drake hurried over and dropped onto the barge. *"Vamonos."*

Eneko muttered something incomprehensible and poled away from the dock. Once they were drifting in the lazy current, the man turned glinting brown eyes on him. "And why were you among the foundries today, Don Dragón? You told your abuelo you were attending classes."

Drake cleared his throat and offered no more than a Spanish *um. "A ver . . ."*

At that equivocation, Eneko shook his head, still more brown than grey. "If you ask me, you are a dragon who needs your wings clipped."

If only he had some — that would certainly make it easier to fly away from trouble. And a bit of fire-breathing wouldn't hurt either. Drake laughed and grabbed the second pole. Best to get them across the river as quickly as possible — and out of range of the German's pistol.

5

"Are you certain you want to join us?" Margot hung back near the church's front step with Dot as Maman chatted with a few friends from the parish. They'd only discovered two weeks ago that they, in fact, attended Mass at the same time and place as her new friend . . . but Dot had always found a seat in the back, and Maman always led Margot to the front.

Dot drew in a breath that shook a bit around the edges, but she smiled and nodded. "It's been ages since I've enjoyed Sunday dinner with anyone. And it was so kind of your brother and sister-in-law to invite me."

Kindness had little to do with it. Lukas had been so impressed that Margot had actually made a friend her own age — more or less — that he'd been hounding her all month to "get the girl here so we can get to know her better."

Maman had chided him for his incredulity. And Lukas had laughed and said, "I was beginning to think my little sister was actually a forty-year-old man, given her choice of companions."

Was it *her* fault that girls her own age were more often than not so silly they made her itch? That the only people she'd ever found who let her be herself were among that motley collection of academics in Room 40? Still. She smiled now at Dot and didn't at all mind that the Lord had finally given in to Maman's prayers on this score. "If at any point you want to leave, please believe that we won't be offended."

Generally speaking, Dot did fine enough once she was out. But Margot had also learned that there came a point in the day when she was just *finished*. When the world got to be too much and she had to get home before the anxiety clawed her to bits.

On the average workday, that time came about ten minutes after her usual dismissal time. Margot certainly didn't want to be the cause of it springing upon her on a Sunday, the day she usually holed up in the safety of her flat after the hour at Mass.

"Your niece is precious." Dot's focus had gone to where Lukas and Willa stood chatting with someone, little Zurie positioned happily on her mother's hip, fingers hooked in her mouth. She'd inherited Lukas's dark hair and eyes, set in a face shaped more like Willa's. She was indeed a pretty little thing, which wasn't surprising. Lukas was as beautiful in a masculine way as their mother was in the feminine, and it stood to reason he'd pass the family beauty along to his children. Though Willa got a glint in her eyes anytime someone praised her daughter's beauty. She had a prejudice against being called *pretty* — and apparently didn't like it applied to her little one either.

Zurie blinked and followed an invisible something or other with her eyes, tilting her head back to watch it. A midge, perhaps, or a dust mote. Or something no one but she could imagine. What *did* babies think about all day? Try as she might to recall, Margot hadn't many memories from before she was two. On the one hand, it seemed babies' worlds must be very boring — nothing but food and nappies and the same rooms day in and day out. But, on the other hand, everything was new and yet to be discovered, which may indeed be the most interesting experiences of their lives.

If so, then it was rather a shame she could remember only fleeting glimpses of it.

Movement beyond Zurie caught Margot's

eye — Mrs. Neville, a busybody forever trying to arrange a meeting between Margot and one of her many grandsons. Given the current ratio of men to women in England, she hadn't any idea why the woman insisted on bothering *her* with nearsighted Thomas or London-stationed Richard when there were any number of young ladies happy to vie for their attention, but Margot didn't much fancy ruining yet another Sunday with the argument.

She gripped Dot's elbow and steered her away from the door. "Mrs. Neville at two o'clock. Hurry and perhaps someone will waylay her before she can catch up to us."

Dot laughed and made no objection to the increase of pace. "Aunt Millie was always complaining of her. Might we begin walking to your brother's?"

"I daresay no one will object." Even Maman understood the desire to flee Mrs. Neville's clutches. She never made any attempt to hinder Margot's escape.

They hurried around a group of chatting parishioners and caught Maman's eye. Margot gave her the prearranged signal for the gossip's approach by checking the watch on her pendant, and Maman gave her a twinkling-eyed smile and nodded toward the street.

89

It was all the approval she needed. She and Dot hurried away. Clouds obscured the sun, and the wind whipped down the street, but it was a warm wind, and Margot felt no need to complain. With Dot still chuckling at her side, they turned left and increased their pace still more.

"Shall we walk or take the tube?" Dot darted a glance over her shoulder. Apparently there was no Mrs. Neville hunting them down, given that she faced forward again without comment.

"Walk. It won't take us long." And she had a key to the townhouse Lukas and Willa let, so even if their housekeeper wasn't back from her own church yet, Margot could let herself and Dot in.

Once they turned the corner at the first intersection, they slowed their pace and Dot let out a happy little sigh. "We'll walk by the park going this direction, won't we?"

"Yes." It wasn't much of a park — neither large nor grand nor a draw from other parts of the city. But it was the nearest one to both her flat and Lukas's house, not to mention the church, so Margot had spent a fair amount of time on its walking paths and benches over the last three years.

"My father used to take us to a park near our home when I was a girl. There was a little pond at the time, and a family of ducks lived there. I used to love to feed them and tease my brother about how he must be a duck too, being named Drake as he is. Though of course he insisted it was for *dragon,* not for a male duck." Dot anchored her hat to her head when a particularly strong gust of wind tore down the street, her eyes alight with memory.

Margot smiled. "I didn't realize that was the word for a male duck in English." No matter how fluent she thought herself, it seemed she always found out something new each day. There was always more to learn. New discoveries to be made.

Dot's gaze remained fixed on the little sliver of green that would eventually unfold into the park. "In Spain, my grandfather and his servants actually call my brother *Dragón.* They refuse to use *Drake* — they still bear a grudge against Sir Frances Drake there, you know."

Margot nearly choked on a laugh. "Are you quite serious?"

"Mm. The Spanish aren't very fond of foreigners in general, and many are anti-British in particular. I daresay our mother agreed to name him that solely because she thought it would be a great joke — though it was a family name on my father's maternal side. She was always laughing and playing jokes on us." Dot's sigh combined wistfulness with contentment. "I'll never forget that about her."

"She sounds wonderful." Margot said no more after that. Dot went silent, her mind probably sifting through memories, and Margot saw no reason to interrupt it.

Another three minutes and they were at the park, both of them turning onto the walking path without any need for discussion about it. That was something she'd come to greatly appreciate about her new friend in their month-long acquaintance — they had the same inclinations and didn't often have to discuss such simple things.

Eighteen. The number flashed into her mind again, for the eighth time since she first decoded that update from Thoroton for DID. She sent her eyes heavenward, along with a mental smile that didn't touch her lips. *Lord, if you call this fellow to mind every time he's in danger, then he courts it far too often. Perhaps you ought to nudge him into a different career.* But she said a prayer for the agent, as she did each time his number came to mind.

"Is everything all right?"

"Hm?" Margot blinked and realized only then that her feet had come to a halt and that her knuckles had fisted in her dress. Another blink made the itch at the back of her neck come into focus. Something wasn't right in the scene before her. "I don't know."

She felt her body settle into the stance that Maman always called *too still.* Each muscle was at rest but ready to move if the situation called for it. She stared straight ahead, but in such a way that she could better attune her attention to the periphery. Her fingertips pressed into the fabric over her legs.

After a minute — or perhaps several minutes, she didn't bother marking time as it passed in these moments — she turned her head to the side. *There.* The man seated at the little wrought-iron table was wrong. As was the game set up before him.

Her legs feeling heavy, she left the path and moved toward him.

It could be nothing. A newcomer to the neighborhood. It shouldn't bother her, Maman would say. Gregory didn't *own* the table, Lukas would have put in. The new bloke wasn't hurting anyone, she could imagine Willa insisting.

But he wasn't *right.* He was shaggy instead of bald, bearded instead of clean-shaven, wore a blue jacket instead of a buff, and he *wasn't Gregory.*

93

Her feet halted beside the table, where a chessboard was not set up. Her throat felt tight. "Where's Gregory?"

Wrong, wrong. Maman would be glaring at her if she were here, her eyes shooting daggers that said, *You're being rude, Margot.* But she couldn't even manage a smile to soften her question.

The man glanced up at her but then back down to his board, his lips moving silently. His eyes didn't seem to focus on her. His fingers twitched, and he coughed.

Dot moved up behind her. "Margot?"

She drew in a deep breath. The English had a saying about flies and honey — though she wasn't sure whether she wanted to catch this particular fly or shoo him away. "I'm sorry, I don't mean to be rude. But Gregory Westrom is usually here this time of day. Are you meeting him? Playing a new game together?"

The man didn't bother looking up again. His twitchy fingers lifted from the table and moved to the game board. For a moment they hovered over one of the black stones. Then, with a spasm, he moved it to another intersection of the lines.

Margot winced. A stupid move, even though he seemed to be playing no one but himself. Though rarely did anyone appreciate her pointing out such things.

Dot edged forward another step. "What game is that? I don't recognize it."

Margot swallowed. That was part of the *wrong.* She didn't know anyone in England who played this game. Didn't know anyone who did at all, aside from the German officer who had occupied their home when they were in Brussels after the invasion. In her head, it was his voice that sounded, though it emerged from her lips in her own tones. "It is called Go. From the Han Chinese empire, but it has become quite popular in Germany."

"Germany?" Dot jerked away a degree.

Margot sucked more oxygen into her lungs. "Apparently its popularity is spreading." She could still feel the smooth round stones against her fingers if she tried hard enough. Still remember sitting for hours at that game board in Brussels, trying not to be too clever in her play, lest the *General-leutnant* realize she was more than what she could safely admit to being.

He'd seen anyway, despite her playing like a dunce. They'd had one honest game together before Lukas had found her and Maman and secretted them out of Belgium, into England. Playing Go had been nearly as much fun as cryptography.

She'd been unable to find a game board here in London, and her mother wouldn't have let her spend the cash on it even if she had. Not to mention that she had no one to play with.

All of which rather begged the question of where this usurper had found a board, and with whom he meant to play. And such a beautiful board, at that, engraved and gleaming. It was a striking contrast to the player, who looked pale and half sick.

"Good morning, Margot. Or afternoon, I suppose."

Margot spun away from the game board and the scruffy man who was reaching now with his spasmodic fingers for a white stone. An ancient woman, Mrs. Rourke, was settling onto her usual bench, drawing a ball of yarn and a crochet hook from her bag.

Sometimes Maman would bring her knitting to the park on a fine day, and she and Mrs. Rourke would ply their crafts together, chatting about the weather and the news and everything in between. Margot usually had a game of chess with Gregory on such occasions.

She summoned a smile for Mrs. Rourke. "Afternoon." And then motioned toward the interloper. "Do you know where Gregory is?"

"Oh. Oh dear." Mrs. Rourke's face collapsed into folds of wrinkles. "Had you not heard? Gregory died. Tuesday last. You know he'd not been well for some time."

True, he hadn't. His trips to the park with the chessboard were about all he could manage. But she hadn't thought he was *dying.* She'd thought . . . well, she'd thought he was part of the park, she supposed. As ever-present as that tree yonder, or the gravel of the path.

Stupid. She curled her fingers into her palm. "I'm very sorry to hear that. Had we known, we would have paid our respects at his funeral."

"Oh, it was a quiet affair, and you and your mother would have been at the office. Just his son and a few of us neighbors came." Mrs. Rourke blinked a few times. "We shall surely miss him."

"As will I." And why, if the friendly old man had only been gone for a few days, was his place already filled at that table? Had the scruffy man no respect? She stepped closer to Mrs. Rourke and pitched her voice low. "So who is this newcomer?"

But the lady just shrugged. "Don't rightly know, dear. First I've seen him. But if he sticks about for any length of time, I'm sure we'll learn."

Margot nodded because it was expected. Smiled because it wasn't Mrs. Rourke's fault. And then turned back to Dot because her friend looked uneasy. It took a bit of effort to keep the smile on her face. "Sorry for the detour, Dot."

"Think nothing of it. But hadn't we better get to your brother's house?"

Margot nodded and said a quick farewell to the old woman. Of course, turning back to the path meant again walking by the game that wasn't chess and the man who wasn't Gregory. Seeing his fingers push another black stone into another stupid move.

Once they were out of earshot, Dot leaned close. "I'm sorry about your friend. Gregory."

"Thank you." It wasn't, of course, just the absence of Gregory and his chessboard that had thrown her. It was the presence of a stranger with Go. No numbers buzzed a warning in her head, but still she couldn't quite settle her nerves. Couldn't quite settle her stomach.

"How well do you know the game? The one he was playing?"

Margot squared her shoulders and forced herself to focus on Dot, and then on the path before them. "Fairly well. The officer

who occupied our house in Brussels —
Gottlieb — liked to play, and I was the only
one around to play with him. I enjoyed it."
And had come to realize, through their daily
games, that he wasn't quite the monster
she'd thought him at first. That a uniform
didn't make a man by nature a friend or an
enemy.

But choice did. And for every ally, one
could be mathematically certain that an
enemy existed too. Gottlieb had turned out
to be a friend, but a fellow Belgian had
proven himself an enemy and had nearly
gotten Willa killed when she came with
Lukas to help Margot and Maman escape.

Gregory Westrom had been a friend. What
of this newcomer, with his German game?
What were the odds that he, too, was a
friend?

Back on the street, Margot led the way to
the redbrick house that looked very much
like every other redbrick house in this section of the city. It was far nicer than the flat
she and Maman shared, and Lukas and
Willa had of course offered them rooms
here. But they'd already been settled in the
flat, and Lukas and Willa had been so newly
married when they found this place. Still,
she and Maman spent enough time here
that Margot felt perfectly comfortable

mounting the doorsteps, ringing the bell, and smiling at the housekeeper who opened the door for her. She stepped inside knowing exactly where to put her coat and how many steps it would take to find her favorite chair in the drawing room. She knew which boards squeaked and how the pipes rattled in the winter.

It wasn't quite home, but it was close enough. And as she motioned Dot to follow her into the drawing room, she said a prayer that it would feel as comforting to her friend as it did to her.

Das Gespenst hunched over the game board and jerked his handkerchief out of his pocket with shaking fingers. He did his best to keep his cough muted, shallow. It had improved with his last brief venture to the Continent, after he'd been released from hospital. It would improve more, he hoped, with his next trip he'd been ordered to take.

But in the meantime, this dratted British damp. He detested England's weather. Why couldn't he have been stationed in Spain or North Africa or South America? His lungs wouldn't be itching like this in those climates.

His gaze flicked again to the old woman with her yarn, then to the park exit through which the two young women had gone. He recognized them both. He'd seen them coming from the Old Admiralty Building on Friday, when he'd stationed himself on a bench near its doors, his back curved against the damp.

His superiors had assured him that it had been an oversight that his ship was torpedoed. They'd assured him that he was trusted, that he was an appreciated asset.

He wasn't entirely certain he believed them. He'd utterly failed to make contact with the agent they'd sent him here to find, so they could have deemed it a failing worthy of termination. He'd have to prove himself anew. So he'd taken his new orders — to try to get his hands on British codebooks — as a challenge in which he could *not* fail.

Codebooks. They would be on every naval vessel, of course, with other officers and agents in the field. But they'd also be there, in the Old Admiralty Building, and those would be guaranteed to be up to date. That must be his target.

But how to penetrate the place? The more he studied it, the more impossible it seemed. He'd watched it for hours, looking for weaknesses, learning the routines of those who came and went. Memorizing each face.

From what he'd been able to glean, every woman who worked there had some connection to the Admiralty. They knew someone within, or someone important. Perhaps . . . perhaps that could prove useful. He could find a secretary to give him access to the place — perhaps one of those two who had just left the park, or perhaps someone else. He'd do a bit of research, watch the building some more. Find the most likely mark. Someone capable of giving him the access he needed. It would be a shame to manipulate or threaten the wrong person and find it got him nowhere.

He tucked his handkerchief back into his pocket and let his fingers brush the handle of the blade he kept close whenever he was on solid ground. He'd not had it with him aboard the *Boynton,* for which he was grateful. He'd have hated to lose *Der Vampir.* When Father had given it to him — not to Heinrich, but to *him* — he'd made him promise to take the best possible care of it. It had been in their family for generations, and the styling reminded him of his Bavarian home every time he looked at it.

He rubbed his thumb over the pommel and then covered it again with his coat.

"Sorry." Yūrei came up behind him, still coughing, though not as badly as he'd been ten minutes ago, when it had sent him inside for a drink to soothe it. He sat opposite him at the Go board.

Das Gespenst summoned a smile for his fellow specter. "Why don't we go inside for our game? Out of this blasted damp?"

"You've read my mind."

Grinning, he lifted the game from its table. With the help of a secretary from the Old Admiralty Building, he'd soon be reading more than Yūrei's mind — he'd be reading the Admiralty's.

6

There were moments when Drake felt guilty for sitting at a bistro on a warm afternoon and ordering a meal. He knew all too well that he was eating far better here than he would be at home in London. Knew that he was eating far better, too, than the poor in Spain. He knew it, but he also knew that if he *didn't* move about and act like the grandson of Francisco Mendoza de Haro, then he could well compromise all the work he was doing.

And today, he wasn't dining alone. He certainly wouldn't begrudge his superior a meal on Abuelo's bill either.

"What do you recommend?" Thoroton studied the menu from his relaxed pose in his chair. He wore the pale linen suit of a Spaniard, but there was no disguising his British features. Even so, he got on well in the country. And should, as hard as he had worked to ingratiate himself.

Drake skimmed the menu, though he ate at this bistro at least once a week. His director had spoken in Spanish, so he followed suit. "I'm partial to the chorizo and rice."

"That sounds good."

They put in their order, both looking out at the pretty street of the Old Quarter while the waiter busied himself at a table nearby. In England right now, autumn had no doubt fully dislodged summer, and rain would be usurping the fair days. But here the sun beat down hot and golden, painting the cobblestones with heat that radiated back up to them at their outdoor table. Around them, chatter buzzed from the other tables, all filled.

It wouldn't look odd for Drake to be entertaining an Englishman — he frequently did, whenever an acquaintance came into town. But more often than not, those acquaintances were other agents, serving with him under this one.

Thoroton reached into the satchel he'd brought with him and drew out a stack of envelopes with familiar script on the outside. His words switched to English. "Here's your post, while I'm thinking of it." As he slid the stack onto the table between them, Charles the Bold offered a lopsided grin. "I suppose it'll be easier once Hall grants you permission to tell your sister where you really are. Then she can just write to you at your grandfather's."

Drake breathed a laugh and tucked the four envelopes into his jacket pocket. "I honestly can't imagine letting Dot in on it. Unless you mind playing courier?"

Thoroton waved that off, his mustache twitching in amusement. "I've been meaning to ask you — more as a curiosity, not because I doubt you've seen to it. How do you keep your grandfather from writing to her of your presence here?"

Drake hid a snort behind his glass. "Oh, that hardly requires any planning. Abuelo's letters are solely responses to *our* letters to him, which he expects every fortnight. They offer advice and reply to whatever we share, but he never volunteers anything at all from what is going on in *his* life."

Lazily trailing a finger through the condensation on his glass, Thoroton lifted a brow. "And if he slips?"

"Then Dot would think I'd merely popped in for a visit on a leave." Coming here was the only way he'd ever see Abuelo. There was never any question of where Dot came by her homebody tendencies — their grandfather never left the house but to go to Mass once a week. Dot had only once met the

106

man she was so like. "Speaking of peculiar people . . . any luck on my opposite number?"

He kept his voice even and light as he asked. Speaking English as they were, it was unlikely that any of the other patrons at the nearby tables would pay any attention, especially if there were no changes in their tones. A trick Thoroton had first taught him.

Obviously he followed suit. "Mm-hmm. I've a few photographs for you to look over. My best guesses." He drew a book out of his satchel next. Poems by Robert Browning. "Here you are."

"Many thanks." As if just so eager to read it, he flipped the cover and a few of the pages until he found the snapshots nestled within. The first bloke he'd never seen before, so he turned another page to where another photo was lodged, and then another before he lifted his brows. "There we are. 'The Pied Piper of Hamelin.' "

Thoroton grunted. "Not my favorite option. Mind yourself."

Drake flipped the photo over and found a name inked onto the back. *Maxim Jaeger.* He committed it to memory and closed the book, handing it back to Thoroton. "I do. Haven't had any exchanges lately." Not since the warehouse, and he was grateful for it.

Well, there'd been an incident on a Sunday when he'd spotted the bloke, but he'd done the spotting first and managed to hide himself before the agent — Jaeger, apparently — could spot *him.*

"Any new poetry you'd recommend, old chap?" Thoroton asked casually.

"As a matter of fact, I've made you a list." After an unhurried swig of lemonade, Drake reached into the pocket opposite the one he'd put Dot's letters in and pulled out a little slip of paper with what he'd discovered in the weeks since he'd found the warehouse with the wolfram. Though not encoded per se, it was written in a shorthand that no one else would likely understand. Thoroton tucked it into the Browning and slid it back into his satchel. No doubt he'd read it as soon as he had some privacy, then burn it.

But the necessary information would make its way to Hall. He'd know about the money that had changed hands between the Germans and a few Spaniards who were more interested in silver than in politics. He'd know about the creaky old ship, the *Erri Barro,* that was due into the harbor soon and had been commissioned to carry the wolfram back out of port with it.

Of course, that meant he'd also know how long it was likely to be before anything came of it. Before they could use the decrepit ship, they first had to repair it.

Thoroton leaned out of the way with a smile when the waiter reappeared with two plates heaping with spiced sausage and rice. "I've been on the hunt for a collection of Victor Hugo's poetry in the original French. Do you think that little shop you frequent may have one?"

Which was to say, there was new information waiting for Drake in one of their usual drop locations — a used and foreign bookshop whose proprietor was sympathetic to the Allies. They never liked to risk handing over too much information at one time. If anyone were to waylay one or the other of them, that would mean too much could be compromised.

Drake thanked the waiter and picked up his fork, nodding as if in thought. "It's quite possible. I'll run in and check for you before they close this evening, shall I? Are you staying in Bilbao tonight?"

"I'm afraid not. I'll be catching the evening train to San Sebastián." Thoroton scooped up a bite of his food and tasted it, grinning in appreciation. "Ah, perfect. An excellent recommendation."

While they ate, they talked in a mixture of Spanish and English about the war and mutual acquaintances, like every other patron here. Nothing that wasn't already in the newspapers, nothing Drake had to take particular note of.

There was no lingering after they'd finished their meal. In different circumstances, Drake would have considered Charles the Bold a friend — but when they met, it was for a specific purpose. Now that said purpose had been fulfilled, Thoroton dashed off to catch his train, and Drake ambled along to the bookshop.

The bell jangled over the door when he entered, and the smell of paper and ink and must greeted him, along with a grunt of acknowledgment from the proprietor, who didn't even look up from the copy of *La Chartreuse de Parme* in his hands. He just held up a finger that said, *Let me finish my paragraph,* without any need for words.

"No hurry, Mateo." Drake smiled and turned into an aisle of bookcases. He would leave with more than just the Hugo that would be hidden behind a dusty tome written in Icelandic — not exactly a book in high demand, which made it a perfect cover. First he'd find a few books in similar taste.

He turned first to the English section, as

he always did. An eclectic selection filled one bookcase, never failing to make him smile. Old Mateo shelved a battered copy of *The Adventures of Huckleberry Finn* next to *Wealth of Nations,* with *Middlemarch* flanking the economic treatise on the other side. Rhyme or reason there was not, not in the foreign sections of the shop. But that was half the fun of browsing these shelves.

After a few minutes, he pulled out a dog-eared copy of Conrad's *Heart of Darkness.* One of these days, he fancied a trip to Africa, and he'd heard quite a bit about Conrad's literary journey up the Congo, inspired by his own travels. Might as well see what portrait he painted of the continent.

He moved next to the French section, which was twice the size of the English. Best to find some poetry, so that the volume of Hugo would have a friend. He looked through shelf after shelf, dismissing the few anthologies he found at first because he already had them. After ten minutes, he spotted *Les Heures Claires* by Émile Verhaeren. He didn't much care for the man's work during his dark period, but this one, he believed, had been written directly after his marriage and reflected his newfound joy. Drake slid it out and added it to his growing stack.

Next stop, that one little corner of Icelandic. He didn't look over his shoulder, didn't do anything other than what he'd been doing all along — sliding out books, looking into them, sliding them back in. Except this time, he slid out one, and then the other, hidden behind it, and replaced only the first.

Hugo he put between Verhaeren and Conrad.

One more. Or maybe two. He moved into the largest partition of the shop, where used books in Spanish took up most of the space. A beautifully bound edition of *Don Quixote* found a place in his stack, even though he knew his grandfather would roll his eyes at him for it — he already had four different editions of what had been his favorite book as a lad, and a duplicate of his favorite. After another twenty minutes of browsing and debate, he selected a slightly worn copy of *Las ilusiones del doctor Faustino* as well. It wasn't his usual fare, but it was considered a monumental work in Spanish literature, so he really ought to read it at some point.

Mateo hadn't stirred from his stool behind his ancient cash register, but when Drake set his stack of books down with a louder-than-necessary *thunk,* the old man looked up and grinned. "Ah, Dragón. Find every-thing?"

"Sí, gracias." He fished out his wallet while Mateo rung up the sale.

The old man chuckled when he came to *Don Quixote.* "How did I know you would be the one to purchase this?"

"I'm predictable." Smiling, he handed over bills and coin enough when the proprietor told him the total, exchanged a few more pleasantries, and then slid out the door.

Spices and greetings tinged the air as he strolled the ten minutes to Abuelo's proud house. Drake called out "Buenas tardes" to all his neighbors, juggling his books time and again to wave or shake a hand.

He knew well that most of these neighbors thought he'd moved in with Abuelo solely to avoid serving in the war. No doubt a few of them looked down on him for it. That had taken a bit of teeth-clenching and spine-straightening to get over when first Hall and Thoroton positioned him here, but at this point he generally believed himself when he recited the refrain that no one else's opinion mattered.

They didn't, not ultimately. *He* knew he was serving his country. It didn't require the daily wearing of a uniform or a medal or being praised as a hero to know he was doing what he ought.

Still. To be thought a coward . . . that had required a bit of thickening of his skin, to be sure.

He let himself in through the centuries-old wooden door, three inches thick, and closed it behind him with nary a creak. When one spent as many hours at home as did his abuelo, one had ample time to ensure that every hinge, latch, and seal was in perfect order.

"Dragón."

Drake's feet had been aimed toward the central marble staircase, but he redirected them toward Abuelo's study, to the right of the entryway, and stepped through the open door with a smile. "Buenas tardes, Abuelo."

His grandfather motioned him in with a wave of his hand, his attention still latched upon the papers currently on his massive desk. "You had a pleasant meal with your English friend?"

"Sí. Charles is always pleasant company. Poetry, the news, mutual acquaintances — always plenty to talk about." And even more *not* to talk about. Drake shifted his stack of books to his other arm.

Abuelo penned something onto the paper in his impeccably elegant script and finally

looked up. He was the very figure of style
— dark jacket cut to fit him perfectly, snow-
white shirt beneath, perfectly matching his
hair, a tie in a shade of deep red that set off
his brows, still shockingly dark. Drake
couldn't recall ever seeing him out of his
bedroom in anything less than formal dress.
Some might find it odd, given that he never
went out to show it off. But plenty of people
paraded into this room throughout the day:
business associates, servants, priests, neighbors. The world of Francisco Mendoza de
Haro was full and colorful, and larger than
one might think, given the walls he chose to
keep around himself.

He didn't smile. He rarely did, though his
eyes seldom lacked for a twinkle of good
humor. "I had a letter from your sister
today. Did you?"

"A few of them caught up to me at once.
I haven't yet had a chance to read them."

"Mm." Abuelo reached for a glass, probably full of Madeira. "Then we will discuss
her news after you have learned it."

News? It was possible that Abuelo was
only just learning of her employment, he
supposed. Regardless, he was anxious to get
up to his room where he could find Thoroton's assignment for him in the Hugo. He
smiled at his grandfather. "Very good. I'll

join you again shortly."

Once upstairs, he let himself into the chamber that had been his since the day he was born, though it was another eight years before he ever stepped foot in it. Dot had the next one down — assigned upon her own birth, and only visited once. Still, it was cleaned every week, the linens changed, the styles updated occasionally, so that if ever she came again, it would be ready for her.

That was Abuelo. Perhaps because this house was his world, he made sure there was a place inside always prepared for those he loved.

Drake's room had, over the years, taken on a bit of the character of a library. In addition to the desk, shelves lined an entire wall. To these he went now, filing most of the books he'd just purchased into their proper places. But he kept the Hugo in his hands and made himself comfortable at his desk. From a drawer he pulled out the dictionary that Thoroton would have used as a key, a fresh sheet of paper, and a pencil.

It took him half an hour to note each line of poetry that was underlined and use the page and line number to find the corresponding entry in the dictionary, but when at last he had the message worked out, he could only stare for a long moment.

Suspect Germans will be trying to use diseases to infect cereal intended for livestock — donkeys and horses. Discover where anthrax and glanders bacilli may be located. Watch for agents.

Drake expelled a long breath and rubbed a hand over his face. How could they justify this? How could a civilized nation really decide it was acceptable to deliberately spread deadly bacteria?

It had been done before, he supposed, recalling the story of blankets of smallpox victims being given to the natives in the colonies. But that hadn't been on the command of the government; it had been the action of a few men with shadows upon their souls. This, though, would have come from the German High Command.

Only animals, it seemed. A fact they would surely emphasize if ever called to task for it. But how could they guarantee, with the current grain shortages, that cereal currently earmarked for animals wouldn't get appropriated for human consumption? How could they know?

Or did they not care?

Drake's eyes slid shut. He wasn't entirely certain how he would go about finding these bacteria cultures — those answers would require some questions he didn't yet know to ask. But he would do some research, put out some feelers, inquire discreetly of some friends.

The clock in the hall chimed the hour, pulling him from those thoughts. Abuelo would be expecting him downstairs again soon — he'd better actually read Dot's letters beforehand.

He pulled the packet of them from his pocket and unbound them, sorting them by date. The first detailed her initial days working in Room 40, how she was being trained to type, a bit about Lady Hambro. Chatty but also decidedly dishonest, as it said nothing about how difficult it had been to force herself from the flat, and Drake knew very well it was a fight she would have had with herself.

The second letter made mention of a new friend she'd made — Margot. This, perhaps, was the news Abuelo was mentioning. New friends were hard enough for Dot to come by that it qualified as noteworthy. *Thank you, Father.* He'd been mentioning his sister's need for companionship in his prayers every night.

When he opened the third, a snapshot slid out as he unfolded the letter. He picked it up and sucked in a breath.

He didn't even glance at his sister's image, smiling from the right side of the photo. He was too busy looking at the figure on the left.

The dark-eyed nameless girl.

She stared up at him with an intensity that a camera should not have been able to capture so well. Her lips didn't smile, exactly, but they didn't *not* either. The corners were turned up just the slightest bit, in a way that put Mona Lisa to shame.

The black-and-white image couldn't reveal details like eye color or the shade of suit she wore, but his memory supplied the image's lack. Deepest brown eyes, so dark they were nearly black. The day he'd seen her, she'd been in dark blue — he couldn't have said whether this skirt and jacket were exactly the same or not, but he imagined them as such.

Just as he imagined the snap of her wit ready to trip off her tongue.

With a corner of his own mouth tugging up in a smile, he turned to the letter, propping the photo up on his desk.

I know I've been chattering nonstop about Margot, so I thought I'd include a snapshot her mother took of us last week at her brother's house. Her brother is Lukas De

Wilde, the violinist — had I mentioned that? I think you'd like her, Drake. It isn't just that she has learned to tolerate my quirks, as Ada has. It's that she understands them and knows when to push and when to let me rest. And heavens, but I think she must be the most intelligent person I've ever met!

He leaned back against the well-worn wood of his chair, eyes shifting again to the photograph. Margot De Wilde, was it? It felt a bit unsporting to learn her name through no cleverness of his own, but he wasn't exactly sorry to have a name to go with the memory. A friend for his sister, not like Ada. Pretty, intelligent, and with those dark eyes that cut him to the quick.

His lips curved into a smile. A reason to look forward to his next trip to London, whenever that might be.

7

Where was she? Margot stood just inside the door of the Old Admiralty Building, clutching her umbrella and staring out into the pouring rain. Most of the day shift had already arrived, though there were still a few stragglers jumping over puddles and hurrying inside.

None, however, were Sophie De Wilde. Margot sighed and glanced at her watch. Five minutes late. Not a lot for some people, perhaps, but quite a bit for her mother. And no doubt it was Margot's fault — she'd grabbed the good umbrella when she left for her weekly night shift yesterday evening, hoping the weather would have improved by the time Maman would need to leave this morning. The other umbrella had been giving them problems for weeks, refusing to go up — or back down after they'd managed to wrestle it into position. It had probably broken outright, leaving her mother to scramble for one she could borrow from a neighbor. Or perhaps even detour to a shop to spend a few precious coins on a new one.

Exhaustion had settled over her shoulders an hour ago. The night shift had managed to break the new codes without too much problem, but Hall had passed her another packet from Thoroton to decipher. "If you have the time," he'd said as he turned for the door. "If you don't, I'll handle it myself tomorrow."

Had they not managed to break the German codes in ample time, she wouldn't have minded handing the stack of HUMINT back to the admiral without its plain script counterpart, but she could hardly nap at her desk as Culbreth and de Grey had done with that packet sitting there. So she'd spent her remaining time scribbling like mad, trying to get it finished before her shift was over.

Now the words were a jumble in her mind as the rain poured down before her vision. Wolfram. Agent Thirty. Anthrax. Cartagena. *Erri Barro.* Codebooks. Agent Eighteen. Bacilli. Madrid. Sugar. Bilbao. Agent Four.

Margot checked her watch again. Was it possible that Maman was waiting at home for her, so she could use the good brolly? It didn't seem the most plausible course of action, but Maman was not always the most logical creature in the world. Most of the time she was utterly rational. But on rare occasions, frustration or joy or some other incomprehensible feeling would trump better reason and make her do the strangest things. Like sit on the couch with a huff after fighting with an umbrella for ten minutes and declaring to the otherwise empty flat that she wouldn't move until a working example arrived.

"Everything all right, Margot?"

Margot looked over her shoulder with a muted smile for Dot. She'd obviously only come back downstairs on some sort of errand, as she had a clutch of papers in hand. *She* had arrived ten minutes ago. Margot lifted a shoulder. "Maman is not here yet."

Dot's brows drew together. "Has she come down with that flu that's been going around, perhaps? She looked a bit pale yesterday."

Margot shifted her weight to her other foot. She hadn't considered that very likely possibility — which proved how tired she was. "Possibly. She *did* seem run-down. But she would have telephoned Lady Hambro to tell her, if so."

"And I daresay she will. If so, I mean. But she may have overslept, or been waiting to be sure her ladyship was in."

True, all. Margot let that possibility slip into the row of them in her mind. Stay or go? Wait or check on her mother?

The numbers were muted, sluggish, as tired as the rest of her. But she *thought* they agreed with the idea of marching out into the cold rain and going home. The powers of three were singing through her mind. No, of four. No . . .

"Are *you* feeling all right?" Dot had come closer and reached now to touch a hand to Margot's forehead. Her own was creased into a frown. Symmetrical lines, equidistant apart. "You feel warm."

She wouldn't let just anybody touch her head like that. But it hadn't taken long for Dot to feel like a sister. And she was too tired to jerk away. "I'm well enough. Just tired." Though now that she mentioned it, her throat was the tiniest bit sore too.

Nothing a cup of tea and a morning of sleep wouldn't fix. With what was meant to be a marshalling exhale but came out as a resigned sigh, Margot lifted the brolly. "All right, enough dillydallying. I'll either find her on the way or see her at home. Good night, Dot. See you tomorrow."

Her friend grinned. "Good morning, Margot. Stay dry — and put a bit of honey in your tea, if you have any. You sound hoarse."

"Yes, Mother." She issued the tease knowing well it would make Dot laugh — rare indeed was the occasion that her friend got to take care of anyone else now that her aunt had left the city.

Then came the draft trying to hold the door shut, the first gust of wet wind lashing against her, the quick *snick* of her umbrella going up, and the drumming of rain upon it. Margot set off with her coat cinched tightly around her waist and her head down as she fought the wind that snuck under her brolly.

Gentle rains were entertaining. She could count to the patter, try to find the pattern in the falling droplets. From the safety of her window, she could even imagine that, were she an inch tall, she could map out a path around them.

Rain like this was too complete. A solid wall, moving in sheets, the drops tripping and pushing one another in their haste to find her umbrella. And her shoes. And the hem of her skirt.

What she wouldn't give just now for a pair of trousers and some boots. Perhaps one of those so-dubbed trench coats that, according to the chattering secretaries, were now all the mode since they were introduced in the military.

Not that she'd had a new coat since her first autumn here, when it had been necessary. Also not, for that matter, that Maman would ever consent to her daughter wearing trousers.

And not that Margot would waste any more than those thirty seconds thinking about, of all things, *fashion.* Good grief, she could only imagine the way Maman and Dot would laugh if they knew.

Thunder rumbled across the sky as Margot hurried around the last corner. She hadn't passed her mother anywhere along the route. That and the throat that really was more than a *little* sore, now that she thought to pay attention to it, made her think Dot was likely right about Maman having caught the cold or flu or whatever it was going around. It seemed Margot had, and they were always in the same places.

Agent Eighteen. Wolfram. Anthrax.

As if a cold was anything to really fuss over these days. Hurrying through a wet English autumn wasn't exactly unpleasant compared to what those field agents faced on a regular basis. She shuddered at the memory of some of the words she'd decoded an hour ago. They reported enemy agents — *opposite numbers,* Thoroton had called them once, which had made her smile — stealing from them, chasing them. Agent Twenty-two, whoever he was, had been arrested last week in Morocco.

Margot wouldn't snivel over a cold or a broken umbrella. She wouldn't.

Finally, the door to their building swallowed her up. She shook the water from her now-lowered brolly onto the front step and then let the door swing shut behind her.

It smelled of damp and mold in this front hallway, as it always did. Maman had tried once to scrub it into lemony bliss, but even wood soap couldn't long hold out against the century or two of damp that had crept into the banisters and floors and walls.

Margot took a moment to wipe her feet — no point in transferring *more* moisture to said floors — and then let them take her on the familiar path. Four steps to the stairs. Up nineteen, pivot on the landing. Up nineteen, pivot on the landing. Again. Again. Her right hand trailed along the banister, counting in time to her feet. A knot in the wood on step sixteen, between the first and second floor. A nick at step three on the next span. The missing rung on the eleventh step of the final stretch of the banister, which *did* change the pitch of her hand running along it, despite Lukas the Pitch Expert swearing it didn't.

Of course it did. It must. Her ears might not be able to hear it, but her mind could.

Then, finally, the corridor that would lead to the familiar door with the familiar number hanging from it in tin: 3E.

She fumbled in her pocket for her key. Until this flat, she'd never lived in anything but a house, with a number all its own. No letters had ever been required by the number. It was a variable, she'd claimed to her mother when they first moved in. Not just 3E, but 3(e) — three of E — with any number of possibilities for what the value really was. Some days she let it be a mere three of one — three times one, a simple three. Some days she enjoyed the chance to let larger numbers swell, and it became 37,518 — three of 12,506.

Today, exhaustion and sore throats and keys that would *not* fit right in the lock inspired a simpler number. Three of six would do, since it took her six attempts to fit the blasted metal into the blasted hole correctly. Eighteen.

Eighteen. That meant something, but she was too startled by opening the door and finding darkness within to think what. "Maman?" Darkness implied her mother *wasn't* there, though that couldn't be, could it? She'd not passed her on the way.

She shoved her wet umbrella into the stand, beside the faulty one that still stood in its usual spot, no evidence of it having been growled over and declared impossible. Pushed the door shut. Switched on the electric lights that they were only allowed to use in the daytime, when they wouldn't shine out the windows and give away their location to any unfriendlies flying overhead.

"Maman?" She must still be in bed. Perhaps the cold had kept her up half the night, and then she'd overslept once she finally found slumber.

But . . . no. A faint light shone from under her mother's bedroom door. She *could* have fallen asleep with the gaslight on, she supposed, but it wasn't likely. Margot hastened to the door, rapped lightly. "Maman?" No answer came. Was she in the toilet? No light shone from under *that* door though.

She cracked the door open, frowning when she realized it wasn't the low gas lamp at all, but the brighter electric one. Maman never turned that on until morning. She'd obviously gotten up to get ready, as usual, this morning.

The door stuck at half-open, bumping into something and going no farther.

That was when panic sank its fangs into her throat. This tiny little cupboard of a room fit only a narrow bed and a minuscule chest of drawers. There was no space for anything else, anything that could fall over and impede the swing of the creaking door. No furniture. And Maman was meticulous about picking up her few possessions.

Which meant it wasn't furniture. Wasn't a possession.

Margot edged through the opening as quickly as she could, braced herself, and yet still felt punched in the stomach at the sight of the white nightgown draping the legs on the floor. "Maman!"

She lay on her side on the rug, her hair a mass of silver-threaded midnight over her arm — unbraided, wavy. Proving she'd risen as she always had, already reaching to undo her hair so she could brush it and pin it up. "Maman."

Margot fell to her knees beside her mother, easing her gently onto her back. It was just a cold. Flu, maybe. Dehydration. She'd fainted. Passed out. Perhaps even bumped her head, but it was nothing that serious.

Her hands shaking, Margot pressed her fingers to Maman's wrist. Where was her pulse, where? "No. No, Maman. Come on.

Wake up. Wake up!"

Her hands — her hands were shaking too badly, that was all. Shaking too much to detect the pulse in her wrist. She reached for her throat instead, where it ought to be more easily found, even if it were weak. Thready, wasn't that what they called it? She could handle weak and thready. Weak and thready left room for hope. For intervention.

But her fingers couldn't find any thumping in her mother's throat either. "God! Sixty-two!" That was Maman's usual resting heart rate. "Fifty-one." Her mother's age. "Nine thousand four." The times she could remember Maman saying she loved her — the times she'd said it back. *Je t'aime, Maman.*

"Mon Dieu, s'il vous plaît. S'il vous plaît, pas ma maman."

She shook her a bit, but Maman didn't stir. Margot screamed out her prayer, but Maman didn't budge.

Telephone. She had to call for assistance.

Lukas. *1532.* He would know what to do.

Hospital. They could help.

DID. The admiral always had answers.

Eighteen.

She pushed to her feet, knocked her knee against the chest of drawers, slid out the door, hit her elbow against the frame.

Telephone.

Lukas.

Hospital.

DID.

Eighteen.

She lifted the receiver, listened for the operator. Telephone.

"This is the operator. How may I direct your call?"

Lukas. "Kensington–1532." Hospital. DID. *Eighteen.*

"One moment, please."

One moment. All it took for a pulse to disappear. For a heart to give up. For the whole world to change. Margot stood rooted to the spot, her eyes scarcely even blinking. They remained fixed on the window, where morning's light was grey and heavy and soaked with autumn rains that distorted the world outside.

Distorted the world *inside.*

Telephone. Lukas. Hospital. DID. *Eighteen.*

"Hello?"

"Lukas. Hospital. DID. Eighteen."

"What? Margot, is that you?"

She couldn't blink. She could only stare at the rain-soaked world beyond the rain-spattered window through her rain-soaked eyes. *"C'est Maman."* No other words would come.

Telephone.
Lukas.
Hospital.
DID.
Eighteen.
Maman. . . .

"Margot. Margot, come away from the window." Lukas's hand rested on her shoulder. Gentle. Firm. Both at once, in different respects.

"Margot, come away from the window." How many times had Maman said that to her, trying to draw her back into the world of which she wanted her to be a part? Eighty-one. Eighty-one times. But not lately. Because lately Margot hadn't had much time to stare out windows. To calculate the number of bricks in the buildings across the street. To wonder. She'd been too busy. Always busy.

The rain had slowed, though it hadn't stopped. The pedestrians were splashing through puddles as they hurried about in search of their midday repast. Every time Margot breathed out, a cloud of vapor settled on the cold pane of glass and then shrank again as she drew in new breath. She could calculate the rate at which it disappeared if she wanted.

But what did it matter?

"Margot." The hand on her shoulder squeezed. "Come, *ma sœur.* You need not stay here. Come home with me — we have canceled the concert tonight. You can let Willa fuss over you."

"No." Droplets still clung to the windowpane. Not racing along their tracks now and joining with other drops in a mad dash for *down,* but just clinging there. Stubborn and small and sure to evaporate into the air if ever the sun decided to break through the clouds.

"Margot." Lukas wrapped his arms around her and, despite her inability to move even a muscle to accommodate him, held on tight. His breath rasped, and his chest heaved. This was how her brother mourned. How he had mourned when their father died, when the world had crumbled even before war had shattered what was left.

It was how he mourned now, when their mother joined Papa in heaven. When the last vestiges of *normal* turned to dust.

She managed to lift a hand, to rest it against his arm. The movement hurt, deep inside. Stillness was her natural state in moments like this. But Lukas needed a touch, so she dug down, despite the pain, and forced one.

She loved him. He knew it. It would be enough for him. Just as his arms around her, though she *didn't* need the touch, was his love for her. She knew it. It was enough.

His tears wet her hair where his face rested against her head. It was only the second time she had ever seen her brother cry. For their father. For their mother.

Then, when one ambitious drop on the windowpane decided to use the wind as an engine and slide a slow, painful inch, he pulled away. "Come. You cannot stay here alone."

Cannot? "No." More like *must.* This was home. This was where she and Maman had made a fresh start. She couldn't just *leave.*

"Margot." Mournful. Not for Maman now, but for her.

Didn't he understand? "No."

He sighed. And he moved away.

The clouds raced over the city. Slate to grey to white. Lightening, turning to fluff, and finally breaking apart enough for a sliver of sunlight to shine through. She ought to move. Help. Make preparations. But her head was foggy and her throat was on fire and that *stillness* wouldn't let her go.

"Margot?"

She hadn't seen Dot coming along the street below, but then, she'd been looking at the clouds. One particularly swift one tumbled over the sky now, its edges shifting and changing and losing bits of itself to the vast expanse of air around it.

Mutters from behind her. Two voices. Three. Dot, Lukas, the landlady. Three. Three of . . . what had it been? Six.

Eighteen.

Only three, when it should have been four. Maman should be standing there with them. Worrying over something with them. Planning something with them.

The racing cloud covered the sun, plunging the street back into midday shadows. The muttering stopped. Silence, then the soft padding of light footsteps. Too light for Lukas. Too light for the landlady, who was as wide as she was tall, within an inch and a half. Dot.

Scraping, scuffing behind her. Beside her. "There." Dot settled into the chair she'd just pulled over. One of them. "If you need to sit."

Her legs did ache. So did her back and her neck and her throat and her eyes and her head. But it didn't matter. She couldn't make them move. Couldn't tell her knees to bend.

Dot said nothing else. She drew a book from the bag hooked over her arm and started reading. With her eyes still locked on the window, Margot couldn't make out the title.

It didn't matter. She was there, and she wasn't talking. This was Dot's love.

The sun emerged again, and it did valiant battle as it tracked across the sky, struggling to fend off the clouds and set the puddles to steaming.

Lukas was by her side again, his hand on her shoulder again. "I need to meet with Father Foster. Did you want to come?"

When she blinked, she saw Louvain out the window instead of London. Felt her childhood home around her instead of this flat with 3E on the door. Heard Maman posing the question, only not. Because it had been Father Pudois she'd been going to see, arrangements for Papa's wake that needed to be made.

She blinked again to clear it. She'd gone with her mother then. She needed to go with her brother now. She nodded.

Lukas stepped closer and reached to brush the hair out of her eyes. Then he jerked his hand away, muttering a French curse under his breath. "You are burning up! For heaven's sake. You are not going anywhere but to bed."

"No!" She had to go with him. If she could convince her muscles to move.

He pushed her down into the chair, a stern look on his face. "No argument. I can meet with Father Foster. You must get well. Do you understand?"

Well? As if there were such a thing today. "Lukas." She blinked, but her head was still as hazy as the fog off the Thames. Sought the words, any words. "Hospital. . . ." That wasn't right. It had been too late for a hospital. Her pulse was gone. Gone. Not sixty-two. Not even thirty. Zero. Too long at zero.

Margot squeezed her eyes shut. "No. DID."

Lukas crouched down. She heard him, felt him, smelled the scent of his soap and cologne. "I already spoke to the admiral, *ma bichette.* He will stop by when he can. He said to take as much time as you need."

Of course he would. That wasn't what she'd wanted either — and on a different day, she may have objected to Lukas calling her a doe. But she wouldn't argue it now. She had something else to say. What was it? What were the words? *Lukas. Hospital. DID.*

Eighteen. "Eighteen."

Lukas shifted again. When she forced her eyes back open, she was aware of him looking at Dot. "Do you know what she means?"

Dot shook her head.

"No." Margot clenched her teeth. She didn't know what she meant either. Her insides itched. "I . . . I don't know."

"Margot." Lukas sounded, now, like Maman always had when Margot had spent too many hours up at her desk when she should have been sleeping or eating or stitching or knitting or running about with other girls her age. He pressed his lips to her forehead. "You are not going out with such a fever. Drink something. Rest. This is no time to have you fainting from exhaustion or dehydration. I am going to need you, *ma bichette.* I can make the decisions about the wake and the burial, but I will need you to sort through the rest with me."

Wake. Burial. Those words weren't right either, not for Maman. The words for Maman ought to have been ones like *smile* and *laugh* and *chide* and *worry.* Always worry — worry for Margot, for Lukas, for Willa, for little Zurie. Worry for money and savings and the future. Worry for Gregory from the park and the other secretaries in the office and Mrs. Parsons from the flat two down from theirs. Worry for everyone but herself.

She couldn't be gone. She couldn't be.

Lukas brushed a lock of hair away from the side of Margot's face. "Do you hear me, Margot? I know it is louder within your head than outside of it right now, but I need you to hear me."

Her eyes hurt. Burned. For all their different ways, he *did* know her. Always had. She forced her head to dip down, to rise again.

"All right." He pressed another kiss to her forehead and levered himself back up. "Dot will stay with you. I will come back when I can."

He slid out of her central vision, out of her peripheral, out of her hearing with a *click* of the 3E door. Three of six. Eighteen.

Eighteen.

Her eyes slid shut again, blocking out the window and the raindrops clinging to it and the clouds on the horizon and the sun chasing them away. Blocking out the faded wallpaper on the walls and the chipping paint on the sill and the radiator to the left of her chair. She could feel the heat coming off it, but still it was cold.

What was eighteen? The door, but no. That wasn't it. That was just today. Eighteen was more than just today. Eighteen was . . .

Spain. Bilbao. *Erri Barro.* Wolfram. Anthrax.

She went even colder. *Eighteen.*

"Here."

Margo raised her eyelids again, though it took three seconds when it should have taken a third of one. A cup steamed in front of her, held in a familiar hand wearing a familiar sleeve of a shirt with 10,360 stitches. Give or take twenty.

"Tea. With honey. It'll soothe your throat."

Eighteen.

Margot reached for the cup, though her hands weren't exactly steady. She would drink it because Dot had made it for her. Because Lukas needed her to. Because dehydration could land *her* on the floor, unconscious, and she wouldn't do that to them now. Because she needed to get well, back on her feet, and able to do what needed to be done.

But it wouldn't soothe her. Nothing could soothe her.

Eighteen.

She cupped the mug in her hands and anchored it against her chest to keep from spilling it. Raised it for a slow sip. Cradled it against her again.

Eighteen.

She clenched her teeth, set her gaze on the windowpane once more. And sent

heavenward the only word she could find.
No.

8

Sugar cubes. Innocuous squares — or they should have been. Drake turned a page in his newspaper and leaned back against his seat so he could see past it without it *looking* like he was looking past it.

He'd found a seat in the back of the train so that he could see each passenger who got on. All from behind the cover of his newspaper, so that no one could see *him*. There'd been the usual moments of tension while the seats beside him filled, but none of the faces that took the adjacent seats belonged to Jaeger, or any of the other German agents whose photographs Thoroton had shown him. He hadn't exactly relaxed, but he'd ticked those concerns off his list, anyway.

That left only the waiting, the anxiousness of that biggest of questions: Was Drake's intelligence correct? Would Jaeger be on this train to Madrid, a sample of the sugar cubes laced with anthrax and glanders in his satchel, along with information on which of the freight carriages at the back of the train had the rest of the shipment? Or was this just a pointless use of a ticket?

Something about the movements of the next passenger to get on caught his attention and inspired him to raise his newsprint higher. Compared to the fluid, nearly languid gesturing of the Spaniards around him, this man's posture was stiff, perfect. He made what seemed to Drake's eye to be a concerted effort to move like his neighbors, but he didn't relax enough.

It was something Drake had studied for hours when he first came to Spain to attend university. He quickly grew tired of everyone pegging him as a foreigner the very moment he walked into a room and treating him accordingly. So he had studied his fellow students, his professors, even his grandfather — whose posture was also always perfect, but without that rigidity.

Drake risked half a glance at the stiff man, peeking around the edge of his paper and then hiding again behind it before the man could spot *him*.

Jaeger.

He was certain of it, though Drake only got a two-second glimpse of his face before he settled into a seat halfway up the train

144

carriage. One didn't forget a face one had first seen from behind a weapon pointed at one's chest.

Perfect. With a bit of luck, he'd be able to search the bloke's bag for the sample and information on the rest of the shipment. He hadn't been sure they'd end up in the same carriage to start out, of course, but he'd been prepared to move through the others if necessary, once the train was moving, and search the freight carriages one by one. This would save him that trouble. He offered up a prayer that the false beard he'd affixed to his face would help conceal his identity.

Usually he could go about his missions without fear of being seen, but this was a different case. Jaeger could easily recognize him through his light disguise, and there was no telling what he might do then. Anonymity was required here.

His neck went hot at the thought of the bacilli sitting just feet away. From the research he'd done, he knew it was stable enough in its current form — it wouldn't infect anyone here, not unless they ingested it or, even less likely, somehow inhaled the dust. But if by chance anyone did, if the sugar fell into human food stores instead of animal . . . The glanders wasn't likely to infect people, but anthrax was a different story. Typical flu symptoms — fever, chills, shortness of breath, fatigue — could lead to high fever, shock, and rapid death if it were inhaled. If it were ingested, lesions in the mouth, throat, and digestive tract would cause debilitating pain, vomiting blood, and ultimately death as well.

A cruel thing to wish even on animals, who would similarly suffer from it. The bacteria originated in livestock, but Pasteur and his assistants had instituted vaccination of sheep and cattle against anthrax decades ago. Science had been doing what it ought to have been — trying to knock it out. Not make a weapon of it. Not until now.

Drake's fingers wanted to tighten around the paper, but he kept them loose. He wouldn't feel sorry for the donkeys and horses the Germans were trying to kill — he'd simply save them the horror, that was all. He'd get the bacilli, he'd turn the sample over to Thoroton to ship to Hall for analysis, he and the rest of the team would reroute the larger quantities to wherever his superiors had decided they should go, and he'd move on to the next assignment.

Jaeger slid his satchel under his seat and cast a glance up and down the aisle as he did. Drake tipped his head down a bit so that the brim of his hat would hide any bits of his face that the paper didn't cover. So far as he could tell, Jaeger hadn't noticed him. No hitches in either his gaze or his posture, no change in his rate of movement as he straightened again.

Good. One complication avoided for now.

A few minutes later, the train pulled away from the station. The seat beside him, next to the window, remained empty — a stroke of luck for which he silently thanked the Lord. In fact, half the train carriage wasn't filled, which could work either to his advantage or disadvantage, depending. Fewer potential distractions to cover him, but fewer eyes to see him. He settled in, keeping his senses alert to the goings-on down the aisle. An opportunity would either arise on its own, or he would make one.

Across the aisle from Jaeger, a woman had settled with her children. There were six of them squeezed into the facing seats, including a baby who began fussing within ten minutes of their departure. Drake buried a smile behind his false whiskers when Jaeger shot the woman a look. Given the strict instruction the woman was giving her eldest daughter, he had a feeling she was the sort who wouldn't hesitate to give Jaeger a piece of her mind if he dared insinuate that her difficulties were an annoyance to him. That could prove entertaining.

His opposite number glanced about, obviously searching for an alternate seat — though moving would require sitting beside someone else, as there were no altogether empty rows. Would he risk moving to a different carriage? Drake prayed he wouldn't.

And he didn't. With a sigh, Jaeger settled in and held his peace. For ten minutes, for twenty. By that point, the harried mother was pacing the aisle with her fussy baby, trying to get the little one to quiet. She'd just reached her own seat again — and hence Jaeger's — when the train went round a bend, she swayed with it, and the baby lost its dinner . . . all over the German.

Jaeger sprang up with an expletive — in Spanish, which testified to how deeply in his cover he must be immersed. Drawing the attention of most of the train carriage, he shouted, "Look what you've done!"

"I'm so sorry, señor!" The woman's face flushed scarlet. She handed the baby to its sister and reached Jaeger's way with her shawl. "Let me —"

"Don't touch me." He sidestepped her, moving down the aisle toward the front of the carriage. The nearest lavatory was in the next carriage in front of them and was no doubt his aim. "Just . . . clean off my seat if you want to be useful."

Drake's eyes fell to said seat. And to the satchel still underneath it. *Thank you, Father in heaven.*

He waited until the agent had vanished and then stood. While the other passengers looked sympathetic, most of them seemed to be in no hurry to help clean up the mess.

Drake opened his own bag, pushed aside the copy of *Les Heures Claires* he'd packed, and grabbed a few other items that would prove useful now. Then he moved up the aisle.

The woman looked up at him with wary brown eyes. "Do you need to pass by?"

"No. I just thought I could help." He offered her a smile and held up the towel he'd packed. "I think this is better to sacrifice than your lovely shawl, *señora.* Here." He handed her the water he'd brought up with him too. "If you can wield this when necessary, I can use the towel."

The wariness melted into gratitude. "Gracias."

It only took a few minutes to get the worst of the mess from the floor. The seat was a bit more difficult, but between towel and water, it too was soon clean.

"Mama!" This cry came from one of her other children, a boy who couldn't be more than three. "My belly hurts too!"

The mother looked caught between exasperation and sympathy, with a dose of plea thrown in.

"Probably the smell." Drake nodded toward the water she still held. "See if he'll drink — perhaps that will settle his stomach. I don't need it." He needed her to turn away for a minute now. Just a minute. With a grin, he pulled out his secret weapon — the cologne he'd grabbed out of his bag too. "I'll just see to the smell, shall I?"

"You are an angel." The woman turned to her children, leaving Drake to spritz the cologne onto the seat.

And to reach underneath it. He didn't have much time now, he knew — Jaeger would be returning from the little lavatory at any moment, unless he decided to go to the dining carriage to give the clean-up time to be finished. Drake couldn't imagine him leaving his satchel unattended for that long though. He was no doubt cursing himself even now for doing so, unless there was nothing important in it.

Doubtful, given the intelligence Drake had found.

Relying on his back to block the view of his hands, he slid the satchel out, silently opened it, and let his eyes scour the contents. There — a small partitioned tray, rubber sealing its glass lid in place. He slid it out, along with the paper shoved in with it. A packing slip. He closed the satchel again and tucked the two items under his jacket as he slid the bag back under the seat.

Standing, he tossed a smile over his shoulder for the mother and her children. "There we go, clean and fragrant. Can I do anything else for you, señora?"

The little boy had settled against her side with a whimper. The other children were reading or looking out the window. Their mother smiled. "No, gracias. You have helped so much already, señor. I am in your debt."

"Nonsense." He folded the noisome towel up into a ball and held it up by way of explanation. "I'll just go and dispose of this. That way." He nodded toward the rear of the train, knowing she would understand his desire to avoid Jaeger.

She chuckled. "Sí."

No one got in his way or questioned him as he exited the back of the train carriage. Once on the little platform connecting it to the next, however, he tossed the towel away into the countryside and went empty-handed into the next carriage. Through it, to the next, and the next, until he'd run out of passenger carriages and there were no more platforms connecting them to the following one.

Perfect. Closing the door behind him, he drew the paper from his inner pocket and, shielding it from the wind, checked the number. Second carriage from the last. The last would have been better, but this would do. Pocketing the slip again, he stretched to the metal ladder going up the side of the freight carriage and gripped it. Swung over. Climbed up.

The wind whipped at him and tore his hat off his head — he made a snatch for it, missed, and indulged in a mutter. That had been his favorite hat, commissioned in Madrid. Blasted wind. It threatened to dislodge his makeshift mustache, too, and in that effort he helped it along, his skin thanking him. That thing had been getting itchy. He strode along the top of the freight carriage, debated jumping versus climbing down and back up between carriages, and decided to jump — it wasn't far, and the tops were flat. He made the leap without incident, and the next, and the next.

Then he landed on *the* carriage. Second to last. He drew in a breath of the warm air swirling around him and then moved to the trapdoor in its roof — easier to access from here than the doors on the side.

A minute's maneuvering and he was in the dark of the swaying box, fishing around in his pocket for his electric torch. Once it was on, he began the search. Crate after crate took up the space in here, along with barrels and bags as big as he was. But after a few minutes of shining his light along each one, he found the stamp that made him pause. *Azúcar.* Sugar.

He sidled over to it like it was alive and ready to bite him. The possibility existed that it was just sugar — normal, precious sugar, in demand and in short supply all over Europe.

Possible. But it would have been the most remarkable of coincidences.

He checked the number on the crates against the one scrawled on the packing slip to seal it in his mind. "Of course it's a match," he muttered to himself.

So then. He checked his watch. Twenty minutes before the train would approach the switch he needed. His pulse kicked up at the thought of this part of the mission. It wasn't risky so much as tricky. But he could do it. He *had* to do it.

He passed the next fifteen minutes in the dark of the carriage, praying more than thinking. Then he thought of his mother, who had said each and every day, *"Do not neglect your prayers, Drake. Neglect your chores, neglect your ablutions, neglect your mother"* — here she would tweak his nose — *"but never neglect your prayers. They are what root you to the Lord."*

Thoughts of Mama led to a few of Father. Then to Dot . . . and from there it was an easy slide to Margot De Wilde.

But he shook away the image of her dark eyes and climbed back up to the trapdoor in the roof. Out, onto the top of the carriage, into the wind. He lowered himself to a seat on the edge. Waited. Watched the side of the tracks for the signal Charles the Bold had promised would be there. A blue flag, he'd said. That was when he had to uncouple the carriages.

He spotted it a minute later, in the distance. And spotted something else in the same glance — a man, climbing up onto the first of the freight carriages.

"Blast!" Not wasting time on any other words, he shimmied down the ladder, praying with everything in him that Jaeger — because it had to be Jaeger — hadn't spotted him.

Knowing very well he had.

Come on, Elton. Don't think about it, just do it. He had a few minutes before the bloke could possibly get to him. A few minutes to do what needed done. He wasn't in any danger, not yet.

But he couldn't uncouple the carriages too early. If he did that, they'd coast to a halt here on this track, and he'd have a major problem on his hands. He had to do it the moment this carriage reached the blue flag — that would leave just enough time and distance for the main part of the train to continue on its track, for this carriage to slow. Not all the way, but enough to allow for another of Thoroton's men to switch the track before Drake reached it. But it needed enough momentum left to then coast to a halt along the siding, where British agents could unload the tainted sugar. Timing was crucial.

But better a bit early and risk drifting to a halt too soon than miss his mark and get there too late — or not at all. And if he had to engage Jaeger, it could well be not at all.

His hand moved of its own volition to check his holster — his sidearm still rested snug and secure inside it. If it came to it, he'd do what needed to be done. But it made his chest go tight. He'd never had to kill a man, and he didn't much fancy changing that. He'd never even fired the gun outside of training. Doing so now, when fac-

155

ing a single enemy, seemed somehow differ-ent from being in the heat of battle, com-rades on either side and the opposite army swarming.

Seemed different by far from the service he was usually called upon to do.

Maybe his opposite number wasn't very nimble. Or was afraid of heights. Maybe he'd slip, or decide to go the safer route and climb down and up each carriage's end instead of jumping from one to the next.

Drake leaned over to check the approach of the blue flag. Estimated that at the train's rate, it would take another thirty seconds to reach it.

Please, Lord.

He reached for the coupler. He'd already read about how to work them, and yesterday he'd even snuck into the railyard to get some practice. He'd take no undue chances with this going wrong.

Fifteen seconds. Ten.

Please, Lord. He glanced up but saw no angry German charging at him.

Now! He unhooked the air lines in one move, tugged upon the pin until it slid out of place in the next, then held his breath as the blue flag zipped by.

For a moment, nothing happened. The two carriages were still moving at the same

156

clip as the rest of the train, and the coupler just stayed there where it was.

Then inertia beautifully began to work. First a narrow gap appeared between the two couplers, then an inch. Three. A foot. A yard.

He stood again, using his handhold on the ladder to leverage himself up. He couldn't risk climbing yet. That would put him in view of Jaeger.

A shout sounded. He couldn't make out any words, given the wind and the screeching of the wheels on the tracks, but it was likely the German, noticing the growing gap between the main train and the carriage with his sugar. Six feet now. More. When it was wide enough that a man wouldn't be able to leap across the distance, the calculus on what he should do changed.

The range of a pistol was significantly longer than what a man could jump, and Drake was a sitting target here at the front of the train.

He drew his own sidearm from its holster and climbed. He'd only gone up three rungs when that voice rang out again. And this time he recognized the word.

"Elton!"

Blast. The German knew who he was, by name. Drake looked over his shoulder, just able to see Jaeger's head and shoulders. Still clinging to the ladder with his left hand, he held out his right and squeezed the trigger. The shot went wild, as Drake had intended, but it had the desired effect as Jaeger dropped to the deck.

It wouldn't keep him down long, but he only needed a few moments. He climbed up the last few rungs, blindly fired another shot to keep his opposite number down, and scrambled onto the roof of the carriage.

He was only a second from safety, ready to swing down into the carriage, when fire pierced his abdomen. Like an echo of the pain, his ears registered the sound of a pistol. The angry Spanish shout. "I will find you! You will pay for this!"

Then he pitched into the black of the carriage. Partly on purpose, partly as the train jerked onto the switched track, partly because his legs gave out.

Barrels roughly caught his fall. He managed to roll off them onto a marginally more welcoming sack of something. But then he could only lie there and try to breathe. Try not to let the dizziness and agony steal his mind.

He wasn't finished yet. He had to see this through. Had to . . . something. Open the door? No. Maybe.

Gritting his teeth, he pressed a hand to his back, sought out the place screaming the loudest. Then moved his hand, wet and sticky now, to his abdomen. Another wet spot that would no doubt be red with his life.

Through and through — he'd thank the Lord for that when he had the power. If his organs were intact enough that he'd live to do it.

For now he . . . he must . . . he should . . .

He slid to the still-rocking floor. Puddled there, leaning against the sack, as the carriage slowed and stopped.

Voices shouted from outside. Something . . . familiar. Clanging at the middle of the carriage, where the door would be. Light. Blinding and white. His gun was still clutched in his right hand, though he doubted he had the strength to lift it were it the enemy who came in instead of a friend. He couldn't even lift his head. But it wasn't pain so much as heaviness now. That was another something for which he should thank the Lord. When he could.

Or when he saw Him. One or the other.

A familiar English face appeared before him. A familiar English phrase slipped from its lips, one that summed up the situation rather well, but for which Drake would have gotten his ears boxed had he ever said it in either his mother's or grandfather's house.

A hand clapped onto his shoulder. "Hang on, old boy. We'll get you out of here. Don't give up on me now."

He tried to speak. Only air wheezed out. But it didn't matter. Thoroton was here. Drake had done his job. Now he could let his eyes slide closed.

9

Margot slid into the chair at her desk, ignoring the stares from the secretaries. From Culbreth and de Grey and Adcock. Ignoring the gaping emptiness of the desk by the door, ignoring the realization that soon it would have to be filled by some other secretary. Ignoring the ache that persisted in her throat and the general discomfort of her stomach.

"Margot. Sweetheart." Lady Hambro perched on the edge of Margot's desk and rested a hand on her shoulder.

She almost shrugged her off, but then she heard Maman in her ear. *Don't be rude, Margot. She's trying to give you comfort.* She forced herself to meet the woman's eyes.

Lady Hambro had been there yesterday at the wake. They all had, every member of Room 40. Paying their respects. Clasping her hand, thumping Lukas on the back. Whispering words that meant nothing.

Absolutely nothing.

The fingers around her shoulder squeezed. "You shouldn't be here, dear. You're ill. I know very well DID told you to take a week off."

Margot blinked and let her gaze drift away from Ebba Hambro's misty eyes and trembling lips. "I'm on the mend. And I have nowhere else to be, my lady."

At home in 3E, Lukas was always there, trying to persuade her to come to his house. He said words like *just for tonight* and *until you are better,* but she well knew once he got her there it would be *just for a week, just for a month,* and then finally *we might as well let the flat go.*

She wouldn't. She *wouldn't* give up the flat.

But she couldn't just stay there all the time either. She couldn't just let this cold run its course. Dot had insisted on staying with her, leaving only to go to work. She'd been tireless, attentive, a perfect friend. A true sister.

But her hands had been shaking that morning, and Margot had caught her looking up the street toward her own flat. If she didn't go home soon, she'd . . . Well, Margot didn't know what exactly would happen. But she knew it wouldn't be good.

So she'd stirred the last of her honey into a cup of tea, told her throat it *would* be better by midday, and dressed for work. She'd resolutely not looked at that closed door to the little cupboard of a room. She would have to open it eventually. Go through the lifeless possessions trapped inside. Decide what to keep, what to get rid of, what to do with the room.

But not today.

Lady Hambro sighed. "You are not alone, Margot. You have your brother and his family. Why not spend a few days with them? Reminisce together, laugh together, cry together. It would do you good."

Margot's answer was to pick up her pencil and a fresh sheet of paper. She had no pneumatically delivered tube of papers before her, but she scratched a few numbers onto the page anyway. Lady Hambro wouldn't know that they were nonsense — nothing but a theorem that had proven unworkable.

In her mind's eye, she saw the look Maman would give her for ignoring someone trying to help.

Margot didn't need help. She didn't need to reminisce. Or to cry. And the idea of laughing — that didn't even deserve a mental response, much less a vocal one. She

163

just needed to *be*. And she could do that best here.

Lady Hambro sighed again and straightened, removing her hand from Margot's shoulder after a matronly pat. "All right. If this is what you need to do, then so be it. But do look after your health, Margot dear. You'll do no one any good if you collapse in a fever — and we certainly don't want the rest of Room 40 coming down with it again."

"I'm on the mend," she said again. Even added what she hoped looked like a smile. Faintly. Perhaps. If the lady had a good imagination. "No fever, I promise you." Not like That Day. The seventh of November.

Eleventh month. Seventh day.

Eighteen.

Margot bit down until her jaw hurt and stared at the useless paper in front of her. No more Eighteen. *Do you hear me, God?* She didn't even know who it was, but the very fact that the Lord had wanted her to pray for *him* instead of her own mother . . . Why hadn't He whispered in her ear about Maman? Why hadn't the numbers insisted she go home earlier? Do something? Help somehow? Why had she come down with that mind-muddling fever on that day of all days?

No. *No. NO.*

She'd say it over and again until that stupid *Eighteen* just stopped, once and for all.

Lady Hambro moved away. Margot waited for her to leave the room, go off to oversee the secretaries stationed elsewhere in the hub, no doubt — or else to tattle to the admiral on her — before she got up and went to fetch a tube full of papers to be decoded. While she was up, she grabbed a copy of today's key as well and then settled at her desk.

Usually her pencil flew. Today it trudged. The numbers that generally pranced and skipped through her mind were playing hide-and-seek. But she didn't need to be at her best. She just needed to be *here.* Because it wasn't *there.*

The morning sprawled on, stretching and stretching toward lunchtime. When she'd have to face the fact that Maman wouldn't appear at her side, prodding her to leave her desk and join the other girls. *Come, Margot. It will do you good.* When she'd have to watch the other secretaries giggle their way down the hall. It was fine out today — they'd spill out the doors, or perhaps even climb up to the roof.

"Margot."

Had it been Lady Hambro's voice, she would have ignored it. Had it been Dot's, she would have held up a hand, asking for a moment to finish the sentence she was decoding. But it was the admiral's.

She put down her pencil and looked up.

Hall crooked a finger.

A bit surprised at how much energy it took just to stand up, Margot followed him out into the corridor and then down it, to his office. He sat, not behind his desk but on its edge. And he looked at her.

If he meant to measure her, she'd make sure his ruler had an accurate reading. She edged her spine straight, her chin up, and willed her eyes to project only ability. A dozen defenses sprang to her tongue, but she wouldn't volunteer them. She'd wait for him to admonish her first, so that she knew which of her reasons would best convince him to let her stay.

"You have become good friends with Dorothea Elton, have you not?"

That wasn't what she'd expected him to say. Not sure what his angle was, her brain scrambled. But she could offer only the truth. "I have, yes."

"I thought so. I must ask a favor of you."

Redirection, perhaps? A ploy to get her to pay attention to something else, anything else? Margot lifted her brows.

Hall let out a slow breath. "I have just received word that her brother has been critically injured. He'll be arriving at Charing Cross Hospital in a few days."

Margot's spine sagged. Drake Elton, of the broken nose and insightful questions, injured? It shouldn't hit her that hard after a whole five minutes in his company, but it did. He did so easily what she struggled to do at all — connect with people, quickly and correctly. It should have insulated him, somehow, against such things.

And then there was Dot. *Poor Dot!*

Her stomach soured a little more than it had already been. Poor Dot and stupid Margot — assuming this was about *her.* It wasn't, and she was a selfish wretch to have assumed it would be. She cleared the regret from her throat. "What can I do?"

"I realize that in times of war, bad news often trips over itself — that in the grand scheme, it is not surprising that her brother would have suffered such an injury while she is trying to be there for you and your family. But I am also aware that Miss Elton's emotions are . . . fragile."

Margot bristled on her friend's behalf. "They most certainly are *not.*"

Hall's lips turned up. "I didn't mean it as

an insult, my dear. I only say it to indicate that I wish to be mindful of her state and not spring this on her in a way that will injure *her.*"

Her chin edged back up from where it had sagged. "I am not questioning your motivations, DID. Just your assumption."

The turning of his lips grew to an outright grin. "So you would have had me let the telegram go straight to her, in the hand of a stranger, rather than one of us delivering the news in a way to soften the blow, is that it?"

"Zero."

The admiral blinked at her. "Pardon?"

"The number of times you've let anyone in Room 40 receive difficult news from the War Office by the hand of a stranger." A week ago, she would have given him a cheeky smile. Today she could only manage the quirk of a brow. "Of course I'm not saying to treat her with *less* care than anyone else. But she needn't be handled with kid gloves. She isn't an egg."

Obviously still amused, Hall spread his hands. "Her brother said —"

"Then her brother's an idiot." She hadn't thought he was. Had in fact been sure he *wasn't.* But everyone was an idiot about something, and apparently Lieutenant

Elton's something was his sister.

The admiral laughed outright at that. "You ought to visit him in hospital and tell him so, my dear. Might get his dander up enough to rally him." He stood up again and tugged the hem of his uniform jacket back into place. "At any rate, I wanted to let you know what news I will be giving your friend during her lunch break, so that you might support her — to whatever extent she may require, be it much or little. I trust you don't object to *that*?"

Rather than answer straightaway, she let the actual news sink in, dig down. Let her brows sink with it. Drake Elton, injured and on his way to Charing Cross. "How bad is he? Will he live?"

His rapid blinks told her nothing, nor did his face. "That, I think, depends on the strength of his will and the grace of the Almighty. He took a gunshot to the abdomen."

Margot winced. "Eighty-seven percent."

Hall lifted his brows.

"The mortality rate of gunshot wounds to the abdomen." She wasn't sure where she'd read or heard the number — probably a newspaper or magazine that someone had left lying about.

"A statistic I pray you will keep to yourself."

She'd physically bite her tongue, if necessary. "Any mitigating circumstances?"

"It went through and through — that's all I know. I daresay your percentages would depend on whether any vital organs were struck, but I haven't that information just yet."

Margot shifted to the side to clear his path to the door. "You'll tell her now?"

After a glance to the clock that verified it was nearly the time the secretaries broke to eat, he nodded.

Margot followed him out his office door, realizing only when they were in the corridor that he'd said absolutely nothing about her presence here today, in direct violation of his order to take a week off. Perhaps he was just glad to have her on hand now, to be there for Dot.

Or perhaps he understood that this was home and the people here were family, every bit as much as Lukas and Willa and Zurie.

They found Dot still at her desk, just reaching down to gather the lunch she'd packed at Margot's flat that morning. Upon looking up and spotting them, her face went blank. Not panicked, not worried, nothing to show an impending falling-to-pieces as

Hall had feared. Just the emptiness of careful control.

Margot gave her a small nod. Approval — support.

The admiral cleared his throat. "If you've a moment, Miss Elton, I'm afraid there's something I must tell you."

Margot could all but see the thoughts ricocheting through her mind. She wasn't being sacked — Lady Hambro would be the one to deliver that news, if it were so. The possibility always existed that he'd simply selected her for a small job of some sort — but why would Margot be on hand for that?

"It's your brother. He's alive," he rushed to say, not giving Dot's eyes time to do more than widen a fraction with dark questions. "Alive but in critical condition, I'm afraid. He's suffered a gunshot to the abdomen. I have no further information about how it happened or the details of the injury, other than that he will arrive in London on Sunday and be taken directly to Charing Cross Hospital, but I didn't want you to read this news in a telegram."

Dot's hands may have been shaking that morning, after spending two nights in a home not her own, but they didn't shake now. She gripped her brown paper bag, yes, but anyone would have. Her nostrils flared, but only once. And her voice came out even and sure. "Thank you for being the one to tell me, Admiral. Do you know where I can discover information on what train he'll be on? I'd like to meet him at Charing Cross as soon as he arrives."

Hall nodded. "I'll request such details be sent to you as soon as they're known."

"Thank you, sir."

Another thing everyone appreciated about Hall — he knew when to take command . . . and when to delegate. At this point he stepped to the side, creating a clear and obvious path between Margot and Dot. "Know that your brother will be in my prayers and that, unless you have objections, I'll ask the others to pray for him as well."

Dot offered a small but steady smile. "I would appreciate that, Admiral. And I know Drake would as well."

He left with a nod, and Margot knew he'd go and do exactly as promised. He'd find Montgomery — their own Fighting Padre, as they'd taken to calling him when he exchanged his clerical robes for a uniform over the summer — and alert the reverend to this latest request for prayer.

Margot slid over to her friend. "I'm sorry, Dot."

"He's alive." She proclaimed it with a nod.

And then winced and gave Margot an apologetic look.

Drake Elton of the crooked nose and insightful questions was alive. Sophie De Wilde of the incomparable beauty and unfailing smiles was not. But the two had nothing to do with each other. And Margot was certainly *not* wretch enough to begrudge her friend that thread of hope. She dug deep until she could pull out a smile. "He is. And God willing, he will remain so."

She paused, tested the words that formed in her mind. No numbers crowded around them, one way or another, to tell her whether they were sound. Just the dull throb of a headache, mixed with the echo of DID's news. She swallowed and said them. "I'll go with you. On Sunday. After Mass."

She couldn't think of a single person who would greet that proclamation with anything other than an objection. *You need to rest* or *It's too soon for you to be out like that after . . .* They'd all be thinking it was stupid to go and look death in the eye at the hospital when it was still haunting her at home.

But Dot just held her gaze for a moment, and then she nodded. "Thank you. I'd appreciate the company."

"And you'll stay at your own flat tonight." Had she been well enough to think of it, she'd have insisted on it before. "It means the world that you were there for me. But I'm all right now."

Dot pursed her lips and studied her with the same sort of intensity Margot would have given a particularly tricky equation. "You can stay with me, if you like. As long as you like. I've the room, with Aunt Millie not being there."

Margot moistened her lips and wondered at the tug of temptation.

She'd never been alone. Never. Not one night in all her life to date. There'd always, always been Maman and Papa and Lukas. And then Maman and Papa. And then Maman. Always. Every day, every night.

She didn't want to be alone. She didn't — and so she had to be, to keep it from controlling her. Right? Especially now. If she went with Lukas or with Dot and stayed with them, she might never have the strength to go home again. To be alone.

Alone.

She'd always thought she was. Isolated, even in a crowd. Different. Unlike the other girls, unlike the other students. Even unlike the others here, to be honest, who laughed their way from the OB in the evenings and went to their dinner parties or concerts or whatever else engaged them in their "real" lives outside the secrets of Room 40.

She hadn't been alone, though. Not really. Not before. There'd always been Maman.

Now there was only Margot.

She cleared her throat and met Dot's eye. "Thanks. And I might take you up on that at some point. But not yet. I need to . . ." Prove herself. To Lukas and to Dot. To Admiral Hall and Lady Hambro.

And to herself. Mostly to herself.

Dot nodded. Stood. Gripped the little paper bag. "The offer stands."

"I know." She fell in beside Dot. They stopped in Room 40 long enough for Margot to fetch the tea and crackers she'd brought for lunch — her stomach still objected at the thought of anything more — and they joined the crowds of laughing, chattering magpies known as secretaries who surged toward the roof and the rare autumn sunshine.

For the first time in her life, Margot left an encoded sentence half-decrypted.

For the first time in her life, she really didn't care.

Der Vampir clattered onto the table. It gleamed in the lights, clean and straight and sure. But Das Gespenst's hands were red. They might always be red.

Poor Yūrei. He'd found Der Vampir and already had it in his stomach before Das Gespenst could stop him. A gruesome way to go — not the way he would have chosen for a friend, and not solely because it meant blood to clean up. He'd had no choice but to finish him off quickly.

For days Yūrei had been begging Das Gespenst to end it for him. He should have done it before now. Quietly, easily. A pillow over his mouth, robbing him of what little breath he could manage to pull into his lungs. That would have been the better way. A way more deserving of a friend — a friend who would never know the favor he'd done him with his death.

He sagged onto one of the hard, simple wooden chairs and stared at the flat around him. Stared at the framed photograph on the wall, at the face of Yamagata Aritomo, the former Japanese prime minister.

A telegram lay on the table before him. It gave him orders, as they always did. Orders that didn't care if his cough was better or worse, if he had pneumonia or didn't, if he killed or was killed. They cared only that he was back in England again. Where they'd told him to be.

Get the codebook, it said. Just as the last had said *Assist in Spain.* He squeezed his eyes shut. He'd never before minded the way they had him travel — he'd welcomed it. England, France, Spain, Africa. He'd been sent everywhere because of his linguistic talent.

But why couldn't they have sent someone else back to England this time? Why that same command he'd been working on for months already? The codebooks, always the codebooks. He pried his eyelids open again, seeing the Old Admiralty Building rather than the flat. He'd tried the direct approach. He'd managed to get inside once, with a fabricated letter inviting him, but it had gotten him no farther than the lobby. Enough to see that security was tight.

Enough to see that young women were there in droves. Pushing tea carts, carrying mops and brooms, acting as secretaries. They would be the weak link. They always were — may his mother forgive him for saying so.

Before this last trip to the Continent, he'd not been certain which of them he should target. But now he knew. Those two from the park — they would be his focus.

He ran his thumb lightly along the blade of Der Vampir. For centuries, it had thirsted. Tasting a bit of human blood here and there as skirmishes and wars charged through

Bavaria. But now it drowned in red. Would it be satiated or crave more?

Which would he?

Exhaustion tickled his lungs, brought the dreaded cough back. The telegram on the table taunted him. Because one task was not enough for them anymore. Perhaps because he had yet to succeed at it. Perhaps because they wanted to keep him busy. Perhaps because they assumed that with *this,* at least, he could succeed, even if he was useless elsewhere.

Identify targets.

Targets. His nostrils flared. He could still smell it. Blood, every time he drew in a breath. They would expect him, require him to obey. To distance himself from everything that happened elsewhere. As a ghost should do naturally. Das Gespenst, that was all he could be. All he could afford to be.

But when he closed his eyes, the waters that drowned the *Boynton* rushed over him again. His lungs ached. His hands were red. It *wasn't* as simple as obedience. Obedience had made him a ghost. And if he were dead already . . . why obey only *them*? Why not obey his own thirsts too? They could do nothing worse than kill him again.

He struggled back to the surface, back to the blade dulled by red and the smiling

178

Japanese face in the photograph and the game board sitting in its position of honor on the side table. Good strategy could harbor two goals at once. An attack here and a parry there.

Obedience could pair with revenge. Revenge on the ones who had done this to him. Who had made him a ghost.

A game. It was just a game. It didn't matter if he was alone, if there was no Heinrich to tell him stories or Yūrei to meet for tea. A ghost didn't need brothers and friends. He only had to *win.*

10

They'd said that whatever drug they'd slipped into his veins would make the journey comfortable. They'd said that he wouldn't even be aware of the trip, that he'd wake up in London and be on the mend. They'd said that rest was all he needed.

They'd lied.

Drake dug his fingers into the miserable cot under him and stared up at the ceiling of the ward in Charing Cross Hospital. It was white. Like all the walls. Like every ceiling and every wall in every hospital in the world, no doubt. All the more plain and stark because he well knew he'd be staring at it for days and weeks to come.

It didn't hurt. Not until he moved. Or breathed too heavily. Or, heaven forbid, laughed at something another of the patients said to one of the nurses. *Then* he was keenly aware of the way that blasted German bullet had ripped through his insides.

He'd been lucky, the doctors had said. Through and through. No vital organs hit. No internal bleeding.

He *knew* he'd been lucky — knew it the moment he pressed his hands to that hot, sticky mess that was his back and stomach on the railcar. But luck didn't make the ceilings any less boring or the pain any less acute when he tried to do something actually *human.*

He would be a shell for the next weeks or months, that was all. An artificial man, delegated to the barest physical duties. Eat. Sleep. Take his medicine. Try to pretend it wasn't embarrassing to have a nurse in her grey uniform hand him a bedpan. Try not to think about Thoroton and the other chaps still in Spain, still working and fighting and discovering and *doing* while he lay here like a . . . like a . . .

His fingers twisted in the sheet as a moan sounded from the next cot over. He was better off than many of the blokes here, and he knew it. He'd had nothing amputated. He hadn't lost any brothers in a mad rush up some hill, into the face of exploding ordnance. He'd not encountered any of that nightmarish mustard gas that the Germans had started using over the summer.

He'd gain his feet again, assuming infection didn't set in.

But he wanted to *do* something. Idleness wasn't, apparently, in his nature. It's just that he'd never realized it until now, when it was his only option.

"Mary," the bloke on the other side of him groaned. "Mary. Mary."

"Mary will be to see you later today, Private." The nurse's voice was cheerful, but not gratingly so. Drake turned his head just enough to see her. She was uncommonly tall, clad in the same boring grey uniform and white apron every other nurse wore, the white kerchief tied over her nearly black hair. She wasn't pretty, exactly, but she looked pleasant. And she turned to Drake with a bright smile. "There's our newcomer, alert and ready for a meal, no doubt. How are you feeling, Lieutenant Elton?"

It would be a long time before the idea of food did anything but inspire pain, he suspected. But he conjured up a grin. "Like I've been shot."

"Astounding." She poured him a cup of water and helped him hold his head up so he could sip it. As if he were an infant. "I'm Nurse Arabelle Denler. I imagine we'll be seeing a good bit of each other until we've got you back on your feet."

"How do you do?" He nearly choked on a chip of ice, garbling the question.

"How polite you are. But as I am far better than you, please don't feel you must engage in such niceties for my sake." When she smiled, a single dimple appeared in her left cheek. The unevenness brought interest to her otherwise plain face. "Where are you from, Lieutenant?"

He had to cough to clear his throat of the vicious ice chip. And of course the coughing lit his entire torso on fire. Which should at least melt the ice. He made no objections to being settled back onto his pillow, knowing well his face had contorted with pain. "Here," he managed from between clenched teeth. "London. And Spain." After he had spent the last seven years of his life in a place, he could claim it as his own, couldn't he?

"Oh, how interesting! When you're well enough, you can tell me all about your foreign travels." She tucked the sheet up around him, precise and efficient, and gave him the single-dimpled smile again. "Have a few minutes' rest, Lieutenant. We'll be bringing your dinner round shortly."

He blinked by way of answer, afraid to loosen his jaw enough for more words lest a moan escape — and the ward was already full enough of those. His fingers dug trenches in the mattress again, though at some point the remnant of drugs in his system must have stolen him away. He jerked to alertness when a clatter sounded at his side, hot words wanting to blister his tongue at the new pain inspired by the abrupt motion.

He would never take movement for granted again. Never.

It was a different nurse this time, this one a bobbed blonde who was beautiful, where the first nurse had been plain. Her sharp green eyes seemed to size him up in a heartbeat too. "May I help you sit up, Lieutenant?"

Risky . . . but no more so than the risk of choking on every sip of broth if he didn't. "Yes, please. Nurse . . . ?"

"Stafford." She slid an arm behind his back and levered him up a bit, fitting another pillow behind him with her other arm in a slick move that proved she did this many times a day.

The chap in the cot across from him laughed. "Call her 'Nurse Stafford' and you'll get a lecture from the ward matron. It's Her Grace."

A duchess? Of Stafford. That made something try to click into place in his head, though he couldn't quite be sure what. "What's a duchess doing *here*?"

Her Grace finished fluffing his pillow and gave him a small smile a second before sending an exaggerated glare to the fellow across the aisle. "My bit, that's what. And *you,* Corporal Henderson — I warned you about outing me to the new arrivals. Just see if I bring you an extra biscuit today."

The Duchess of Stafford. He knew the name, though he'd certainly never met her. But from where? Ah. He had it. "Did you ever get your Renault?"

Her hands stilled, and her brows lifted as she looked down at him again. "Are we acquainted, Lieutenant? Forgive me, if so — I don't recall how or when."

"No." He shook his head but then regretted it. Though how a simple action like moving his neck could make pain light up in his stomach he just didn't know. Still, he forced a smile. "Visited friends in the Cotswolds a few years ago. Had a meal with one of your drivers."

"Ah." Her smile reappeared, and she positioned a tray over his legs. "A new car seemed a waste in times like these. But I broke the new stallion. And when this dratted war's over, I'm going to make my ace of a husband teach me to fly a plane."

The duke was a pilot? Somehow that was just as shocking as learning that his wife was a nurse. "In the RNAS?" It had to be either the Royal Naval Air Service or the Royal Flying Corp.

"The RFC — he was one of the first to sign up, fool man, and no one could talk him out of it." Pride saturated her voice though, not irritation. "Stationed at Northolt, though, not on the front — which is why the boys and I are in London. We still get to see him several times a week. We're lucky." She moved a bowl of not-steaming broth onto his tray. "Shall I?"

For the first time since he'd arrived here this morning, he actually looked around the ward. There were two rows of cots on each of the walls, facing each other. Almost all were filled with soldiers. White bandages everywhere, stumps where limbs should have been, some chaps with faces as pale as the sheets they lay on.

He swallowed and ignored the throbbing that hadn't yet ebbed from the effort of sitting up. Or waking up. Or just being, perhaps. "I can manage, I think. Thank you, Your Grace."

She sighed. "Another hopelessly proper patient, I see. Very well then, Lieutenant. Your sidearm." She handed him a spoon.

"And your bayonet." A knife, presumably to butter the bread she also slid onto his tray. "Use them wisely, or I shall strip you of them and submit you to the humiliation of being fed by a woman."

It was all he could do to force his lips into a smile and keep his face clear of the wince that wanted to overtake him when he lifted his arm.

This was going to be fun.

He waited until she bustled to the next bed, the next patient, before he tried lifting his arm again. Never before had he been aware of all the muscles required to complete such a simple act. Dip the spoon. Raise it again. Aim it at his own mouth.

He managed the first spoonful all right. On the second, his arm shook. By the third, he'd worn it rather than eating it — good thing it hadn't been more than warm.

Nurse Denler appeared at his side, her lonely dimple in place. She spread a napkin over his chest. "I know that look. But we cannot accept defeat so soon, Lieutenant Elton. You'll not regain your strength by eating so little." She pried the spoon from his fingers and sat in the wooden chair positioned between the cots, angling it toward him. "Besides, from what I hear, your sister will be coming soon to visit you. You'll want to be finished and cleaned up by then, won't you? Best to let me help."

Of course Dot was coming. He hadn't really paused to think about that yet — that Charing Cross meant London, the very neighborhood where she lived and now worked. Of course she'd come. Likely every day, while he was here.

She'd see him weak and in pain and no doubt want to know how he'd come by his injury.

He had no intentions of telling her. Let her assume he'd ended up in one of the many battles raging on the Continent.

Jaeger's face filled his vision. Contorted with rage, closer than it had ever been in reality, obliterating all else in the room.

Across the aisle, the duchess shattered the illusion as she shouted something in a language that sounded a bit like French, a bit like Italian, but wasn't fully either, to his ear. And the men laughed.

Nurse Denler did, too, low and warm. "Another reason she serves here, I think. To give the men stories to tell when they go back to the field, or home. Tales of the duchess who fed them, served them, and then yelled at them in Monegasque."

It *would* make a good story. But Drake wasn't sure to whom he'd tell it. "Back to the field" would mean Spain and Abuelo's house — but if he remembered correctly the words Thoroton had spoken while Drake was being put on the train, his grandfather hadn't been informed of his injury. Rather, Charles the Bold had sent a telegram in Drake's name, saying he'd decided to extend the little trip he'd been on and was debating spending the winter in London with Dot.

Abuelo would frown — why would he choose to winter in England rather than the temperance of Spain? — but he wouldn't think it out of character.

And when could he reasonably expect to go back to Spain, anyway? That same muddled recollection of his superior had contained some instruction about enjoying Christmas with his sister, hadn't it?

Christmas. That was a month and a half away. So much would have happened in that time — the wolfram would have been loaded on *Erri Barro,* and the frigate would have set out to sea. He'd wanted to be there, one of the team on the English ship sent to intercept it. Thoroton had told him he could be. That he could see it through, from discovery to confiscation.

No chance of that now.

"Finished?" Nurse Denler frowned at the

bowl — still over half full. "Would you like the bread and butter?"

Solid food should sound good, shouldn't it? But the thought of it just made him hurt. "No. Thanks."

"All right." She stood and lifted the tray from over his legs. "Try to rest until your sister comes. Do you want to lie back down?"

Move again? Only to want to return to this position so he could actually see Dot when she got here? He risked a shake of his head — a minuscule one.

Given the increased noise in the ward as men were roused for their dinners, he didn't really expect to rest. But he must have dozed for a minute here and there, because it seemed like only a moment before he heard his sister's familiar voice saying his name and felt her familiar fingers on the top of his hand.

He blinked awake, glad it wasn't with a jerk this time. Saw Dot with her curls pinned back in their usual chignon, her smile obviously trying to strike a note between bravery and normality, the blue-grey eyes they shared suspiciously shiny.

Then his gaze tracked just past her, to a second figure hovering by his bed. He might have thought it another nurse, except instead of white, he saw blue. A blue dress under a belted blue coat. And above that, hair of dark chocolate pinned in a plain bun, a slender nose in a slender face, and those dark eyes that had haunted him for the last month.

Blast it all. Why today? When he was dressed in a soup-stained pajama shirt and couldn't move without the risk of crying like a baby?

The ever-helpful Nurse Denler arrived with another chair, and Margot De Wilde sat.

Drake tore his eyes from *her* and looked back to his sister. "Hello."

Dot sighed and wove their fingers together. "How are you feeling?"

"I've been better." He couldn't think of a time he'd been *worse,* as a matter of fact, but he'd embrace the British stiff upper lip just now.

Dot, of course, saw through him. He could tell by the way she narrowed her eyes and tilted her head. But instead of calling him on it, she turned a bit to include her friend. "This is Margot De Wilde, my friend from the office. Did you get my letters? If so, you know who she is."

"I did." His smile was no doubt far from suave and handsome, but the introduction gave him an excuse to look at her again, anyway. "I thought you didn't have a name. Your parents forgot to give you one, if I recall." It took a ridiculous amount of energy to deliver the sentence.

But he was rewarded with a snap of amusement in her eyes and the slightest hint of a smile in the corner of her lips.

Dot's brows arched upward. "Have I missed something?"

"We met the day you had your interview." Drake reclaimed his hand from her so he could plant it against the mattress and try to ease himself up another inch. It didn't feel right being below the level of their eyes. But he couldn't accomplish the move on his own, and he certainly wasn't going to ask for help. He cleared his throat. "Sort of. She wouldn't tell me her name."

Miss De Wilde folded her arms over her chest, her smile growing another fraction. "You didn't ask what my name *is,* Lieutenant. You asked if I *had* one. And then if I weren't going to tell you."

Dot laughed, which turned a few male heads their way. Drake sent a scowl at his neighbors. Until he knew what kinds of blokes they were, they weren't going to get away with ogling his sister.

"Oh heavens! I wish I'd heard it. I

wouldn't have been half so nervous if I'd had a good laugh before going in there." Dot shook her head and leaned back in her hard wooden chair. "She's very literal," she said in a stage whisper, shielding her mouth from Miss De Wilde's view.

Miss De Wilde let her smile bloom heart-stoppingly full. "What is the point of language if we don't use it with precision? When others fail in this, then it's instructional to point it out with exaggeration."

Drake kept his gaze on her. "It was a lesson, was it? I had just assumed it was custom in Antarctica not to name one's children. After all, your parents must have been penguins."

Her lips settled back down into neutral. "Nonsense. They were albatrosses."

Drake would have liked to laugh, if it wouldn't have been agony.

Dot had no such compunction and released another chuckle. "Antarctica?"

"Where she claimed her accent was from."

"And I imagine she said it with a straight face." Dot grinned. "I could never."

"No," Drake agreed. "You were always miserable at lying."

"Lying is easy." Miss De Wilde leaned back in her chair too and folded her hands in her lap. "Especially when one doesn't actually mean to be believed."

Blast, those *eyes.* They exuded challenge and questions with every second. And here he was fighting just to stay upright. It wasn't fair. And he knew well it wouldn't be long before exhaustion and pain won out.

But in the meantime . . . "And when one *does* mean to be believed?"

Her gaze met his, bold and unflinching. "Then it's a simple matter of mathematics."

He let his brows ask the obvious question.

She acknowledged it with a tilt of her head. "The correct ratio of truth to falsehood, combined with the proper rate of respiration, blinking, and the angle of one's spine. Ratios, rates, and angles — mathematics."

He could see why Blinker Hall called her *my dear.* She was clearly a girl cut from the same cloth as their director. He looked back to Dot. "Perhaps you'd better tell me how your new position is going before I begin to wonder if we ought to believe a thing this young lady has ever told you."

Dot sent him a look. "I'd rather hoped *you* would tell *me* what happened." She motioned to his stomach.

Blast. He'd not had time to come up with a proper cover story. But hopefully his wince would suffice for now. "Perhaps when the pain and medicine have allowed me to sort through it all myself?"

His sister sighed. But she relented and began to tell him about how she'd finally begun to settle in and feel a proper part of "Blinker's Beauty Chorus," as the secretaries were apparently called. "And Margot and I have such fun on our daily walks and meals!"

Fun didn't seem like a word Margot would use very often — at least, not one she would have defined in the way most people did. But then, Dot was a bit of an odd duck herself, so perhaps their definitions matched.

He wished he could have enjoyed the telling more, could have done more than smile when the tale called for laughter. But the longer she talked, the more aware he became of the pain shooting from his midsection down his legs and up into his neck. He had to move, to lie back down. Even a slight shift might help. But when he tried it, his attempt ended in a wince he couldn't hide.

Dot's fingers landed on his again. "Oh, look at me. Rambling on and tiring you out. We've already been warned we mustn't stay more than a quarter hour, and no doubt we've been here that long. Sit still, Drake." She pressed harder on his hand. "Don't injure yourself. Let me fetch a nurse to help you."

"You needn't go yet." Once they left, it would just be the pain again. He'd rather suffer this position a little longer, with their company.

"Nonsense. You're exhausted." She leaned over and planted a kiss on his cheek. "But don't worry, we'll be back tomorrow. And every day, after work."

We? He darted a glance at Margot De Wilde and her dark eyes. She made no correction, but then, she wouldn't, would she? Not now. She just wouldn't come back if she didn't want to.

Dot was already on her feet, chasing after an as-yet-nameless nurse who was passing by the door. "Nurse! Excuse me!"

Drake dug his fingers in again in the effort to keep his face clear of pain for Margot De Wilde's sake.

She shifted, and for a moment he thought she'd get up and chase after Dot. But no. She slid over to Dot's chair and leaned down. Actually leaned down, closer to him, until the scent of lemons met his nose.

Then she said, "You're an idiot, Drake Elton."

He was too tired to so much as lift his head from the pillow it had fallen back against. "Am I?" She could well be on to something. Surely only an idiot would be more concerned with how he appeared to a veritable stranger than with his actual condition.

"You told the admiral that your sister is emotionally fragile."

His eyes had drooped, but he forced them fully open now. "I don't believe I ever used those exact words."

"They were the ones he used with me, and I daresay they got at the heart of whatever your exact words were. And if you think that about her, you're an idiot."

Her eyes positively burned. Her cheeks had a pretty flush to them. But somehow he had a feeling that if he said so, she'd slap him. And he wasn't exactly in prime condition for such a response. So he settled for a tight-lipped smile that she probably interpreted as condescending. "I appreciate that you feel the need to champion her. But I've known my sister a fair bit longer than you have."

"I think she doesn't *need* a champion. Going out every day when it's so difficult — that is bravery, Lieutenant. That is strength." Now she stood. No emotion clouded her face — she probably kept it off with ratios and proportions and rates and angles — but those eyes still snapped beautifully. "You of all people should know that." Pushing the chairs back to make room, she stalked into the aisle and out the door.

Drake let his eyes slide closed and tried not to smile.

A moment later, Dot's step sounded, along with a second set. And Dot's voice hissed in his ear. "What did you say to her? She was upset."

She could tell, beyond all that careful control? They *must* be friends. Drake peeled his eyes open. "Didn't say anything." Much.

She scowled at him. "Be kind to her, Drake — her mother just died on Wednesday, very unexpectedly."

"What?" He jerked, winced, hissed with the pain, and made no objection when Nurse Anonymous elbowed Dot aside to help him lie down. Why hadn't she said something sooner? Or why hadn't he been able to tell that something so massive had just struck? Or, better still, why had Margot De Wilde even come here today, so soon after such tragedy? As the nurse settled him, he ground out between his teeth, "I wasn't unkind. I wouldn't be. She's your friend."

But she wasn't like Ada, that was for sure. Margot De Wilde wasn't the sort of friend he'd be kind to but avoid whenever he could. No, Margot De Wilde was a different sort of friend altogether.

Dot huffed and came around to the other side of his cot. "All right. I won't badger you." She leaned down, kissed his cheek once more. "Rest well and *get* well. Do you understand me? I'll tolerate nothing less than a full recovery."

Her words were so strong, so brave — like Margot claimed *she* was — but he saw the shadows in her eyes. The ones that said *You can't die too.* And if Margot *didn't* see those . . . maybe *she* was the idiot.

Perhaps he'd tell her so sometime. And see what her ratios did for her then.

11

Emptiness surrounded her. Somehow it wove through the usual chatter of the room, snuck in behind the *thunk* of the pneumatic tubes, edged out the scratching of pens and pencils, the clicks and clacks and *dings* of the typewriters. So much busyness.

But empty. Margot squeezed her eyes shut, but that only amplified the problem. Her desk wasn't empty. The room wasn't empty. The building wasn't empty. But that part of her own mind where it never had been before . . . *that* was all silent, echoing darkness.

Like a grave. She blinked her eyes open again and just stared at the half-blank page before her. Instead of the neat columns of numbers and decrypted words she'd written down, she saw that gaping black hole into which they'd lowered Maman last week.

"Her heart," Lukas had said last night. That's what the doctor had decided it must

have been. He'd never detected any problems with it before, but the cold she'd caught, the fever she was probably running, could have exacerbated an unknown condition.

But that couldn't be, and she'd said as much to her brother. "That's how Papa died." Why she had to remind him of this, she didn't know. Shouldn't he have seen the obvious when the doctor said such nonsense? "It's highly unlikely that Maman would have died of the same condition. Do you know what the chance of that is?"

Her brother had sighed, his face going hard. "Is the chance zero?"

"Of course not, but —"

"Then it does not matter, does it? Even if there is only a five percent chance, then that means it happens occasionally. And it did. It happened now. For whatever reason, however unlikely, they are both gone, and from the same malady."

"No." She'd said it last night over dinner. She thought it again now over her stalled work. Perhaps it had made sense that Papa's heart had failed him — he was not in prime physical condition. She could recognize that now. Hours at a desk had taken their toll, and he wasn't exactly trim. But Maman was different. Maman was nearly militant about

taking her exercise. Maman never overin-
dulged — and seldom indulged at all these
days — on sweets. Maman's heart ought to
have been in perfect condition.

There was something else. Some other
cause. There *had* to be. She didn't know
what, but she couldn't shake the idea that
somewhere in her mind lay the answer. That
it wasn't random at all, it was purposeful.
Someone was to blame.

She stared, and she listened. She waited
for God to speak, one way or another,
through the numbers in her head. Beautiful
proofs for a *Yes, pursue this.* Unsolvable
equations for a *No, this will get you nowhere.*

He always spoke. Always. And she listened,
because God was smarter than she was —
the only being about whom she could say
that with certainty. She didn't always understand His ways, but she'd learned to trust
them. Learned that when harmonious figures sang through her mind, she ought to
act.

But there was nothing. *Nothing.* No yes or
no. No stay or go.

God had gone silent.

She curled her fingers into her palm. Drew
in a breath. Picked up her pencil. She didn't
need those numbers to do this work; she
needed only time and half a brain. Finish

this, then think of the other.

The last word finally found its place on the page a moment before Dot appeared at her elbow. "Ready?"

"Mm." She stood and went a bit mechanically about her duties — tidy her desk, drop the handwritten decrypt into a basket for a secretary to type up, toss the original coded message into the bin to be filed with every other message they intercepted. Then she was shrugging into her coat and cinching the belt around her waist.

Visiting the hospital again wasn't exactly something she *wanted* to do. She didn't mind visiting with Lieutenant Elton — despite idiocy over his sister, he was a pleasant-enough chap to have a conversation with — but the hospital itself . . . it had been worse than she'd thought it would be. Harder on her. But she couldn't let that rule her.

Dot had proven herself a true friend last week. Margot would do the same.

Besides, going home to her empty flat wasn't exactly appealing.

"Are you going to Mr. Herschell's dinner party on Saturday?" Dot asked as they stepped out into the chilly air.

Margot glanced at her with what she hoped was a quelling look. "Why would I do that?"

Her friend chuckled. "Because everyone is invited, and from what I hear, he and Mr. Serocold will be performing for us. Sarah said they're talented musicians, the both of them."

Margot smiled. She could see musicians of far more talent whenever she pleased — she had only to tag along with Lukas and Willa. But Serocold and Herschell, two of the cryptographers, *did* have talent, to be sure. Maman had dragged her to a similar dinner party over the summer.

Tedious thing. At least until she'd been on hand for one of the always-entertaining debates between Dilly Knox — confirmed atheist — and William Montgomery — who'd even come to said dinner party in his clerical robes.

To Dot she only said, "I don't imagine I'll want to attend, no."

"It could be good for you. To get out and do something, I mean." Her cheeks flushed, and Margot didn't think it was from the sting of the wind. "I know I am a fine one to speak of the merits of getting out."

"I am out every day." Though come to think of it . . . "Do you mean *you* want to go?"

"I don't know. I *won't*. I know I won't.

Not unless you needed the outing and required my company."

A rather elementary equation, this. A single variable — Dot's desires — combined with the known quantities of her fears and Margot's presence. But the fears were substantial and negative, so the result would be too, unless the variable were large enough to overcome it. And the only way for Dot to make it so was to call upon her desire to be there for someone else. For Margot.

No, perhaps not so simple an equation. Because that same variable of Dot's desires must be on the other side of the equal sign as well. She *wanted* to go. Or at least, she wanted to want to go.

Margot didn't. But she'd learned long ago that wants must often be sacrificed when it came to maintaining relationships. "I'll think about it. See how I'm feeling on Thursday and Friday."

Her throat no longer ached, but she was still rather exhausted by day's end. A blessing that allowed her to fall into bed and go immediately to sleep without having to look overlong at the flat. At the closed door to Maman's cupboard of a room. To all the empty places that should have been filled with laughter and chiding and French phrases.

She focused on the street that would lead them to Charing Cross Hospital and changed the subject. "How long do you suppose your brother will be in hospital?"

"The doctors said it will be weeks." Dot sighed. "Drake will be gnawing at the bit long before then. Perhaps I'll be able to convince them to release him to my care, since my flat isn't far. I can set up Aunt Millie's room for him."

Margot hadn't yet pieced together all the details of her friend's family. Most of it, but there were still a few gaps. "Where does he usually stay when in London?"

"At a club, lately. He'd been attending university in Spain before the war, so after our father died, we agreed it was best to let the house, and I moved in with Aunt Millie." She didn't say with words how hard the change had been on her, but a wisp of it echoed in her eyes. She'd moved, she'd made a new home. She hadn't been willing to do it again when Aunt Millie evacuated. "Drake wasn't at home enough to warrant keeping a room for him."

A Lord-inspired move, no doubt. Margot had already learned that their father's shipping business, which her brother had planned to take over once he graduated, had suffered greatly in the first days of the war, with three-fourths of their vessels being struck by U-boats. Perhaps after the war they would rebuild the line, but that was hardly possible while Drake Elton was in the Royal Navy.

The hospital loomed large and quiet ahead of them. Margot could all but feel her remaining energy drain away another half a percent with every step she took.

But she would treat it as she did everything else — a mental exercise. She counted the steps as they entered. How long it took to travel down the corridor, up the stairs to the lieutenant's ward, down the next corridor. How many doors on each side of the hallway. Calculate the hour by how far into the rooms the light from the windows stretched.

Dot turned in at the appropriate door, but Margot halted, her ears nearly twitching. From somewhere down the corridor came a French diatribe in a cultured female voice. It acted like a magnet upon her bones, pulling her toward it.

"Margot?"

She motioned Dot on. "Go ahead. I'll find you in a moment. I want to see who's shouting in French."

Dot disappeared into the ward with a chuckle. Margot followed her ears down the corridor, to the entrance of a small administrative room in which two women stood. The younger was the one doing the shouting, her words complete with a few uniquely Gallic gestures of her hands. She was dressed in serviceable grey, like the nurses, but jewels winked at her ears and from her fingers. And her curly blond hair had been shorn above the shoulders. Somehow Margot couldn't imagine the strict matrons allowing that for just any nurse or volunteer.

The matron in front of her, in a crisp white apron over a dowdy grey dress, wore a pinched expression on her face. "I'm terribly sorry, Your Grace, but I'm sure whatever you're on about has a reasonable explanation."

Margot leaned into the doorframe. "She said that she's tired of being given only the neat and tidy jobs after years volunteering here, just because her husband's a duke, and that if it wouldn't be too ironic for words, she'd complain to him of this preferential treatment. But then any changes would be a result of *more* preferential treatment, and so she's thoroughly stymied, and she knows nothing will change, and so she'll just shout about it for a moment, get it out of her system, and then pretend to be a reasonable British lady again."

The duchess spun on her, amusement sparkling in her eyes. "Had I known some-one was handy who could understand me, I would have made the rant in Monegasque."

Margot lifted her brows. "My Italian is passable too — I probably still could have pieced the gist of it together. *Je suis dé-solée.*"

Her Grace tilted her head and studied her. "Northern France or Belgium?"

"Louvain." Margot mirrored her position. "Given the reference to Monegasque, may I assume Monaco?"

"*Oui.*" She smiled. "Though not recently. I suppose eventually I ought to claim to be from either Yorkshire, where my father lives, or the Cotswolds, where I now do." The lady held out a hand, masculine style. "Brook Wildon."

"The Duchess of Stafford!" the ward matron practically shouted, exasperation bringing her up onto the balls of her feet. As if ready to pounce on Margot if she dared to greet so lofty a personage by name.

Margot shook the duchess's hand. "I believe you've met my brother at one of his concerts. Lukas De Wilde. And I am Mar-got."

"Oh yes, you're the mathematician! He's mentioned you. Fondly. Tell me . . ." Brook reached into a bag slung onto her shoulder and pulled out a few papers. "It's really very fortuitous that I should run into you. I've been trying to find someone to discuss this with, but none of my friends care in the least, and my husband, who first introduced me to these concepts, is a bit busy at the present time. Have you read Professor Einstein's latest paper on how general relativity describes the creation and fate of the universe?"

Margot's fingers itched — not like her insides did when someone said something stupid, but in a way that made her reach out and take the proffered paper with more enthusiasm than could possibly be polite. "I have not been able to find any recent copies of the *Preussische Akademie der Wissenschaften, Sitzungsberichte.*"

"It's rather difficult to get anything originally published in German right now, to be sure. But my grandfather has connections." Brook waved a hand. "Keep that one, read it, and then I would love your thoughts, if you've the time. Are you volunteering here?"

She nearly nodded, just because of all the positivity thrumming through her head. But she caught herself. "No. I'm just visiting a patient with a friend." Unable to resist, she thumbed through the journal.

"Then take this too." A calling card appeared in Margot's vision and tucked itself into the page of the journal she'd opened to. "When you've had a chance to read it, just jot me a note, and we'll arrange tea or dinner or whatever is most convenient for you."

"I will. Thank you so much, Your Grace." She dragged her gaze off all those beautiful scientific words long enough to smile at the lady.

Said lady positioned a hat over her short curls with a grin. "Excellent. So glad to have met you, Margot. I'll let you get back to your friend, and I to my boys, before my father can spoil them beyond recognition. *Bonne soirée!*"

"Merci. À vous aussi." Margot's eyes ran down the index of the journal. All the articles looked interesting, but she made special note of where Professor Einstein's began — page 142. At least with all the codebreaking she'd been doing, her German was more or less fluent. She ought to be able to follow the professor's words. And the numbers, of course, would speak for themselves in that language unique to them, independent of German or English or French.

The matron huffed and took Margot by

the elbow, propelling her back into the corridor. "I ought to take that from you, young lady — it is surely a sin to fill your mind with that rot."

"I beg your pardon?" Margot closed the journal and tucked it under the arm opposite the matron.

"How the universe was created, she said. And its fate! As if we don't know the former and can ever know the latter. That is in the Lord's hands, not man's." The woman's brows met above her nose in a frown.

Margot's neck itched. "We can know it was created by God and still ask questions as to *how,* madam. That is not a sin. And if you think it is, then I find it curious that you work in a hospital, because is not medicine to the human form as theoretical physics is to the universe? Seeking to understand the order by which the Lord set the world in motion?"

A *hmph* was the matron's answer to that. She stared at where the duchess's figure disappeared down the stairwell. "Blessed as we are to have such a patroness, that one is not fitting company for a girl like you. You ought to dispose of that card. Bobbing her hair as she's done — and I've heard she's even been seen in trousers! Hardly a good influence on an impressionable young thing like yourself."

"An *impressionable young thing*?" A wave crashed over her, making her head feel tight and her throat close off and her heart pound so hard that the words *unknown heart condition* flickered through her brain.

She hated being called *young*. Hated it. Too long she had been dismissed, her ideas ignored solely because she hadn't been alive as long as others. She'd thought those days were beyond her now that she'd been part of the adult world for so many years. But no, this frumpish lump of a woman would speak down to her simply because her skin was smooth with youth. And *impressionable*? As if she hadn't mind enough to make it up for herself? That she would just follow someone else's *fashion* choices?

As if it even mattered if she did?

Margot yanked her elbow out of the woman's grasp. With one hand she pulled the pins from her hair, and with the other she reached for a pair of scissors sitting on a wheeled cart outside one of the ward doors. The scientific journal smacked onto the floor.

"What in the world are you — ?"

"Well, if I'm *so* impressionable . . ." She held out the long, dark coil of hair and, with

213

a single *snip,* cut it off.

Still that wave crashed and roared and bubbled, making her breath come too fast. She slammed both shears and hair onto the cart and bent to snatch up the journal. "There. Now you know you may as well judge me as you do anyone else who doesn't conform to your narrow-minded views."

The woman made a sound that was half gasp, half squeak of protest.

Margot marched into Lieutenant Elton's ward, still fuming. For a few steps. Then the steam dissipated. The pressure in her chest eased. Her eyes burned. She stopped, eyes fastened on a seam in the tile floor, and tried to regulate the ragged edges of her breath.

In — two, three, four. *Out* — two, three, four. Eight beats. Six seconds. One cycle. Two. Three.

Trace the seams. Measure the tiles. Twelve inches by twelve inches. Twenty-six tiles from one wall to the other. Three hundred twelve inches. Eight yards and two feet.

Hair tickled her neck in a way it hadn't done since she was six — the first time she'd taken a pair of scissors to her hair, to eliminate the need for the ridiculous ribbons Maman had insisted on tying in it. That day, she'd learned what happened when she crossed one of Sophie De Wilde's invisible lines, and she hadn't been able to sit at her desk chair without pain for hours.

But Maman wasn't here to see. To judge. To punish. Or to decide that it wasn't deserving of punishment.

She had never drawn the lines in the same place twice. The second time Margot had cut her own hair, at age ten, it had simply been because it was annoying her, not in rebellion. Maman hadn't punished her that time, and it wasn't because she'd left it longer — below her shoulders, no ends tickling her neck. It had been because it hadn't been meant to hurt anyone.

"It is the heart that matters," Maman had said as she evened out the edges that second time. *"The motivation."*

She squeezed her eyes shut. The matron *was* a narrow-minded hag. But Margot's actions wouldn't actually hurt her. They were merely a statement. So did it deserve punishment?

"Margot! What did you *do*?"

Apparently Dot thought it did. Or deserved outrage, anyway.

Margot opened her eyes to find that she'd apparently made it to Lieutenant Elton's bed, more or less. Her friend had stood up, eyes as round as zeros, fingers reaching out

215

to touch the blunt edges of Margot's hair.

Margot swallowed. "Made a statement to the matron about the opinion in which I held her judgments, I believe." Riding that wave of whatever-it-had-been. The one that left her empty when it ebbed.

For the first time in their acquaintance, Dot looked baffled by her. "Why? Why would you . . . Everyone will say you're . . ."

"The better question is," Drake Elton put in from his place propped against pillows, "what did the matron say to instigate the reaction? We all know she's a judgmental nag."

Her insides went a bit softer. Margot offered him a smile for taking her side, despite the fact that he had no real reason to. Then she looked back to Dot. "I don't care what anyone says." She meant only to blink, but her eyes stayed shut for a long moment. Squeezed. "She just made me so . . ."

"Angry?" Now Dot's voice was soft. The kind of soft that meant she was trying to be understanding, and perhaps probe a bit. Maman had always excelled at that particular tone.

Margot forced her eyes back open. "Of course not. That wouldn't be logical."

"No." Dot drew the word into three syllables. "It would be emotional. You've had a trying week."

Trying. The English word came from the French. To examine, to separate the good from the bad. Is that what losing her mother was supposed to do? Cull and test and examine her? Or bits of her? Or perhaps just try *her,* as a whole, and sit in judgment?

No. There could be no purpose to it. None. Not from God.

But someone else could have had a purpose. A black one. Hitting directly at Room 40, perhaps. Or at Margot.

Margot sucked in a breath and angled away. "Do you mind if I leave? I don't mean to abandon you, but I know well I didn't cut it in a straight line, and —"

"Oh, it's straight." Dot's lips twitched. "Just . . . diagonal."

That was enough to make her twitchy, and she squirmed her shoulders in protest. "Short I don't mind. Crooked won't do."

Her friend laughed. "No. It won't do at all. Do you need my help?"

"Willa can fix it, I imagine. You enjoy your time with your brother." She sent him a tight smile over Dot's shoulder. "Sorry to have caused a ruckus."

"Are you kidding?" His grin looked almost nearly without pain. "This is the most interesting thing to happen here in days.

You've made yourself the heroine of the ward."

With a shake of her head more amused than she'd thought it could be, Margot tucked the journal and the duchess's card into her handbag and calculated how long it would take her to reach her brother's house — and how many horrified looks she'd have to ignore on the walk.

12

"Ignore your brother."

Margot kept her gaze on the mirror, but she moved it from the reflection of Willa as she snipped at the back of her hair to Lukas, who stood glowering in the doorway. An image that might have looked more intimidating were Zurie not gurgling happily in his arms and smacking his cheeks with chubby hands.

"No, do not ignore me. I am only saying what everyone else will. Short hair on women is scandalous."

Willa smiled as she worked. "He doesn't mean that, because he knows well that I cut mine the year before he met me, and he would never *ever* imply that I committed some grave social error in doing so."

Lukas's reflection frowned. "That was different. You cut yours so you could sell it and buy material to make your brother a coat. That was a selfless reason, not one made from frustration. Or fashion — not that Margot ever thinks of something as trivial as fashion."

Snip. Snip. Willa cut hair in the same way she played the violin — with precise, well-planned movements. The tension in Margot's shoulders eased. She would be even and symmetrical again in no time.

"You know how rebellious I am, luv. Keep saying how unbecoming it is, and I'm going to cut my own."

Lukas's reflection intercepted little Zurie's hand, which made the baby giggle. His scowl only darkened. "Absolutely not. I forbid it."

Margot's gaze went to Willa in the mirror. Her sister-in-law only grinned at the command. "And why not? Will you not love me anymore if I have short hair?"

"That is not it, as well you know. But if you cut yours, then it would not be but a day before suddenly I was thinking that short hair was the loveliest style ever to come into fashion, and it is embarrassing to constantly be changing my opinions based on whatever you do. Spare a man his pride, *mon amour.* Take pity."

Willa laughed. Lukas kissed the baby fist he held captive. Zurie squealed in delight.

Margot rolled her eyes. But with amusement. "It is only hair." How many times would she have to say that? It was part of the reason why she'd not resorted to scissors since she was ten. "It will grow back, if I decide I want it to."

"And in the meantime, you'll look chic and on the cutting edge of fashion." Willa laughed even as she said it, obviously anticipating the scowl Margot now directed at her reflection. "There, Lukas, I gave her a reason to grow it back out. See what a good wife I am?"

A buzz sounded from the hallway, and Lukas spun out of the door. "That will be your sisters, I imagine. I will let them in."

"I don't know why I did it." Margot said the words quietly, almost changing her mind about saying them at all. But that was the truth that had settled as she walked here. She wasn't usually so impulsive, especially not about something a stranger said. It didn't matter. It could have no effect on her life what some random woman in a hospital thought of her. But she had let it — she had *made* it affect her by reacting as she had done.

She didn't care about the hair. It would grow, or it would not, if she decided she liked it this way. She'd cut it before. She was hardly like one of those girls who thought they wanted to be fashionable and then bawled their way out of the barbershop.

But the irrational action — that bothered her.

Willa put the scissors down and leaned over until her head was next to Margot's, their faces sharing the reflection. They looked nothing alike — Willa's hair was a fair brown, straight and silky, her nose flatter, her complexion that perfect English rose — but they were sisters. Love and Lukas had made them so, and it was the only reason Margot entrusted her with such an unsettling truth.

It was why she made no objections when Willa slid an arm around her shoulders. This sister of hers wasn't much of a toucher. Only with those she loved best, and only in moments when it mattered. When Willa put her arm around her, Margot knew it meant something.

In many ways, they spoke the same language.

"Margot. I know you think it's weak to give in to emotions. But you just lost your mother. That can't go unanswered by your heart."

"It hasn't." It wouldn't. She would discover what had really made her mother fall and breathe her last. She would go over every minute of her last days until she had answers.

"It has. This isn't something you approach scientifically, as a puzzle needing to be solved. This isn't a matter for your head." She lifted her fingers and rested them against the side of Margot's head.

Margot drew in a breath. "Everything is a matter for the head. The mind controls the heart — or can. We do not *have* to be swayed by every emotion that comes along."

"No. Not each one. But sometimes they crash over us, don't they? Too strong for us to swim against, to fight off. And then we do illogical things like cut our hair off in the middle of a hospital corridor. Or go with someone into occupied territory to rescue his mother and sister."

She didn't know what to say to that. Worse, she couldn't hold Willa's reflected blue-green gaze. She looked down, even though she could count on one hand the times she'd ever been the first to avert her eyes in a conversation.

It wasn't wrong to feel emotion. She knew that. Especially in something like this.

But it was dangerous. So dangerous. Emotions didn't obey the rules. They existed somewhere outside the set of axioms that governed the rest of her life. They confused her.

Chatter and feminine laughter in three different tones filled the hallway. Were it anyone else giggling, she would have gone tense again, but Willa's sisters she knew well. And knew that they deserved every lighthearted moment they could find or create. They'd lived hard lives, all of them, before the war had set their family of orphans on a different path.

Elinor was the first to enter, looking as though she stepped from an advert, in a smart suit and with perfectly coiffed hair. She held something in her hand that she brandished like a weapon, held aloft to rally the troops. "I bring curlers and wavers!"

Margot would have leapt from the chair if Willa weren't holding her down. "No. Absolutely not. I only wanted you to trim it — and how did they even know?"

"I told Lukas to telephone them." Willa narrowed her eyes at her. "Sit still and stop squirming like a child, Margot. You're as bad as Jory. This isn't about fashion — this is about blending in."

"I fail to see —"

"She's very right." Rosemary edged over to the dressing table and set down a bag of her own. "Something we learned long ago:

Look right, and you'll draw *less* attention, not more. If you're going to have short hair and you don't want everyone ogling you for it, you have to style it like the other girls are doing."

Margot groaned. She certainly hadn't thought of *this* when she picked up those scissors, or she would have come up with a less bothersome way to snarl at the matron.

"We'll put it in terms you can understand. That's why we brought Lina along." Elinor motioned to the auburn-haired completion of the trio. Evelina wasn't a direct adoption into their family — she'd married their eldest brother, Barclay, two years ago. "She understands mathematics better than the rest of us."

Evelina made a show of cracking her knuckles. "I've borrowed Fergus's text so I can get my phraseology right. We're talking about waves, Margot. So let's think in terms of amplitude and altitude, all right?"

Elinor nodded and unfastened the bag she'd brought. "Now, you're going to want to start with these clips. I'll show you how, but for tonight we're going to use one of those Marcel heated curling irons."

It took a ridiculously long time for the sisters to finish their instructions, though that was largely because they were constantly interrupting one another. But Margot thought she was a pretty good sport about it. She took note of how wide each section of hair needed to be, the volume each clip could hold, what diameter she needed in an iron, and which direction to rotate either an iron or a clip to get the desired effect — though she still wasn't sure she actually desired the effect. She practiced a few times on her own, and she didn't say what she was thinking about how difficult it would be to get the back into the silly little curlers by herself.

She wasn't going to point out that she now lived alone. She *wouldn't.*

She'd remember the process, though, and do what she could with it. At least since she could simply go to bed with her hair wound around the pins at night and take them out in the morning. A bit of pinning and, according to Elinor, she'd be finished. At least since she'd solidly refused the offer of the pomade the blonde had brought.

At last, they deemed the style complete and let her face the mirror again.

Margot wrinkled her nose at her reflection. "It isn't me."

"It is now." Willa smirked and smoothed down a tuft of her daughter's hair. Zurie had at some point abandoned Lukas, it seemed. "Unless you want us to make you match your niece."

Right on cue, Zurie lunged for Margot, chanting, "Go-Go! Go!"

A game board flashed before her mind's eye. A strange man in the park, playing it. He'd been there a few more times, though not regularly.

Zurie's fingers found her new waves and latched ahold of them, earning a laughing reprimand from the others. Margot didn't much care if the style was destroyed, but she also didn't object when Willa took the little one back. She liked Zurie, and she would like her even more as she grew up a bit and could carry on a conversation. But she never experienced whatever tug these other young women must feel, to make such silly faces and coo over each new addition to their family.

"Let's show Lukas." Rosemary tugged her to her feet and gave her a helpful push toward the door. "You know, Go-Go, I could work wonders with that dress, too, if you let me —"

"No. And you're not allowed to call me that if you're over three years old."

Rosemary gave an exaggerated sigh. "You're hopeless. But we love you anyway."

A minute later, she stood obediently in

front of her brother while he regarded her with lifted brows. His silence stretched long enough that Margot's fingers curled into her palms. "What? I know it looks strange, but —"

"Non. Ce n'est pas ça." He shook his head, blinked rapidly. "It isn't that at all. You look . . . you look like *Mère.*"

"Now you're just being ridiculous." She'd always taken after their father, not their mother. And Maman had certainly never had short hair. Though she *had* occasionally styled the sides in waves, for special occasions. It had been years since Margot had seen her make such an effort. Before Papa died.

"Look." Lukas reached into his pocket and pulled out his wallet. From within it, he slipped a small photograph. "I had it with me in Paris. Before the invasion."

She took the thick paper, her throat going tight when she looked down at it. Maman, smiling at the camera, looking beautiful and polished. She remembered the portrait — it was what Papa had wanted for his birthday the year before he died. But she'd thought all the prints of it were gone, like everything else from her past.

"I didn't know you had this." Each feature was so familiar. So beloved. The darkest hair. The sparkling eyes. The perfectly proportioned face, symmetrical and un-equivocally beautiful because of it. And waves on the sides of her hair.

Even so. Her brother may see their mother in her, but only because he wanted to. She handed the photo back and forced her tone to go light. "Does that mean you won't disown me?"

His smile was crooked. "I did not disown you the other times, did I?"

"No. But I was a child."

"You were never a child." Chuckling, he put the photograph back into his wallet, that back into his pocket, and then stepped closer to fold her into his arms. "But you are still my baby sister."

He said no more. But he didn't have to. She knew all the things he didn't voice.

After a moment, she pulled away with a muted smile. "I'd better get home. It's getting late."

"You do not . . ." *Have to.* But he didn't say that again either. Just sighed and nod-ded. "Be careful. It is dark already."

He was coming a long way, this brother of hers. It used to be that he wouldn't think of allowing her to travel the distance home alone. But as that had proven impossible to keep to, given their very different hours with his concert schedule and her work, he'd settled for making sure she could defend herself against any attacker. Willa and Barclay had taught her all she needed to know.

She said good-bye to the other girls and soon slipped out into the night. The November air was cold but welcome, chasing a few bits of residual clutter from her mind. She buried her hands in her pockets and strode along, from gaslight to gaslight, from Kensington back toward her flat in Chelsea.

Fog had crept in from the Thames at some point while she was inside. It would protect them tonight from biplanes and zeppelins. She watched it swirl in front of the nearest light, moving so slowly that it nearly looked immobile. But it wasn't. Nothing ever was, it seemed.

At the corner, she paused. Looked toward the park, cold and dark. She didn't have to see to know where Mrs. Rourke usually sat with her crocheting. Where the stranger had taken up residence at the wrought-iron table instead of Gregory, playing no one at Go.

He wasn't there now, of course. Even from here she could see the silhouette of the empty chair. But why was he ever? *Who* was he? And where had he come by that game?

"Have you any spare change, miss?"

She didn't jump, but she did jerk her head

toward the voice more quickly than if she'd noted the figure before his words snuck through the fog toward her. There, someone shuffling toward the light.

Male. Twenty-two to twenty-five, were she to guess. Five feet eleven inches, if he'd been standing up straight, which he wasn't. He was hunched against the chill and hobbling with that distinct gait that suggested a missing limb. Hair of an indeterminate color in the dim light. A cap pulled low against the cold. A scarf that was more holes than knit — Maman would have been appalled.

He didn't come any closer. Whether the distance was out of respect or because he knew he'd get nothing from her if he scared her, she could only guess. But she opened her handbag. The journal that the duchess had given her still protruded from the top, but she reached in around it and pulled out her change purse. She never carried much on her, not unless she was going to the shops. But she counted out what she had and held it all out in her palm. "Here."

The man hesitated, edged a bit closer, and then took a single florin. "I won't take all you have, miss. You've no doubt a husband and little ones at home."

"No, I haven't. Take it all." She followed his hand and spilled the coins into it. Maman would have given more conservatively, always mindful of the house in Brussels that would need repair and the accounts that might be drained when they were no longer frozen.

But Margot's equation was different.

The man's fingers closed around the offering. "I don't — I mean, thank you. I hate to have asked. To have *had* to ask."

He must be new to such hard times.

"I'll work for it. If I can. That is . . ." He edged back half a step. No expression of pain accompanied the awkward movement, so perhaps the injury wasn't as new as the low circumstances. "There's not much I can do these days."

And she had nothing that needed done, regardless.

Or did she? "I do have one small task that you can accomplish. Not now, but sometime this week." She pointed to the park, and to the empty table and chair. "Sometimes there is a man there, playing a board game with white and black stones. He'll tell no one his name. But if you could determine who he is, I would very much appreciate it."

The stranger frowned. "All right. May I ask why?"

"Because I don't like unknowns. Every x

in an equation ought to be solved for."

"Then you'll want to know *my* name as well." He stuck out a hand. "I'm called Redvers — Red, for short. Red Holmes."

She shook rather than holding her hand out, wrist limp, for him to bow over. "Any relation to Sherlock?"

He laughed, making her glad she'd emptied her change purse for him. "Not that I've yet discovered. So once I've found out who that other bloke is, how am I to let you know?"

Well, that was a good question. She could only imagine Lukas's outrage if she told him where she lived. "If you're in this neighborhood often, you could simply make it a point to be on this corner around five-thirty. That's when I usually walk by." When she walked this way, which she typically only did if coming from her brother's, or if she fancied a turn through the park. But she'd take the long way until he reported back. And then he wouldn't know her actual path, in case he was less savory than he seemed.

He nodded and slid the hand with the coins into his pocket. "Thank you, miss. I'm grateful. I won't spend it on anything but food, I promise you."

Yes, definitely new to his current plight. She nodded and kept her features schooled.

"I trust not. Have a good evening, Mr. Holmes."

"You too, miss. Thank you."

He hadn't asked her name, and he backed up again to give her room to go by. She nearly smiled. In the French sectors of Belgium, people tended to get much closer than the English did in general. Stop to ask someone for directions, and they all but embraced you. But she'd taken rather naturally to the more generous spaces between people, and she appreciated now that he was obviously taking pains to keep from alarming her.

A nice man, she would guess. On hard times thanks to whatever battle had stolen part of his left leg. Of no more use to the army. She could only imagine how long he'd been recuperating, the agony as he learned to use a false foot. But none of that showed on his face now. No pain, other than that of failure. He must have been trying recently to find work and been turned away.

There ought to be something though. It was a simple matching operation. Perhaps when he told her the name of the Go player, she would ask him what skills he had.

And in the meantime, she could at the very least provide him with a better scarf. Maman always had a stack of extras. *"You never know when you might see a neck in need of warmth,"* she'd said no fewer than eight times.

She hurried home, checking over her shoulder to be sure no one was following — cold or not, she wouldn't have the fellow finding out where she lived. In the door, up the stairs. Noting absently the squeaky stair, the missing rung, all the markers. She kept her stride open and long as she moved to 3E. Three of E. Three of — no.

Just 3E. No more equations there.

She let herself in and locked up behind her. With one hand she turned on the low gaslights while she dropped her handbag on the table with the other. Then she turned and made it two steps toward the bedroom doors before she stopped.

The scarves were all in Maman's room. Behind the door that she hadn't opened in a week. The door she'd not really planned to open again until someone called her on her cowardice. In a month or two. Or three. Or four.

She hadn't said anything to Red Holmes about the scarf. He wouldn't know if she changed her mind.

But *she* would know.

Margot stood rooted to the spot for five seconds. And then ten more. And another thirty before she drew in a long breath and forced herself forward. Right foot — *one.* Left foot — *two.* Another halt.

"You're stronger than this, Margot." She clenched her hands into fists and wished she hadn't spoken aloud — it made the flat seem all the emptier. *Just go.*

Go — white stones and black, the outlines of squares. Strangers in the park.

Go-Go — innocent little eyes in deepest brown that wouldn't look upon their *grand-mère* again.

Go!

She rushed forward — *one, two, three, four, five* — and gripped the doorknob. Pushed it open.

Cold air wafted out, and on it rode the light, floral scent of Maman's soap. Lily of the valley.

She blinked and fumbled for the knob that would turn on the low lights.

It looked the same as it always had, each and every time she'd come in here. Someone had made the bed. Righted the disorder that had been caused when they came to remove her. Dot, she'd bet. Or Willa. Lukas wouldn't have had the heart.

But it didn't look like Dot or Willa. It looked like Maman, smelled like Maman.

She wasn't sure if it brought comfort or pain.

Best not to dwell on it. She went for the chest of drawers and opened the topmost one. A rainbow of clothing met her eyes. To the left, various scarves and even a shawl. Whites, greys, browns, a black. She pulled out a grey one, but before she could command herself to close the drawer and retreat, she saw blue and red and pink and yellow articles to the right of the scarves, all with slips of paper pinned to them.

Christmas presents. She knew it the moment she pulled out the little cardigan with *Zurie* pinned to it. As if Maman had really needed to remind herself for whom the tiny thing was intended. But she'd always been meticulous about the oddest things.

Margot turned and set the gift on the bed, along with the scarf. Zurie would get it for Christmas. One last gift from her grand-mère. Turning back to the drawer, she saw that the next slip said *Lukas.* A new scarf in masculine blues and greys, with gloves to match. Moving that aside, she saw a beautiful shawl for Willa. Then stared at the last slip. *Margot.*

She blinked, and blinked again when the first one didn't clear her eyes of their blurriness. At first all she could see was the bright red. A color she never would have chosen for herself, but exactly the sort of brilliant hue Maman always pushed her to wear. It wouldn't be a shawl — Margot never wore shawls. It was too wide for a scarf. With hands trembling more than she cared to admit, she extracted it. Fold after fold lengthened. Sleeves shook themselves out.

A long cardigan, belted, open at the front, cabled on the sleeves. The sort of thing that would be perfect on a spring day, or an autumn one, when a coat was too heavy but the air too cool for nothing. The sort of thing that Margot had wished for, though the words had never crossed her lips.

But she'd known. Maman had always known. She'd known, and somehow she'd found the time to knit this without Margot ever seeing her work on it. The evenings when Margot had the night shift, probably. Or after Maman had shut her door and supposedly retired.

She took off the pin and let the paper flutter to the floor. She slid her arms into the sleeves. She buttoned the belt into place. And then she looked up, catching her reflection in the mirror.

A stranger looked back at her with short waves in her hair, Maman's handiwork lending style to her figure, a flash of color she never sought but which even she knew suited her complexion. She wrapped her arms around her middle and felt her mother embracing her.

"Maman." She whispered the name into the room — a plea. A prayer she knew the Lord wouldn't answer. He wouldn't give her mother back to her. Couldn't, because He'd created a world of rules and laws and mathematical certainties, and that world didn't involve women rising from the grave a week after they'd died and been buried.

The floor greeted her, though she wasn't aware of her knees having buckled until they smacked into the unforgiving wood. But her knees didn't matter. The pain was welcome, even. A muted echo of her heart.

Arms still wrapped around herself, she leaned her head against the bed and breathed in the lily of the valley scent that equaled Maman. The breath knotted, heaved, her diaphragm rebelled, and something hot and wet scalded her cheeks.

"Maman," she whispered again into the room. But the only answer was the sound of her sob.

13

"Look sharp, men." One of the patients who was a day or so away from being released back to his unit scurried into the ward. His eyes were wide, and he followed his own advice, cinching the belt on his dressing gown and standing far straighter than most of the blokes in hospital could hope to do. "There's an admiral on his way in. Coming for *you,* Elton."

Drake pushed himself up a few more inches, glad he could manage the feat today without having to call for a nurse like an infant. It would be Hall, he assumed. He'd had a feeling DID would come by before another day or two could pass.

What surprised him when Hall strode into the ward a minute later wasn't the way he homed directly in on Drake's bed. And it certainly wasn't the way his presence filled the room, despite the fact that he was neither tall nor particularly fierce-looking, and made all the men who were awake try to salute. What surprised him was the very familiar bag clutched in his hand. Drake's bag — the one he'd had with him on the train. The one he'd *left* on the train. Thoroton must have retrieved it for him and sent it along.

"At ease, men," DID said with a smile as he turned toward Drake's cot. He set the bag down and took a seat without any ado. "Lieutenant Elton. How are you feeling today?"

"Ready to escape." He still hurt like the dickens and hadn't attempted to stand since he'd fallen into that train car, but he was awake far too much for the monotony of hospital life to be anything but agonizing. He added a smile. "And report back to duty, I mean."

Hall snorted a laugh. "Right. You look it. Though actually, that's what I've come about. I know you're the type who will improve faster if you've something to occupy your mind."

"Yes!" He nearly shouted it, though he caught himself in time. Any patient who dared to raise his voice in anything but a scream of pain would be chastised immediately by Nurse Wilcox, the same ward matron who had so infuriated Margot De

Wilde the other day. He couldn't help smiling over the memory of her stomping in, her hair an absolute wreck and fury dripping from every beautiful line of her face.

Hopefully DID would chalk the smile up to something other than thoughts of Margot De Wilde. Though as distractions went, she'd proven an interesting one. She hadn't rejoined Dot on her daily visits, but his sister had endless stories to tell from their six-week-long acquaintance.

"I do realize that five days in hospital is hardly enough to have recovered after such a scrape, and I'll not have you pushing yourself beyond your capabilities and *slowing* your recuperation. However" — Hall lifted his chin and looked down at Drake like a schoolmaster would look at a particularly bright pupil who was acting particularly stupid — "if you promise to abide by the dictates of your doctor, I've made arrangements."

Drake nodded, afraid to part his lips lest that forbidden shout of joy emerge.

The admiral nodded too. "Very well, then. Tomorrow you'll be moved to your sister's flat. I've arranged for your doctor to pay you a visit every day, and we can hire a nurse as well, if needed. If their reports are good, then I'll begin sending a bit of work home for you with your sister."

"With my . . ." Drake pursed his lips. "But, sir —"

"You'll have to tell her, Lieutenant." Hall's tone left no room for debate. "Thus far she is willing to believe that I am the bearer of information simply because *she* is under my command, but that will not hold up if we move forward with this plan."

"Yes, sir." Training had him agreeing. But training didn't answer the questions. How was he supposed to inform his sister that he was an intelligence agent — not just a sailor — without sparking the fear that lived deep inside her? How was he to admit that when she thought he'd been on the battleship *Royal Oak,* seeing little action, he'd really been with Abuelo in Spain, balancing the image of a spoiled university student with the reality of dodging German bullets?

Or *not* dodging them, as the case may be.

Margot De Wilde seemed to have a formula for telling a convincing lie. Did she also have one for delivering a hard truth?

"Very good. Now." Eyes snapping with amusement, Hall leaned forward. "I've yet to get a straight answer from either Miss De Wilde or your sister about what happened here the other day to result in shorn locks. But I suspect it's a story I want to hear."

It was certainly one that had been making the rounds in the ward — always at the expense of the cantankerous matron who had dared to insult their duchess. As Drake told the admiral the tale, his neighbors butted in now and then with their own observations of how Miss De Wilde had stridden in, looking to be the epitome of furious pride. And how Dot had been the only one in the room who seemed more horrified than impressed.

The admiral chuckled in all the right places, going so far as to lean back in his chair and slap a hand to his knee at one point.

The duchess herself made an appearance as they were wrapping up the tale, stealing the attention of most of the men and giving Hall the chance to lean forward and say quietly, eyes still twinkling, "Don't waste your time, Elton."

Drake lifted his brows. "Pardon?"

"Pursuing Margot De Wilde. I see the interest in your eyes."

His brows pulled down again. Hall was famous for reading people, but even so — Drake was usually better at hiding his thoughts than that. Perhaps it was the fault of the injury and medication and endless hours on this blighted cot. But DID *had* seen, apparently, so what was the point in denying it? He weighed the question for a moment before coming to the conclusion that admitting it could actually prove an advantage. He could ask the admiral questions he couldn't ask his sister without announcing to *her* his interest in her friend. "Is she spoken for?"

The admiral barked a laugh. "Heavens no! She wouldn't hear of it. Which is my point. In the last year I have watched no fewer than half a dozen men try to get her attention, and she is utterly oblivious to them all."

Drake shifted, winced, and covered it with a smile. "That's a positive for my cause, sir, not a negative."

"Elton . . ." The amusement in the admiral's eyes faded into mild concern. "I don't usually take it upon myself to interfere in such matters, but Margot is a special case. She is vulnerable from the loss of her mother, though she'll never admit it. I won't have you taking advantage of that."

"I wouldn't!" The very suggestion made him go tense. Which in turn made fire scream through his middle.

"Not in any reprehensible way. But you ought to know that she has goals for her life, for when this war is over, that don't include a husband keeping her at home to raise a brood of children. Education, for starters."

Drake settled back against the pillows, darting only a glance to his right when a chorus of laughter broke out near where the duchess and Nurse Denler were arguing — or pretending to argue — over who would make up the empty cot that was apparently to be filled this afternoon. "She hasn't already got an education?" According to Dot, most of the secretaries had attended university, at least for a while. Dot was one of the few who hadn't.

"Not as much a one as she would like. Though I believe she was enrolled at university in Louvain before her father passed away. When she was twelve or thirteen."

University? At such a young age? He knew his surprise showed on his face. Even so, it didn't stop a corner of his mouth from tugging up. "Dot did say her new friend is the most intelligent person she's ever met."

"Mm. I rather agree with her." That statement said considerably more than Dot's claim, given that Admiral Blinker Hall, Director of Intelligence, knew far more people than Dorothea Elton. Still.

Hall shook his head. "And I see I've only managed to intrigue you more. Well. I shall leave it to Margot, then, to convince you of the futility of your thoughts."

"It is surely understandable to be intrigued. I look forward to becoming her friend, at the very least."

"An infinitely wiser goal. And now I had better be off." Hall stood, tugging his jacket into place, and motioned to the bag he'd set on the floor. "Would you like me to hand that to you?"

"Please. And thank you for bringing it, sir." Thoughts of the bag, and hence the other items he'd had on his person that day, bruised the happier thought of a pretty Belgian who could out-think him. "One moment more, if you please. I'm afraid my memory is a bit muddled after I fell. The case I'd slipped into my pocket, with the sample . . . ?" It hadn't broken, had it? Because if it had, if the tainted sugar had been crushed — Drake could be fairly certain *he* hadn't ingested or inhaled any, given the fact that he was still on earth and only in bullet-induced pain, but what of the workers and other intelligence agents who had swarmed the car?

Hall offered a reassuring smile and positioned the bag beside Drake on his cot. "Thoroton sent it ahead of you — perfectly preserved. You apparently protected it as you fell."

His relief was palpable. "Good. Thank you, Admiral."

"The thanks go to you for a job well done, Elton. Get back on your feet, and perhaps we'll get you into the field again before this war is over." He turned away, then paused and leveled a finger at him. "Tell your sister. By Monday. Understood?"

Drake sighed. "Understood. And I will, of course, caution her to keep it to herself. Although — what of her new friend? Can Miss De Wilde know?"

"I see no harm in that." Hall's lips twitched.

Drake nodded. "Then good day, Admiral." He saluted as best as he could manage and, after the admiral strode away, opened his satchel. There wasn't much inside it. A change of clothes. The newspaper he'd been hiding behind more than reading. The volume of poetry he'd brought with him.

This he pulled out and opened to the slip of paper he'd been using to mark his spot, his mind still spinning through those last moments. His fingers stilled. "Admiral?"

Hall had made it halfway to the door, but he turned with lifted brows and hurried back to Drake's bedside, his face clear of anything but question. "Yes? What is it, lad?"

Drake stared at the page, but it wasn't the French clouding his mind. It was the Spanish shout from German lips. Garbled by the wind, but still clear. "Jaeger."

Hall sat again, probably so that their words could be quieter. "Yes? His name was in Thoroton's report. He was the agent accompanying the shipment."

The one who shot him — that would have been in the report, too, at least as a supposition. "Was he apprehended?" They could surely have had someone waiting when the train arrived.

But Hall shook his head. "Thoroton reported that he'd disembarked the train at some point before the next station."

Drake's fingers tightened around the book. "He'll be seeking retribution. Either on the team in Spain or on me here. He ought to be watched."

"He will be." Hall pitched his voice lower still, leaning to within a few inches of him. "Don't let that worry you — I keep accounts of every German agent still in England, and they're only free if I've deemed them to be of more use to me that way. If he enters the country, I'll know it. And if necessary, we can make use of the identity of one of the German agents we have in prison to communicate with him, sending a message in a name he would recognize. We've done it before, with others, to great success."

A nod, a smile to show how well he appreciated the admiral's cleverness. But Drake couldn't convince his grip on the book to loosen. Perhaps it was only fear — a visceral, purely instinctual reaction to the man who had shot at him twice and struck him once. A few inches either direction, and that bullet would have killed him. It was surely nothing but the finger of God that had directed it through his abdomen in a way that dodged all vital organs and arteries.

But perhaps it *wasn't* only fear. Perhaps it was a premonition born of the instincts he'd sharpened so carefully over the last three years of service. And if that were the case, he'd have to sort out why he thought so and what it might mean. What particular dangers the man could pose. When Drake's mind was less clouded with pain and medication, he'd work it out.

Margot clutched the glass, praying it would tether her to sanity. Somehow, though, she suspected that the fizzing soda had no such miraculous properties. It couldn't combat the dozens of chattering people, the crowds that moved in chaotic patterns through Herschell's house, the too-warm temperature that made her wish she'd agreed to a dress with a shorter sleeve.

Beside her, Dot actually seemed to be having a decent time. She wore an evening dress in green, had a necklace sparkling around her throat, and swayed a bit to the beat of the music. Two couples were attempting to dance in a space not designed for it, while Serocold laughed and launched into another verse of the song he was playing on the piano.

Margot could appreciate the rhythm, strong and sure. She could calculate the intervals and knew intellectually that some chords were more pleasing than others because of them. She understood the mathematics behind the music and loved it because of the rules it followed. But it never made her feet tap or her body sway.

"I haven't been to anything like this since Nelson left." Dot was smiling and sipping at her own glass of fizzing red liquid. "And not often then, I confess."

Margot had already heard all about the man Dot had planned to marry. He seemed like he'd been a good sort. But at this point, the loss was stale enough that her friend's voice never seemed strained or *too* sad when she mentioned him. Margot looked out over the crowd. "I attended one of these over the summer." When Maman had made her.

Maman had also insisted she have a few evening dresses in her wardrobe for such occasions. Willa had come over this afternoon to tell her which she ought to wear. And, Margot suspected, to make sure she waved her hair.

She'd nearly refused to do so again after the flutter it had caused among the secretaries.

A man she didn't recognize, but who bore a bit of a resemblance to Herschell, approached with a smile. Aimed, wisely, at Dot instead of her. "Good evening, ladies." He looked young, maybe nineteen or twenty, and wore naval blue. "Would one of you like to dance?"

He said *one of* but looked only at Dot. Which suited Margot fine.

"Oh." Her friend looked to her, obviously debating whether it would be rude to abandon her.

Margot produced a smile and waved her fingers toward the improvised dance floor. "Go. Have fun."

Fun. That would be the quiet of her flat and that journal the Duchess of Stafford had lent her. She'd already read through the whole thing twice, but she'd like another go at Einstein's article before she dared to talk of it to the duchess. Her German was good, but it hadn't recently been focused on mathematical and scientific phrases, and she wasn't altogether certain she'd been translating each word properly. She'd brought a massive dictionary home with her this afternoon, though, to help her remedy any mistakes.

Once Dot put down her glass and joined the sailor on the not-a-dance-floor, Margot edged backward until she'd found a nice corner to disappear into. By her calculation, they could leave in another twenty-three minutes without it looking rude. Assuming Dot *wanted* to go. With a bit of luck, the sailor wouldn't be charming enough to outweigh her friend's urge to return home. Surely she'd want to go and check on her newly installed brother.

Culbreth drifted to a halt in front of her, along with Sir Malcolm — one of DID's staff. "A bit scary, isn't it?" he was saying.

Sir Malcolm hummed his agreement. "I'm just grateful we managed to intercept it. Can you imagine the chaos it would have caused if they'd made it to our armies? There was enough sugar there to have killed thousands of animals. Horses, donkeys —

we'd have been in quite a spot."

Margot lowered her glass a bit. Sugar. Dead animals. She'd decoded something about that, but the details wouldn't quite surface. Which was troubling. She frowned at her soda and tried to sort through it.

Wednesday last. That was it — the day she'd come home with a fever and found Maman.

No wonder the details were playing hide-and-seek.

Culbreth was shaking his head. "I can't quite fathom it. Using a disease like anthrax to gain the upper hand. It doesn't seem right, does it? Deliberately spreading something we've tried so hard to eradicate?"

"The huns are scrambling for any advantage they can find, that's what. We've got them on the run."

Anthrax. Margot took another sip of the soda.

"Yes, but what if some of that sugar had made it into human consumption? Can you imagine the results?" Culbreth, though his back was to her, was surely frowning. She could hear it in his voice. "I looked it up — nasty thing, that. Gave me quite a start, too, to see how many symptoms of infection resembled the flu, what with that bout of it going round the office."

The synapses in her brain finally fired in such a way that she felt the jolt all the way to her toes. This was what had been bothering her ever since she stumbled home that morning and found Maman.

Anthrax. Sugar cubes. A perfectly healthy woman falling prey to death for no good reason after contracting the flu.

Maman hadn't just died. She'd been killed. Targeted — and perhaps more of them would be too. One of the agents the admiral had left in play must have been contacted, given *something* tainted with anthrax. And he must have decided to use it against Room 40. The people under Admiral Hall, who was waging war so effectively against the Germans' intelligence operations.

The soda in her cup sloshed as her hand trembled. She slid the glass onto an end table nearby and pushed through the crowd of familiar faces, toward the lavatory, muttering her apologies as she bumped into a few colleagues on her way.

They all just smiled and moved aside, oblivious.

But she wasn't. Not anymore.

14

Drake had never considered himself a coward. But apparently he was one, as evidenced by the fact that every time he opened his mouth to tell Dot the truth about his wartime activities, he closed it again, the words still unsaid. He'd meant to get it over with as soon as he'd settled into her flat on Saturday, but she'd been busy alternately fussing over him and then herself, preparing for her outing.

His sister. Out for an evening. Of her own free will.

Perhaps it was the shock that rendered him speechless.

No, because he'd been speechless still the next morning as she dressed for Mass, and he had remained so even after she'd returned.

Now here they were, mere hours left in Sunday, right up against his admiral-imposed deadline for telling her, and he knew he had only an hour or two of wake-fulness left. He'd managed to shuffle his way to the sofa in the main room, given that Margot De Wilde was due any minute, and it had cost him a ridiculous amount of energy.

He should tell her now, before Dark Eyes arrived. He should.

He *would.*

To prove it to himself, he cleared his throat. "Dot . . ."

"Here you go." Cheerful and smiling and utterly oblivious, she handed him a cup of steaming, fragrant tea. "Just the way you like it."

"Gracias."

She kept smiling, but her eyes frowned. "De nada." She shook her head. "Thinking of Spain, are you?"

A slip — one he usually only made in the first week or two after returning from time in Spain. His subconscious must be trying to help him along. "Perhaps so. After spend-ing so many years there at university, I —"

"Oh! That reminds me!" Dot sat in the chair at right angles to his sofa, bouncing upon the cushion in whatever excitement she'd just recollected. "I've been informed that Margot's birthday is next week!"

For a long moment he could only blink at

her. "How does my being at university in Spain remind you of Margot's birthday?"

She laughed. "Because she was talking the other day of how she hoped to attend university after the war is over. And thinking of her reminds me of what I just learned last night about her, though she never would have admitted her birthday on her own, I suspect. She isn't one for a fuss. But I'd like to host a small dinner party for her. You wouldn't mind, would you? Just her and her brother and his wife?"

"Of course I don't mind. But if we could backtrack a bit, I —"

A knock sounded on the door. Not the usual quick *rat-a-tat-tat,* but a measured, slightly slower version. *Rap, rap, rap, rap, rap.*

"There she is." Dot hopped to her feet again with enviable ease. "And I'm sorry. What were you saying about your university days?"

Maybe it would be easier to tell it to her back as she scurried away, toward the door. He glanced at her retreating form.

Nope.

Besides, he would only be interrupted again by her opening the door and greeting her friend. He'd just have to tell her and Miss De Wilde both.

Perhaps it would be better that way. Perhaps Dot wouldn't overreact in the presence of company.

He didn't bother answering her question directly, and she didn't seem to notice, given that in the next moment she was unfastening the chain, turning the lock, and opening the door with an exclamation of greeting.

Drake couldn't drag himself to his feet fast enough to stand like a gentleman when the ladies entered the room, but he managed to sit up a bit straighter, anyway. And he'd donned a real shirt and trousers for the occasion. Nothing constricting, no waistcoat or jacket, but he was at least out of his pajamas and dressing gown.

Not that Margot De Wilde did more than glance at him with a generic smile, the same one she'd have given anyone. A blow to his self-confidence, to be sure. He may not be the most handsome bloke in the world, and girls may not fall over themselves vying for his attention, but it would be nice if he weren't entirely invisible to her.

"Sit, sit." Dot waved her friend toward the chairs. "We've another half an hour before the food is ready. Would you like something to drink, Margot?"

"Not yet, thank you." She shrugged out of her coat and passed it into Dot's outstretched hand. Then she turned her dark eyes on him while Dot went to put her coat somewhere. "How goes your recuperation, Lieutenant?"

"Very well, thank you." He took a sip of his tea and prayed silently for a way to broach this conversation with his sister.

Miss De Wilde — would she ever give him leave to call her Margot? — shifted on her seat a bit. "I don't believe Dot ever mentioned which ship you were on. I'm afraid I'm not aware of any that saw action last week."

Sometimes the Lord answered prayers at an alarming rate. He cleared his throat and tracked Dot with his gaze as she came back from her bedroom, all smiles. For now. "The *Royal Oak*. Though, actually . . ." Blast, but the truth was hard sometimes. He'd pay her the respect of looking her in the eye when he delivered it though. "Actually, I wasn't on a ship at all."

Dot reclaimed her chair, looking only mildly curious. "Oh? Where were you, then?"

He wanted to look at something else, anything else. But he didn't. "On a train from Bilbao."

A bit of bafflement entered her eyes. "Were you visiting Abuelo on a leave? You didn't mention such intentions. And how would you have got shot on a train?"

"It wasn't leave. Or a visit." His fingers tightened around the delicate china cup she'd given him. "I haven't been on a ship for years, Dot."

Now her expression flattened into disbelief. "Nonsense. You are always such a joker."

"I'm not joking. DID has instructed me to tell you the truth. He pulled me from the *Royal Oak* in my first months aboard. Because he needed men on the ground in Spain, gathering intelligence. And my records included that I'd been educated there."

Dot went still. Utterly still.

Miss De Wilde — Margot, in his thoughts if not in his speech — leaned forward. "Interesting. You're part of Thoroton's network, then?"

For a beat, he stared at her, surprised she knew the name. But then, she'd probably typed up the decrypts of his reports or something. Perhaps that was why the admiral had smirked when he'd asked if it was all right for her to know the truth. She most likely already knew a large part of it, just not his name. He shook himself and nodded. "Stationed in Bilbao mostly, where I could stay with Abuelo and use my already-

261

existent reputation there as a cover for my real work."

Dot had folded her hands into her lap, but it wasn't a peaceful pose. Her every muscle looked tense, and her breath came too fast. "Do you really mean to tell me that you're one of the admiral's spies?"

"Agents." Semantics, but *spy* had such a negative connotation. It implied untrustworthiness, deceitfulness, duplicity.

His sister didn't seem to care about his correction. Her nostrils flared. "And you were shot how, exactly?"

Though his throat was dry, he didn't imagine the hot tea would really help it much. "I was . . ." How much to say? He was telling her the truth, yes. But discretion was surely still called for. "I was part of a team tasked with identifying and intercepting a shipment of sugar cubes tainted with anthrax. The German agent accompanying the shipment got in a lucky parting shot."

"A lucky shot?" Faux peace abandoned, Dot leapt to her feet. "You could have been killed!"

"A fate just as likely were I a regular soldier. More likely." He set the teacup down and swung his feet to the floor, wincing a bit in the process. "I'm far safer than most chaps I know. Eating well, living in

Abuelo's luxury while my friends are starving and dying in the trenches. If there's guilt to be felt, Dorothea, it isn't about being in a dangerous spot and not telling you — it's over having it easy, all things considered. Over not being haunted by the experiences that eat up my friends — deaths on their consciences, second-guessing, wondering at —"

"Having it *easy*? I know the number of agents lost in the field, Drake! I type up the reports every day!" Rivaling sparks of fury and fear in her eyes, she spun away, toward the window.

"Not in Spain." This from Margot, whose dark eyes seemed to bore into him as effectively as Jaeger's bullet had done, though it made his pulse hammer instead of slow. "We haven't lost any agents in Spain. Though we have gained much valuable intelligence."

He lifted a brow. "Is that a compliment?"

"For the effectiveness of the organization, yes. Whether any of that belongs to you in particular, I cannot say without more information." She lifted a brow in return, a smile playing at the corners of her mouth. "Though DID seems to like you well enough, so you can't be too useless a source."

A laugh sputtered out. And dug claws into his stomach. He pressed a hand to the spot that hurt the worst.

Margot nodded toward Dot's back. "Your sister's been typing up the reports from France. Different tale for our agents there, unfortunately. We've lost far too many, either to death or arrest."

"I can imagine. But France is occupied territory, Dot. Spain isn't."

His sister drew in a deep breath and let it slowly out, but she didn't turn back around.

Margot tapped a finger three times on the arm of her chair. She opened her mouth, closed it again, clenched her jaw. Even having met her only a few times before, Drake had a feeling that hesitation wasn't her normal mode of operation. But after a few seconds she met his eyes again. "How long were you investigating the anthrax?"

He couldn't think why she'd ask. But she'd have a reason. "Several weeks."

"How likely is it that any of the tainted sugar or grain made it to England?"

He reached again for his tea, mainly to give himself a moment to consider. She didn't seem to be asking from fear — or if so, her fear didn't reveal itself like his sister's did. "Nothing is outside the realm of possibility, of course, but I discovered nothing

264

to hint at it. Why?"

Dot turned around, her drawn brows focused now on Margot rather than him. "Yes, why?"

What an interesting young woman she was. She didn't flinch under their regard, didn't shift, didn't look away. She didn't raise her chin or straighten her spine. She just blinked. And answered them. "Because the symptoms my mother was apparently suffering before her death are consistent with anthrax."

Dot took a tentative step forward, her hand stretched out a few inches toward her friend. "Margot . . . they're also consistent with a heart attack."

"She was perfectly healthy."

"We both know these conditions aren't always apparent."

Still Margot showed no signs of either defense or offense. Her posture didn't change, nor did her facial expression. "The statistical probability of her falling prey to the same ailment that felled my father four years ago, when considerations such as diet and location and exercise are so vastly different, is considerably lower than the probability that one of our abundant enemies has been at work."

Dot's eyes went wide, and her arms spread

out in a gesture that said, *Look about you.* "In what world is a heart attack *less* likely than — than assassination?"

Drake willed his sister to look over at him so that he could give her a sign to shut up. She was Margot's friend, and she ought to know better than to say something like that, even if she thought it. He could scarcely believe she just *had.*

His fault, he suspected. She was reeling from his news and lashing out.

Margot didn't miss a beat. "In *my* world. We lived for months under the same roof as a German general who never hesitated to share with us how readily the High Command would kill anyone deemed an enemy. We watched our entire town be torn to pieces and burned. Any family whose military-aged son had escaped the country could be arrested. They dismantled our factories and sent the pieces to Germany so that we cannot rebuild after the war."

"But that is different than being targeted."

Why was Dot fighting her about this?

Perhaps Margot was wondering the same. She finally changed her expression and lifted her brows. "We were hunted before, for my father's work. My brother was shot because he was recognized as being the son of Professor De Wilde. Willa was shot and held prisoner trying to help us escape from Belgium. Agents of both the English and German Crown made it quite clear they would do anything to get their hands on his work in cryptography."

Who *was* this girl? Or perhaps it was more a question of who her father had been, and if in fact she and her mother *had* been in possession of his work. He didn't know yet which question to ask. But he'd dealt in this world long enough to see the sense in her words.

Dot, he granted, hadn't. She huffed. "Terrible. But years ago."

"You think the threat evaporated? While the war yet rages on?"

"No." Drake's interjection, quiet but sure, had his sister spinning on him, her eyes asking why he was encouraging her friend in what she no doubt thought was a fruitless and unhealthy inquiry. Which it might be.

Or she might be right. And if she were right . . .

He transferred his gaze from Dot to Margot. "Have you mentioned your concerns to DID?"

"Not yet. I only just made the connection last night."

He nodded. "We should bring it to his attention. I have no evidence to say you could be right, but I have none to say you're wrong either. I'll do what I can to remedy that for you."

Now she moved — her shoulders sagged, just a bit. And she let out the tiniest puff of breath, so small he likely would have missed it had he not been paying close attention. "Thank you, Lieutenant."

"I'm really not accustomed to answering to that, given that I have been undercover for all these years. Call me Drake." He tried for a grin, though it no doubt didn't look all that charming. And likely wouldn't faze her regardless. "One of the conditions of my inquiry."

"Very well." No, not so much as a pause or a shift to indicate any effect.

"You're both ridiculous." Dot stormed between his sofa and Margot's chair. "I'm going to fetch the potatoes from Mrs. Colton's oven."

Silence whooshed in with the closing of the door. Drake shifted to a more comfortable position, absurdly aware of how weak and unlike himself he was just now. He couldn't ask her if she'd like anything and actually get up to fetch it if she did. He couldn't rise and amble to the window to fend off any awkwardness. He couldn't do anything but sip at his tea and wait for her to speak.

She didn't.

He cleared his throat and slid the cup back onto the end table. "I suppose I thought you might have more questions for me."

How could her blink be so powerful? Perhaps because of the way it first hid and then revealed those eyes. "Were you lying when you said you had no evidence to support or dismiss my suspicions?"

How could she sit so still? No movements in her fingers or her legs or anything. Just a spine stiffly aligned and each limb arranged as if she were a doll. "Of course not."

"Then what good would more questions do me?"

A smile tugged at his lips, though they didn't seem to curve up evenly. "Well, one never knows what unexpected details one might learn through the right questions. For instance, why have you dismissed the attention of the half-dozen men who have tried to catch your eye this past year?"

He was aiming at a response, and he got one. She jerked as if he'd hit her with a dart. "How do you expect to get any useful information from a question whose very premise is flawed?"

Press his lips together as he might, still

the grin slipped through. "Oh, I just got plenty. I learned that the admiral was quite right when he described you as oblivious to the attention, as evidenced by your shocked reaction to my question. And the fact that you think my premise flawed not only corroborates that, it shows that you genuinely think the idea ridiculous. Though I haven't yet determined why you'd think so."

She stared at him for a long moment, her mouth a bit agape. Then she shook herself and returned to her previous perfect posture. "Several reasons. First of all, I have no interest in such attachments, so the idea *is* ridiculous. Secondly, there is no reason for the admiral to have mentioned such a thing. And finally, no one would show such interest anyway."

Drake lifted a finger. "What is so ridiculous about finding someone to support and encourage you through the ups and downs of life?" He lifted a second finger. "The admiral had reason to mention it in response to *my* interest." The third finger joined its friends. "Which goes also to your third point. And why would you think no one *would* show interest, anyway? You're intelligent —"

"More intelligent than any young man I've ever met. They don't like that." She didn't look apologetic. If anything, the twitching of her lips looked smug.

And why not? Why apologize for one's strengths? Of course, she no doubt assumed she was smarter than him too. And maybe she was. He didn't know her well enough to say, but Dot certainly thought so.

His smile didn't budge. "Plenty of men take no issue with that. Especially given that you're also beautiful —"

A snort interrupted him this time. "Hardly."

He lifted his brows. "Are you quite serious?"

She looked at him as though he were daft. "My mother was beautiful. As is my brother."

Now it was his turn to interrupt with a snort of laughter. "I'm sure your brother greatly appreciates being called that."

"Oh, he knows he is. And he's made a living from it."

"I suppose his musical talent had nothing to do with that?"

She finally leaned back a bit in her chair, and her smile went light and bright. Interesting — speaking of her brother made her relax. "His talent made him a professional violinist. His beauty made him a celebrity."

He chuckled, since that was probably true.

"And you think you bear no resemblance to him?"

"I know I don't. I take after my father."

The professor whose work had apparently brought enemies down upon them at the start of the war. He lifted his cup again and saluted her with it. "Well, I'll have to respectfully disagree on the beauty question, and I daresay many other men do too. But if romance is of no interest to you, then I suppose our opinions don't matter."

"Not in the least." She tilted her head to the side, apparently unaware of how it lengthened her neck and made her jawline look so fetching. "And why are you even saying such things?"

Never in his life had he met anyone quite like Margot De Wilde. Drake took another sip of his tea to give himself time to school his lips. "It's called flirting."

She stiffened again. "But . . . *why?*"

"Because you're intelligent. And you're beautiful. And you're interesting."

And baffled, apparently. Which only made her all the *more* interesting. She shook her head. "But to what purpose? Is it meaningless, to pass the time? In which case, I'd rather talk about something else. Or are you angling for a fleeting amorous encounter? Because I'm not the type. And if you're interested in courtship, you ought to know now that I have no intention of marrying."

He studied her over the rim of his cup. She looked completely serious. "Ever?"

"Not for the next decade, at the very least. I have plans."

"Mm." He ought to call his interest ill-advised and leave it at that, then. He was in no great rush to find a Mrs. Elton, especially while the war dragged on, but he certainly didn't mean to wait another decade to do so. But still . . . puzzling her out would prove an entertaining distraction while he was laid up. "University, Dot said. What then?"

"A professorship, ideally."

Drake couldn't keep his brows from drawing together. "I've never known of a female professor."

"They're rare. The second in England just attained her status in 1913. And both that I know of are professors of English literature. I am well aware that I will face maddening prejudice if I dare to enter the sciences or mathematics. But I'll do it anyway."

"And woe to whoever stands in your way?" He smiled so that she knew he meant it to be encouraging. Mostly. He wasn't sure why some people always had to be rocking whatever boat they were on, but if it was for a real purpose and not just because they liked the rocking, it was different. And this young lady didn't seem to subscribe to movement for its own sake, that was for sure. "So university, a doctorate perhaps, and then a professorship. Marriage only when you've achieved all that?"

"If then. With marriage comes children — they are one of the purposes of the institution after all — and while I'm a proponent of them in general, I have no interest in procuring my own specifically." She changed the angle of her head, as if she were listening to something, and then flinched. "My mother hated it when I spoke this way. Once her own children were grown, grandchildren became her *raison d'être.*"

A woman who had no interest in either marriage *or* children. He *would* be intrigued by such, wouldn't he? Because the chances of winning her heart were all but non-existent and promised a headache even if he succeeded. He liked a challenge, but this would cross over to the absurd.

She blinked at him again. "You failed to answer my question, Drake, about the purpose of your flirting."

"So I did." And he heard the neighbor's door close, indicating Dot would return in another moment with the potatoes that wouldn't fit in their own crowded oven, which would effectively end the odd conversation anyway. "You can be sure it's not with the goal of a dalliance — I'm not the type either. But whether it's to no purpose or the ultimate purpose . . . I suppose I was testing the waters."

Brows lifted, she stood. "Are they shark-infested enough to convince you of the futility?"

"I haven't decided. When I do, I'll let you know." His mother would have given him a tongue lashing for even considering courting such a girl. One who was unsure about marriage and wanted no children? Who intended to work outside the home rather than in it, even when war or finances didn't demand it? Oh yes, she'd have had a strong opinion on that.

But as he watched Margot move to the door so she could open it for his sister, he knew that her answers hadn't done a thing to squash his interest. If anything, they'd raised it. Because never in his life had he met anyone like Margot De Wilde. Never would he again, he suspected. But did that mean he ought to pursue her romantically? Would it be worth the certain headache — and likely heartache?

He was none too sure. But he had nothing but time, just now, in which to decide.

15

"Why are you going this way? Not that I mind your company for a little longer."

Margot turned the same corner as Dot, where usually she would continue straight along the street on the shortest route to her flat. They'd walk by the park if they went this way, and she needed to see if Redvers Holmes was waiting. She had the grey scarf in her bag, though today was warm enough that he wouldn't need it. Who was to guess as to tomorrow, though? It was November, after all.

She touched a hand to the knitted belt of the cardigan Maman had made for her. It could well have been intended as a birthday gift, rather than a Christmas one. Her mother wouldn't mind her wearing it now. Today. It had seemed like a whisper of assurance when her eighteenth birthday had dawned warm enough that she didn't need her coat. Just this. A piece of Maman.

No numbers to say *It's all right. She wouldn't mind.* Or *Save it until Christmas.* No numbers other than those painted onto the thermometers. They had two, because England still used the imperial measure, but Maman couldn't get used to Fahrenheit and had invested some of their precious funds into a centigrade thermometer too.

There were no numbers for anything these days. None to tell her whether today had been the best day to approach the admiral about her concerns. None when she'd dropped a note to the Duchess of Stafford into the post, requesting that audience to discuss Einstein. None to tell her whether today would be the day that Redvers Holmes would be waiting by the park.

"Margot?"

She darted a glance at Dot and realized she'd yet to answer her friend about her direction. "I asked a new acquaintance to see if he could discover the name of that fellow at the park, and he said he'd meet me there one evening at five-thirty to let me know what he's discovered." She didn't mention that the chap had begged a few coins from her, or that she had a scarf for him in her bag. No numbers told her not to, but even so. Pride she understood without assistance.

Dot shook her head. "You always have to have answers, don't you?"

Her rebuke wasn't about the Go player in the park, Margot knew. It was about her determination to discover if Maman had been felled by anthrax. Margot had seen her press her lips together today when she asked DID if she could speak with him.

It was statistically inevitable that she and this new friend of hers would disagree about something. Probable that the something would be important.

But she wished *this* hadn't been their first disagreement. This, of all things.

If the numbers hadn't told her to befriend Dot to begin with, perhaps she'd shrug it off and simply drift away. But the Lord meant for them to be friends. She wouldn't forget that now, despite the fact that the numbers had gone silent.

And so Margot said quietly, "I realize you don't think my questions about Maman's death are worth asking. But I have to ask them. I have to know. I'm sorry if that bothers you."

Dot touched her arm, then withdrew her fingers. "It doesn't *bother* me, Margot. It *worries* me. Because I don't want you obsessing over this instead of simply healing."

Healing? Margot sucked in a long breath and scanned the distance ahead of them. She'd already lost one parent. It wasn't a wound that *healed* per se. It was simply one she'd learned to live with. Like Red Holmes's missing limb. Something that had once supported him, gone forever. He'd learned to walk again, and so would Margot. The flesh could be stitched, a prosthetic attached. It didn't bleed forever.

But healing meant returning to a state of health, being restored to the original condition. Drake Elton's gunshot wound would heal. Red Holmes's amputation would not.

"Death isn't a gunshot, Dot. It's an amputation."

Dot's pace slowed. "I beg your pardon?"

"It doesn't *heal.* We're never restored fully, whole again, after we lose someone. We just learn to go on with the pieces missing."

Holmes was there, coming even now from the park with that peculiar gait reserved for those using artificial feet with ankle joints — the ankle that released the foot all at once when he put down the heel, rather than rolling onto and back off the ball. She didn't know how long he'd had the thing, but it must have been a few months, at least. From what she'd read on the subject, it took a considerable while for patients to adjust to the wearing of such a device, and he seemed to have mastered it as much as it allowed.

She would too. She'd learn how to walk without Maman, as she'd learned without Papa. But it would never be the same. She would never stop missing them.

Dot was frowning into the distance. "Who did you say you're meeting?"

"I didn't. But a young man named Redvers —"

"Holmes! Red!" Dot lifted a hand and picked up her pace, leaving Margot behind.

They knew each other? What an odd turn. Margot hurried to keep up, arriving just as Holmes was tipping his hat and bowing a bit at the waist.

"Miss Elton! How do you do? I haven't seen you for ages."

Dot held out a hand, beaming. "Not since the war began and you enlisted." She turned to include Margot in her smile. "Red and Nelson were great friends. And Red worked for my father."

"What a small world." She smiled. But she didn't want to. Not because it wasn't lovely, that the man she'd decided to trust was indeed trustworthy, an old friend of her new friend. But because she'd done it on

281

her own, on a whim. God hadn't told her to. He'd given her no indication one way or the other. Her fingers curled into her palm. Was this how it would be from now on? A silent God, leaving her to her own devices?

Holmes still had Dot's hand pressed between both of his. "I'm so sorry about Nelson. I can't say how sorry I am."

"I know. I am too. I still miss him." She angled a smile toward Margot. "But I've learned to go on with the pieces missing."

He released her hand. "And your brother? How is he? I've heard nothing of Elton for several years."

Dot waved a hand in the general vicinity of her flat. "Home thanks to a gunshot wound, at the moment, but the doctors think he'll make a full recovery. He'll be here through Christmas, which is a pleasant change. You ought to come and visit him sometime, I know he'd like that. Oh!" She looked at Margot again, her eyes wide.

Had it been Maman, Margot probably would have been able to read whatever thoughts she was silently shouting. But she didn't know Dot quite so well yet. She could only lift her brows in response and wait to see what she was thinking.

She didn't have to wait long. Dot straightened her shoulders and said, "You ought to join us on Saturday. We're having a small dinner party to celebrate Margot's birthday. Just us and my brother and her brother and his wife. You'll give us an even number."

Six. More even than five, to be sure. It was, Margot supposed, a better number for a dinner party. She saw no particular reason to object.

Aside from the fact that Holmes clearly wasn't comfortable with it. He glanced down at himself, muttering, "Oh . . . how kind. But I don't think . . ."

He was wearing the same clothes he had been the other night, and they were none too fine. Not ragged, not yet, but probably also not clean. Certainly not what one wore to a dinner at the home of one's former employer's daughter.

Margot pressed her lips together. He was about the same size as Lukas. Half an inch shorter, perhaps, but his shoulders looked to be the same breadth. And her brother had plenty of clothes. He could lend him a suit of them, and Willa's sister Rosemary could do any alterations needed. Rosie was brilliant with a needle. They'd be happy to help. They always were.

"Of course you'll come." Margot nodded, as if that settled it. It wouldn't have done so for *her,* if she were the one resisting. But perhaps Holmes just needed someone to do for him what Maman had always done for her — insist and leave no room for argument. She'd find a way to inform him later of how to go about avoiding embarrassment. For now, she turned a bit toward the park. From this distance, she could just make out a figure sitting at the wrought-iron table. "Did you have any luck playing detective, Mr. Holmes?"

He chuckled and turned as well. "Well, I'm no Sherlock, I daresay. But I did, at that." He shuffled a step closer to her and pitched his voice to a lower volume. "It was two days before the bloke showed up, and when he did, he wouldn't talk to me — as you said was likely to happen. But I followed him to his flat that night and got his name from his box. John Williams."

"Well, that's easy to remember." Dot slid to the other side of Margot, smiling in an easy way that proved she had no stakes in this game.

Margot wasn't quite sure why *she* did, but the thought of John Williams playing Go in her park just wouldn't leave her alone. "Thank you, Holmes. I appreciate your finding that for me."

"Oh, I found more than that." When he grinned, he didn't look like a footless soldier who had to beg a few shillings from her. He looked like a friend of Dot's who knew his way around the city. "Did a bit of asking about. Seems that until the war began, Mr. Williams had been in Japan, part of a diplomatic envoy. Spent a decade there. When hostilities broke out in '14, he decided to come home and enlist. He was an officer on a minesweeper, the *Ariel*, that was sunk by a U-boat in August. One of the few survivors. According to my sources" — here he leaned closer, speaking more quietly still — "he hasn't been right since. In the head, I mean."

Dot pressed a hand to her chest. "How very sad!"

It was, of course. But it was also very enlightening. "Japan." Margot nodded and recalled the look of the board he'd been using. It had been exquisite — lovelier than the one on which Gottlieb had taught her. He'd probably acquired it in Japan and brought it back to England with him. Though the game originated in China, it was so ubiquitous in Japan that most of the terms of play were Japanese rather than Chinese. "That makes sense." Not a German connection — a Japanese one.

It ought to make the unease settle. But it didn't, exactly. It just inspired her feet to move away from Dot and Holmes and toward the hunched figure of John Williams. The last time she'd tried to speak to him, he'd barely even looked at her. That was all right.

She slid into the seat opposite his and didn't look at him either. She looked at the board, at the game he was playing with no one, and took a moment to take in the positions of the pieces. He was even then taking his fingers off one of his black stones after moving it. She rested two of hers onto a white.

It was cool and smooth and familiar, sucking her back three years in time with that single touch. She sat across from Gottlieb instead of Williams, in the warm home of Madame Dumont, who had taken them in as if they were family, though they'd never met her before that long, grueling march from burned-out Louvain to occupied Brussels. The crisp London air disappeared, the babble of voices was French in her ear instead of English.

But in Brussels, she wouldn't have made the best move she saw, not often. She'd had to pretend she wasn't as smart as she was, pretend she wasn't the daughter of her father, pretend she wasn't the "crypotography machine" he'd apparently bragged to too many people about having created.

Today she was just one more cog in the machine of Room 40. Allowed to be who she was. Able to play however she pleased. Today Maman certainly wouldn't be hovering behind her, glowering warnings with wide eyes.

Margot blinked away the pain of that and moved the stone under her fingers.

Williams grunted. She darted a glance up at him, expecting protest to be upon his face. But the corners of his lips had turned up. Just a bit. He still didn't look at her, but he looked at the board in a new way.

A few minutes must have marched by, though she hadn't cared to mark them. Then Holmes appeared at her side with a softly cleared throat. "Beg your pardon, Miss De Wilde." Dot must have filled him in on her last name. "I'm going to see Miss Elton home. And don't worry." He pitched his voice low. "I'll find a way to bow out of your dinner party."

"Nonsense. Come." Eyes still on the board, she reached into her handbag and pulled out the scarf that was taking up much of the space inside. "My mother knitted this for you." Maman hadn't known it, but it was nonetheless true. "And if you meet me back here in an hour, I'll take you to my brother's house. He'll ensure you have the proper attire for this party, if that's your concern."

"Very kind, miss, but I oughtn't . . ."

She looked over, up, into his eyes. "We all fall on hard times, Mr. Holmes. The kindness of a stranger saved my life once, and my mother's. Please. Let me do for you just a portion of what she did for us. It is a small enough gesture. Lukas will not miss one suit of clothes."

Though one suit of clothes wouldn't solve this man's ultimate problem either. The missing variable in his equation was surely equal to a larger number than that. But it could help. Could perhaps put his feet — organic and artificial both — on a path toward restoration.

She watched him wrestle with his pride though. It took the form of his hands twisting in the knitted length he still held. He didn't want to take it, any of it. Didn't want to *need* to. But he also apparently didn't want to go on as he had been. He shoved the scarf into his pocket — leaving one end trailing out — and nodded. "Anything you need me to do, miss, you just ask. Anything at all."

Williams drew her attention back to the board when he slid a black stone to a new position. One not entirely stupid.

Margot pursed her lips and considered her next move. "Very well. At the moment, I need you to see my friend safely home, if you would."

Even without looking, she could see his smile. "A real hardship, that, but I'll manage it. And be back here in an hour." He moved half a step but then stopped. "Will you be all right here alone?"

It was her own park in her own neighborhood. Moreover, she didn't intend to move for the next hour. "We will be quite busy until you return. Isn't that right, sir?"

Her shaggy-haired opponent steepled his hands, rested his chin against them, and stared at the board with bright eyes. His grunt this time clearly said, *Your move.*

She slid a white stone to a better position.

Williams's smile bloomed full this time. He nodded his approval and studied his own pieces.

Holmes breathed a laugh. "Enjoy your game, Miss De Wilde. I'll see you in an hour."

Das Gespenst sat in the park long after the chill chased everyone else indoors and the gaslights turned on. The clouds had rolled in, bringing damp air. Cold.

He hated every damp breeze of this blasted island, but he was at least learning to control the ever-present cough. It was better if he didn't try to talk. He could just grunt and let everyone think him an idiot.

His eyes wandered toward the park entrance where the girls had stood two hours ago. The thirst for revenge tickled his lungs, drowning him as surely as the waters of the *Boynton* had tried to do. He'd have his day. He must. And it could well be the same day he handed over the codebooks to his superiors. How perfect would that be?

Margot De Wilde and Dorothea Elton. He'd hardly been able to believe it when his research had led him back to them — and then when they'd come right up to him. Mother would say it was the hand of God, delivering his enemies to him on a silver platter.

More like a small world, this one of intelligence. Everyone was connected to everyone else. It hadn't been surprise so much as certainty filling his veins when he'd learned her name. *Of course* they were connected. They were all connected. And now all he had to do was forge his own connection. To them.

To one of them, at least. One would do. Get one, and he'd have them both, as inseparable as they were.

Margot De Wilde. He traced a finger along the pattern in the iron of the bench. Who'd have thought she'd know how to play Go? It made perfect what had otherwise been sufficient. He could use the game to get to know her. Use her to get at his true enemies.

From what he'd seen, no one else in this part of London knew how to play. It would just be her. And him. A new game.

He had to know what kind of opponent she would be. How many strategies he would need to employ. How many uses he could find for each move, each play.

He'd soon know. With each move, he'd learn more.

He dug his fingers into his leg. His chest ached, all the way down to his soul. But he wouldn't let it stop him. If anything, it must motivate him. He must succeed. He'd have his revenge, and he'd hand over everything the High Command asked for. Their targets. Their codebooks. And then he'd make a demand of his own — relocation.

He was ready to be finished with this godforsaken island.

A smile tugged up the corners of his lips. Heinrich would have enjoyed this ghost story. A tale of hauntings and recompense and evening the score. It wasn't his brother's

291

usual type of yarn, but still he would appreciate it. Not every tale was one of glory. Of heroics.

What did playing the part of a hero ever really get one, anyway? Death, that's what. An enemy's bullet. A pathetic medal sent home to one's wife.

Das Gespenst. He closed his eyes and drew the name close. Let every other name — and he'd had no fewer than half a dozen — fade away. He'd be no one. Everyone. Faceless. Nameless.

Heinrich had a name, and it would be carved for eternity in a slab of granite in the cemetery. Their mother and Ilse would take flowers every Sunday until they too were just a few letters carved on other slabs.

All that nobility, all those stories of glory and feats of honor and bravery, forgotten.

Margot De Wilde had a streak of the heroic in her, too, trying to provide as she was for the crippled man. She, too, would learn that it was a weakness. And *he* would be the one to teach her. He'd use it, as surely as he used Go.

Das Gespenst opened his eyes again and stared into the world that lost its color a little more with every minute. Daylight fading, night oozing in, stripping it of green and pink and orange and leaving muted grey behind. She wouldn't understand, she with that noble streak. Just as Heinrich had never understood.

It couldn't be about nobility. Or honor. Or bravery. It could only be about the game.

16

Drake counted it a victory when, on Thursday, he managed to get himself out of bed before his sister left for work in the morning. It still hurt like the dickens if he made too abrupt a movement, but he'd not touched the pain medication in two days — not because the doctor hadn't given him a stern look and told him to keep taking it, but because he couldn't get a bit of the work done that the admiral had been sending home with Dot when he did. The stuff muddied his mind.

He could handle this amount of pain, though. He tired easily, yes, but that would only get better by pushing himself a little more each day. Today, that meant shuffling out of his bedroom while the scents of tea and porridge were still fresh.

He paused a step into the main living area of the flat. Dot stood in front of the door. Overcoat on, hat pinned in place, handbag looped over her arm. And rosary beads clutched between gloved knuckles. Watching her lips move, he could tell where she was in the prayer. *When Jesus is twelve years old, He goes with His parents to Jerusalem for the feast of Passover.* Her lips paused for half a beat, and her fingers moved to the next bead. *After the feast of the Passover, Mary and Joseph unknowingly set out for Nazareth without Jesus. . . .*

He held his place while she finished, not wanting to disturb her. Were it anyone else, he might have thought she'd forgotten to say her prayers earlier and wanted to squeeze them in before she left home. But not Dot. Dot waited to say them until she was standing there before the door. She waited until she most needed the strength the familiar words imparted. *Mary keeps all these things in her heart.*

She drew in a deep breath, tucked the beads into her pocket, and lifted her chin. Her hand shook as she lifted it to the door's latch, but she gripped it anyway.

His throat went tight. Margot was right. His sister was strong. Courageous. Every day she left this flat, she had to put on her armor like a knight errant and make herself slay the dragon of the world outside that door.

She was strong. She was courageous. But it never took away the fear. "Have a good day, Dot." His voice came out quiet, barely audible in the room.

She didn't look back at him. If she did, it would ruin her routine and she might not reach for the door again, he knew. It had happened before. But she nodded, pulled the door open, and stepped out without a word.

Drake sighed and continued his shuffle toward her small kitchen. He prayed that, eventually, routine would make it easier. And he was proud that she did it even when it was difficult.

As usual, a small pot of bland porridge sat on the stove for him. In days past, he'd reheated it whenever he managed to pull his aching body from bed. Today it was still warm, and he had only to spoon it into his bowl.

A few minutes later he'd fixed his tea as well and sat at the table, papers spread out before him. DID had sent a bit of everything home with Dot this week, obviously trying to discover what Drake could best do here at his sister's house rather than in the field. This latest packet didn't have any codes that needed to be cracked — he could muddle through when he had the key, but how they ever managed to break one without that he honestly didn't know. But Hall apparently thought he did a decent enough job of analyzing what *others* had put into plain script, because there were quite a few decrypts here.

The challenge, as always, was determining what to do with them. What they meant — not in terms of what the words said, but in terms of what impact they could and would have on British operations.

Drake flipped through the first few pages as he ate a spoonful of porridge that might as well be tasteless. No butter, no sugar. What he wouldn't give for a dollop of Mother's favorite strawberry preserves to swirl through the gruel. Anything would help.

He tried not to think of the spiced sausage and eggs that would have been on Abuelo's table this morning.

Dot had brought the newspaper in as well. When he moved a few of the decrypts aside, the headline caught his eye. ACE PILOT GROUNDED AND FACING COURT-MARTIAL. His eyes went wide when he saw the grainy photograph. He hadn't seen his old school chum in years, but there was no mistaking the face of Phillip Camden. Or, as the article called him, Black Heart.

He read all the way through the piece before pushing himself to his feet and moving to the telephone. The article still clutched in one hand, he waited to be patched through to Admiral Hall.

"Yes?"

"Morning, sir. It's Elton." When his side protested his standing so long in one position, Drake granted it a reprieve and sank to the hard wooden chair Dot kept beside the telephone table. "Did you see that article in yesterday's *Evening Standard*? About the ace who's been grounded?"

"Mm. Camden, wasn't it? I couldn't quite make sense of what had happened from the article. Had half a mind to pull a few strings just to satisfy my curiosity."

Drake wouldn't mind a few more answers either, but that was hardly his point in calling. "Sir, if you've the power, may I suggest you arrange to have him allocated to your command rather than put on trial? I know Camden rather well — we were at school together as boys. I think you'd find him just your sort of chap."

Though it was a bit hard to tell over the static-filled line, Drake thought the admiral's snort sounded amused. "You think a criminal is my sort?"

"He's not a criminal. Just . . . unconventional. It does have a tendency to land him in hot water" — never *this* hot before, but with raised stakes came raised consequences — "but there's nothing untrustworthy about him."

"Hm." Yes, definitely amused. "Perhaps I'll pay the fellow a visit. Though what exactly makes you think he'd be an asset to me?"

Drake's lips quirked up at the many memories that bombarded him. Phillip Camden had a way of getting into scrapes — and out of them — with flare enough that people tended to see his attitude more than his mind. But the mind was always what was behind them. "When we were twelve, he created a code and taught it to all the boys in our class so that he could give us secret messages as to when we ought to cause specific disturbances."

A laugh crackled over the line. "Did he, now? Well then, perhaps I'll bring him a few puzzles and see what he can do. Thank you for the tip, Elton."

"You're quite welcome, sir."

They said their farewells, and Drake set the receiver back in its cradle with a bit of satisfaction. He didn't have a clue what Camden had actually done to turn himself from one of their best pilots to someone the press was determined to make into a villain. But whatever it really was, Camden was too great an asset to the country for them to just toss him away. Drake didn't trust them *all* to see that, but Blinker Hall would. Though whether the admiral could manage to get someone from the RFC transferred to Admiralty control rather than army, he really didn't know. Why couldn't he have joined the RNAS instead? Then he'd already be a navy man.

Drake spent some more time on the decrypts in need of analyzing and then, when the clock chimed the ten o'clock hour, put it all away and pushed himself back up and toward his bedroom. The doctor would stop by in another half hour, and it took Drake a ridiculous amount of time these days to get dressed. But he was determined to do so, just to prove to the doctor that he was well enough to handle the task.

He'd scarcely gotten his shirt buttoned, however, when a knock sounded on the door. Scowling, he checked his watch. A full fifteen minutes earlier than the doctor had said he would be. "Coming!" he called. Not all that loudly, as volume required more muscles than he currently had to spare, but he could probably still be heard in the corridor. Maybe.

A glance through the peephole, however, made his brows rise. It wasn't the doctor. He opened the door with a smile that he knew held a question within it. "Red. Good morning."

Redvers Holmes offered a smile more sheepish than confident. "Sorry to drop by unannounced, Elton."

"No trouble at all — I've certainly got time enough on my hands for a visit. Won't you come in?" He stepped aside, holding the door wide. He'd been more than a little surprised on Monday when Red had escorted Dot home, but he'd been happy enough to renew their acquaintance.

"Thank you." Red swiped his cap off his head as he entered. He walked slowly, but the oddity in his gait from the prosthetic was barely noticeable at that pace.

Drake could still barely keep up. "Sit down, please. Make yourself comfortable. Would you like some tea?"

"No, no, don't go to any trouble on my account." He darted a glance at the kitchen, however, in a way that said he'd *like* a cup, just didn't want to *ask* for one.

Drake turned into the room with its still-warm kettle. He put it back on the stove to heat and spoke across the half wall separating the kitchen and living area — an arrangement that had probably horrified Dot when she first saw it. No maid, no cook, and not even a decent wall to separate the kitchen from the more formal part of the flat. "No trouble at all. I insist."

He kept his tone casual, but his intent wasn't. He'd tried to sound Red out the other day on where he was living now, what he was doing, but the fellow had been vague in all his answers, and it would have been rude to press. He had a feeling the truth wasn't very rosy. All the questions he'd asked himself about his old acquaintance kept delivering up the same answers: he was hungry and cold and in need, but too proud to admit it.

Well, a friend knew to give whether it was asked or not. He'd make sure to serve him a sandwich before he left too. "What a pleasant surprise it was for Dot to run into you the other day. I didn't quite catch the story of how your paths crossed."

"Oh." Red chose the chair that would face both where he stood in the kitchen and the sofa. "Thanks to Miss De Wilde. She'd . . . hired me to do a bit of sleuthing for her."

Drake measured a spoonful of tea into the teapot. "Are you an investigator now?"

"No. Not that I'd be opposed to such work. Or any work. I . . ." He broke off with

302

a stumbling chuckle. "Sorry, old boy, this is blazing awkward. I was actually wondering — that is, I know the war hit your shipping company hard, but if you've any positions . . ."

Drake's heart sank. "Not here in England, I'm afraid. I sent the few ships we had left to join my grandfather's fleet in Spain until the war is over. Those blasted U-boats, you see." He poured some steaming tea into a cup. "Wish I had better news for you. But with all our crewmen either down with the ships or joining the navy, there wasn't much choice. Didn't make sense to keep the offices open either. Once the war's over, Abuelo and I plan to relocate half of everything back to London, but in the meantime . . ."

In the meantime, he had no job to offer Redvers Holmes. Would that he had. But there would be *something* he could do to help. There was always something. He had only to ask the right question.

Red sighed. "Assumed as much, but I thought I'd ask. Work's rather hard to find when a chap only knows physical labor and can't do it anymore."

"You have some education though, don't you? I know you and Nelson were chums — from school, I'd assumed." With the shortage of men in London right now, he ought to be able to find a job in an office somewhere.

Red's cheeks flushed to match his name. "I was never much good with letters and figures. They tend to, well, jump around on me. But I've a good memory. And my hands aren't impaired, and I've always been good with *them,* much to the dismay of my father, who always claimed the Holmeses were better than that." He snorted. "Glad he can't see what's become of us now."

The question had yielded an answer, anyway. Education might lend a bit of pedigree, but it didn't guarantee a position if one couldn't put it to use. Something else, then. Drake picked up the cup and saucer and made his slow way toward the sitting area. "I'd offer you sugar, but Dot has forbidden me on pain of death from touching her stash before the dinner party this weekend."

"I never take any, regardless." His smile flashed bright. Then faded. Red took the cup when Drake eventually reached him with it.

Drake sat with a *whoosh* of breath and a wince. "I'll be happy to put out some inquiries for you, Red. As you can see, the war has indeed hit us hard." He waved to the small flat — a far cry from the house the Eltons had once called home. "But some of Father's old friends have fared better. One of them may be in need of a trustworthy worker — I can certainly vouch for you."

"I would appreciate that. Thank you." Red stared into the cup. "Sorry, Drake, I hate to have to ask. But every door I've knocked on has been shut in my face when they see me limping on this blasted foot." He scowled at the tea, then seemed to realize it would better serve a different purpose and sipped at it. "I've half a mind to remake the thing. Would if I could get any parts. If I can eliminate the limp —"

"Well now. That's something I can probably help you with." He motioned to the small table between them, which Dot had stocked with what she thought he might need to work, including paper and pens. "Write down anything you might need. And you're welcome to do the work here, if you'd like. I believe there's a set of tools."

His friend's eyes lit. Then faded, like his smile had. "Thank you. Of course, I can't impose on your hospitality for the length of time it would require to —"

"Nonsense. I'd be grateful for the company. Much as I love my sister, we do bore each other after a while." He smiled. "Seriously, Red. You could come by every day, and I'd be nothing but grateful for the change of pace. I don't do well with convalescence, it seems."

Red took another sip of his tea. "If you're certain . . ."

"Very certain. All my other friends are deployed, as you can imagine." Or facing court-martial. Or gone forever, like Nelson.

Red must have heard the unspoken additions. His nod was the sort of slow that came with the burden of too many brothers lost. "It seems the blokes still in the city aren't the ones I'd ever run with. Even when I could run."

Drake nodded and glanced at the clock. The doctor would be coming any minute, and he was likely to scare Red off. "You can certainly run better than I can just now. I say, I don't suppose you'd feel up to a few errands for me? Just around the corner? If it's too much, please don't hesitate to —"

"It would be my pleasure. Walking is no trouble for me at all anymore, I assure you. After six months on this thing, I like to think I've mastered it." He sat up straighter. "Do you have a list?"

"I'll make one while you finish your tea. My physician will likely stop by while you're out, but then we can have lunch, if you agree. I do hate eating alone day after day."

"That would be lovely."

"Wonderful. I'm in your debt." He smiled and reached for a piece of paper, hoping that Red wouldn't call him on the bluff. Or partial bluff, anyway. Heaven knew Drake couldn't manage a trip to the shops in his condition, and he hated to keep asking Dot to make stops for him, knowing how eager she always was to get home. But this could work well. It wouldn't feel like a handout to Red, not if he was doing something for Drake in return for the meal.

If he played it right, he could assure himself that Red was getting at least one solid meal a day. It would do, at least until he could help him find a permanent position.

He would make a list of all his father's friends whose businesses were still in operation. Perhaps even get the admiral's opinion — though he'd already asked Hall for one favor for an old friend today. Much as he liked his superior, he didn't want to push his luck. Someone would know of something though.

The phone jangled. Drake jerked at the unexpected noise and then hissed at the pain that coursed up his side in protest.

Red jumped to his feet. "Shall I answer for you? Or bring it to you?"

"I don't think it'll stretch this far, but if you would?" By the time he got to it, it would probably have stopped ringing.

Red picked it up after the third one, though, answering with a chipper "Good morning, Elton residence. Holmes speaking." He listened for a moment, brows scrunched together. "Hello? Anyone there?" After another moment of listening, he shrugged and hung up. "No one."

Innocent, surely. A dropped line. It happened often enough. But Drake couldn't convince his fingers to loosen around his pen. "I imagine whoever it was will call back." It was the same thing he'd said to Dot on Tuesday night, when *she* had answered to an empty line. No one *had* called back, though. Not until now.

Drake sucked in a breath and forced himself to get back to his list. He wouldn't worry over wasted telephone calls. He'd focus instead on helping his friend. Tracking down anything he could on the anthrax question for Margot. And convincing Hall in whatever way he could that he was still useful, even when he couldn't answer his own blighted phone.

That was certainly worry enough for one day.

17

He was *looking* at her. Margot slid another bite of food into her mouth and did *not* look over at *him.* Despite the all-too-knowing grin that Willa shot her from across the table, proving that Margot wasn't the only one aware of how Drake's eyes kept drifting her way when he had absolutely no reason to let them.

Infuriating man. She'd been happy enough to consider him as a likely friend, until he had to go and ruin it all with that flirtation nonsense. She'd hoped he would have let such ridiculousness go by now, but apparently not. Did it never occur to him that she'd like to eat her dinner without someone staring at her and making her too conscious of every bite she took?

Smile, Margot, Maman said in her head. *A long look is a compliment, and how do we respond to compliments?*

She shot a glare at Willa, since she didn't

want to encourage Drake with even that much attention. Her sister-in-law just chuckled into her water glass, which thankfully went unnoticed by anyone else, since Dot and Holmes and Lukas were all laughing down at their end of the table. She hadn't caught what had inspired the amusement because she'd been so busy ignoring *him,* seated to her right, at the head of the table, that she'd apparently ignored everything else too.

She forked her last bite of chicken and lifted it to her lips. Counted her chews. Swallowed.

And why wasn't Willa helping her? She, of all people, could commiserate with Margot's discomfort over having anyone linger so long over her *looks.*

Finally, at long last, Willa seemed to have had her fill of smirking and leaned forward. She'd say something biting and clever to him, no doubt. Willa was an expert at biting and clever. Or perhaps she'd just deflect his attention. Strike up a conversation that would force him to pay attention to *her* rather than to Margot.

So why did she turn her head toward the opposite table end? "Dot, this chicken is divine. May I get the recipe from you? Lucy would love to make it, I know. She considers it her own special challenge to make sure no one in the family notices the shortages."

Some help *she* was.

Dot, face aglow, launched into a discourse about how pleasurable it had been to learn to cook when she and her aunt got this flat. Had she actually launched into the recipe, Margot might have paid attention — recipes were just mathematics, after all. But they were mathematics she usually happily left to theory.

Other than when she'd come here or gone to Lukas's, she'd had nothing to eat that required more cooking than porridge since Maman . . .

It wasn't lack of ability. It was lack of incentive. Cooking for one just seemed pointless.

"Did you have a happy birthday, Miss De Wilde?" Drake's question was low, quiet, as if he'd asked a more sensitive question that he wanted no one else to hear.

She gripped her fork. If she didn't look over at him now, it would be not only rude but telling. Proving she was deliberately ignoring him, and hence paying him attention through her inattention. She blinked and glanced his way. "As happy as could be expected this year. Thank you for asking."

He smiled. Scientifically, she noted that

his color was better this evening and the shadows under his eyes not so deep. According to Dot, he was making great strides of progress.

Good. The sooner he healed, the sooner he'd leave.

He picked up his own water glass but didn't drink from it. "And how old are you now? My sister didn't know."

A question she'd grown tired of answering when she was six. "Two hundred sixty-three."

"Really?" He drank now, chuckling as he did so, then set the glass down with a grin. "And here I wouldn't have pegged you as a day over two hundred sixty-one."

A bit of her irritation slipped off her shoulders, blast him. He *was* the sort of person she liked, if he'd just keep his interest relegated to the confines of friendship. "It is my skin-care regimen, you see. I'm militant about it. It's all I can ever think about."

He laughed, splaying a hand over his side as he did so. "Exactly the impression I had of you. Why, it's certainly all you've ever talked about in our previous conversations."

Her lips pulled up, and her shoulders relaxed a bit. Perhaps she could simply ignore his too-long glances. Pretend his

313

interest was no different from any of the men in Room 40. She'd hate to deprive herself of a friend, after all. "May I ask you a question, since you're so fond of them?"

His brows lifted. "Of course."

She nodded in the general vicinity of his face. "How did you break your nose?"

"Ah." Leaning back in his chair, he seemed to lift his hand experimentally from his injured side. Apparently it passed the test, as he reached for his fork again. He'd eaten only half his food, and everyone else was finishing off their last bites. Perhaps he wasn't quite as well as he pretended. "Got in a bit of a tussle with some older boys when I was a lad, that's all."

"Over what?" Dot, possibly. He seemed the type of brother who wouldn't mind a few fisticuffs if it meant defending his sister from bullies.

But he didn't look at his sister. He looked upward, and to the right. "My mother. Or her faith, more precisely. The neighbor lads thought it their Christian duty to throw a few literal stones at her for being Catholic."

Margot's blood went hot. In Belgium, everyone belonged to the Catholic church — that was simply the way it was. But when the Germans had invaded, they'd made it clear that part of their hatred was rooted in

314

what they called their different faiths — as if the same Christ had not bled and died for all. "I hope you broke *their* noses too."

That wasn't the attitude God would want her to have about it, she knew. No false equations flashed through her mind now to tell her so, but they had often enough before when she'd had such thoughts.

Drake's grin looked better suited to the lad he had been than the man of twenty-four she knew him to be. "I may have knocked out a few teeth — baby ones, lucky for them. And got in a bit of trouble for it too."

"I can imagine. Their mothers?"

"No. Mine."

Margot chuckled. "Our mothers were much alike, I think." She darted a glance to Lukas, who was smiling across the table at Red Holmes, saying something clever and witty, no doubt. No one would ever know, to look at how the two bantered, that they'd only met the other night, when Lukas happily handed over a suit of clothes that he claimed didn't fit his current tastes anyway. Rosemary had made a few quick alterations, and the result . . . Well, the result was that Dot had been looking at Holmes even when conversation didn't call for it.

Margot sighed. Whether to him or someone else, Dot would no doubt marry within a year or two. She'd move off into the world of housewives and mothers. Margot would shift into academia. Would they still be friends, when Dot was set on multiplying and Margot on limits? Simple arithmetic and calculus may have had a bit in common, but the one didn't necessarily understand the other.

Drake leaned closer. Not by much, just an inch and a half, but it brought her gaze back to his face. It was serious now, the blue-grey eyes he shared with Dot absent the spark of jesting that tended to be there whenever he spoke. "I'm sorry, Miss De Wilde. For making you think of sad things tonight, when you ought to be celebrating."

Smile, Maman said in her mind. *Reassure him.* But she couldn't. She could only press her lips together and tilt the corners up a stingy few degrees. "It isn't your fault. And really, I've never understood the need to celebrate another year going by. Age is a pointless measure of who we are, anyway."

"Oh, here we go." Willa rolled her eyes, stood — Dot had stood too — and reached for Margot's empty plate. But despite her words, she was grinning. "You've got her started on age. I'm evacuating the table before she makes me feel alternately like an old biddy and like a child."

"It's a valid complaint!" One she could fall back on easily now, rather than lapsing into a silent contemplation of how much she missed Maman. How empty her flat was every single day. How tired she was growing of sandwiches and toast, and the fact that there was no one to share anything more interesting with. "Our number of years is completely irrelevant when it comes to our life experiences and our mental age. An eight-year-old who has lived on the street for years already, for instance, is hardly the same *age* as a pampered child of a lord on a manor in the country."

The point she had made to Willa, who had found herself on the streets when she was six.

"True enough." Drake rested his arm on the table in a way that would have made Maman scold her had Margot done it. But then, she had a feeling Drake did it to try to alleviate the discomfort in his side. Maman likely would have let that one pass. "But your early life was not the sort to demand you grow up quickly, was it?"

She arched a brow. "Perhaps not in terms of loss and hardship. But I was attending my father's university when I was twelve. I could out-think and out-reason adults old enough to be my parents and grandparents. Yet they dismissed me solely because I was still in short dresses. It was infuriating."

No one else at the table was paying her a bit of attention — they were all helping to clear the dishes away, laughing about something else.

Drake didn't seem inclined to move yet though. He studied her. Not like he'd been doing before, but for an actual purpose this time. Or so it seemed to her. "I imagine it would have been."

She leaned back in her chair. "I spent my last years in Belgium wishing I were older simply so that people would stop treating me like a child — I didn't feel like a child." Other than a few rather childish reactions to the Germans, of course. But plenty of adults fell prey to those as well. She summoned up another fraction of a smile. "And then my first years here needing to pretend to be older so that I could work in Room 40. So age really doesn't mean much to me. I feel as though I've been eighteen for years already."

"Eighteen, is it?" His grin smacked of victory. And the teasing light returned to his eyes. "I would have guessed older. Not a thing I'd usually dare say to a female, but in light of our current conversation . . ."

Margot grinned back. "You can say you thought me forty, and I'd only thank you."

He chuckled — bracing his side again as he did so. He was probably tiring after sitting so long on that hard chair. But he was an adult. If he was tired, he could move. "We'll stick with eighteen. Solely because I'm rather fond of the number." His gaze flicked to the others, none of whom were paying them a bit of attention. Still, he dropped his voice down as if in conspiracy when he said, "It was *my* number, you see. In Spain. Agent Eighteen."

"It was . . ." Her smile froze. Her blood froze. Her very heart froze, and she could only stare at him. "*You?* You are Eighteen?"

Maybe it shouldn't have surprised her. After all, given the number of agents in Spain and the fact that she knew he was a part of Thoroton's network, she could have easily calculated the chances of it being him. Could have. But hadn't.

She pushed away from the table, tossed her napkin into the place where her plate had been, and spun away. Perhaps it made sense, in a way. Who better for God to tell her to pray for than her new friend's brother? Dot would have been devastated had he been killed in the field. Her last close relative, gone.

It was for Dot. Surely. That was why God had whispered *Eighteen* into her ear over and over again.

Her fingers curled into her palm, bit into the flesh. Though she wasn't aware of giving them the instruction, her feet had taken her to the window. The curtains were drawn, of course — it was dark outside, and the blackout restrictions were in place. She gained nothing by standing here. She couldn't see out. Couldn't track the clouds. Couldn't watch raindrops race and tumble down the glass.

But she could feel the cold radiating off it, and she could see her own window in her mind's eye instead of this one. Those grey clouds that had broken up and chased each other across the sky on that wretched day. She could hear Lukas, now as then. Smell the tea Dot had pressed into her hand that day.

She could hear that blighted number echoing over and again in her ear. *Eighteen. Eighteen. Eighteen.*

Her palms stung from where her nails, always kept short and utilitarian, dug into her palms.

"What did I say?"

She jumped at the voice, so close to her side. The wrong voice. Not Lukas or Dot or the landlady. *Him.* Her head snapped his way, that blood that had gone cold now raging. *"You."* It came out low, accusatory. As if he could help that God had brought him to her mind. "I prayed for you."

His brows knit over that knot in his nose, and he reached out a hand to the opposite window frame to brace himself. His hand shook, but she suspected it wasn't from her revelation. "Thank you? Though I'm not certain why you sound so angry about it."

"Not *now,* after you came home. *Then.* Before." She dragged in a breath, huffed it out. "Eighteen. God kept bringing the number to mind, ever since I decoded that report from Thoroton for DID. Not long after Dot and I met."

His fingers bit into the wood like hers did into her palm. "Wait. That *you* decoded?"

"I'm not a secretary, Drake." She spat it, hurled it at him, hoping it would hurt him and not quite sure why she hoped that. Or why she thought it would. She was nothing to him, and his preconceived notions being challenged couldn't really affect anything. "I'm a cryptographer."

"You?" Incredulity flickered across his face, chased by denial, amusement, and then simple blankness. "All right. You're a codebreaker. And you decoded one of

Thoroton's reports for the admiral. So you read about Agent Eighteen and . . . ?"

She squeezed her eyes shut. She didn't want to look at him. Didn't want to be talking to him, frankly, but unfortunately the powers of her mind stopped rather short of moving her by sheer will through time and space, and there were far too many people between her and the door who wouldn't let her storm out of her own birthday celebration. Blast them all. "And God kept bringing the number to mind at odd moments. Telling me to pray. That first day, the Tuesday. And then a Sunday in the park, after Mass. And —"

"Tuesday and Sunday," he muttered. When she peeled her eyes back open, she saw his brows were furrowed again. "The day I ran into Jaeger in the warehouse. And then in the city." His gaze clashed with hers, tangled. "Your prayers may well have saved my life those days."

"Bully for you." She jerked her head back toward the blank window again and folded her arms over her chest.

He shifted closer, something tense and pain-filled in his movement. His side, no doubt. "Do you really hate me that much? That you begrudge having prayed for me?" Or maybe not his side.

322

She pressed her lips together, but still pressure built inside her head. Blast and blast again. She shook her head. "Of course not. It isn't you at all. It's just . . ." She wouldn't say it, wouldn't tell him. Why should she? It was none of his business. He was nothing to her. Nothing but the brother of a friend.

Nothing but the man God had told her to pray for when she *should* have been praying for her mother. Something hot and wild heaved its way from her stomach upward, making her shoulders convulse. She squeezed her eyes shut again. "That day. She was lying there on the floor, already gone, and all that was going through my head was that stupid number. My mother was dead, and God was concerned for *you.*"

"Margot." He stepped closer, so close she could smell his soap. So close she could tell that he was blocking the view of her from the others. Shielding her from their attention as brine scalded her cheeks. "I'm so sorry."

"It isn't your fault." It was *His.* She shuddered and leaned into the window frame, trying and failing to wrestle it all back down. "I should have been praying for her. Not you. That morning, when I was just *standing* there, waiting for her to come. He should have brought her to mind then. Should have told me to go home, but no. He let me get that stupid fever that muddled my mind, and He said *nothing*. No numbers to warn me or spur me home or *anything*. He just let her die and didn't let me help."

"Maybe you couldn't have." Fingers brushed her shoulder, retreated. "Maybe He wanted to spare you that pain."

"What?" How did that make any sense at all? Prying her blurred eyes back open yet again, she turned her head to glare at him.

He was too close. Under normal circumstances, she would have backed away or made him do so. Just now, she knew it was to keep their conversation private, and with that she could agree. No one else needed to hear her falling apart. "I could have saved her. If I'd just gone home earlier —"

"Why do you assume that?" His face a careful mask of dispassion and yet, somehow, empathetic, he held her eyes. "Do you hold the powers of life and death in your hands?"

As if that deserved a response. She pursed her lips.

"Margot, sometimes there's simply nothing we can do. You want to think you could have helped, that a few minutes or hours would have made a difference. That she could be here still." He spread his hands. "But what if it wouldn't have? What if, no matter what you did that day, she would have died? Do you think it would be easier now if you'd seen it happen? If she'd been in your arms?" Now his face contorted. "It wouldn't be. Trust me. I was with my mother in the boat when it overturned. I tried to get her to shore, I tried to save her. I was barely more than a lad, but I thought it was my fault that I couldn't. I watched her face mottle and her soul fly away. You never forget that. Never. You ought to be thanking the Lord for sparing you such a memory."

She shook her head. "Better bad memories for me than her dying alone."

"Really? You think she'd have wished that on you? What if her last prayer was for you, that the Lord spare you that?"

She jolted and pressed that last inch into the window, away from him as much as she could manage.

Because she could imagine it. Maman, feeling the pain, knowing her last minutes were upon her, and thinking not of herself or how to get help, but of her children. Praying that God spare them whatever pain He could.

But He shouldn't have listened. He should

have told her anyway.

Drake swayed a bit on his feet, but he didn't move off, didn't reach for any support. "I know nothing makes it easier. I do, I've been there. Logic can't make it *feel* less."

Her chin edged up. "I am no slave to my feelings." She wouldn't be. Couldn't be.

His smile looked sad. And understanding. "Then cling to the logic. If you trust the Lord enough to listen when He asks you to pray for a stranger, you must trust Him in this too — that He knows better than we do when it is time for us to die."

How many times had she said she trusted the Lord because He was the only being in the universe she could be sure was smarter than she? She hadn't questioned Him when He took Papa home. But somehow this was different. "I cannot accept it. Not this time." Her words emerged bare and skeletal, clattering against each other like dry bones.

He opened his mouth to respond, but before he could, Lukas appeared, frowning and fierce. "Margot, what is the matter?" He shot an arrow of a look at Drake.

Margot touched her brother's arm to still him. "We were talking of Maman. That's all."

She could feel his muscles relax, even as

he sighed and focused on her again. "It is supposed to be a celebration of your birthday tonight, *ma bichette.*"

As if she could help but think of her mother when celebrating her own birth. It was such a ridiculous thing to say that her shoulders wiggled against the itch of it. "Don't be stupid, Lukas."

He wasn't, and so he could puzzle out quickly enough the idiot thing he'd said. He rolled his eyes.

She lifted her chin. "And if you don't stop calling me a doe, I'm going to —"

"What should I call you instead? *Mon nombre?*"

She had to give it to her brother — he knew how to cheer her. "That would do."

"You are ridiculous. But I shall still give you your gift. Come."

She let him take her hand and tug her toward the couch. And she sent Drake a long glance as she stepped around him. One that apologized, she hoped, for Lukas assuming *he* had made her cry. One that said she appreciated him listening — and not being offended at her for all but accusing him of being the reason she hadn't saved her mother.

One that said, perhaps, that she hoped

they could be friends . . . if he'd just stop *looking* at her as he did.

18

Drake blamed his exhaustion on the churning waves crashing around inside him, knowing very well that had little to do with it.

She'd prayed for him. Whenever he faced the threat of Jaeger, she'd been praying.

Had it been old Mrs. Colton from the flat above Dot's who said so, he simply would have marveled at the Lord's care. But it wasn't. It was *her.* While her dark eyes had been haunting him, his number had been echoing in her mind, bidding her to pray.

Did it mean anything? That they were somehow connected, other than through his sister? She'd say no, he suspected.

But his heart said yes.

Were the others not chattering and passing Margot a few wrapped packages, he may have splayed a hand over his chest to try to dampen the ache there. He'd have to be a fool to pursue this course. And he wasn't.

He didn't need the headache and heartache of chasing after a girl who wanted nothing to do with him.

But not *nothing*. There'd been something in that final glance of hers. Something that acknowledged that there was more connecting them than Dot. Or there could be.

Not romance though. She'd call him a fool for even considering it and pretend he didn't exist again while sitting a few inches away, as she'd done through dinner.

"Here." Her brother — who at least didn't still look ready to finish what Jaeger's bullet had started — handed her a rectangular gift that shouted *book* in its dimension. "I had Barclay scouring the bookshops for months to find this."

He had no idea who Barclay might be, but Willa, who sat on the end of the couch closest to him, leaned over to say, "My older brother. He has a . . . knack, let's call it, for finding whatever anyone might need. Hence why Admiral Hall has hired him to do just that."

Drake produced a smile for her, though she turned back to face Margot before she really saw it.

Margot had gotten the paper off the book and laughed when its title was revealed.

Dot scooted forward on her chair. "What

is it? Something about mathematics, no doubt."

"Yes." Grinning in a way that nearly stopped his heart, she held up the book.

"No." Her brother sent her a mock scowl.

Dot lifted a brow. "Poetry?"

Margot nodded. "Mathematics. Meter and rhythm and rhyming patterns. All mathematics."

"Hardly." Lukas's eyes were definitely twinkling over his frown. "Music. Poetry is but music without the instruments."

Willa rolled her eyes and leaned back comfortably against the couch. "Spare us the familiar debate, you two. And do explain why you had my brother hunting for this *particular* book of poetry, luv."

"Émile Verhaeren is one of Belgium's most beloved poets." His expression softened into a smile. One flavored, it looked to Drake, with honeyed memories. "*Les Heures Claires* was the book we first began our music-or-mathematics debate over, when Margot was . . . what? Nine?"

Drake's throat went tight. *Les Heures Claires.*

"Eight." She ran a hand over the cloth binding. Her amusement shifted into longing. "It burned along with all our other books. In Louvain."

331

Dot shot a look at Drake. "Isn't this the one you're reading now?"

All eyes flew to him, and he nodded. "I found a copy in my favorite bookshop in Bilbao. Had it with me when I was . . ." He motioned to his side.

Lukas turned wide eyes on him. *"Parlez-vous français?"*

Nodding, Drake said, "*Oui*. In addition to Spanish and Italian and Latin. Spanish is, of course, my best language after English, but French is a close third."

"I've always been a dunce at languages." Dot chuckled at herself and cast a look at Red, who'd pulled over a chair from the dining table. "You?"

"I always reckoned English enough."

Drake looked between his sister and their old friend. Measuring. Gauging. Her eyes lit when she looked at Redvers Holmes in a way he hadn't seen them do since Nelson signed up. And now that he paused to think of it, her smiles had been rather more abundant than usual when talking with him too.

He let out a slow breath. Finding the bloke a good position just got a bit more imperative.

"Here. This is from Drake and me." Dot handed Margot a small package that con-

332

tained a few decorative hairpins and grinned. "Mostly me."

He certainly hadn't chosen them. "Entirely Dot. She's just too good to allow me to arrive empty-handed to the celebration, so she added my name to the tag."

Margot lifted her eyes to him for the slenderest of seconds before focusing on the package, but it was a sliver of attention large enough to pierce.

Blast it all, he'd never get her out of his head now. The eyes, the prayers, even the poetry had all conspired against him. He was doomed. Which left him with one vital question.

What could he do about it?

"Oh, how lovely." No particular excitement emerged with Margot's words as she lifted the crystal-encrusted pins from their box. "Thank you, Dot."

His sister laughed. "I know you don't care a whit for pretty baubles. But they'll help keep your hair out of your face without the need for the pomade you detest."

"Oh!" Now her face brightened. "Thank you *very* much, then. And there are ones with metal flowers as well." She held these up, presumably for Willa to see, since the other men seemed about as interested in them as Drake was.

But he took mental notes on Margot's reactions. Pretty things — useless. Useful things — priceless. Mathematics over music. Logic over feelings. She was obviously a subscriber to the virtues of sarcasm, and when one could engage her there, she went from stony silence to smiles. She said she didn't want a husband and children, but family was obviously of the utmost importance to her.

She sought solitude. But if she really wanted to be alone, she wouldn't be so angry at God for letting her mother die that way.

He let it all tumble through his head while Dot served the cake she'd made with the sugar she'd been saving. He'd never win Margot over through conventional means. Never gain her heart if he appealed to it outright. But there had to be a way. She was no island — she was anchored to Lukas, to Willa, to Willa's family. She'd formed a quick attachment to Dot and seemed to have taken to Red.

Drake let a bite of cake melt on his tongue. It would be easier if she were just another girl. Like Ada. But he'd never liked Ada. He had no interest in *just another girl.* This one, though. He apparently preferred dark eyes to ready smiles. Sarcasm to sweetness. Codebreakers to secretaries.

Codebreaker. He straightened a bit in his chair, barely even wanting to wince. She must be a talented one indeed, for DID to have hired her to the position contrary to convention. Obviously she loved it. That was the life she wanted to pursue, even after this madness of war was over. Numbers and equations and puzzles.

He could use that. Convince her he could be a part of it.

An hour later, their guests were all moving toward their coats and the door, laughter still ringing out. No one expected Drake to shuffle along with them, but he at least stood and added his farewells. And, when Lukas De Wilde stepped over to shake his hand while the others were all by the exit, Drake seized the opportunity before it slipped away. Who knew when he'd see her brother again?

"May I ask you a question?" He kept his voice low, though it was doubtful the others would hear him over Dot and Red's laughter.

Lukas smiled. "Of course."

The smile likely would shift in a moment. Drake braced himself. "May I court your sister?"

Well, the man didn't shout in laughter at

the absurdity. Or scowl either. He just went very still and held his gaze for a long moment. "Mr. Elton . . . I personally have no objections. But my sister very well may."

"I know." His eyes drifted to her. She was standing at the door, between Willa and Dot, buttoning her coat. With them but not one of them. Loving them even if she wasn't like them. It could be done. She was capable of such attachments. "But I have a plan."

"Oh?"

He looked back to Lukas and smiled. "It's a simple matter of mathematics."

Margot had never had any particular feelings toward the night. It came, it went, at calculable times. She didn't fear the darkness, and she didn't love it. It was, and so she moved through it the same way she did the sun or the rain or the fog. Deliberately.

Tonight she strode home along the familiar streets with her birthday gifts tucked in her handbag, rather grateful for the solitude. The dinner party had been nice, all in all. Bout of tears notwithstanding, the night had been pleasant — perhaps even thanks to the ridiculous storm of emotions. She felt strangely better for having vented her anger to somebody.

Why it had to have been to Drake Elton

— but it had. And she was . . . all right with that. Her bag thumped against her side, heavy thanks to the book of poetry, and the corners of her lips tugged up. He at least had good taste in poets. And spoke French. Why that should count as a mark in his favor when there were certainly people aplenty in the world who spoke it whom Margot did *not* like, she didn't know. Still. The tally marks under his virtues column had increased quite a bit tonight.

Eighteen. The number didn't echo in that part of her mind where the Lord spoke. It just echoed. Would always echo, she suspected. The number she'd thought of the day she went inside to find her mother gone. The month plus the date of that terrible day. The birthday that came far too quickly on the heels of that loss. The number of the agent she'd prayed for, not knowing who it was. Eighteen. The number, even, of the year soon to dawn.

She reached a corner and hesitated. The air was cold, the night was dark, and the quickest route home was straight ahead. Maman never would have considered turning to the right instead, just to walk through the park. Not now.

Margot pressed her lips together, paused for one more second, and then turned to the right. There was no *reason* to walk through the park. But she wanted to, and there was nothing to stop her.

At the park's edge, she turned onto the little brick path, following it by the bench where Mrs. Rourke was obviously not sitting with her crochet hook. To the wrought-iron table where neither Gregory sat with his chessboard nor Williams with his Go.

Only . . . that wasn't quite true. There was no *person* seated at the table. But the Go board was there.

How very odd. She moved over to it, frowning into the shadows. Why would Williams have left his board set up? It was a stupid thing to do — anyone could come by and steal it. Even if few in London knew how to play the game, any thief could see that it was a valuable board.

But there it sat, safe and whole and set up for the beginning of a game. Or rather, she saw as she drew nearer, a game just begun. One black stone had been moved.

She edged closer and saw a slip of white fluttering in the breeze, secured partly under the board. A slip of white with black ink on both sides. She read the top first.

Margot De Wilde. I waited throughout the afternoon and found myself a terrible substitute for you as an opponent. Perhaps you'll stop by soon — I had to flee the damp of evening for a while in favor of a cup of tea. But if you happen by before I return, do make a play.

Her brows scrunched together. He surely hadn't been out here all evening, waiting — with the cough he obviously struggled against, that couldn't be good for him. But no, the paper was damp, proving it had been there awhile. Had he left the board unattended for hours? Stupid. Stupid enough to make her itchy. But perhaps he had fallen asleep after his cup of tea. Heaven knew he wasn't well. And this time, at least, no one had stolen the game.

The breeze shifted and she saw the bottom of the paper. *Sente.*

Her eyes narrowed, and she snatched the slip of paper out. A lot of nerve Williams had, claiming with that *sente* to be on the offensive, to have the initiative, when the play had only just begun. She dug around in her handbag until she came up with a pencil. Using the empty space in the middle of the board as her table, she drew a line through *Sente* and wrote *Moyo. Prepare to be gote.*

The plays were all potential now — *moyo.* But she didn't ever play on the defensive. *She* would not be *gote* — she'd force him into it. After anchoring the paper again, she touched a finger to a white stone. Cold. Hard. And slid it to her opening position.

Then she left the park and went home without a backward glance.

Das Gespenst waited until her figure had vanished from sight. Until her footsteps had faded into the night. Until the cold, damp English breeze had snaked for another long minute through his jacket. Then, for the first time in ten minutes, he moved. Away from the tree against whose trunk he'd been leaning, in whose shadow he'd been hiding.

If other people were out tonight, they weren't in the park. He hadn't been sure, of course, that she would come this way either. More often than not she didn't. But when he saw where she'd gone earlier, rather than stopping by for a game . . . well, he hadn't wanted to wait for another day to get a read on her, and this had seemed like an easy enough way. And if she'd gone straight home after her dinner at the Eltons', he simply would have packed up the board for now and set it up again tomorrow afternoon, waiting for her.

Eventually she would have come. But he wouldn't complain that *eventually* was *now.*

Gliding over the meters without a sound,

he remained, as always, on alert. But no one else watched or walked or waited here. It was just him and the board and the slip of fluttering white.

He plucked the paper out even as he took in her move. Then he glanced down at the sheet, and his lips twitched. She had *kiai* — fighting spirit. It would serve her well in Go, if she had the skill to match it. And their first game had indicated that she did.

But that wasn't what he'd really needed to know. What he'd needed to know was if she had kiai in life. And her note proved she did far more adeptly than one move possibly could on the game board.

She would prove an interesting enemy.

After another glance around, he tucked the paper into his pocket, swept the black and white stones into their pouches, and packed up the game. He pursed his lips.

Enemy wasn't the right word for Margot De Wilde. *Adversary.* That was it. Or *opponent,* perhaps. *Enemy* implied hatred, and he had no such feelings for the Belgian girl. No, hatred was too powerful a force to spread out to just anyone on the wrong side of this war. He would reserve his for those who truly deserved it.

Though night and distance shrouded it from his sight, Das Gespenst turned to face the Admiralty's Old Building. He had an enemy. But it wasn't Margot De Wilde. She would be a fine conduit, though, to the one who was. She kept odd hours, the same as some of the men. None of the other secretaries did. She must be trusted indeed, if her hours had to match her boss's. Valuable to them.

Perfect for him.

Tucking the board under his arm and clearing a tickle from his throat, he put a foot on the path that would take him out of the park. A whistle came from his lips once he gained the street — just an average Englishman, making his way home. That's all he was.

No one looked twice at him as he moved to his building. He drew the key from his pocket, paused for a moment to collect the post from the little box that said *John Williams,* and flipped through it as he jogged up the stairs. Just an average Englishman going home for the night.

19

Drake squeezed his eyes closed for a minute, leaning back his head and stretching a bit. He'd been reading for hours, and both eyes and side demanded a break from it. But he still had a mountain of files to read through.

How the devil did Hall compile so much data? They read every single letter that left England by post. Every telegram that was sent wirelessly was intercepted — which was pretty much every telegram that had to leave its own country, given that cutting the underwater wires had been the first move when war was declared back in 1914. Agents all over the world were reporting once a week.

An answer to every question seemed to be at Hall's fingertips. The problem, of course, was finding said answer among so much chaff. The sheer volume of information . . . well, Drake had no idea how many people were currently employed as he was, doing nothing but reading over it all. But even if it were hundreds, they weren't likely to get through it in any kind of reasonable time.

He rubbed at his neck and then pushed himself to his feet. Time for a turn around the flat. Get the blood flowing again and convince his muscles to strengthen. It took him a long moment to straighten and stand, but it was faster than he could do it last week. He was improving. If he didn't have any setbacks, he might even be able to join his sister at church on Sunday.

His steps were slow and measured, but his mind sped quickly enough to make up for his physical shuffle. He'd flagged a few items to send back to the admiral — the bits relevant to the questions for which he'd been tasked with finding answers. He'd made a list of any other details that seemed as though they could be important to someone else, though they weren't relevant to his tasks. He'd put a considerable dent in the considerable pile of papers.

He passed by the window and looked out as he walked by. Frowned. The same man had been standing on the corner there, leaning into the doorway of a shop, since his last turn about the flat an hour ago. Or was back, perhaps. But still. It was odd. Drake paused a moment and looked down.

The chap wore a hat that obscured his face from this angle and a grey overcoat that looked like countless other grey overcoats out on the street. Perhaps it wasn't the same man, just another in a similar jacket, in a similar position.

But no. The fellow was rather tall, taller than the other chaps who strode by. It made him stand out. And it wasn't just a *similar* position. It was the *same* position. Drake had been well trained in noting such little anomalies that set one man apart from the rest. This fellow had chosen the doorway of a shop that was closed, and he had a newspaper raised in front of him to the exact level it had been an hour ago. And his head was at an angle Drake knew well — the one he himself had employed on the train, when *he* was the one hiding behind newsprint.

His pulse kicked up, even as his logic tamped it down. It could be anyone. There for any reason. Maybe it was just some bloke waiting for somebody. Innocent. Or even not-so-innocent, but of no relevance to *him.* He could be a detective, hired by a wife to track a straying husband. A police officer undercover, looking for a suspect. A man ducking out of work and not wanting to be spotted.

It could be Jaeger.

Drake's nostrils flared, and he stepped closer to the window. He couldn't tell from up here if that thought had any evidence to support it or not. He'd never gotten a good measure on Jaeger's height to know if it matched this tall chap's, and he couldn't see this man's face.

Look up, he willed the figure. *Let me see you.*

He waited for one minute. Two. The man shifted a few times, but his face remained concealed under the brim of his hat and behind the paper. Though at one point he turned it to the side, revealing his hair.

Dark — darker than Jaeger's. And longer.

He breathed more easily. There were ways to change hair color, yes. But it wouldn't have had time to grow that much.

Drake shook himself and turned from the window. He was just stir-crazy. He'd been laid up and kept inside for over two weeks, and his brain was simply fabricating some adventure for him. That was all. It made him jump at shadows — not out of fear but out of boredom. He meandered the room for another few minutes, deliberately *not* looking out the window.

The phone jangled. He was only a few steps from it, so he could actually reach it before it stopped. He picked it up after the second ring and didn't even sound too breathless when he said, "Hello, Elton residence."

Silence stretched. His shoulders went tense. Then, "Is this *Drake* Elton?"

The words didn't ease the tension. The voice . . . Did he know it? Or was he still just starting at shadows, prey to his own thoughts? "Yes it is."

"Good." The chuckle that thrummed over the line made a chill crawl up Drake's spine. "You will pay. Know that. Not quite yet, but you *will* pay. Know I am here."

"Jaeger." His hand went so tight around the telephone that he feared he'd crack it. It had to be. He'd never heard him speaking in English before, and his voice was distorted a bit over the phone lines, but he still recognized it from the train. He moved as far toward the window as the cord would allow, but he couldn't see down to the street below.

No answer came, just silence. Drake waited for a moment, then put the receiver back in the cradle. He stared at it for a moment, filtering through the questions in his head.

Had it been Jaeger? Yes. He recognized his voice, and he'd said the same words he had on the train. That Drake would pay.

Where was *here*? England, obviously — he couldn't have made a telephone call from outside the country. London? Possibly, though he couldn't be sure at the moment. That was surely something Hall could help him discover. How did he learn Dot's phone number, though? Did he also know where she lived? Was he watching them?

He strode back to the window now, too fast for his side. But he didn't care about the pain.

The man in the grey overcoat was gone.

It didn't mean anything. He knew it didn't. He'd already convinced himself it wasn't Jaeger out there. But it could have been someone he hired to watch the window, couldn't it? To let Jaeger know that Drake was in.

Had he been the one to call before and hang up when someone else answered? Like Dot or Red?

Drake spun back to the telephone. A minute later he'd been patched through to Hall's line and had explained the situation to his superior.

DID's silence was sharp as a hammer's rap. "Impossible. He cannot be in country."

It didn't sound like an accusation of lying. Just like denial. Drake eased down onto the hard wooden chair by the telephone table.

"It was him on the line, Admiral. I recognized his voice. He couldn't have called from anywhere else, could he?"

"No. Blast." Something hit something else in the background. "Someone has missed something. Rest assured, I shall find out who and what. And we'll determine from where that call was placed and through what switchboards it went. In the meantime, I'll gather anything I can find on Jaeger. Perhaps there will be a clue somewhere in his history that could help us locate him now."

"Perhaps." He turned to face the window again, though from his seat, he could see nothing but the windows of the building across the street. "Do you think . . . What if he comes after my sister, Admiral?"

Another beat of silence, this one not quite so sharp. "For now, Lieutenant, comfort yourself in the likelihood that those other calls *were* him, and that it was only you with whom he wanted to engage. That suggests he will only target you, and perhaps your work — since it was *his* work, not his person, with which you interfered. I find it highly unlikely that he would react to your having foiled a sugar shipment by attacking your family. That would be too emotional a response for a man who is clearly a professional in matters of espionage."

The band around Drake's chest loosened. "Excellent point, sir. Thank you."

"While I have you here and we are speaking of sugar — have you found anything yet to corroborate Margot's suspicions about her mother?"

Drake glanced at the second stack of papers he'd been plodding through, which contained every mention they could find over the last year of anthrax or sugar or grain. "Nothing, sir. Only about the shipment in Spain, and more in South America. I trust you've already seen to those?"

"We are investigating, though the German agent in South Am is as slippery as they come. But nothing that mentions us here?"

"No. Not yet." He'd been through most of the material already, somehow both hoping and dreading that he'd find something. "Though there's a bit of a difference in tracking tons versus a few ounces of the stuff."

"But if it were truly an attack on us here, then an agent would have had to either enter our borders or contact someone already here. *That* would leave a trail."

"It would. But thus far, nothing." And the more he read, the more he didn't think he *would* find anything. All intelligence they'd intercepted pointed only to infecting animals with the anthrax and glanders. Not people. Surely if an order had been sent out with such instructions, it would have garnered a response, a reply to that, and so on. "It would be outside their usual instructions, that much has become clear."

"Mm. Well, I put nothing past the huns, in general. But my instinct says Margot's suspicions are unfounded in this case." A pause, and the sound of something tapping. "Finish going through what I've already sent, but after that, if we've nothing to warrant further attention, I'm going to call that investigation complete. Your attention ought to be focused on Jaeger."

Drake didn't dare contradict the admiral. And didn't really want to . . . for his own sake. For logic's sake. But for Margot's? "Sir . . . Margot . . ." He didn't even know what to say. How could he, when he knew her so little?

But Hall obviously knew her quite well, given his long sigh. "Leave her to me, Elton. You just focus on what I've given you — and on recuperating. We need you back in the field, and we need Jaeger *out* of it."

"Yes, sir." What else could he say?

But when he hung up, he just stared at the stack of work for a long moment. He didn't think he'd find anything in there to tell him that someone had killed her mother with anthrax. But how could he stop until he had answers for her?

On the other hand, if there were no answers to be found, how long could he really keep searching for them?

He passed a hand through his hair and glanced at the clock. He had hours yet before Dot would be home. Time aplenty to finish his work for Hall for the day. For now, while he was alone, he'd put a bit of effort into his other mission.

For a change of scenery, he set himself up at Aunt Millie's small desk in the bedroom he'd taken over. By the time he pulled out scrap paper, some of his good stationery, and *Les Heures Claires,* the entire surface was filled. With only a moment's longing for his desk at Abuelo's, he set to work.

He may not be able to give Margot answers on her mother. But maybe, just maybe, he could find the equation for her heart.

"Margot. What in the world are you doing?"

Margot glanced up only briefly from the newspaper she had spread over her desk. And only then because it was Barclay who spoke, and she hadn't seen him in nearly a week. "Taking my lunch break."

His silence spoke eloquently as he looked over her shoulder at the marks and circles obscuring some of the print on the page. "Margot."

She knew how it looked. But she also knew she was *not* mad. "DID said one of the German agents in custody mentioned their suspicion that we communicated with our agents through coded messages hidden within newspapers. Why would they assume that unless it was a method *they* were using? If my mother was targeted, there could be information to be found here."

She could only hope he wouldn't remember that it was the method her father had used to train her. That would make it seem a bit . . . desperate.

Given the look he shot her, he *did* recall. "Margot. If you need help with something, you know well you can simply ask me."

She'd be lying if she said she hadn't considered doing just that, after Drake confessed last night that he'd been called off the investigation. Barclay certainly had connections she didn't — the very ones that made him an invaluable asset to Admiral Hall. After years of scavenging and thieving through the city, he knew the ins and outs better than just about anyone.

But his connections to the intelligence

world were all through Mr. V, the man who had recruited her to Room 40 to begin with. V answered directly to Admiral Hall. Using Barclay's aid in this question would lead her right back where she started, and the admiral had been firm this morning. No more Room 40 resources could be dedicated to the question of her mother's death.

"There's nothing you can do, Barclay. Though I thank you for the offer." She dug up a smile that probably bore only the slightest resemblance to a real one. "What are you doing here today, anyway?"

"What, I can't come and visit my favorite cryptographer for no reason?" With a grin, Barclay leaned against her desk in that way he always did, as if he had all the time in the world and nothing better to spend it on than a conversation. He had a way of looking instantly relaxed that clashed with the Wavy Navy uniform he now wore. "V said Hall had a task for me. I appear to have arrived a bit early, so I thought I'd take a minute to bother you." He made a show of looking around. "Where's Dot? I thought you took lunches together."

"Usually. But she's having lunch with a . . . friend today. From outside the OB." It wasn't jealousy that had wriggled through her when Dot had shared, with pink cheeks, that she was meeting Redvers Holmes at noon. A bit of sorrow for herself, perhaps. Such a new friendship, and already they were being pulled separate directions. But Margot wouldn't begrudge her any happiness.

"So instead you decide to pass your lunch with newspapers and sad questions?"

She opened her mouth, sure a clever retort would find its way to her tongue, but all words went silent when the admiral strode into the room. His all-knowing gaze took in the newspapers with a blink. His lips thinned. But then he focused on Barclay. "Sorry, Pearce. Did I keep you waiting long?"

"Just long enough that I could say hello to my little sister."

Despite herself, a corner of her lips turned up. Barclay was the only person in the world who seemed to think that liking a person made them a sibling. Well, one of his adopted sisters *had* married Margot's brother . . .

Hall chuckled and slid a hand to his inner pocket. It emerged again with a folded paper. "See to this, if you would."

"Yes, sir." Barclay didn't even ask what it was. Just took the paper and straightened again. And then he leaned over to press a kiss to Margot's forehead. "See you on Sunday, Margot." In a whisper he added, "If you need me, you've only to ask."

"Bye, Barclay." She wanted to ask, even now. But she knew she shouldn't. She may be willing to risk irritating Hall herself, but she certainly didn't want to land Barclay in any hot water for pursuing what the admiral thought to be a waste of time.

He watched Barclay exit and then turned back to Margot. The sigh was, no doubt, over the newspapers spread across her desk. He too would know well what she was doing. But it was her own time. She could spend it however she pleased.

Perhaps he realized as much. Or perhaps he didn't want to open the debate again. "When your break is over, my dear, I've a task for you: a new recruit who needs to be trained."

Margot set her pen down and frowned at her superior. "Since when do I train new people?"

Hall grinned. "Since the new chap has a chip on his shoulder that has already put off half the fellows here — and the rest haven't met him yet. I didn't think you'd be prone to such reactions."

He must be quite a chap if Hall was determined to bring him on board despite not fitting in well with the rest of the team. "Who is he?"

The admiral tapped a finger to another of the newspapers on her desk. "Black Heart."

Her brows flew up before she could stop them. "We've brought an RFC pilot into our numbers?"

"He has talent with more than aircraft. And I enjoyed pulling one over on the people who wanted to make an example of him. Took a few tugs on odd strings to get him here, but worth it, I hope."

She chuckled and nodded. "All right. Consider me your new trainer. Where can I find this *Cœur Noir*?"

"I have him sequestered in the little storage room at the end of the hall for now, until he stops snarling at everyone." The admiral lost the battle to another grin. "Apparently being threatened with court-martial and a firing squad has put him in a bit of a foul temper. Nothing you can't handle though."

Margot smiled. "As long as snarling back is acceptable."

"No arguments from me. Though Camden *is* an old friend of Lieutenant Elton, apparently — he's actually the one who suggested I bring him into the fold. If you wish to be kind for his sake."

Her brows lifted again. "And why would that affect anything?"

"Oh, no reason." Lips twitching, Hall spun away. "Let me know how it goes. I'm off to meet with the press and convince them to stop lambasting my newest recruit."

Margot shook her head and picked her pen up again. If the articles she'd read over the past few days were an indication of the journalists' inclinations, they weren't going to be happy about letting their prize story go. But DID had the press corps wrapped around his finger. He fed them enough juicy tidbits that they wouldn't nip at his out-stretched fingers now.

Heaven knew these papers spread before her didn't seem to have any hidden messages in them, just their overt ones. She kept looking for the telltale signs — letters too bold, or not aligned properly — that would alert an operative to a message, but thus far each oddity she had circled hadn't followed up on its promise.

When the voices of the others began filtering back through the hallways, Margot folded up the newspapers with a sigh. She would keep looking through the old editions she had in a box at home. But for now, training. She certainly hoped this Camden fellow was a quick study.

She gathered up a few newly arrived encoded telegrams, today's code, paper, and pencils. Then she aimed herself for the room at the end of the hall that had been a storage room. Margot tapped on the door and opened it, nearly dropping her supplies when the occupant all but leapt at her like a caged lion.

"Have you come to let me out of this prison?" He was tall, dark, and seething. Margot noted the features that would have made the secretaries go aflutter — the strong jaw, the chiseled lips, the clear blue eyes, et cetera. But they were secondary to what interested *her* more — the intelligence snapping in those eyes, and the bad attitude coming off him in waves.

This was sure to be fun.

She stepped into the room and set the papers and pencils on the scratched-up table that someone had shoved in here, up against the boxes of papers. There were no windows, just a bare bulb hanging from the ceiling and a lamp. She'd leave the door open. "I should think you of all people, sir, would recognize that this is *far* from a prison."

He snarled. Then drew in a breath and made a quick bow. "Forgive me, miss. You've probably come to bring me tea, or to see if I've anything for you to type up."

One of these days, people wouldn't just assume she was a secretary. Or a tea girl.

No, that was wishful thinking. People would always assume it. But maybe one of these days it would stop making her itch in protest. She spread her now-empty hands. "Do I look like I've come with tea?"

He folded his arms over his chest, still clad in the olive-green RFC pilot's uniform. How odd it was to see olive green here, instead of naval blue. "You could have left your cart in the corridor. Heaven knows it wouldn't fit in this cell."

She motioned to the equally empty space outside the door. "There are no tea girls on our floor. And I am not a secretary." She pointed to the chair obviously brought in with the makeshift desk. "Now sit down. Unless you *want* to go to prison, you have a lot to learn."

He scoffed. *Scoffed.* "And I suppose you're going to teach me, darling?"

The admiral had said he wouldn't mind if Margot snarled at him — she wondered how he'd feel about it if she employed a few of the moves Willa had taught her for self-defense. A knee to the groin might bring this chap down a much-needed peg.

She settled for a scathing look. For now.

"I suppose that depends on how big an idiot you are. Sit."

He sat, but with a smirk that said he was merely playing along for his own entertainment. "Right. Sitting. Now what? I suppose you're going to bring in a typewriter and teach me how to type up a few papers while filing my nails?"

"Well, apparently, first I'm going to teach you how to avoid the firing squad." She perched on the edge of the table and glared at him. "Admiral Hall has gone out on a limb, bringing you here when everyone in England is calling for a court-martial. I highly suggest you show your gratitude in some way other than by provoking every single member of his staff."

The smirk died away into a glower. "I didn't ask the admiral to fetch me from prison."

"No. Drake Elton did. For some reason, he deems you a friend, whether you know the meaning of the word or not."

"Elton?" He sat up straighter and looked genuinely struck. For a moment. Then the smirk reappeared, and he swept his eyes down the length of her. "Are you his sister? Dora, isn't it?"

Men could be such imbeciles. "No. And no." She picked up the tube she'd brought with her, opened it, and pulled out the intercepted telegrams within. "Are you ready to get to work, or do you need a few more minutes to prove yourself a reprobate?"

He waved a hand. "By all means, darling. Teach me something."

He was about to learn how *not* darling she was. "That top sheet there has today's code on it. Since you're obviously so much smarter than a mere woman could possibly be, why don't you just go right ahead and decode those telegrams?"

He sent her an arched look but picked up the day's code and one of the slips of paper from the tube. "Might take some time, but infinitely doable."

"I'm glad to hear it. Then you'll be ready for your first night shift in a few days and will be able to do it in reverse — break the code with nothing to go on but the telegram written in it." She pushed off the desk and gave him an empty smile. "Have at it, then. Cheerio."

She pivoted to the door, fully intending to leave him to his own devices for an hour or two and see what came of it.

But the doorway was blocked by Dilly Knox, who stepped inside with raised brows. "Is DID angry with you, De Wilde?

To assign you to *him*?"

Margot grinned. "No. He just knows I'm not going to butt heads with him like a ram, as the rest of you do."

"Mm." Dilly glared at Camden for a moment and then held up a paper in his hands, his eyes softening back to normal when he looked again to her. "I could use your help, if you have a moment. This just came in. I haven't compared it to all our codebooks yet, but it doesn't look to me as though it's in the usual ones, and I was afraid it would be another of those that seem to be in that new code. You hold the lot of them in your head better than I do, so I thought perhaps you could . . . ?"

"Ah, fun." It was something like holding up a random piece and trying to determine which of five puzzles it belonged to. One had to look past the portion of image that was so incomplete, the colors that could belong in any of the blank spots, and instead look at the shape of the thing.

Behind her, the chair scraped. "Wait just a blighted moment. Do you mean to tell me —"

"Do shut up, Camden. My feeble feminine intelligence requires a bit of quiet for such tasks." Margot read through the page and then let her eyes slide shut. Let the organization of it turn into numbers in her mind, let the numbers shift and slide until their patterns matched up with others.

When she opened her eyes again, she found Dilly to be the one wearing a smirk, directed at the grounded pilot.

Margot handed the paper back. "I believe it's a variation of 2310. You'll need to determine the variance, of course, but that seems to be its pattern."

"Ah. Good man, De Wilde. You've saved me a few hours of trial and error." He stepped back into the corridor with a mock salute. "Best of luck with your delinquent."

"Much appreciated." She turned back to said delinquent with raised brows. "Any questions before I go?"

He held up a pencil, bemusement on his face. "You're a codebreaker?"

Not quite as insightful as the ones Drake tended to ask. But then, they were old friends, not identical twins. "Obviously."

"But you're a woman."

"Excellent powers of deduction. What was your first clue?"

He sighed, and a fair bit of his bravado seeped out with it. He looked . . . tired. And maybe a bit broken.

Margot decided to take pity on him. A little, anyway. "It's like this, Camden. DID will hire whoever can do the job. A banker. A music critic. A girl. A supposed criminal. It doesn't matter what you were outside these halls. In here, all that matters is that you can do the job. So do the job. All right?"

He rubbed a hand over his face. "It's been . . . a nasty week."

"I imagine." The papers hadn't been very clear on exactly what he was being blamed for, but it involved the deaths of members of his squadron. That kind of horror gave a man an excuse for surliness. What she didn't quite know was how to reach out to him through it.

Drake would know. He'd have a clever question to ask, one to poke through the resistance and get to the heart of the matter. The heart of his old friend.

All Margot could do was draw in a breath and say, "My mother died three weeks ago."

He looked up, shoulders still stooped but combativeness gone. "I'm sorry to hear that."

She heaved out the breath she'd drawn in, wishing for just a bit of Drake's ability to communicate. "I didn't say it for sympathy. Just . . . the work helps. Helps me, I mean. Maybe it'll help you too. Give you something positive to focus on. A way to let go of all that nastiness, at least for a few hours at a clip."

He leaned forward and rested his arms on the table. "Probably. But I don't know that I'm ready to let go of it."

Margot nudged a few boxes over and sat on them. "We haven't the luxury of that indulgence just now. You're an officer in His Majesty's Royal Flying Corp. It's your duty to do your bit." She tapped a finger to the papers on the table. "And right now, *this* is your bit."

For a long moment, he just sat unmoving, staring at the papers. Probably seeing something far different, far removed from a storage room in the OB. Then he blinked, nodded, and pulled the papers forward. "All right, then. I'll save the moping for my own time. Show me what I'm doing here, Mademoiselle Codebreaker."

She smiled, happy enough to get down to business.

20

Drake knew well his sister — and his doctor — would have his head if they could see him now. But that sure knowledge hadn't stopped him from slipping on his overcoat, planting a hat onto his head, and wishing this building had a lift as he slowly took one step after another until he was on the ground floor, out the back door, and on the blessed street.

Fresh air was a heady thing. For a second, he could do nothing but breathe it in, forgetting his purpose in hobbling down here. Forgetting the way Dot would fret. The way the physician would scold. None of that mattered. It smelled of cold and rain and the exhaust of the car that had just rattled past. Of the bread baking in the shop down the street. It smelled of London and of *freedom*.

He might never go back inside again.

Or at the very least, he might begin making a trek down here every day, when no one was at home to berate him for it. Assuming, of course, he could get back up the stairs after *this* outing. Which was probably going to be a bit more difficult than coming *down* had been, and that was challenging enough.

Blasted gunshot wound.

But he couldn't sit there anymore, looking out at the same dark-haired man in the grey overcoat who had been there the past two days. He wasn't quite sure what he intended to discover by investigating from the street, but surely more than he'd been able to glean from Dot's flat.

Hall had paid him a visit yesterday to tell him that the phone call of the day before had been placed from a coin-operated telephone box a street over from where he now stood. He'd delivered the news with a tight mouth that proclaimed him unhappy with the discovery and with warning flashing in his eyes.

Jaeger had been here. One street over. He knew Dot's telephone number. He knew where she lived. He knew Drake was there.

His blood felt as cold in his veins as the November air. Jaeger now knew all of this . . . but what did he mean to do with the knowledge? What, exactly, would he deem the proper payment for a foiled shipment of anthrax?

Try as he might to cling to the admiral's insistence that a professional win would not be met with a personal vendetta, Drake had begun doubting that logic the moment Hall told him about the call's origin. Because he was *here.*

That felt blighted personal.

He had to know if the man in the overcoat was linked to him somehow. So here he was, on the street, with a grey overcoat of his own. Some of his sister's facial powder in his hair to make it seem grey, too, a stoop to his spine that didn't require much thought to maintain just now, and an old hat on his head — his father's. Dot must have kept it. Drake's favorite was no doubt still tumbling about the countryside in Spain, unless a local had rescued it after the wind stole it from his head on top of the train.

He'd brought a cane with him too — the one the doctor had given him but which he'd refused to use in the flat. He didn't need it, not in general. There was nothing wrong with his legs. But it would help with the image he was trying to project now. With a bit of luck, no one would look past the overall image to his unlined face.

Usually he made it a point not to stoop in pain when he was walking. Now he let himself and exaggerated it until his spine curved over the cane. Head tucked down so that passersby would see Father's old hat more than Drake's young face, he hobbled toward the abandoned shop whose door the mystery man liked to lean against.

He'd been there twenty minutes ago, whoever the bloke was. And, yes, he was there still. Drake's pulse kicked up a few beautiful beats per minute, but he did no more than glance at that doorway. He'd chosen the back entrance of his building so that whoever-he-was wouldn't be alerted. Now he shuffled across the street, aiming for a bench positioned at a bus stop at which buses never stopped anymore. Most of London's buses had been sent to the front to move soldiers and supplies.

He settled onto the bench, his back to the bloke. Drew out a newspaper to unfold in front of his own face. And a mirror too. Careful to keep it shaded enough that the sun wouldn't send out a homing beacon, Drake angled it until he could see the man behind him.

For five minutes, the only movement on the street came from everyone else bustling by. No one paused to question him, no one seemed to even notice he was there. Then, at just the time the chap had vanished each previous day, he moved. Folded his paper and tucked it into his overcoat's inner pocket.

He kept his face down, so that an observer from the windows above wouldn't see his features. But Drake was now at the perfect angle for that. Thanks to the mirror, that tucking of his chin actually presented his face to him.

Familiar . . . maybe. Drake frowned and tried to memorize each angle and plane. It wasn't Jaeger — of that much he was certain. But some chord of memory still jangled. Another of the blokes Charles the Bold had provided photographs of, perhaps? He couldn't be sure. He hadn't paid close enough attention to any of them but the one he'd identified as his opposite number.

But he was paying attention now. Whoever he was, Drake would be able to identify him in an instant if they crossed paths anywhere else.

Dark hair, long enough to brush his ears on the sides and collar in back. A trim beard that hid a nearly delicate mouth. Brows with an inquisitive slant to them.

The chap strode away, his pace just fast enough to blend in with most other pedestrians going about their business. Drake had no hope of keeping up with him, and frankly, he didn't intend to follow just now anyway. He'd only wanted to see him.

And now he had. The next step, which would be considerably trickier, would be to discover whether he had anything to do with Jaeger.

He sat for another few minutes, working it out in his mind. How could he learn the man's identity? Following him was certainly his best recourse, and it would be made easier thanks to the man leaving his post at the exact same time every day. Drake himself couldn't keep up, but . . . Red could. The changes he'd made to his prosthetic recently had been ingenious. His stride now was sure and smooth, and he could walk at a normal pace.

Red had done a bit of sleuthing for Margot, right? Maybe he'd be willing to do a bit more for Drake. Heaven knew the money he'd pay him for it would be welcome.

He should be coming by soon. They'd have tea, and Drake would pretend he needed the break from his work. He pushed himself off the bench, admitting another rather unwelcome truth to himself — he'd only dared come down here because he knew that help would be arriving soon, should he need it to get back up the stairs.

But pride insisted he try on his own first. Pride, and the fact that he was none too certain that Red wouldn't tattle to Dot if he found him down here.

"Elton?"

Drake looked up, trying to place the voice, managing it only when he saw the face it matched. He began to smile for the old friend he hadn't seen in seven years.

The smile turned to an *oompf* of protest when said old friend landed a fist in Drake's stomach. He doubled over, the searing pain that exploded through his abdomen making it impossible to so much as shout a plea to stop.

Phillip Camden wasn't given the chance to hit him again anyway — Red flew in from somewhere or another, pushing the idiot back with a shout that seemed nothing but wordless din to Drake's ears.

His knees buckled. The bench was still there behind him, and he collapsed onto it, clutching his side. Though he almost wished for the ground, where he could have curled up in a ball until his vision cleared of the white-hot agony.

After an eternity, Camden's blistering words made it through the ringing in his ears. ". . . didn't *ask* you for your help, you blighted —"

"Don't you go a step closer or I'll —"

"This is between me and —"

"I don't know who you are, you idiot, but when you go around punching a man who was just shot, it becomes *my* business."

Drake drew in a breath, rather experimentally, and slid his hand to his injury. He couldn't detect any fresh blood. The blighter had landed his fist on the side opposite the wound. That was something. Perhaps it would be only pain and not a reopening that would set him back another week or two.

"He probably deserved to get shot if he goes around interfering with everyone else like he did with —"

A solid *whack* drew Drake's attention from the street just in time to see Camden stagger back and Red's fist recoiling from where it had met with the idiot's jaw.

Apparently Drake had a bodyguard. And apparently he needed one.

His next breath still hurt, but not quite as much as the previous. He forced himself to sit up a little bit straighter. Camden wasn't taking a return swing at Red, anyway, just glaring at Drake as if his eyes were flame-throwers.

That told him quite a bit, really. Drake tried to smile, though it felt more like a grimace. "You know, Cam, we civilized people usually greet old chums with a 'hello' rather than a fist."

Camden pushed Red away and dabbed at the corner of his mouth, still staring at Drake. "You ought to have stayed out of it. It's no concern of yours if I rot in prison or am executed."

Had Hall told him Drake was the one who'd suggested he recruit him? That was a bit surprising. But apparently so, as otherwise Camden couldn't possibly have made the connection. "I didn't do it for you." His smile emerged a little surer this time. "I did it for your mother. Don't you remember when I kept you from getting expelled when we were twelve? She sent me biscuits every week for a year."

Camden's laugh could better be termed a breath. But his shoulders sagged, and the flames shooting from his eyes died down to coals. Stepping around Red — who probably would have lunged at him again if Drake hadn't given him a little shake of the head — Camden fell onto the bench beside him. "She'll probably start a campaign for you to be knighted for this."

"Then I'll practice answering to *Sir Drake,* because once your mother sets her mind to a thing, it's all but guaranteed."

There, a hint of a smile. Just a hint of one, in one corner of Camden's mouth. But it sure beat a fist.

Camden sighed and rubbed a hand over his jaw, which was reddening. "You were shot?"

"Only a bit."

"Only a *bit*?" Red, looking just as irritated with Drake now as he was with Camden, stepped forward, glowering. "You nearly died, and you are nowhere near ready to be on your feet out here. What were you thinking coming outside on your own?"

Camden sent Red one of the smirks that had landed him in the headmaster's office at least once a week in their school days. "You know, Elton, you seem to have got cheated on the nursemaid front. She isn't pretty at all."

Red's fingers curled into fists again. "Are you spoiling for another fight, you —"

"Yes. He is." Drake held up a hand to keep Red that crucial step away. "Kindly don't oblige him."

Camden only glanced briefly at Drake, but the glance was directed at his abdomen, which he hadn't yet convinced his hand to release. Camden pursed his lips. "That's not the side I hit, is it?"

Drake forced his spine a little straighter.

"Luckily not or I'd be on the ground instead of a bench."

Camden swallowed. He wouldn't apologize — he never did. But he nodded and said, "I'll owe you one."

And a favor from Phillip Camden was worth more than an apology from any other man anyway. Drake grinned as best he could. "Excellent. I shall be sure to collect at the most inconvenient moment possible."

Camden produced a smile too. A fleeting one, soon gone. "I think your nursemaid would like you to get back inside now, Elton. She looks ready to cluck at any moment."

Red looked ready to take another swing at him, more like.

Drake cleared his throat and hoped Red had the sense not to rise to the bait. He motioned him forward. "Could you give me a hand up, Holmes?" He usually would have tried to regain his feet without help, but if Red was busy supporting him, he wouldn't be able to engage with Camden again.

Red stepped forward without taking his wary gaze off Camden and hooked a hand under Drake's elbow.

Shocking was the fact that Camden hooked one under his other and helped get him back to his feet, somehow managing the act with a look on his face that denied he was doing it to be kind. Camden didn't believe in ever being caught in an act of kindness.

Drake directed his thanks only toward Red, who was muttering something about the apparent dangers of choosing the wrong sorts of friends and leaning down to retrieve the cane Drake must have let fall in the scuffle.

Dropping his hand back to his side, Camden took a step away, smirking again. "Now, now. Don't chide, miss. I'm not *such* a bad friend. I would have paid him a visit days ago had it not taken me this long to pry from his sister where he could be found."

He always knew which buttons to push, didn't he? Drake leaned into Red to keep him still and willed the chap's eyes not to blaze a response, though guile had never been Red's forte. For his own part, Drake kept his smile clear. "Settling in at the OB, are you? How goes the training?"

The smirk faded — proving either that Red hadn't reacted or that Camden was genuinely interested in the subject, one or the other. "Not as riveting as prison, but I suppose it'll do. De Wilde assures me I'm *'not a complete dunce,'* which I believe is the highest of praise."

Drake felt as though another fist had landed in his stomach. "Margot De Wilde?" *She* was the one training him? This man as notorious for charming the females as he was for provoking his chums?

Perhaps Drake should have thought it through a bit more before suggesting Hall bring him on.

But the lift of Camden's brows was absent its usual challenge. "Is that her given name? Everyone in the office just calls her De Wilde, as if she were a man. Frankly, it seems most of them forget that she isn't."

Red shifted. "That makes no sense. How could one forget she's a girl? She's pretty —"

"Pretty can't make up for terrifying." Camden's smirk this time seemed to be, if Drake weren't mistaken, at his own expense. "I tried flirting with her yesterday, and she calmly informed me that if I didn't desist immediately, she had no fewer than one hundred and twenty-three ways to make my life miserable, sixty-five percent of which had been field tested and were without fail."

Drake's lips twitched up too. That sounded about right — though it wasn't how she'd responded to *him,* at least. No threats, just . . . questions. He ought to have known, he supposed, that he needn't worry she'd succumb to Camden's charms. *Charm* didn't seem to be what drew her.

Hopefully he knew what *would* though. He'd had Red drop a few letters in the post for him yesterday — one to Abuelo, and the encoded letter for her. It ought to be delivered to her today. Tomorrow at the latest. And she'd realize it was from him in about two seconds, so he might soon know how she'd respond to it. His throat went tight.

As for Camden . . . Drake cleared his throat and lifted a brow. "And you didn't take her threats as a challenge?"

"I prefer my women with a bit of softness to go along with their pretty faces, thank you." That glint reentered his eyes. "Your sister turned out quite well, Elton. When last I saw her, she was just a scrawny little thing, but I do believe she's one of the loveliest girls in the OB."

Red's fingers went tight around Drake's elbow. Drake kept his smile easy though. "She's spoken for, of course." Or would be, as soon as Red worked up the courage.

Camden chuckled. "You think I'd let that stop me if I were determined?"

A good point. "And she's Margot De Wilde's dearest friend."

"Oh yes, I already worked that one out." He winced. Actually *winced,* which made

Drake all kinds of curious as to what Margot had done or threatened to do to him. Camden clapped a hand to Drake's shoulder and then angled away. "I need to get back to the office. But I'll drop by sometime when your nursemaid isn't here for a proper visit."

"Mm. So long as you leave your fists at home."

Camden's smile looked like it always had — carefree and more than a little mischievous — but his eyes were absent the light that had filled them when they were lads. They sparked, but somehow darkly. "Don't worry, old chap. No more fisticuffs until you're well."

Drake lifted his chin. "Not forgiven yet, am I?"

"My mother might keep you in biscuits for life, but I won't thank you for this. You should have left me to rot."

Red huffed out a breath. "Look at that. Something on which we agree."

With one last glare, Camden strode away. Silence pulsed in his absence for a few moments. Then Red said, "What have you done to your hair? It's all grey."

Drake laughed and turned to the street they must cross. "I was doing some reconnaissance. And have a bit for you to do tomorrow, too, if you will." As they made their way across the largely empty street and through the front door of Dot's building, Drake gave him a bare outline of the suspicious character and how he was in need of a spot of help in following him.

"You know I'm happy to help," Red replied, though the words did nothing to erase the confusion in his tone. He must be wondering why Drake thought he had enemies here in London, why he'd be willing to pay him to help root them out. But Drake couldn't tell him that, so hopefully the speculation would remain unspoken.

He heaved a sigh and looked up as they crossed the threshold of the building and came to the never-ending rise of stairs. "Why couldn't she have found a flat in a building with a lift?"

Red chuckled and gripped his elbow again. "We'll manage it. One step at a time." Then, "Who has spoken for Dot?"

That hadn't taken long. Drake grinned and hooked the handle of his cane over his arm so he could grip the handrail. "No one. But I didn't want *him* getting ideas. Camden's the sort of bloke who would defend a friend to the death — but not one to be trusted with one's sister."

"Ah." Relief saturated the short syllable.

Drake shook his head and took the first step. Then the next. "Though if you're so worried, *you* could speak for her."

Those fingers on his elbow tightened again. "Why would you even suggest that, Elton? I'm no better a prospect for your sister than he is. I've no income, no future—"

"You're a good man in bad circumstances, Red. But circumstances change. Yours will too." One of the queries he'd sent to his father's old friends would surely pan out. Or some other opportunity would arise. Red wouldn't be left like this forever, not when he was willing and able to work.

"Even so. What's the best I can hope for? Manual labor. Hardly something that could support a girl like your sister, who's used to the finer things. Who *deserves* the finer things."

"My sister can get on quite well whatever her lot — and don't you dare sell her short by implying otherwise." Not to mention that Dot was part owner in their shipping company as well. A fact that did neither of them any good at the moment, but it would someday, when the war was over.

Not that it would do anything but make Red feel worse about himself just now. He wasn't looking for a wife with means. He was looking for the means to provide for her himself.

As they made their way to the first landing, silence overtook them — a rather brooding one. Had the discomfort in his side not been increasing with every step and his energy flagging by a proportional degree, he may have smiled at the frown furrowed into his friend's brow.

They were just turning to the next flight of stairs when Red said, "How do you suppose he convinced her to tell him where she lived?"

"If I were to guess . . ." He paused not for effect, but to suck in another breath and grip the railing better. Couldn't Dot and Aunt Millie at least have found a flat on the ground floor? "He asked."

Red's scowl didn't lessen any. "And she simply *told* him where he could find her?"

"Where to find *me*." Blast, but when had these stairs grown as tall as the Matterhorn? "She knows we're old school chums."

"But —"

"Trust me, Red. I know the type of fellow my sister likes, and Phillip Camden isn't it. She's never gone in for the sort who is chasing a different girl every week."

Red didn't look quite convinced, but Drake couldn't spare the breath to offer any more encouragement just now.

Funny though. All the exertion didn't at all distract his mind from winging a few streets away to where he imagined a certain letter being dropped into a certain post box.

Margot obviously didn't care for Camden's type either. But did she care for *his*?

21

"So intriguing." The duchess was leaning back in her chair, her teacup dangling from her hand and her trousered legs crossed in what looked like a pose for an advert in one of the fashion magazines Maman had always liked. "I know it's all still theoretical, but it sounds very revolutionary, doesn't it?"

"Indeed." Margot sipped the last of her own coffee — apparently what the duchess preferred to serve in her dainty little teacups — with a smile. She and Maman hadn't been able to find or afford decent coffee since moving here. The very scent was enough to take her back to Belgium. If she closed her eyes, she could almost imagine that she heard Papa chuckling over his own cup. "Einstein's mathematics are certainly sound. I don't know how one could prove his theories, but they *could* be true. Which is quite amazing."

The duchess hummed and sat forward to

386

slide her cup onto the end table by her chair. "The mathematics themselves are a bit beyond me, I confess. But the ideas . . ." She flashed a smile. "If my grandfather keeps sending me what journals he can find, can I keep passing them along to you? I've so enjoyed getting to talk to someone about something other than this dratted war."

Margot could only blink for a long moment. Surely she'd wake up and find this had been nothing but a dream. Because surely nowhere in this world did a place like this still exist. The beautiful Stafford townhouse, the tea cakes with real sugar in them, the hostess who could converse intelligently about something other than children and clothes and aide meetings. "Of course, Your Grace. I would be delighted."

"Good. And you can call me Brook. After all" — her smile went impish — "apparently I have already proven a terrible influence on you. The ward matron has done nothing but scowl at me ever since you cut your hair. It looks lovely, by the way."

"Oh." Margot lifted a hand, not to touch the waves that she rather thought she'd mastered creating by now, but to motion the compliment away. "It was more for a point than for fashion. I don't much care whether I'm in vogue."

Brook opened her mouth but got out no reply before there came a genuine cacophony from the entryway. Doors opening, closing, the butler's shuffle, and what sounded like a dozen — or perhaps two — enthusiastic little voices calling out, "Maman! Maman! *Tu ne devines jamais ce que on a fait!*"

Instantly the duchess's face lit, and she leaned forward with her arms outstretched for the miniature people who came barreling into the room. Boys, apparently. The larger probably around five, the smaller perhaps three. They were dressed similarly in short trousers and knee socks, the caps that matched their jackets both askew as they hurled themselves into their mother's arms.

"What did you do?" Brook asked in response to her boys' claim that she would never guess. "Grandpapa didn't take you to the sweets shop again, did he?"

"I learned my lesson after you left me with them last time."

Margot turned her head to see a full-sized person following the boys at a more sedate pace. A gentleman, obviously, and presumably either the duchess's father or father-in-law. He wore a small smile that seemed perfectly at home in the corners of his mouth and a jacket with four gleaming black buttons, and he'd taken five steps into the room before he seemed to notice that it held someone other than his grandchildren and their mother. But when he looked over at Margot, it was with a ready smile.

"The zoo!" the bigger of the little ones exclaimed, switching without any seeming thought from French to English.

"How fun!" Over her son's head, Brook said, "Papa, this is Margot De Wilde, about whom I was telling you earlier. Margot, my father, the Earl of Whitby."

"How do you do, my lord?" Margot slid her empty coffee cup onto the table nearest her and held out a hand to shake.

Lord Whitby took it with a sparkle in his eye to match his grin. "Ah, the mathematician! Yes, Brook was telling me how excited she was to find someone with whom to discuss that journal. And your brother is the violinist, I believe?"

"He is, yes."

Apparently that was far too much boring talk for the boys to suffer. The littler one bounced on his toes and tugged on his mother's arm. "Maman, there were *lions*! Roary lions, but they no roared."

Brook chuckled and pulled the smaller one into her lap, holding the larger close with an arm about his middle. "And these are my boys. William is the elder — the Marquess of Abingdon."

"Bing," the boy pronounced with a grin not unlike his mother's.

"And my baby is little Lord Ambrose."

"Just Am," the little one corrected, one finger hooked in his mouth. "Not baby."

"Of course not." Brook took off both their caps, somehow keeping her grin out of her voice. "Did you behave for Grandpapa?"

"What would have been the fun in that?" Lord Whitby made himself comfortable in another of the chairs. "But I kept him from tumbling into that 'roary' lions' den, so I deemed it a successful outing."

Ambrose gave a belly laugh. "Grandpapa say lion eat my hand if I pet him."

Bing smirked. "I told him if it did, he'd have to get one of those false ones that our new factory is making."

"You have a prosthetics factory?" Interesting. Many of the nobility Margot had met over the years seemed to think it beneath them to have a hand in anything related to a trade.

"There is a rather great need. It seemed a good thing to invest our resources in." Whitby arched his brows at his daughter. "Though remind me to speak to you of that later, my dear. We still need to find more management. We may need to run an advert."

Margot sat up straighter. Blinked. Listened. Waited for the numbers to chase her thoughts.

Nothing.

She folded her hands in her lap and drew in a breath. She couldn't not speak just because God was still silent. "May I ask what sort of qualifications you require? I've a friend in search of a position. He is himself just recently back from the war, injured. He wears a prosthetic foot — and has actually altered it rather cleverly."

"Really." Eyes alight, Brook looked to her father. "Have you a card to give her, Papa? Someone with some engineering talent would be just the thing."

"He would indeed." Whitby reached into his pocket and came out with a card, which he rose to hand over. "And we're trying to hire mostly veterans who have been injured. I daresay we would have a position for him somewhere, regardless of his skills. Has he any education?"

"Some, though I'm not sure of specifics." Margot held the card for a moment. It was just a rectangle of card paper, cut at perfect right angles in the typical aspect ratio.

But to Redvers Holmes, it could be the

future. She smiled and tucked the card into her handbag. "Thank you. I'm sure he'll be pleased to know of the opportunity. And now I had better say farewell and get home." It was already dark and no doubt cold, but she still wanted to stop by the park and see if Williams had made another play.

"I'm so glad you could join me." Brook nudged Ambrose back to his feet and stood.

Her father took to his feet, too, with a huff. "Are you in trousers again? Brook Elizabeth —"

"I was riding!" She didn't look repentant. If anything, she looked as mischievous as her sons.

"When? And why didn't you change before your guest arrived?" With a shake of his head that did nothing to disguise the amused glint in his eye, Whitby turned to Margot. "Forgive my daughter. She thinks social conventions are in place solely to be challenged."

"A proclivity I inherited straight from my recluse of a father." Still grinning, Brook came over and clasped Margot's hands. "Come again soon, please. And I'll pass along the next journal."

"Thank you. And thank you for having me." She smiled, squeezed the duchess's hand, and then shook the earl's again too.

And could all but see Maman smiling at her. She'd managed a social engagement with two of England's finest, and not once had her mother's memory had to chastise her. Of course, they'd mostly been talking about mathematics and theoretical physics. But still.

The little ones said a farewell, too, and then Margot was shown out. The Stafford car sat waiting to take her home. She'd tried to turn down the offer, but Brook had insisted that the tube station was too far, at least after dark.

As she settled into the back of the automobile, handbag in her lap, she let her eyes slide closed. At home, she'd find the stack of newspapers still waiting. She'd gathered all she could find from the weeks surrounding Maman's death, but she'd only made it through half of them.

There was nothing there. Not in the ones she'd searched. Granted, that meant nothing, but . . . but it drained her to pore over the newsprint for hour after hour and find nothing. Nothing.

Was it really not there? Or had those numbers gone just as silent as the ones from the Lord?

She drew in a long, slow breath. At work she was fine. Her mind worked more or less as it always had. But at home . . . all she could do was notice how *empty* the flat felt. Her mother wasn't there to chide her for thinking about nothing but work. Every time she went to the kitchenette, there seemed no point in cooking anything just for her.

Maman would have liked Holmes. And Drake. And this unconventional duchess and her father.

I could stand to be alone if I could still hear you, Lord. She directed the silent words upward. But even to her ears, they sounded more accusatory than inviting. Because she shouldn't *be* alone. And yet, she ought to be capable of it. She could be. She *would* be.

Once out of Westminster and back in her own neighborhood, Margot instructed the driver to drop her at the park. As he puttered away again, she hurried over to see if the Go board was set up.

It was. She took a moment to study the play and identify Williams's latest move, smiling at the slip of damp paper anchored to it this time, proving it had been waiting for hours. *Yosu-miru.* A probing move. She answered it with a move that took one of his stones but no doubt revealed to him a bit of her strategy. She'd been making each move with the eye toward *sabaki* — a flexible position that wouldn't easily be attacked.

She looked around, half expecting to see Holmes there simply because she had the card to give to him. But no one lingered in the night, and as the first needles of a cold rain stung her face, she had to grant the wisdom of that. Opening the umbrella she'd long ago learned never to leave home without, she hurried to her building, gathered her post from the box, and jogged up the stairs.

Once inside, she tossed everything into its proper place and flipped through the three envelopes. One was a bill for funeral expenses — she'd check their numbers and then split it with Lukas. But the other two were odd. They were both in the same handwriting, to her, but with no return address. Heart thudding almost painfully, she noted that they each had a number in the place where the sender's direction ought to have gone. 1 and 2.

She opened 1 first. Inside rested a small slip of paper, no bigger than one inch by three. *Les Heures Claires* was written upon it.

Her chest eased. What had she thought? That this was something from whoever had killed her mother? It could be, she supposed. But if so, it was rather odd that he'd reference the book of poetry that Lukas had given her for her birthday. The one that Drake Elton had also been reading.

She ripped open the second envelope and pulled out a folded sheet of paper. When she flattened it and angled it toward the low gaslights, her lips twitched up. Numbers. Whole paragraphs of beautiful numbers.

Rather obvious of him. But . . . clever too. He knew she couldn't turn down a puzzle, apparently. Bypassing that imposing stack of newsprint that wouldn't speak to her no matter how hard she searched for hidden meaning, she turned to her room with its tiny little desk. With its volume of poetry. With its fresh paper and ready pen.

The code was simple, using the poetry book as the key. Like a breath of spring air compared to the work she did at OB 40 every day. And fun because of it. It took her only a few minutes to work it out, flipping back and forth and back again in the book and then writing down the word that corresponded to each three-part number. Page, line, word on the line.

Only once she'd finished did she bother to really read what he'd written her. And even then, it wasn't the words that struck her — they were flattering nonsense, praising her dark eyes and her wit — it was the fact that he'd written them. Like this. That somehow, though he'd barely known her for a few weeks, he knew her so well.

What was she to do with this? With a man who'd apparently decided that yes, he would pursue her? He'd already said if he did so, it wouldn't be casually. This, then, was his declaration. He was courting her.

She pressed her hand against the page as too many thoughts swirled, a jumble of words and impressions and feelings where orderly numbers should have been. He was mixing her up. And for some reason, she liked it even as she hated it.

This wasn't the path she'd set out upon. Get through the war, go to university, conquer academia — that was her future. That was it. She had no intentions of letting a man pursue her when she was only eighteen. There was time enough for such thoughts later. In a decade, perhaps. Or two.

And yet . . . she didn't know who some future man in a decade or two might be, or how well she'd like him. But she knew who Drake Elton was. And she *did* like him.

"No. I'm not doing this." She wouldn't give up her dreams just because a field agent with a broken nose asked her the right questions and sent her puzzles in the post. She wouldn't be the sort of girl she just *wasn't,* concerned with finding a husband and holding his attention. She didn't know how to be that girl.

When I close my eyes, you are there. When I turn my heart to prayer, you are there. The words, penned in French, jumped off the page at her.

She leaned back in her chair, straightening her spine, and stared at the wall. There were a hundred and sixty gaudy orange flowers on this wall, faded to a shade nearly not-glaring. Three hundred and twenty once-green leaves. Twenty-two vertical stripes behind them. Four inches between each row.

When I turn my heart to prayer . . .

She hadn't been able to pray since she lost Maman. Not really. She hadn't really tried. Because before, she'd never *had* to try. God had always been there, waiting, directing. She'd never had to do more than reach out to Him, and there He was. Filling her mind with numbers. With the assurance that He'd set the world in order, and so it wasn't chaotic. There were equations. There were formulas. There were *reasons.*

She didn't know how to reach Him now, when it wasn't easy anymore. She didn't know how to find Him when He wasn't just right there. She didn't know how to know Him when the numbers were silent.

Her eyes dropped back down to the encoded letter. She didn't know how to do this either. She didn't know how to deal with someone who could pinpoint her so easily and yet who envisioned such a different future.

Cold rain hissed at the window. The kitchen sat empty and aroma-less with no supper upon the stove. The newspapers towered on the table, unsolved and uncaring. She should cook something. Or read something. Or try to find a pattern in the ice on the window.

Instead, she took the decoded letter in hand and sprawled on her bed to read it again, brushing away a wave of hair that fell against her cheek in the process. It was nonsense, most of it.

But it was beautiful nonsense nonetheless.

22

The days had been rather mild for November in London, even given the rain. But Drake had nothing but the rain to blame for the absence of the man in the doorway across the street. He hadn't been there since the day Drake had gone down to get a look at him — two days ago.

It was the rain. He hoped. Because if it wasn't the rain, then it was most likely that whoever he was had spotted Drake after all.

Red was due any minute, and Drake had hoped to send him out today to follow the bloke. But with no bloke to follow, what was he to do?

He paced the flat, which he'd been doing as much as he could manage. He had eventually made it up the stairs the other day, but he probably wouldn't have, had Red not been helping him. And that wouldn't do. Not for long. Who knew what he might have to do to evade Jaeger?

The doctor had told him not to push — but then, the doctor had also praised his progress when he *did* push, saying that morning, "See there? The proper amount of rest and your body heals itself."

Ha. He'd given up on rest and had taken to walking whenever he wasn't working. Around the flat, down the corridor outside their door, down a few stairs and then back up. Not many at a time — he wouldn't strand himself and then have to listen to Dot berating him for it. But a few, repeated, was the same as more in the long run.

He slanted a glance at the table. Beside his stacks of newly decoded intelligence that he'd been reading through today, he had another letter he'd ask Red to post, to Margot. He'd sent a new one each day, and she had to be getting them. She'd be coming for dinner tonight. And whether she addressed the subject or not, he'd at least make sure the letter wasn't just sitting there. That would be awkward.

At least if she wanted to pretend she didn't know they were from him. Though she must.

A knock sounded on the door, and Drake was able to get to it in almost normal time. He opened it with a smile for Red, who was positively beaming back.

"I've found a position!"

"Come in." Drake stepped back and motioned his friend in. "That's wonderful news. Where?"

"The prosthetics factory — the one owned by Lord Whitby and his daughter, that Miss De Wilde gave me the card for. I had my interview this morning, and they've offered me a position. A good one. I'll be helping develop new devices, with room to advance. I could be a manager someday, they said, if it all pans out." He sank to a seat with a look of blissful awe on his face. "They even advanced me my first pay. Can you believe it?"

"Of course I can." Grinning, Drake settled on the couch he'd not had to resort to lying on at all yet today. "I told you, Red. Circumstances change. You'll be the perfect man for that job, and kudos to them for realizing it."

And to Margot for having mentioned him to Lord Whitby. And to Red himself for following up on it when other men would have been too proud to chase a lead they hadn't found for themselves.

He only let his gaze slide once to the window, outside of which no man in a grey overcoat was waiting to be followed.

And he wouldn't be followed now, even if

he came back. Not by Red, at least. "When do you begin work?"

"Monday. I can't stay long — I need to find some clothes. The suit De Wilde gave me won't work for business, I suppose. I'll need something appropriate for daytime. Brown, perhaps, or grey. The advance will cover it. They were quite generous."

He'd borrowed a suit from Lukas De Wilde? For Margot's birthday dinner, Drake assumed. Which must have been her doing. And she must have done it subtly, because Dot hadn't said anything, and it was the sort of thing she would have mentioned, solely as praise for her friend.

Praise she deserved. She hadn't even known Red then — but she'd gone out of her way to be kind. To help him.

Did she realize she had such a soft heart under that barricade of mathematics? Or perhaps for her it *was* mathematics. One man in need combined with one man with plenty equaled a fine solution.

"I can't quite believe it." Red scrubbed a hand over his face. "I'd almost begun to think . . . but this changes everything. Everything."

"I'm so glad for you, Red." And more than a little relieved. He still wasn't sure where his friend had been living, or if he managed to purchase any meals aside from the ones he shared with them here. "You're still joining us tonight, aren't you? You certainly should. We can celebrate." They'd all agreed last time that they'd make it a habit — the four of them, sharing a meal of an evening. It would guarantee Red got one, that Margot didn't have to take hers alone, and that Dot and Drake had some extra company to keep from annoying each other.

"I wouldn't miss it. Though I'd better go and do that shopping now. I had to come by straightaway, though, to tell you. Do you need anything while I'm out?"

"Just a letter to post, if you would." He nodded toward it and stood. "And actually, if you're going to be dropping by a haberdasher, I could use a new hat. Fedora, size seven and a quarter."

Red quirked a brow. "Planning another jaunt out of doors, are you?"

Drake smirked back. "Well, I'm not going to be staying inside forever. The goal's to get out and about, after all."

"Were it up to your physician alone, you'd still be in hospital."

"Yes, well. Thank the Lord for Admiral Hall and his powers of persuasion." He sidled over to the money tin and drew out two pound notes. "This ought to be enough,

I'd think. Though if not —"

"If not, then I'll cover it and you can reimburse me later." The words were casual, but Red's tone was elated. "Color?"

"Grey or black. Use your judgment."

"Until this evening, then. Cheerio."

He left with every bit as much enthusiasm as he'd entered, leaving Drake to smile and shake his head at the empty-again flat.

Having had enough of pacing for a while, he settled at the table to finish today's stack of intelligence review before the quiet was interrupted by Dot and Margot bustling in to start the meal.

Something more to make him smile.

He'd found a routine for the work. Reading through each telegram, each diplomatic report, with a pencil always in hand. He'd underline anything that struck him as important, note it on a separate paper, and then mark each paper with a few words at the top to sum them up, in case they needed to be referenced later.

Not exactly like being out in the field, finding the HUMINT to prove or disprove the SIGINT. But he at least knew he was being useful. And it kept him busy, which certainly improved his disposition.

Soon enough the clock struck the hour that was his signal to finish for the day. He gathered all the papers together and slid them into the folder for Dot to take back to the OB tomorrow. He then went and tidied himself a bit, caught between wishing for the wardrobe still in Spain and glad he didn't have the choices to worry over. It wasn't as though Margot were the type to really care about whether his jacket was single- or double-breasted anyway.

Still. He knew he looked sharper in the suits Abuelo had provided than he did in these — the ones he'd left in London for when he visited. At some point he'd have to fetch his uniform from the flat where he'd stored it, but he couldn't exactly get across the city easily just now, and Hall hadn't mentioned it.

He emerged from his room a few minutes later and didn't even have the chance to consider how to fill the time before he heard the key in the lock and laughter outside it. Dot and Margot. His pulse sped accordingly.

She followed his sister through the door, still smiling. And directing it at him. "Hello, Drake."

A smile. That was all. A hello. Simple things. But they felt far from simple, and his speeding pulse went bumpy. "Evening, ladies. May I help with anything?" Now that he could spend a bit of time on his feet, he wouldn't mind helping his sister with meals in general.

But she always waved him away, as she did now. "Just be ready to answer the door when Red arrives. And keep us company, of course. After you put away the work DID sent home for you."

Dot's hands weren't shaking — sometimes they were, if Margot didn't walk home with her to keep her distracted. Sometimes she had to take a few minutes in her room, to take some deep breaths and just be out of the out-there. But tonight she was smiling and seemed at ease. It didn't look like a front.

Though he'd make sure. "Can I at least get anything out for you while you relax for a moment and catch your breath?"

She knew what he was doing, of course, giving her an opening to excuse herself. Hence why her smile was soft. "I'm fine. We slipped out right on time, and I've been looking forward to this."

He took the new packet of work and put it with the completed bundle and then took Dot's coat from her and held out a hand for Margot's. She held his gaze, those dark eyes intent. She apparently understood too. Of course she would. Dot hadn't tried to hide her difficulties from this new friend. She shrugged out of her coat and held it out to him. "Thank you."

"Certainly." The way she held the coat, he couldn't manage a brush of her hands. But if he positioned himself right when she left, he could help her back into it. Maybe let his hands rest for just a second on her shoulders.

Knowing well that his smile probably revealed the nature of his thoughts, if she cared to decipher them, he turned toward the coatrack.

When he turned back, it was with a question on his tongue. "So what frustrated you two today?"

Margot paused mid-reach for a pot, brows lifted. "Do we look frustrated?"

"Not at all." He smiled and leaned against the table edge. "But there's always something."

"The ribbon on my typewriter broke." Dot, never too shocked by anything he asked, pulled the flour canister forward. "And it was brand-new too. What about you, brother of mine?"

"Hm. Well, the neighbor above us kept playing that same phonograph record over and over, at top volume. I was about to tell Alexander that his ragtime band was sacked."

Dot laughed. And looked to Margot. "What about you, Margot?"

She had such an interesting way of moving. Not fluid and graceful like a young lady who had studied the social arts, but rather each move was brisk, efficient. As if she calculated the most effectual order of movements and performed them accordingly as she did the simple tasks of meal preparation. A striking contrast to Dot, who paused in the center of the kitchen area even now and spun in a circle, obviously trying to remember what she'd been about to do next.

Margot set the small saucepan onto the stove. "Well, we added two more telegrams to our unbreakable stack — more and more keep coming in that are encrypted in a code we've yet to break. I'm sure we could crack it if we had time and examples enough, but we don't." She pursed her lips a bit at that last part.

Drake smiled. "Does it bother you to have unbroken codes?"

"It makes me itchy." She wriggled a bit in demonstration, as if she had an itch there between her shoulders, in the most difficult spot for one to reach on one's own back.

A chuckle joined his smile. "Why not do

it on your own, then? In your own time, I mean?"

Margot was already reaching for the sack of potatoes and selecting a few. "I'm not certain we've enough to work with. And besides, DID hasn't given me permission to take them home. I offered, but he insists that a bit of free time is necessary for one's mental health and ought not to be filled with the same sort of work that employs one's days."

That did indeed sound like something Hall would say. He demanded the best from his people, but he was also always cognizant of their need for time away from the office. "At what point does it become critical enough to demand attention during working hours?"

"Soon, I should think." Margot carried her potatoes to the sink. "If the codebook isn't recovered from a U-boat or zeppelin before long, anyway. That's of course the fastest way to solve the problem, if we can get our lads to the wreckage before the Germans."

"Is Hall still offering prizes to anyone who recovers something useful?"

She grinned. Directed at the potatoes, but still. "Much to his superiors' dismay, yes."

"Then I imagine if there's a codebook to

be found, you'll have it." He pushed off the table and joined them in the kitchen. "I can peel those for you."

Dot sighed. "Drake, just go and sit down. It isn't big enough in here for all three of us."

"I'm not going to sit there being useless while there's something I can do." In proof, he nudged his sister out of the way — perhaps with a bit of exaggerated force just to earn her frustrated grunt — and reached for the paring knife.

She grumbled a bit but eventually moved off to pull from the icebox the cut of beef she'd bought yesterday.

Margot fetched a second knife and joined him at the potatoes.

He worked to keep his smile at a minimum. It was nice though, working side by side with her. Even doing something as mundane as peeling potatoes — a task their cook had set him to countless times when he was a boy, always at her elbow trying to beg a biscuit or snack and asking *"too many infernal questions."* When their business was back up and running smoothly, he'd probably be able to hire a cook again. When he married, his wife wouldn't have to prepare their meals herself, unless she wanted to. But this was nice. He wouldn't mind repeat-

411

ing it day in and day out for the next five decades or so.

If this young lady beside him could be convinced to give him a chance. Would she mention the letters tonight? Probably not. But she also wasn't avoiding him, so she must not mind them.

Perhaps *not minding* could become enjoying. And enjoying could become looking forward to. And then if ever he stopped, she'd miss them. Miss him.

"Have you heard from Red yet about his interview?" Dot asked from the other side of the kitchen.

Drake skated his knife down the side of the potato, careful not to waste any of the meat. Cook would always give him a mostly playful cuff if he wasted anything, even in prosperous times. "He stopped by, yes, in quite a jovial mood. I'll let him tell you the details though."

"So then it went well?" She rooted around in the cupboard for something or another. "Oh, I'm so glad!"

"I imagined you would be." Laughter seeped into his tone, he knew. And he didn't exactly try to stop it. "Perhaps now you two will make the courtship official instead of pretending you don't know what I'm teasing you about."

Something hit the back of his head and then fell to the floor. A dish towel, he saw with a chuckle. And noted that the childish response had Margot biting back a grin.

"I wish you'd just *stop* the teasing." But his sister didn't exactly sound put out. "We've only just got reacquainted, and when we knew each other before, there was Nelson."

"Yes. But isn't that in part what creates a bond between you now? That he meant so much to both of you?"

When he glanced over his shoulder, he saw a soft smile on Dot's face. "It is. We can reminisce together . . . and yet somehow, it isn't awkward. We can remember, but his ghost isn't there between us."

His first potato finished, Drake reached for the next. "Where do you see yourself when the war's over? I know Nelson had intended to move to the country. Is that what you want?"

"No. It was never really what I wanted. London is home, you know that." She hummed a bit, no doubt tilting her head in that way she always did when really considering something, though he didn't turn round again to see. "I think I would be happiest somewhere here in this neighborhood I've got to know so well. I don't need a large house like we used to have — to be honest, I quite enjoy taking care of the place and cooking my own meals. Perhaps a bit larger than this one, eventually. If I have children."

"When," he corrected.

"There are no certainties. I know that very well. I'd rather given up the idea of a husband and family — there are too few of our generation left, and I certainly don't intend to go out in search of the ones remaining."

"But now?"

"Well. We'll see, won't we?"

Her smile was audible. Drake sneaked a glance at Margot to see what she thought of the conversation, but she looked intent on her potatoes now. He already knew *she* didn't particularly want a husband and family. But what did she think of Dot's wanting them?

She would look at it academically, he imagined. If it would make Dot happy, then she would consider it the thing Dot ought to pursue. If not, then not. "What about you, Margot? At which university would you most like to teach someday?"

She looked up at him, surprise in her expression. She didn't answer, but just stared.

He lifted a brow. "Why are you so shocked

by the question?"

"Because no one ever credits my goals as viable. Certainly no one ever thinks I'd have a choice in a university." She hesitated, looked about to say something else.

His gaze moved to her eyes, tangled there in hers. She was probing, trying to discern if he really believed in her dreams or if he was only asking to placate her. To make her *think* he did, to win her over, before beginning a campaign for her to be content with the normal role of a wife.

He couldn't blame her for the probing. Frankly, he wasn't quite sure himself where he stood. He'd always imagined himself married to a woman who fit the mold his mother had set forth — to raise their family, to be there when he got home of an evening, to be the pillar of strength behind him while he went out into the world to support them.

There was nothing wrong with that image. His mother had thrived in the role, as Dot would do. But it was what they *wanted.* Not so for Margot.

And he couldn't quite imagine anyone else in that traditional place by his side, not now that he'd met her. He didn't know what marriage to her would look like. Didn't even know if she'd agree to it anytime soon, whether she came to care for him or not. But one thing he grew more certain of with every conversation they had.

She was worth waiting for. Worth seeking hour by hour, day by day, month by month. Year by year. Even if it took him a decade to convince her to be his, it would be worth it. And the wait would only make him appreciate her all the more.

His work in the field had taught him patience. Perseverance. Lessons he'd use now, with her.

For now, it was enough to peel potatoes by her side, if that's all she'd grant him. He smiled and turned back to it, only glancing over at her now and then. "One thing I've learned about you already, Margot De Wilde — you're a formidable force when you've set your mind to a thing. You'll find a place at whatever university you want. So . . . which do you fancy?"

Her posture shifted, her shoulders easing into the relaxed posture that they'd taken on when speaking of her family. Of people or places she loved. "King's College. Several of the cryptographers are from there — I think I'd be a good fit."

And it was in London. Excellent. "You don't mean to go back to Belgium?"

"To visit. But it isn't home anymore. Assuming, of course, that I'm allowed to stay here."

Dot laughed. "I imagine DID can pull a few strings for you, Margot."

"I'm counting on it."

Drake smiled into his spuds. He would count on it too.

23

I love to watch you and try to imagine the thoughts pouring through your mind. Are they ordered and calm or a whirling dervish that would mystify me? I picture them like a whirlwind, each thought a bejeweled raindrop. Beautiful storms of brilliance.

Margot let the words play through her mind again, as they'd been doing all morning when she ought to have been paying attention to the liturgy. Against her will, her eyes tracked Drake where he exchanged a few discreet murmurs with an old friend he'd discovered was in the parish. It was the first he'd made it out of the flat for Mass. He seemed to be reveling in it.

"You seem rather intent on a certain someone." Willa at least whispered the words, though she made no attempt to disguise the amusement in them.

"I haven't the foggiest notion what you mean." Margot snatched her gaze away from

Drake and focused it instead on Zurie, who made a happy noise and then lunged for her. They were making their way to the exit by means of a side aisle, and the going was rather slow.

She caught her niece, dropped a kiss upon her curls, and waited to see if being pre-occupied with thoughts of a man made any urges for a little one of her own spring to life. But she found, as always, that her love for Zurie in particular didn't seem to extend to the thought of babies in general. Was there something the matter with her?

Each thought a bejeweled raindrop.

Hardly, just now. More like a rain puddle, cloudy and grey.

Willa chuckled and looked over at where Drake was moving toward the narthex with his friend. "Right. No notion at all, I'm sure. You do know he asked Lukas's permission to court you, don't you?"

"What?" Her gaze snapped back to Willa from where it had strayed to him again. Something buzzed in her veins, and she wasn't quite sure if it was anger or pleasure. "When was this?"

"Oh, at your birthday dinner." Willa lifted her brows and adjusted Zurie's little ruffled bonnet. "Hasn't he followed up on it? I thought perhaps with all the dinners you'd been eating over there . . ."

"No. I mean, he's attentive, but he's attentive to everyone. His sister and Holmes as well as me." The only thing different in his treatment was the way his eyes lingered. And the letters.

He looked up now and caught her gaze — which had again gone his way, blast it all. Smiled.

Bother. Drat. Blast. Why did he do this to her? It wasn't that she looked at him and went all weak-kneed over his knotted nose or his silver-blue eyes, the way the secretaries said happened when they saw a handsome man. Not that he was unpleasant to look at, but what were good looks, really? Just inherited features from parents, arranged symmetrically.

He praised her beauty in those letters. But no more often than he praised her mind. Her heart.

Was this really how Drake Elton courted a girl?

Half of her mouth returned his smile before she could help it. Which made her all the more frustrated when she turned back to hiss a quiet reply to Willa. "I'm not going to fall in love, so stop smirking at me like that. He's a friend. That's all."

Willa pressed her lips against a laugh that

would earn her a few scalding glares if she let it loose and took her daughter back. They were finally only a few steps from the narthex, where conversation wasn't quite so restricted. "I thought I'd have to wait decades to see you like this. Rather delicious irony that of all the girls to fall in love at a young age, it happens to *you.*"

"It has not!" And wouldn't. Just because she liked him, just because his words, written in code, kept playing through her mind, didn't mean she was *in love.*

"There you are." Lukas edged his way to them once they left the sanctuary, through the crowd of parishioners who seemed none too eager to go out into the cool December air again. "What have you made my sister scowl about this time, mon amour?"

"The fact that she's sweet on Drake Elton and doesn't want to admit it." Grinning like the mischief-maker she was, Willa turned toward the aisle. "We'd better get home, luv. My family's probably already there."

Lukas, of course, was too busy staring at Margot with questions in his brows to follow his wife. "Is she right? You actually like this fellow? I thought him on a fool's errand when he said he meant to win your heart."

"My heart isn't in need of winning, thank you." And she'd prove it if she must. A quick plotting of the most efficient course through the milling masses — bypassing Mrs. Neville, of course — and she was sidestepping her way over to where he stood just outside the doors. She'd simply tell him she wasn't interested in being courted. Perhaps if he heard the words outright, that would be that.

Though she'd said as much the first time he'd flirted with her, hadn't she? And yet here they were, apparently involved in something romantic without her ever once having agreed to it. All she'd done was read the letters. Did that equal agreement? Complicity?

A rotund gentleman shifted into her way, requiring an immediate course correction to avoid plowing into his well-padded back.

Drake would probably be embarrassed if she just went up to him now and said, "We're not courting." Which might help her cause, ultimately.

Though he'd no doubt stop sending the letters then too. Which shouldn't make her pace slacken . . . but it did.

And she didn't want to *hurt* him. Or, to be honest, embarrass him. He'd been nothing but kind to her. And he was a good man. The best sort of man, always watching for a way to help others. He certainly didn't deserve a public dressing-down for the crime of liking her, did he?

She cleared the doors. He'd wandered a bit along the sidewalk with his friend, but he stood now ten paces away, tracking her. As she neared, he turned a bit so he was facing her more than his friend. Waiting for her.

Never had she imagined she'd find herself in this position. Her words to him that first time he'd flirted had been perfectly true — men usually forgot quickly enough that she was female when they realized she was smarter than they were. That she didn't enjoy flirting. That she had no interest in the things a girl was supposed to want.

Why was he different?

His friend said his farewells and moved off as Margot drew nearer. Still, with each step closer, her desire to put him in his place about this courting nonsense dropped by another twelve percent, until it was so low upon reaching him that she couldn't summon the words to her lips.

Instead she asked, "How are you holding up? Tired?"

He smiled, silver eyes sparkling. "I've quite recuperated from the walk here, actually. Though I think my pace on the return trip will have to be rather slow." His head tipped toward hers a bit. "Perhaps you'd walk with me? I'd love to hear your thoughts on Father Foster's homily. When he's visited me as I recuperated, I found him to be a thoughtful man."

"Oh." She couldn't exactly admit that she hadn't been paying that much attention — he'd ask her what had distracted her, and then she'd either have to scramble for a lie or admit that she kept seeing the numbers from his latest letter, arranged like poetry on the page.

12.15.3 67.3.8 112.9.9

She blinked them away and smiled. "Of course." They'd be eating together at Dot's flat anyway. There was no point in refusing to walk with him. Especially since Dot and Holmes were exiting the church now too, her hand in his arm.

Her friend had no qualms about falling in love. No question about what it meant for who she was if she did so. She could simply enjoy it, bask in Holmes's smiles, celebrate his new victories knowing they could become her victories as well. She could encourage him and not feel as if she were compromising her identity in doing so.

Drake picked up her hand and looped it through the crook of his elbow, setting it on his forearm. He wore gloves, and so did she.

But still she was acutely aware of the touch. And not in a way that made her itchy or eager to pull away.

She looked up to meet his gaze. "You set the pace." For the walk, she meant. And yet it sounded like more in her ears.

Perhaps it did to his as well. He gave a low, slow smile and led her along the sidewalk.

They'd barely gone three steps when an olive-clad figure stomped into their path, his scowl as dark as the circles under his eyes. "De Wilde! I thought you'd never come out. It's impossible."

Drake's arms tightened a bit under her fingers. Interesting. She blinked at Camden. "I take it your first night shift didn't go well?"

"How could it? It's impossible. I don't know how in blazes any of you ever manage to find the new variations. I tried every conceivable one and couldn't make sense of it." He flicked his eyes toward Drake, nodded. "Morning, Elton."

Drake gave him a rather pointed look. Probably because he hadn't actually said *in blazes,* though Margot had gotten rather accustomed to filtering the men's talk for herself as she processed their conversations.

Margot motioned him to move out of the

425

path. He could walk with them if he wanted, but they'd be holding up everyone else if he just stood there.

Not that Phillip Camden seemed to mind inconveniencing anyone.

"Are you certain you were using the right telegrams to try to break it?"

He walked backward in front of her rather than falling beside. Presumably so he could keep frowning at her. "There are *wrong* telegrams?"

She sighed. The others with the night shift last night should have briefed him on procedure, though they probably *hadn't* simply to teach him a lesson. "They're not all in the same code, you know. If you're trying to find a variation for 13040 with a message sent in 7500, you're going to get nothing but a headache for your trouble."

"Well, how can you tell —"

"The form. Weather reports, for instance. They always appear the same. And are always in the same code."

He muttered something that didn't have a less offensive interpretation for her to provide for her own mind.

Drake let out an exasperated breath. "Camden! Language."

Camden smirked. "Sorry." He said the same thing, more or less, but in French.

426

He knew very well that she spoke French, too, but Margot interjected before Drake could chide him again. "I think the fellows pulled one over on you, Camden. I told you that you ought to try to get along."

"I'm not interested in making friends." Did he know that pain flashed in his eyes with the proclamation?

Drake certainly wouldn't miss it.

She lifted her brows. "Then you'd best learn how to function among enemies."

He muttered another something that would have made Maman blush.

This time Drake responded with a sigh. "Would you like to join us for dinner, Cam?"

The invitation brought the pilot's feet to a halt, necessitating that Margot and Drake stop too. He glanced over her shoulder, his search halting quickly. Margot turned to find Dot and Holmes strolling not far behind them. "Will your nursemaid be there?"

Margot's brows drew together. "Dot?"

"No, he means Red. Yes, he'll be there. And do stop antagonizing him. I think you'd actually get along if —"

"As I just said. I'm not interested in making friends." He faced them again, his face hard. And then he stepped out of their way.

427

"Thanks for the invitation, but no thanks. The role of fifth wheel has never suited me."

"Cam —"

"I have tomorrow off, though. I could do with a game of chess, if you've the time."

Drake's face shifted from determined to satisfied. "Whenever you'd like. I'll be at home."

Camden spared a nod for Drake, another for her, and then strode off as if he were going somewhere of the utmost importance.

They both watched him go. Margot shook her head. "Has he always been so . . . ?"

"No. Not quite. Always gruff, always a troublemaker, but never with those shadows."

"Has he told you what happened?" Thus far it was an unsolved x in the equation that was Phillip Camden.

Drake shook his head. "Perhaps he will tomorrow. But I doubt it. I don't think he's ready for that. Sharing it with someone would mean letting go of it a little, and he's holding it tight. It may help him just to be with someone he knows won't judge. Won't ask."

A breath of laughter slipped out. "*You?* Won't ask? I rather thought that your specialty."

The way he grinned down at her made

her wonder if the observation somehow equaled encouragement in his mind. That they were growing familiar enough to tease each other, perhaps. "Part of the art of asking a good question is knowing what *not* to ask, you know."

Like *not* asking *her* if he could court her, perhaps? She turned her attention straight ahead. If he'd reasoned it out like that, then it was frankly a tally mark in his favor. "Could we take a turn through the park, if you've energy enough?"

"So eager for a few extra minutes with me?"

Teasing or flirting? Either way, she met it with narrowed eyes but the beginnings of a smile. "Don't flatter yourself. I want to see if Williams is there or has made another play at Go. He hasn't had the board set up for days."

"I have no idea who and what that is."

She explained briefly as they walked — the new face, the game they'd played the day Holmes and Dot were reacquainted, how since then he'd been playing her via notes, the board left out waiting for her. She'd been meaning to come by the park earlier in the day to try to catch *him* and not just his note, but time and short hours of daylight hadn't cooperated.

Drake frowned at the entrance of the park. "And that doesn't strike you as odd? Someone playing a game like that? Why not just sit there and wait for you?"

"Well, the weather's gotten colder, and he doesn't seem quite healthy. Given that I'm rarely there in the warmest part of the day, I suppose he simply sets it up then and comes back to check my move the next day."

"Isn't that a bit careless? Who's to say someone won't just pinch the board?"

"I certainly thought of that." But she could only shrug. "He lives nearby. Perhaps he keeps an eye on it."

They turned in, and his eyes began to scan everything in sight in a way that wasn't exactly casual. "This Williams bloke — what do you know of him?"

She tugged him down the correct path. "What Holmes discovered for me. He was part of the diplomatic retinue to Japan until war broke out. Returned home, joined the navy. Was on a minesweeper that sank in August. Discharged." She decided to leave off the bit about him not being quite mentally stable. Drake looked dubious enough as it was.

She stopped at the wrought-iron table, smiling to see the board there again. No white note fluttered this time, but that was all right. She stepped up and studied the stones' arrangement, withdrawing her hand from Drake's arm so she could fold her arms over her middle while she considered.

Drake only glanced for a second at the game before moving a step away. He stared at a tree a few dozen paces off, his fingers twitching.

And why was she considering *him* instead of her next move? "Is everything all right?"

"I don't know. It doesn't feel right. How do you know this chap can be trusted?"

"Drake. It's just a game, in a public park. What harm could there possibly be?"

He still stared at the tree, as if expecting something other than a squirrel to jump out from behind it. "That's the question, isn't it? And I don't have the answer." He pivoted back to face her, his smile a bit forced but no less warm for it. "Perhaps you could teach *me* how to play. If you'd rather actually finish a game this century."

She made a show of thinking about it, tapping a finger on her arm. "I don't know. It's a complicated game. You might not have the capacity."

As she'd expected, he laughed in outrage — and made a playful lunge for her, which she *hadn't* foreseen. "Are you insulting my intelligence?"

She dodged him, her pulse picking up. Just like it always had when Lukas would chase her. But not. Not at all like that. Biting back a smile, she put the chair between them. "Well, I have no proof of your mental prowess, have I?"

He grinned and sidestepped the chair, trapping her between him and the table. He didn't draw too close, but even so. Even so. "Of course you have. I like you, don't I? What could be a more accurate proof that I'm smart?"

She felt as though she'd just sprinted up a flight of stairs. And had absolutely no idea how to parry that. So she turned to the game board. "I don't have the game. This is the first set I've actually seen in England."

"So teach me on this one. It's out here, isn't it? One doesn't leave a board in public if one minds it being played. I'm sure you could return everything to its current position when we were through."

She could. And the idea of sitting across from him for hours, strategizing and counter-strategizing, was an appealing one. She'd learn much about him through a game of Go. The way he thought, whether he would sacrifice one stone for another.

She touched a finger to a white stone and slid it into her chosen play in *this* game.

"All right. I don't imagine we have time for the lesson today. Dot won't want to wait dinner that long. But perhaps the next time it's set up."

"It's a date."

No, that wasn't what she meant. She opened her mouth to say so, then jumped when his hand brushed against the small of her back. There was no good reason to do so — it was a move that her brother made all the time, as did Hall and Barclay. Completely innocent. Gentlemanly. So why did it feel so new?

He was smiling. Probably because he knew well why she jumped. "Ready, then?"

No. Not nearly. But he was only talking about dinner with his sister. Not dates or romance or anything else. Careful not to meet his gaze lest he see in her eyes what a muddle he'd made of her, she turned back toward the walking path and drew in a long breath. In two beats, out two beats. Count the bricks. Measure the steps. Focus on the mathematics of the walk, not on the man beside her.

Das Gespenst muttered a curse under his breath and kept his back against the tree for a full minute after their voices faded into the sounds of the city. Only then did he dare to peek around the massive trunk.

That had been close. Too close. Curse that man for his instincts — he'd quite obviously been searching the park the moment he stepped foot in it, and Das Gespenst had barely had time to move from his casual lounge on a bench to the cover of the tree.

The man was too observant. And had kept staring right at the tree where he'd hid — obvious from the way his voice traveled.

Good thing he'd been more set on flirting with the girl than with finding *him,* or he'd have had to run. Which would have been disastrous, as it would have brought even more attention.

Coughing into his glove, Das Gespenst emerged slowly from his cover, not trusting them not to turn back into the park at any moment. His chest still ached a bit from the cold that had kept him inside the last few days.

Blasted English damp.

But no one else came into the park, leaving him free to approach the Go board. Would she really teach him to play? On *his* board?

His fingers curled into his palm in protest. No. That wouldn't do. Then they'd both be hovering around here, and he'd have to find a new place to blend into the shadows.

Blighted man would no doubt spot him otherwise.

Well then. A slight change of plans, that was all. He pulled out the small velvet bags that held the stones and swept the white and black pieces into their respective pouches. His game with Margot De Wilde would just have to be paused for a while.

But that was all right. He'd already learned all he needed to know from her play anyway. The next step would have to be a little more . . . involved.

24

What if they were right?

Margot sat at the table in her empty flat, staring at the stack of newspapers but unable to make herself pick up another one. Never in her life had she let other people's doubts stop her from doing what she knew was right.

But she didn't *know* this time. There had been no whisper of beautiful proofs in her head. No nudging of the Pythagorean theorem telling her to follow, to walk, to do. To search newspapers for answers. To find an assassin.

She'd been clinging to her belief that it couldn't be coincidence. But then yesterday Drake had responded to one of his sister's jokes with, *"You're asking the wrong question, Dot."*

And the words had stuck fast in her mind. He hadn't said those exact words to her, but it was what he'd been getting at that evening at her birthday dinner, wasn't it? That she shouldn't have been asking why God hadn't sent her to help — that perhaps she couldn't have. Perhaps there was a different way she ought to be looking at it.

You're asking the wrong question. She tapped her pen against the table and let her eyes drift to the letter that had been waiting for her when she got home, as usual. Quite a stack of them had grown on her desk in the last few weeks, as November had marched into December. Each one somehow made her feel as though she knew Drake a little better. Understood the workings of his mind a bit more. He never wrote questions in them — those he seemed to save for their thrice-weekly meals together. They were filled instead with his insights. What he'd learned from each thing he asked her.

She pulled forward the stack and flipped through a few. Frowned. They were out of order. Why were they out of order?

She certainly had no one to blame for it other than herself — she must have been careless last night after she'd reread them. Not her usual state . . . but then, he muddled her. Made her think of a future she hadn't before. Entertain ideas she'd always dismissed.

He knew how to ask the right questions. And with each day that went by, she admired that more. It wasn't an easy thing, wasn't really a *natural* thing.

It wasn't a thing she was so sure she was good at. A few months ago, she would have claimed the opposite. Because a few months ago, God still spoke to her whenever she asked Him for direction.

With a huff, she pushed up from her chair. After dousing the gaslights, she strode to the window and pulled back the blackout curtains. Winter darkness, virtually untouched by the few dim streetlights here and there, stared back. She rested her forehead against the cold glass pane.

It *seemed* like the cold radiated into her flesh. But was it that, or was it the heat transferring *out* of her skin?

Was it Margot's predisposition to see numbers in the chaos that had led to Maman's death? Or Maman's death that had made Margot see an order where there was none?

What if it was random? A heart attack?

But what if it wasn't, and she gave up the search, and the killer struck again?

Groaning, she pushed her forehead off the window and rubbed at the cold spot on her head. She didn't know what questions were right, what answers were worth pursuing.

She just knew that the evening stretched out long and endless before her, and she didn't want to spend it alone with her newspapers.

The duchess had sent round another journal. She could read that. Once upon a time, a free evening plus a new scientific journal equaled guaranteed happiness.

But that was when Maman would be there on the couch, knitting. Somehow having that company, even when silent, made a difference.

She glanced at the clock. It was only six. Early yet. She could go and spend the evening with Lukas and Willa and Zurie.

No. It was Tuesday. They were in Poplar, eating with Willa's family at Pauly's Pub.

She could take the tube to join them, but by the time she got there, it would be seven. They'd be finishing up, preparing for the hour's ride home to get Zurie into bed.

Her gaze found the letter. Forcing her to admit that she didn't really want to visit her brother tonight anyway. She wanted to see Dot.

All right, she wanted to see Drake. Maybe he knew what questions to ask.

Dot wouldn't mind if she dropped by. Nor would Drake, she was sure. If anything, he'd give her one of those smiles. The kind that

439

said she'd surprised him, and he liked it.

Before she could reason herself out of it, she grabbed her coat, hat, handbag, and keys and left.

The parallel lines of the hallway led to the parallel lines of the banister, which led to the parallel lines of the doorway, and then the curbs on the street. Never intersecting — barring calamity that brought it all crashing down.

She'd thought that's what she wanted — to track a course parallel to everyone else. Always close, but always separate. Never intersecting.

But even parallel lines intersected in infinity — that was the non-Euclidean theory that allowed for revolutionary thoughts like the ones Professor Einstein proposed. Irrelevant to everyday life here on earth. But crucial in understanding the heavens.

Did she want to be confined to the earthly, then . . . or set her sights on the heavenly again?

She paused at the first corner, less to check for the traffic that wouldn't be there after dark than to let *that* question whisper through her soul. It almost, nearly felt like the demand of an equation. *Solve for x.* Find the thing that was missing. Put it back.

A horn honked somewhere in the distance,

and she hurried across the intersection. Habit had her turning into the park when she reached it. The Go board hadn't been there since that day after Mass two Sundays ago. But she checked every day. It seemed odd that Williams hadn't been out in so long . . . odd enough that on Sunday Margot had asked Holmes to give her the direction for the building he'd trailed him to. She'd written him a note, just asking after his health and if there was anything she could do for him. Saying she missed their game.

Her feet came to a halt at the little wrought-iron table. The game board was there again, with a fluttering slip of white paper. She reached for it with relief.

More writing marched across the small page in neat, parallel lines longer than normal. Not just the words of play. An actual note, the likes of which he hadn't left since that first one.

Thank you so much for your concern, Miss De Wilde. It means the world to me. I have been under the weather — pneumonia, I fear. But I have missed our game too. I will make more of an effort to continue it. Your prayers would be appreciated. JW

She'd been right to be concerned, then. Sitting on the cold chair, she made the move in the game that she'd already had planned and then fished about in her handbag for something to write with. Flipped the note over and used her handbag, lumpy as it was, for a table.

You have my prayers.

She paused a moment, pen still hovering over the period. Habit made her say it — never had she turned down a request for prayers. But then, no one had really made such a request since Maman died.

She wouldn't let the note be a lie. She wouldn't.

Squeezing her eyes shut, she gripped the icy edge of the table and drew in a long breath. It shook. *Eternal Father . . .*

Her fingers bit harder, until she felt the many layers of paint dent under her nails.

Eternal Father. Please put your hand on Mr. Williams. Clear his lungs of any pneumonia. Touch him, Lord, and make him well. Eighteen, thirty-six, fifty-four . . .

She sucked in another breath. That wasn't so bad.

Eighteen.

Her eyes flew open again. It wasn't the

Lord. She didn't think so. It wasn't that resonating voice deep within, just the memory of it. An echo.

An accusation.

She knew now who Eighteen was. And like a roulette wheel spinning, she watched numbers cartwheel through her mind. Only they weren't just numbers. They were dates.

Breath catching again, she stood and darted off. Back to the street and down it, toward Dot's building. Through the doors, up the stairs, to the door that had become nearly as familiar as her own. She knocked and forced her respiration to even out again.

After ten eternal seconds, the door opened, and Drake stood silhouetted against the lamplight. Smiling. As if she deserved his smile. "Margot. Dot and Red went out to see a moving picture —"

"Good." She didn't need her friend to hear this anyway. To blame her. Not yet. She pushed her way in and then spun a step from the door to face him. To face the truth. "It's my fault you were shot."

Drake closed the door slowly, silently, and turned to her without a twitch in his countenance to betray anything but pleasure to see her. "No, it's not."

"Of course it is." Didn't he see? She closed her eyes, and it was there, right there.

Glaring at her. "The date. The date you were shot. The seventh of November, right?" Seven plus eleven. Eighteen. Always eighteen.

"Yes." He drew the word into three syllables. *Three times six. Eighteen.*

Her hands shook. "The same day Maman died. When He *wasn't* asking me to pray for her. He wasn't telling me to go home. He was telling me to pray for *you.*"

Warm strength enveloped the shaking. His hands clasping hers. She'd forgotten her gloves, apparently. "I know. You told me."

"But I didn't. I didn't tell you that I *didn't.*" She forced her eyes open again, forced herself to look up at him. "I wouldn't. I was so angry. She was gone, and all I could hear was *Eighteen.* I told Him no. I refused to pray. The very day — probably the very *minute* you were shot."

His thumb stroked over her hand. "Good."

"What?" He was supposed to be cross. Cross would make sense. *Good* certainly didn't. "How could you —"

"I'm glad it happened the way it did. That I got sent home to recuperate. That I'm here now. With you."

He was an idiot. But it didn't make her itchy. It made her weak. Liquid. Blurring her eyes. She shook her head. "No. You could have been killed. I should have —"

"Margot." He moved closer, tightening his grip on her hands. "I *wasn't*. Focus on that."

"But —"

"Are you the only one in the world with faith enough to pray for someone when you don't know why?"

Faith enough. She'd had it, then. She thought. But had she, if she'd let it go so easily? Turned her back on him? On Him? "I certainly hope not."

"Do you know for a fact that no one else was asked to pray when you said no? If perhaps someone else's prayers kept that bullet from hitting anything vital?" One of his hands dropped her fingers. Touched her cheek instead. "God was in it. I know He was. He didn't abandon me."

"But I shouldn't have either. It should have been me."

"Mi alma." His lips pressed to her forehead and lingered there, warm and sweet. "I love knowing that it was *ever* you. That our Lord wove that bond between us. It doesn't matter if it wasn't you that one time."

"But it *does*. Of course it does."

"It doesn't." His hand was so warm against her winter-chilled cheek. His face was so calm behind the mask of her tears. "Do you know what matters? That you *wish* it had been you."

He shouldn't be so kind about it. Not about this, when he could have been killed because of her stubbornness. Her anger. And she hadn't even regretted it, not until just now, when she realized the dates had been the same. She hadn't regretted it — she'd resented it. Her fingers went tight around his. "I'm sorry though. So sorry." To think of the pain he was still clawing his way out of. How devastated Dot would have been if she'd lost him.

How empty *her* life would be right now if he weren't in it.

"Margot." His voice was just a whisper, bare and raw. "I'm going to kiss you now."

It should have made her start. Jump away. List a few of the threats she tossed so easily at other men if ever they made the mistake of getting too close. But it didn't. It just made her suck in a breath. "Why?"

His lips, a mere two inches from hers, smiled. "Because I don't recall ever wanting to do anything more. Do you mind?"

"I don't know." She should. A kiss would lead to a different kind of courtship, wouldn't it? One that was more than letters and codes and dinners with his sister. And she didn't want a different kind of courtship. She liked this one. That wasn't one.

Except that it was. She'd always known it was.

His fingers moved on her cheek in an unfathomably soft caress. "I won't, if you don't want me to."

"I don't not want you to. I just don't know if I *do* want you to." She wasn't supposed to be like this. Befuddled and swamped by *feeling.*

He eased another inch closer. "How about an experiment, then?" His fingers released hers, but they didn't move far. Just to her wrist. "Scientific. Mathematical. We'll examine the increase of your pulse. The change in respiration. Dilation of your pupils. To determine if you want me to. What percent of change do you think equals a *yes*?"

How could he make her laugh even now? It should have changed the numbers, that laugh. Added in another element that threw off the equation. But somehow all it seemed to do was draw her closer to him. Perhaps it worked as a coefficient of the want, simply increasing the end desire rather than offsetting it.

Apparently it was her *yes.* Because in the next second his lips skimmed hers, and she didn't want to pull away. She wanted to count the seconds of that first touch, how long her breath stayed balled up in her chest, determine the angle when he tilted his head and try to determine why it made the sensation that much *more.* She wanted to measure it all out and yet wasn't sure if it was a second or a minute, whether she was tumbling or flying, leaning in or pulling away.

In. Definitely leaning in, because his arms slid around her. Hers slid around him. And it felt odd, because she'd never held a man like this. And yet it didn't, because there was none of the unease she usually felt with a casual touch. Perhaps because it wasn't casual. It was purposeful. Every contact — hand to back, arm to shoulder, lips to lips — meant something. And they all added up to one very clear conclusion.

Willa was right.

Blast. Now she pulled away, shaking her head as she backed toward the door. "No. I don't want things to change. I like it how it is — how it was. Just . . . pretend that didn't happen."

He looked *amused,* drat it. "Impossible."

"No it isn't! We'll just . . . erase it. Cancel it out with an opposite. Rebalance the equation." She waved a hand, as if the past minutes were a chalkboard she could erase with the gesture.

And now he was smiling, while she gestured like an idiot. "I don't want to cancel it out."

Her hands were shaking again as she reached for the door latch. "Well, I do."

"What are you afraid of, Margot?"

Change. Being alone. Losing him. It would hurt all the worse if she let herself give in to this. She shook her head and pulled open the door. "I'm just your friend. Your sister's friend."

"I love you."

He said it so easily. Calmly. Confidently.

Her panic was in proportion — an exponential one. "No. You don't. You can't. *I* don't. Just . . ." But she didn't know what she meant for him to do. She just knew she couldn't do this. Because she'd lost her father, she'd lost her home, she'd lost her country, she'd lost her mother. She couldn't lose anything else, but it always happened. Inevitably. And she didn't have positives enough to offset all those negatives anymore. She'd run out, run dry, run empty. *Run away.*

"Margot!"

She nearly tripped on the threshold, but running was her only option. So she'd take it.

25

"Margot!" Drake picked up the handbag she'd dropped as she'd groped for the doorknob and ran after her. He wasn't as fast as he used to be. His side objected, but not loudly enough to stop him. He couldn't let her leave like that. She could try to disappear from his life.

Worse, she could fall headlong into the fear he'd seen flashing through her dark eyes like lightning. Let herself believe the only way to outpace it was to deny even possessing what it threatened to take away.

He reached the door to the building just as it was clicking shut from her exit and swept out onto the sidewalk in time to see her plow into someone on the corner.

It didn't slow her down for long.

But it slowed Drake. Because it wasn't just *someone.* It was someone in a grey overcoat, with longish dark hair, a trim beard, and an inquisitive slant to his brows. Someone who, upon spotting *him,* took off at a run on the street perpendicular to this one.

Drake sped to the corner, glancing first straight ahead toward Margot's retreating back and then down the intersecting street, where the man's grey coat flapped behind him.

If he'd still doubted that the man had something to do with Jaeger, that made it certain. If he were just an innocent neighbor, he wouldn't run from him like that. And why did he now? He must have spotted Drake that day he'd come down and known he would recognize him. He must have.

He could follow now. He wasn't at his fastest, but the man didn't seem to be moving at that impressive a clip either. He might be able to catch up.

And then what? Tackle him? Smack him with Margot's handbag? The man must know he was injured. And a well-placed brolly to the side could undo all the weeks of healing.

Moreover, he didn't matter. Not compared to Margot.

The debate had only taken a second. And he didn't regret his decision for a moment as he ran after her. He only hoped that no Good Samaritan would think he was chasing her for cruel reasons and would decide to intervene. Though he could always claim he'd seen her drop her handbag and was just trying to return it.

He didn't call out again — the less attention the better — and she still didn't look over her shoulder. Maybe she thought he wouldn't follow. Or didn't *really* mind that he did. Either way, her pace slowed as she made the turn that would take her home, and he closed the distance between them.

Which was a good thing, or he might have lost her when she made the unexpected detour into the little park they'd walked in after Mass for the last few Sundays.

"Margot." He dared to call to her again only once he'd entered the park, too, and followed the winding brick path to where the table and chairs were set up by the bench. She was there, of course, collapsed onto one of the hard chairs by the table with the Go board. Gasping for breath. Or crying. Or perhaps both. "Mi alma?"

She shook her head, shoulders heaving. "Don't call me that. I'm not your soul."

She knew the phrase? Always surprising him, this one. He eased down beside her chair and slid her handbag into her hands. "Why does it scare you so?"

Her hair was a ruin under her hat, those

carefully measured waves flying every which way — and looking all the more charming for their disarray. He gave in to the urge to smooth them down and was rewarded by her meeting his gaze.

"I'm not scared."

Part of him wanted to smirk, to call her on the obvious lie — point out, perhaps, that she didn't deliver it with her usual mathematical precision. But what would that achieve? Instead he took a moment to think. To try to see down to the depths of her heart through those depthless eyes. "Sometimes running away does speak to courage instead of fear. To wisdom. Sometimes running away is necessary. Though I certainly hope not in this case."

She gasped again and dashed a sleeve across her eyes with the look of someone who detested the tears she wiped away. "I don't *know.*"

There was meaning there beyond the words. "What don't you know?"

"What to do. What's right. What's wise. I don't know whether to turn this way or that, whether to go or stay, whether to . . . to kiss you or to run away."

"Do I get a vote?"

She sent him an exasperated look. But it eased her. Just a bit. "Drake."

He caught her fingers in his. "You don't *have* to know."

"Don't I?" She shook her head. "You want to change things. But I don't know what changes are good and what are bad right now. I can't . . . I can't tell the right way to go."

"Then don't go anywhere." He gave her fingers a squeeze and her eyes a small smile. "I'm not changing anything, mi alma. All I did was say the words I'd already been thinking. Kiss you like I'd been dreaming of doing. It was already there. Latent energy or whatever it's called. Already factored into the equation."

She almost, maybe smiled. Then turned her face away. "But it's not just you. I'm not certain about anything anymore. He's gone silent."

"Who has? The Lord?"

She nodded, sniffed. But didn't look at him again. "I could always hear Him. Ever since I was a child."

He shifted a bit, settled in. "Like when He asked you to pray for me?"

She lifted a shoulder, tilted her head. "Like that, but not just that. Numbers would appear. Directing me. Beautiful proofs for encouragement, unsolvable equations to dissuade. But He's gone silent."

"Has He?"

Her gaze dropped to their hands. "Or I've gone deaf. Either way, it's . . . too quiet. Lonely. How am I to know what to do? Whether I'm making a wreck of everything?"

He let the night wrap its arms around them for a minute, content to study her in the moonlight. It was cold, and he'd not grabbed his coat as he chased her from the flat. But he could warm up later. "The way the rest of us do, I suppose. You choose what seems best and trust."

"But that's *stupid.*" Now she looked at him, eyes ablaze. "Life isn't just guesswork."

"And faith isn't just feeling. We have to *know* He's still there, unchanged, even when we can't feel Him. When the grief's too loud to let us hear His voice."

Her scowl was fierce and quick. "It was never *feeling.*"

"Of course it was." He countered her scowl with a grin. "It's just that you feel in numbers."

"I . . ." She halted, pursed her lips.

Which of course made him want to kiss her again, but he didn't need a lightning bolt from heaven to tell that now wasn't the time. So he settled for a chuckle. "Are you going to argue with me?"

Her answer was a sigh that had her gaze sinking again.

"Margot." He lifted her hand and chafed her fingers between his equally cold ones. "God understands how you're feeling — that you're mourning, that you're angry, that you can't accept the way this has happened. But He's still there. His hand is still sheltering you. He'll wait for you."

Serious eyes looked up again. Accepting. Challenging. "*He* will. I know." *But what about you?*

She might as well have shouted the question, it came through so clearly. Because it wasn't just that her dreams hadn't accounted for this. It was that her heart was still broken from the loss of her mother.

Drake lifted her fingers a few inches more and pressed a kiss to her ink-stained fingertips. "As long as it takes, mi alma. I'll wait on you."

She didn't believe him. He read it in the pull of her fingers and the flicker of her eyes. "You're not a man who can sit and do nothing, Drake."

"Who said waiting was inactive?" He stood. And held out the hand she'd just pulled her fingers free of.

He'd chosen his words carefully, so that he'd remember his own intentions. He wasn't waiting *for* her. He was waiting *on* her. That kind of waiting wasn't impatient, didn't sit there tapping its foot. That kind of waiting was service. Selfless. Unflagging.

She sat still for a long moment, searching his eyes. Probably trying to find the tell of a lie or guess at how patient he really meant to be. Then, with a deep breath and a slow move, she put her fingers in his.

With every gasping, painful breath Das Gespenst cursed this wretched island. The coughing fit finally subsided, but still the chill wracked him. And yet perspiration trickled down his back from the unexpected dash down the street. Hot and cold. Feverish, probably.

It had slowed him. He knew it had. He was lucky Elton had decided to chase Margot De Wilde instead of him, or this night would have ended far differently. He wouldn't be hunkered in some random alleyway trying to quell a coughing fit. He'd have been caught, forced to draw his thirsty dagger without a careful plan — dangerous in itself. And then they just would have had to see whose weakened state inhibited him the least. Elton, with his bullet wound. Das Gespenst, with what he had to think was pneumonia.

After he'd managed to breathe without a new coughing fit for a few minutes, he pushed himself off the cold stones and stepped out on the street to get his bearings. He'd grown fairly well acquainted with the whole neighborhood that the Eltons and De Wildes both claimed as home. It took him only a few glances to realize that he'd ended up not far from the entrance to the park opposite the one the girl favored.

His chest ached as he walked, begging him to turn toward his flat instead of the Go board. But he didn't want to leave it out all night. And he wasn't altogether certain he'd be able to drag himself down here again tomorrow. He'd barely managed to convince himself to search her flat while she spent the previous night at the Old Building.

What he'd found had been interesting. What sort of secretary played at codebreaking? It was rudimentary, the code Elton wrote to her in, but still. His instincts must have been right — she must work near codes. She would be his way in, as soon as he had strength enough.

He approached the park carefully, moving from one tree's shadow to the next until he could be certain they weren't here. The wrought-iron table beckoned him forward. She couldn't have been in any state to make

458

a move, not given how upset she'd been when she flew so unexpectedly out of the Eltons' building — she had never been there for less than an hour before.

But she *had* made a play. And a clever one at that. He nodded his approval and made a note of what she'd done before reaching for the slip of paper anchored under the board.

Heinrich would have loved this touch — the perfect irony to the ghost story, when the liar told the truth. Confessing his weakness knowing she wouldn't know whose weakness it was or believe it if she did know. Using it to his own advantage.

She'd written something on the back. He flipped it over. Paused.

She was praying for him. He'd asked for it simply because it seemed the thing to say — not because he expected her to respond to that. *Get well* was more what he'd thought she'd say.

His breath still burned when he drew it into his lungs. His muscles still ached. Maybe she wasn't really going to do it. And it surely wouldn't matter if she did. There may well be a God up in heaven, but if so, He surely didn't concern Himself with a ghost roaming the earth. If He'd favored anyone, it was Heinrich. And look how that had ended.

Even so. It meant something that she would pray for him. Meant something about her. He folded the paper into a precise square and slid it into his pocket.

His gaze traveled through the darkness to where the Old Building stood out of sight, proud and stiff. He'd known from the start that Margot DeWilde wasn't his enemy. But she was proving herself the best sort of opponent.

The kind he could admire.

He gathered the stones yet again, slipped their pouches into his pockets, and tucked the board under his arm.

He wouldn't hurt her, if it could be helped. Not directly. Despite the company she'd been keeping — what a strangely small world was this sphere of intelligence — she was a worthy opponent. He would respect that. He would do what he must to get into the Old Building or get her to go in on his behalf, but Der Vampir wouldn't taste her life's blood.

Heinrich wasn't the only one with a streak of honor after all.

26

Margot's lips twitched up at the string of curses echoing down the corridor — colorful enough to make her glance over at Camden, who wasn't paying any mind to the diatribe underway. She could only imagine how Drake would chide the men out there if he heard them. There were ladies in earshot, after all.

But the reason for the cursing was far more interesting to her than the words themselves. She pushed away from her desk and peeked into the corridor.

"What is the point of it all if they don't listen?" Commander James stood in his office door, facing both Hall and Knox.

"There are at least fifty-five a month! Fifty-five U-boats slipping through those blasted antisubmarine nets, and the Admiralty is doing *nothing*!" Knox hadn't said *blasted*, of course.

"Because the vice-admiral won't believe

it." Hall bit off a choice word of his own. "Jellicoe has to take a stand and make a point of it. Force their hand, prove us right. Turn a few floodlights on, I think. That's all it will take to force the U-boats to dive into the nets instead of skimming over them as they've been doing."

Margot turned back into the room. She'd decrypted countless telegrams about this over the last few weeks — messages from one German U-boat to another, giving advice on how to avoid the explosive nets — but there were still those high up in the Admiralty's chain of command who couldn't be convinced that their intelligence was worthwhile. Hall's eternal headache.

"What's going on out there?" Camden had finally looked up from his work. He'd only just been moved out of the storage room, now that the others had gotten used to his insults. Or learned to ignore them, anyway. More or less.

Margot took her seat again. They'd take their lunch break in a few more minutes, but she had time to finish her current decrypt first. "They're yelling."

Camden gave her the same look Lukas always did when she answered the question he'd asked rather than the one he'd meant. "Brilliant. About *what*?"

"The usual. A vice admiral failing to heed the warnings we send them. This time about the U-boats still bypassing the nets." She picked up her pencil.

"What's the blasted point of all this if people are just going to ignore it?" He, of course, didn't say *blasted* either.

Margot rolled her eyes. "The question of the hour, it seems. You ought to step into the corridor and share your very new outrage on the subject that no one else has ever once expressed before."

Camden grunted. But he also smiled. "You're a sarcastic little thing, did you know that?"

"I was unaware."

"There you go again."

"It wasn't going again. I hadn't stopped."

He snorted a laugh. He must have finished whatever he'd been working on since he stood, stretched, and meandered over to the window. And given that he didn't make a point of bumping into anyone's chair, he must have been rather pleased with how that one had gone.

She turned back to her own, ignoring the continued debate in the corridor and the mutters from Culbreth and Adcock about a line that was giving one of them trouble. The words in front of her took her six weeks

463

back in time. *Wolfram. Erri Barro.* It only took her a few more minutes to finish up.

Which was good, since Camden said from the window, "Elton and his nursemaid are coming this way. I take it we're having another cozy lunch for four?"

"Unless you've decided to be our spare wheel today." She offered a cheeky grin, knowing well he wouldn't even consent to being in the same room as Holmes, though she still wasn't certain why. She'd asked, but he'd only made a snide comment about some people having no sense of humor.

Holmes couldn't always manage to get away from the factory for a lunch hour, but when he did, he'd taken to swinging by the flat for Drake on his way to meet Dot.

She'd be glowing afterward. And Margot didn't exactly mind the company either, but she could be fairly certain her face didn't shine over it — if so, the chaps would never let her live it down.

Margot pulled her lunch sack from under her desk and looked over to the station by the door, occupied now by a thirty-year-old secretary who'd been with them for two years. Margot pressed her lips together. Six weeks wasn't enough to obliterate a habit of three years, apparently. Maybe eventually she'd stop looking for Maman there. Maybe eventually the ache would subside at least a little. Maybe eventually she'd be able to accept that all her theories, all her leads, all her mathematics had led her nowhere in the question of what really happened.

She ought to be glad there was no evidence that anthrax had been smuggled into the country. It meant no one else was in danger of being infected with it.

As long as it didn't instead mean that they'd just missed something.

"Ask the nurse what I ought to do about —"

"Shut up, Camden." She fell in behind Culbreth, who was making his way to the corridor with his lunch. Camden's chuckle followed them out.

Culbreth sent her a look over his shoulder. "You're a brave soul, talking to him like that."

"He isn't so bad. He just does a good job of hiding that fact." She wasn't quite sure who he was behind the wall of pain that stood behind the towers of rudeness, but she knew that once a week he went to play chess with Drake during his lunch. And he came back quieter and less surly. Evidence that, under it all, he appreciated his friend.

"Miss De Wilde, your lieutenant is here." One of the secretaries strode by with a grin, her arms full of files she must have been bringing up from a lower level.

"He isn't *my* . . ." She cut herself off with a huff when the young woman laughed and passed her. The other girls never listened when she insisted they weren't a couple.

And they had a point, if she were being honest. How long could she really maintain that one plus one just equaled one plus one and not grant that it was two?

But he'd been true to his word this past week, since the night he'd kissed her. Nothing had overtly changed. He hadn't kissed her again, didn't hold her hand, never made mention of that L-word again. His encoded letters continued to arrive day after day.

But the irony of that didn't escape her either. This *was* his love for her. Respecting her needs. Letting her work through the fears she'd tried to deny were fears.

I dream of a thousand tomorrows, he'd written to her in last night's letter. *Each one a jewel to be cherished at your side.*

She paused at Dot's door and glanced in to catch her friend's eye.

"Coming," Dot sang out with a smile, her fingers not slowing on the typewriter keys. "Did Drake and Red make it today?"

"They did. Though they've not come up yet."

Dot hit one last key with a flourish and then whipped the paper from the machine and tucked it into a basket. A moment later she'd grabbed her food and coat, too, and they continued down the hallway and to the stairs. Drake never took the lift up — he still seemed to think he had to use every possible moment to stretch himself, exercise, and strengthen.

And there he was on the stairs, talking to Montgomery, their Fighting Padre. Laughing with him. Margot's feet slowed. Holmes caught sight of them and hurried to greet Dot, but Margot hung back so that Drake could finish his conversation.

How did he do it so easily? She leaned against the railing and let herself study him. The line of his spine, of his shoulders, the way he always kept his focus on the person with whom he was speaking. The smile that bade the other smile back. The questions that inevitably drew the truth out of them.

He'd taken to wearing his naval uniform again, making him look like he had the day he'd first stepped into her path and asked her if she had a name. *"He cuts a fine figure,"* one of the secretaries had said with an appreciative grin just the other day.

He'll soon be going. That was what the uniform said to Margot. He was well again, sooner than the doctors had expected. Healed. They'd already granted him medical leave until after Christmas, but that was only six days away. He'd be sent back into the field after that. Back to Bilbao. Maybe even in time to help with the capture of the wolfram on the *Erri Barro,* if there were more delays — which seemed likely. He'd be leaving her.

And she'd miss him.

How does she do it? Drake had slipped just inside Room 40 while he waited for Hall, so that he could watch her while she worked. He'd done it before, whenever he could. And smiled to realize she didn't even notice.

She always sat at her desk just like she did now, so intent upon the papers before her that the rest of the world might as well not exist. Pencil flying, columns of numbers queuing up and marching down the page in parallel lines. It took her seconds to render code into plain script. Seconds. No doubt she worked through his letters just as fast, or faster — heaven knew his code wasn't as sophisticated as the ones she rattled off the names for so easily. 7500, 13040, 18470, 89734.

Her mind amazed him. The way she processed the world, turned it all into theorems and equations and endless strings of numbers. Dot was right — she had to be the most intelligent person he'd ever met. She outdid him by far. Held her own here among England's brightest. Would no doubt achieve great success outside the OB someday too.

He couldn't quite imagine what life would be like if ever she agreed to marry him. He had no idea how many years it might take to even convince her to do that. There would be headaches in the meantime, and heartaches, and countless lonely nights when his arms ached for her.

But it didn't matter how long it took. He'd never be able to look at another girl like he looked at her.

"Elton. Thank you for waiting."

He started and turned with a smile for Hall, not really minding getting caught staring at Margot. "Not a hardship, sir."

The admiral smiled and motioned him to follow. "You've made great strides with her, I've noticed."

"Have I?" Sometimes he wasn't sure. She'd still never once mentioned his letters. She never leaned closer to him when she didn't have to. She'd certainly never said she loved him — he wasn't sure she ever would, even though it may be true. Words weren't her language.

Perhaps someday she would say it, somehow, in numbers.

Hall chuckled. "She's given up arguing when people refer to you as her young man. I would count that as a victory, were I you."

Drake's lips twitched up. "And so I shall."

The admiral led the way into his office and motioned him to close the door behind him. "She just provided a decrypt that will interest you. They have finally finished loading the wolfram onto the *Erri Barro*. She is finally scheduled to leave port."

Drake's pulse kicked up as he took a chair. "And we're ready to intercept?"

"We are. Whenever she enters open waters, we'll set upon her."

He'd wanted to be there, part of the prize crew. And yet he wasn't at all sorry he was here instead. "Are they certain she's seaworthy? I've seen her, sir — she's in sorry shape, and that's a heavy load for her to carry."

"Hence the many weeks of repairs. But I imagine we'll soon know how she fares. Now." Hall pulled a stack of clipped papers forward and slid it across his desk to Drake. "I'm sorry it's taken so long to compile this information. We've been able to discover precious little about this Jaeger chap. But

I've had a team combing through all entrance records, looking for him or his compatriots. There are half a dozen or so who could well be working with the Germans. A few have been detained already, a few have left the country again already. But these are still at large."

Throat tight in anticipation, Drake took the papers and flipped through it. Looking not just for Jaeger, but for the man in the grey overcoat.

His fingers paused on the fourth page. "This could be him."

"Jaeger?"

"No. The man outside my building, the one who ran from me. The height, weight, and age are right, and the description matches." Tall — six foot four. Not too many men could answer to that. He frowned. "Niall Walsh. Irish?"

"Claiming to be an American of Irish descent, but I have my doubts. The story he gave the custom agents didn't check out." Hall blinked and tapped a finger to his desk. "What's more, he's vanished. He was apparently on board the *Boynton* when she was sunk, was rescued, hospitalized . . . and then nothing after his release. He let his flat go afterward, but I can't track where he's gone. No hotels or boardinghouses in the city have seen him, but he hasn't left the country again, so far as we know. My people are checking other cities, but thus far, nothing."

"Mm." He kept reading, that page and the final two. Sighed. "None sound like Jaeger himself to me. But that supposedly Irish chap could be the one watching my flat for him. If we find *him* . . ."

"Right. I'll put a few more lads on it." Hall made a note and gave him a distracted smile. "I believe that's all. Oh, except that I did send Thoroton a note this morning with the good news from your doctor, that you've been given the all-clear to return to the field. He'll be expecting you by the new year."

"Excellent." He said the word easily enough. And hoped it sounded truthful. He *was* looking forward to seeing Abuelo again and getting back into the work he was so well suited for, doing something other than reading all day.

But . . .

Hall angled him a knowing look. "She'll be here when you return, Elton."

Apparently he was utterly transparent. Drake gave him a sheepish smile and stood. "Yes, sir. I know." And every man had to say farewell to his sweetheart these days, it seemed. He was nothing special. He ought to simply be grateful to have had this much time with her. And that he wasn't being sent to the front lines. Just to Spain. Back to his grandfather's luxurious house and Thoroton's efficient team.

But he was going to miss her.

27

"Is it too soon, do you think?" Dot worried her lip between her teeth — and still was smiling. "I shouldn't be even hoping for such a thing quite yet, I know. And he's only been at Lord Whitby's factory for a few weeks. But he's already been promoted once. It seems *right*."

Were it anyone but Dot speculating on whether or not her sweetheart meant to propose to her over Christmas, Margot would have rolled her eyes and strode away over the parade grounds and home without a backward glance. But it *was* Dot. And so she rolled her eyes and stayed at her side, happy enough to take the path that would lead her to Dot's flat instead of her own. "Of course it's right. Does it even require conversation?" Because even with Dot, she didn't quite know how to *have* such a conversation. What if she wanted to start talking about weddings? Gowns? Flower arrangements? Margot shuddered at the very thought.

"When I'm with him . . . he makes me feel as though I'm the only girl in the world. As though none of my quirks matter in the least. That we can stay in or we can go out, and it's all the same so long as we're together."

"Well, it would be stupid to consider marriage to someone who *didn't* think that way, wouldn't it?" Margot pulled her scarf a bit tighter and tucked her hands into her coat pockets. The air had gotten downright icy throughout the day and was bitter now, with newly fallen night around them. They might actually get a bit of snow if warmer air didn't sweep in off the ocean and return them to last month's relative temperance. "Though you can be sure Red, at least, isn't going anywhere. There's no reason to rush into anything. Why not enjoy the courtship?"

And give Margot a few more weeks or months of friendship before they spun into their different world. She didn't want to think of how everything would change once Dot got married. Would she even keep working at the OB? Or would she settle happily into the new role of housewife, tending the little flat Holmes had so proudly invited them all to the other night, and leave this world behind?

She'd be gone. Into Chiswick instead of Chelsea. Drake would be in Spain. A quick close to a short chapter. *Do you remember the autumn of 1917,* Lukas and Willa would say to each other, *when Margot actually had a friend and a beau? Whatever happened to that?*

She shouldn't pity herself. She must be happy for Dot. Happy for Drake, that he would return to the work he loved. Happy for Holmes, that asking for spare change on a street one night had somehow led to a solid position under the Earl of Whitby, a new home, and a woman who loved him.

Margot's fingers traced the edge of a florin in her pocket. She'd had a role in that, however small. She'd done the right thing even without any numbers to tell her it *was* the right thing, and she'd made a difference in a man's life. In her friend's life too.

Still, she felt the cold as she walked beside Dot. Because they weren't moving in parallel lines at all. It had looked that way for a while, but now she could clearly see the distance between them widening. Their paths would diverge, not intersect in infinity. Perhaps they had intersected at that one point, the day they met, and had been at such an acute angle that it had just *seemed* for a while to be equidistant.

Movement caught her eye, a flash of deeper darkness, even as Dot said, "What in the world is —"

And then a scream cut her off. First a masculine one, more a battle cry than a scream. And then Dot's piercing shout for help.

Margot spun toward the movement, letting her bag fall to the ground, trying to assess the situation that looked like nothing but a blur. A dark-colored coat, a man's hat, Dot's flailing limbs.

In one-eighth of a second, the details came into focus: the man's shaggy dark hair, his trim beard that hid a nearly delicate mouth, curled back in a snarl. He'd materialized from the alley like a specter.

Williams.

She hadn't seen him in weeks. And never like this. The stoop was gone, as was the distant look to his eyes. Intent gleamed there now. Malicious intent. It glinted wicked and bright off the blade that Williams held aloft, aimed at Dot.

Why? Why would he do this?

A quarter of a second for it all to process. That was all she could afford. Then Willa's voice in her ear, teaching her how to walk

477

the streets safely at night, alone. *"If anyone ever attacks you, don't try to recoil. Meet them, move into them. They never expect that. Then use their momentum to keep pushing them in the same direction they'd been going. Don't try to knock them back, especially if it's a man. Use their strength against them."*

She'd practiced on Lukas, who had proven a terrible combat partner, and then on Barclay, who had been the one to train Willa to begin with. He'd worked with Margot until she had the move down, applauding her when she'd sent him tumbling over and again to the floor, not minding the bruises.

It came back to her now. She pushed Dot out of the way and met Williams's advance, grabbing his knife-wielding arm rather than trying to avoid it. Pulling on it, pulling on him, wrenching the arm around as she stepped past him.

He grunted in pain, and the knife clattered to the ground. Margot was vaguely aware of Dot scrambling for it but more intent upon turning to face him again as he spun on her.

There was no moonlight to show her his face, just the weak gas lamps that didn't quite reach them. She couldn't make out his expression, but he hesitated a second before making a rush at her.

478

She stepped forward again, met him, and brought a knee up into his groin that sent him to the ground.

"Run!" Dot, with that wicked knife in her hands and Margot's bag over her shoulder, grabbed her by the arm and jerked her away.

Probably the best advice at this point, while Williams was immobilized. And he was coughing, wheezing with every groan. That would buy them another minute or two that might offset how much slower Dot's pumps would make them.

They ran.

Familiar streets sped by, but they didn't slow until they reached Dot's building, other than to look back and make sure he wasn't giving chase. They were both gasping for breath as they pushed through the doors and stumbled up the steps, neither of them accustomed to such a pace.

Dot's hands shook as she fumbled her keys out of her own bag. Not trembling, but actual, violent shaking. She dropped the keys. She choked on a sob as she tried to pick them up and couldn't seem to get hold of them.

Margot moved forward, ready to help, but the door opened even as she did, and a frowning Drake filled it. "Dot? What's the matter?"

Margot pulled her friend up rather than the keys and propelled her into her brother's arms. Then she fished the slips of metal off the ground and followed the siblings inside.

"Mugger," Dot managed between sobs.

"What? Are you all right?" He moved his wide eyes from Dot to Margot.

Margot sucked in a much-needed breath, not ashamed to admit there was a bit of a tremor in her own hands, now that the danger had passed. "We're all right. We got his knife from him. He didn't take anything, and he didn't hurt us."

At the word *knife,* Dot pulled away from Drake, fingers pressed to her lips. She let the two bags — her own and Margot's — fall to the floor and made a mad dash toward her bedroom.

"Dot!"

"Give her a minute." Drake touched a hand to her arm to stop her from following. But his frown furrowed deeper in his brow than she'd ever seen it as he looked at the door she'd slammed shut behind her.

Margot wrapped her arms around her middle. And when Drake moved his hand to her back instead of her arm, she leaned into him just a little. He apparently took it as permission to pull her to his chest, and she didn't mind that either. Her arms were trapped against her stomach, between them, but she buried her face in his uniform's shoulder. "We're all right," she felt the need to say again. And then a third time.

"I know. Praise the Lord." He pulled away, framed her face in his hands, and pressed a firm kiss to her forehead. Then he stepped away, his own hands shaking. Putting space between them when she knew well he wanted to eliminate it instead.

This was Drake's love.

He heaved a breath and passed a hand through his hair. "Tea. The kettle is on. You need tea."

She didn't need tea. But she'd take it, and she'd drink it, and maybe the warmth of it would chip away at the cold inside. So she nodded.

While he moved toward the kitchen, she slid out of her coat. And then, armed in the cardigan Maman had made her that she'd worn as an extra layer on this cold day, she bent down to retrieve the fallen bags. And her trembling hands pulled out that vicious-looking knife that Dot had apparently slid into Margot's handbag at some point.

She set it on the table, where the lamp-light could flash down its blade and gleam golden against the wooden handle. She was no expert, but it looked costly. Well made.

"This was his weapon?" Drake set two cups on the table and moved to her side, staring at the knife.

She nodded. And slid a few inches closer to him. Partly for him. Partly for her.

Drake reached for it, obviously more familiar with such weapons than she was, given how easily he flipped it this way and that, testing its balance, she guessed. "It's a beautiful piece."

Margot blinked at him. "It's a *weapon.* It isn't beautiful. Equations are beautiful. Sunsets are beautiful. Poetry and music are beautiful. Knives —"

"It's the mathematics of it that makes it so. The symmetry. The angles. The perfect ratio of weight between the tang and the tip." His smile flashed only briefly.

He held it closer. Her gaze settled where his had, on the metal closest to the wood. "There's something etched into the guard."

She leaned closer, even rested her fingers on his so she could steady it where she needed. "It looks like *d-e-r* something. *V-a-m . . .*" She straightened. "It's German. *Der Vampir.*"

Drake's brows flew upward. "Is that a cognate? 'The vampire'?"

Margot nodded. And shuddered. "A morbid name for a blade."

"Certainly not one you'd carve into a kitchen knife." He set it back down and rubbed a hand up and down her back. "How did you manage to disarm him?"

"Willa and Barclay taught me. Self-defense, they say, is every girl's best friend."

His hand hooked over her shoulder. Held tight. "Remind me to thank her on Sunday. Can you tell me what happened? Describe the man?"

She nodded. But somehow, with his arm so comfortably around her and the warmth of the flat seeping in, she became more aware every second of how weak her knees felt. And how much she didn't want to admit to him that he'd been right to wonder about Williams. "Could we sit first? With that tea?"

"Of course."

He carried the cups while she moved to the couch, casting a long look at Dot's closed bedroom door. "Should we check on her?"

"Only if she's in there more than half an hour. She knows how to calm herself and never thanks me for interrupting her process."

Margot clasped her elbows. She still had much to learn about her best friend, to be sure.

Drake slid the tea onto the end table and motioned for her to join him. "Red said he'd be here by six-thirty. If she hasn't emerged before then, we'll go in."

She nodded and forced her feet to move again. Six steps, a two-hundred-seventy degree pivot, and she sat beside him.

He pressed a warm cup of tea into her hands. And waited.

She took a sip and then began, detailing everything she could recall.

"I recognized him," she said only after the rest had been summarized. She looked up from the tea into Drake's silver-blue eyes. "It was John Williams. He didn't look like he had at the Go game — he'd been hunched over then, disheveled-looking, always a bit unfocused in the eyes. He was different tonight. Standing tall — far taller than I thought he was."

Drake went stiff beside her. "How tall?"

"Probably . . ." She closed her eyes, visualized the distance she'd had to look up into his face, calculated. "I'd say between six-four and six-four-and-a-half, depending on the soles of his shoes."

He hissed out a breath. "What about his hair? The color of his coat?"

Her brows drew down. "Dark — longish. The first time I saw him he was in a blue coat, but this one was grey. Why?"

He scooted forward a bit and angled in. "That night you ran from the flat — the bloke you ran into. Was that him?"

"I . . ." She drew back, and not because it was the first time they'd ever referenced that night when she'd run out into the darkness with her lips still warm from his, with her ears still ringing with his claim that he loved her. She hadn't been paying any attention at the time. Her eyes had been blurred with tears, and she hadn't looked up. But she must have had impressions. "I didn't look at his face. It could have been, I think. The height seems right. Why?"

Drake muttered something in Spanish and looked away.

Margot scooted an inch and an eighth closer. "Drake — *why*?"

"Because that sounds like the man who's been watching the flat."

"This flat? But *why?"* He was just a former emissary to Japan. A sailor. Not right in the head, but harmless, she'd thought.

She'd obviously been wrong. Had he been following her? And watching Drake and Dot here? Planning this attack? It didn't make sense. What could he want?

"I can't be certain. But I suspect he's working with the German agent who shot me on the train, the one in charge of getting the anthrax-laced sugar where it was meant to go."

No, that made even less sense. "That can't be. He was here before you were shot. And why would you think the man who shot you has anything to do with this?"

"He's called me on the telephone. It was Jaeger's voice. We haven't been able to locate him, but the man you call Williams — he knew who I was that night, and he knew I'd been watching him, that I knew who *he* was. Minus the name. He must be an agent on the ground, here, one Hall's men have missed. We thought we'd identified him as a bloke who's called Niall Walsh, but he could well have another alias."

Margot stood, her tea sloshing in its cup. "Why didn't you chase him down that night? Apprehend him? Get answers?"

"You were more important." But he winced and looked away. "Though maybe I should have. I'd feared reopening my wound, but I probably could have stopped him, or at least taken his knife. Then he couldn't have attacked you two today. I'm sorry. At the time, the choice had seemed obvious."

He'd chosen her, soothing her fears, over the best chance he'd probably ever had to apprehend a German agent hunting him down? "How is that obvious? I was acting like a . . . like a silly *girl.* You shouldn't have let that stop you from finding him! Don't you think I can weigh the situation and see that apprehending a German agent is a bit more important than wiping away my ridiculous tears?"

And for that matter, why hadn't he bothered mentioning this little detail before now? That he'd been in danger all this time, hunted down? Perhaps they could have pieced it together sooner. Realized that her Go partner was working with his opposite number. She spun away, too many factors enumerating themselves for her to sort while she was looking at him.

His hands rested on her shoulders. "Nothing's more important than soothing your tears, ridiculous or warranted. You matter more than a dozen German agents."

She tried to shrug his hands away, though they settled right back where they'd been. And she was stupidly glad of it. "Don't be absurd. One is never greater than twelve."

"It is when you love the one."

She huffed out a breath.

"You're thinking I should have told you all this sooner. About the man following me. About Jaeger." He pulled her toward him four inches, until her back brushed his chest.

Her eyes slid closed. "I've been obsessing over what killed my mother, wasting hours of time on newspapers that told me nothing. I could have been working on this instead. Finding answers that obviously *are* there. Because *he's* there." Had been for so long. Could he have had anything to do with Maman's death? No, that didn't fit. Not if he'd been hovering outside this flat. It must have to do with something else.

"I'm sorry." His thumbs rubbed at her neck, digging into the knots of tension and bidding them loosen. "I'm used to protecting the women I love — hence why I didn't even want to tell Dot what my position in the navy really was. But I should have told you sooner. You're right."

"Not to appease me. Because I could help. You know I could."

"I know you could." His voice was a whisper at her ear. "I didn't want you to have to. I didn't want to bring that danger to your door."

She turned, dislodging his hands but catching them in her own. Facing him. "It was already there. I don't need to be coddled, Drake. And I won't coddle *you.* He could have killed your sister. He was aiming a knife at her."

He knew that. The sobering truth of it turned his eyes from silver to lead, heavy and dark. His fingers tightened around hers until it nearly hurt. "We need to stop him."

We. One plus one. But the truth was, it didn't always equal two. Sometimes the whole was greater than the sum of its parts. Sometimes, when two things worked together, they were stronger than they should have been.

Pounding on the door made her jump, her gaze breaking away from his, her pulse hammering as fast as it had when she'd run here fifteen minutes ago. As fast as it had when he'd kissed her.

"Drake! Open up!" Red's voice called out.

Margot released Drake's hands, and he strode to the door, jerked it wide, even as the one to Dot's room cracked open too. "What is it?"

Holmes's chest was heaving, as if he too had run all the way here — or as close as he could get to running with his foot, anyway. He looked past Drake, to Margot. "I saw police swarming all over a building of flats on my way here and stopped in to see what the hubbub was about. It was Williams's building."

She looked to Drake, then back to Red.

"What has he done now?"

"Williams?" Red shook his head. "Williams apparently hasn't done anything for more than a month. They found his body in the basement. The bloke who's been living there, the one I followed . . . apparently he isn't Williams at all."

"Walsh, then." Drake charged toward the stairs, his face a stony mask. "And he'll be on the run."

28

Drake stood in the center of Williams's unfamiliar flat, knowing well he was only here because Hall had once again pulled strings. Margot stood beside him, her fingers gripping his. To give strength or receive it? He wasn't sure anymore.

Dot was at home, with Red and their upstairs neighbor to chaperone. And to fuss over them. Camden had been standing sentinel at the door when they'd left. Hall hadn't sent him, but Cam apparently had heard him barking out an order for an armed guard and had volunteered for the job.

Heaven help anyone who tried to cross him.

"I don't understand." Margot's eyes stayed fixed on the portrait that hung, framed, on the wall. The real Williams, it seemed, smiling as he posed for the camera, shaking the hand of an important-looking Japanese official. Not the man either he or Margot had seen before. "Why would he have assumed Williams's identity?"

"I don't know. Perhaps he thought his Niall Walsh cover had been compromised." Drake's glance skidded around the room, not sure where to rest. The police had already been all through it, looking for any hints as to who had murdered the poor man. Muddy boot prints marred the floor, papers had been left out on the table, drawers upended.

"Who is this man?" Margot had looked away from the portrait at last. But her gaze settled on the grey overcoat hanging neatly in the corner. Apparently he'd had to flee from the bobbies too quickly to grab it.

But it was the one he'd been wearing outside Dot's flat. The one, according to Margot, he'd been wearing earlier that evening when he'd attacked them.

"I don't know. I only know who he's not. Not Jaeger." Jaeger hadn't operated like this, killing innocents for his own convenience. The warehouse clerk, all those people on the streets between them, the family in the train carriages. Abuelo, for that matter, and the household there. Jaeger had known who Drake was, called him by name. But he'd never hurt anyone else to get to him.

Professional, Hall had said. Opposite numbers. But it hadn't been personal.

Yet it had been Jaeger's voice on the phone. He was involved. Somehow.

Margot's fingers slid free of his, and she wandered through the small, three-room flat. For a moment, Drake just watched her unique way of wandering. She didn't do it aimlessly like other people. She wandered with precision. Two steps, a halt, a three-hundred-sixty degree turn. Two more steps, another halt, another turn. Taking in everything. Seeing numbers, probably, to account for everything. Boards in the floor. Books on the shelf. Pillows on the bed. Slices of bread on the plate on the table, where Walsh or whatever his name really was must have been sitting down to eat when the police had knocked on his door.

Not *his* door. Williams's door.

Drake moved, too, after a minute. Less precisely, but perhaps more purposefully. He was no stranger to poking about, finding information, investigating. The police had said they'd taken nothing with them, that there was nothing to give them a clue as to the killer's identity. Nothing, they insisted, to indicate that the man living here was even Williams's killer rather than a random squatter.

493

He knew better. Drake opened every drawer, checked every loose board, pulled out every book.

"Margot." The volume in his hands was in German, but he recognized a few of the words. It was a guide on the game Go. And it had telltale yellow papers sticking out of its pages like bookmarks.

She appeared at his side and drew in a sharp breath. "Telegrams."

"Telegrams." He opened to the first one, made note of the page number in case it mattered, and handed it to her after only a cursory glance. "In German."

"In code." She sank onto the edge of the little wooden chair by the bookshelf. "Blast."

"What?"

"In the mystery code. I'm all but certain of it. The one we haven't broken yet."

He extracted the others too. "What about these?"

She took them, her eyes going over them not word by word but seeming to swallow them whole. Then she let her eyes slide shut, her lips move without sound. And she nodded. "All the same."

Drake re-marked the pages in the book with pieces he tore off a blank page on the desk. "How long will it take you to break it?"

"Too long. Weeks. Months. We don't have enough examples of it."

"Not even when combined with what you have on file?"

"These *are* what we have on file. Some of them, anyway. The originals." She stood again, her dark eyes troubled. "We need to get this all to the admiral. We can check the sources, see where they were sent from. That might give us a clue as to what code we're looking for and where we can find a codebook."

In this flat would be nice — but he had a feeling this bloke hadn't left such a thing lying about. He nodded and looked around again. "Let me just make certain there's nothing else of interest hiding here first."

"All right. I'll stare at these a bit longer. See if I have any epiphanies."

He let a smile tease the edges of his mouth as he turned back to the bookshelf. If anyone could crack a code just by staring at it, it was surely Margot De Wilde.

He didn't find anything else hidden in the tomes, nor in the cupboards in the kitchen, nor anywhere else he checked. After a thorough search, he moved back to Margot's side. "I suppose those are our only clues."

She wasn't staring at the telegrams any longer though. She was staring at a small notebook opened to a blank page.

"What is it?"

She picked it up, angled it toward the light. "I thought so."

He bent down to match her view and could just barely make out indentations on the page. "What does it say? Something important?"

"It's what he used to write the notes that he left with the — wait a minute." Frowning, she stood and spun in a faster three-sixty. "Where's the game board?"

Drake spun, too, even though he knew well it hadn't been anywhere in here. "I don't know. Could it be set up in the park?"

Her answer was simply to look at him for a second and then take off for the door. Drake followed in her wake, pulling the door closed behind him and nodding his thanks to the bobby stationed in the corridor.

Williams's flat wasn't far from the park. It only took them a few minutes to reach it and walk the familiar paths.

But the table was empty. No game. No notes. Certainly no Niall Walsh.

"He must have it with him."

Drake shoved his hands deep into his pockets. "He didn't grab his coat, but he grabbed the game?"

"Priorities, I suppose. Which tells us what?"

He grinned. "I'm rubbing off on you. That, mi alma, is the question. It tells us he's going to use it again. To communicate with you."

"Well then. It's his play." She tucked her hand into the crook of Drake's arm — without prompting, without invitation — and tugged him along the path. "We need to get to Hall."

They didn't speak as they hurried along. He had to imagine that her mind was working through everything like a moving-picture reel. His certainly was. Drawing up all the details again, examining them, asking what each piece could mean, then flipping to the next.

Wondering, always wondering, where Jaeger fit into it.

The OB was officially closed for the night, but it wasn't empty. It was never empty, especially not on the floor that the intelligence hive had taken over. The night shift was there, waiting for the new codes to come in shortly after midnight. And Hall was still there, pacing his office like a caged lion.

He charged out of his door as they drew near. "There you are. What did you find?"

They briefed him as succinctly as possible, Margot handing over the telegrams. The admiral's lips pressed together as he blinked, taking it all in. "We have these in our files?"

Margot nodded. "And a few others besides."

"Then let's see what the others are, where they came from. See if that lends us any aid."

Drake didn't know what to look for or how to help as they pulled down box after box and riffled through them, so he just leaned into the threshold and set his mind toward prayer. The best possible use of his time just now anyway.

"Here they are." Margot pulled out what was clearly a logbook, and Hall handed over a stack of papers. The other intercepts, he assumed, in the code in question.

She flipped page after page, ran a finger down the charts.

"Well?" Hall looked over her shoulder.

"All the ones our fellow had in the book originated in Berlin, which is no surprise. It looks like they were sent to a variety of locations, though. France. Spain. Ireland. Here."

"He must have got around, whoever he is. What of the others?"

Margot checked the papers, flipped a few more pages in the log, and then looked up with bright eyes. "There are a few intercepts with reverse locations — originating here or the other places and sent *to* Berlin. And others from Berlin to South America, more to the Continent. But a few went to zeppelins."

Drake straightened. "Does that mean zeppelins would carry the codebooks?"

Hall slapped a hand to his knee and stood up from where he'd crouched. "It's likely." His eyes met Drake's.

Drake knew exactly what he was thinking. "A zeppelin just went down yesterday in France." It had been part of the information he'd sorted that morning. He'd flagged it, because he always flagged it. Hall must have reviewed his flags already. "The French reported nothing salvageable from the wreckage."

"Bah." Hall took a step past him, his brows drawn. "I'll offer a reward for anything useful brought back. That'll inspire some of our chaps to scour the area, widen the search. I only pray we've time enough. It will take at least a week for our lads on the ground to be given leave to hunt through the wreckage and then get anything they find back to us by ship. I do worry that —"

"I'll go."

They went still, both of them. Hall, in front of him. Margot, behind him. Both of their eyes drilling into him. Drake straightened his shoulders. "We need answers now, or this bloke's going to vanish on us."

Hall shook his head. "By the time you could get there, the others might as well —"

"Camden can fly me in." He summoned a smile. "Assuming you can help him get his hands on a plane again, sir."

Hall lifted his brows. "You're going to ask *him* for a favor? I know he is your friend, Elton, but he hasn't been in the best frame of mind recently. I wouldn't count on his good graces."

"He owes me one." He turned to Margot. "I'll get you the codebook."

She gripped the logbook until her knuckles went white. "No. Let the others do it. We can wait."

But they couldn't. "You know well we can't. He attacked you and Dot tonight. He lost his flat to the authorities. He'll be on the move, and if we don't act now . . . I have to."

She must be clenching her teeth, given the tic in her jaw. "I'm sure there's someone else who can do it."

Drake lifted his brows. "Perhaps. But this is at least in part because of me, linked to Jaeger. I need to see it through. And Camden will know what we're looking for. It's the perfect, quickest solution, Margot."

Hall's footsteps sounded, padding away. "I'll see to that plane."

Drake turned to face her. He pried the logbook from her hands and set it aside so he could take those hands in one of his. "I'll be all right."

"You don't know that. The number of planes shot down —"

"Is irrelevant." He used his free hand to brush her hair from her cheek. "Camden is the best pilot we have. He can get me there and back safely."

"You can't even be sure there's a codebook to be found. It could have burned up in the wreckage."

"Maybe. But I have to try. You know how you hear numbers? I get urges. Impressions. Feelings, maybe, though I know you consider that a curse word." He grinned, but it only earned him a shake of her head. "This is right."

A bigger shake of her head. "It doesn't feel right to me. It feels wrong. Really wrong."

He tilted his head, let that settle. Was it only his pride that made him want to seek out these answers himself? To get back into the thick of things? No. If it were that, he'd rather scour the streets of London, hunting down this man who didn't have his grey overcoat anymore. He'd want to stay close to her, to Dot, where he could protect them. Because it made him antsy to think of leaving them here alone when that bloke was still at large and obviously dangerous.

But still that urgency thrummed in his chest. "Can you trust me, Margot? Can you trust that I'm certain? That this is the Lord leading me?"

She made a noise he couldn't quite classify — a squeak of protest? A whimper? — and gripped his wrist. "I don't want to lose you. I can't. I can't lose anyone else right now."

He could promise to come home, but she wouldn't believe him. She would have numbers to prove how many promised it and failed to deliver. And she had a point. There were never any guarantees. Even being sure God wanted him to do this didn't mean he'd come home safely. Sometimes God's will meant bullets searing flesh. Death coming too soon. Sometimes God's will was to let man taste the consequences of his folly and his hatred and his supposed self-sufficiency.

Sometimes God let people die. Let His children break. And then pieced them back together into something new. Something that He could use for His glory instead of theirs.

He nudged her chin up, bent his head down. Caught her lips with his. They tasted as sweet as they had the first time. Were as hesitant and yet as welcoming. He savored each second, lingered one more. And then pulled away. "I need to go and talk with Camden. Why don't you come and stay with Dot? You shouldn't go home alone."

She shook her head. "I'll stay here. I need to work."

He sighed, knowing well there'd be no talking her out of it. And it was quite possibly the safest place she could be, so he wouldn't argue. With a brush of his fingers down her neck, he stepped away. "All right. I'll let you know before I leave, if there's time. I don't know if we'll have to wait for daylight to take off or not."

She folded her arms across her middle, the red cardigan hugging her tight. "Drake."

He paused a step away, lifted his brows.

She couldn't seem to wrap her lips around whatever it was she wanted to say. She squeezed her eyes shut, opened them again. Dragged in a breath. Met his gaze. "Eighteen." It had the sound of a word pulled by force from her mouth. Strenuous. Weighty.

The word that had bidden her to pray for him. The word that had echoed in her mind on that day so fateful to them both. The number that meant him in her mind.

He smiled and took a step backward. "I love you too."

And she smiled.

None of the words Das Gespenst knew in any of his five languages was strong enough. He'd managed to grab only his lightweight blue jacket for his shimmy out the window, and it wasn't nearly enough against the chill. He'd been hunkered down in this alley all blasted night, careful to shrink his frame with a hunch in his back. A cough threatened to attack his lungs after the hours spent in the cold damp.

Blast it all. Who *was* that girl? She was from a genteel family — she shouldn't have known such moves.

It had been so simple a plan. Give Dorothea Elton a slash across the shoulder to prove himself serious, then grab her and hold the knife to her throat. Demand Margot De Wilde fetch him the codebook the High Command wanted. And then, while she was fetching that — only then, once his assignment was being completed — a sweet taste of revenge.

Elton.

It had seemed so beautifully simple. So perfect, that they were all connected — the universe handing him not only the summation to one of the tasks he'd been sent here to achieve, but revenge as well. A bit of recompense for all this war had taken from him.

He leaned his head back against the brick wall behind him and kept his eyes trained on Dorothea Elton as she made her way inside the Old Building, accompanied by an armed guard. In, no doubt, to be with her friend. Connected. Together. But they couldn't stay in there forever. They'd emerge, those young women, either together or separately.

He wasn't out of moves yet. He would get the High Command their blasted codes. He would deliver them a fine target for their bombs.

And he would have his revenge.

29

Margot blinked awake slowly, not quite sure where she was or why there was such a babble around her. Something soft was under her back, something warm tucked around her. But it took an entire six and a half seconds to realize that she was in DID's office, on the leather sofa he kept against the wall. And the corridors were alive with the thrum of many voices going about their daily tasks.

She sat up, eyes searching for a clock. The last she'd known, Drake and Camden were in a Sopwith, flying across the Channel with the first hint of dawn. And so she'd come in here, sat down, thought to breathe for a minute. She'd tried to pray.

She'd managed only to clench her fingers together and say, "Please. Please." Would God count that as a prayer? One of the mutterings of the soul that the Spirit made sense of before the Father?

Instead of a clock, she became aware of a different type of face. One pinched, shadowed, and pale. Dot's hands were clenched too. And still shaking. "Morning."

Margot shoved her hair out of her face, wincing at the snarls in it. It felt strange, like it wasn't at the right angles. She tried to force it flat with her fingers. "Morning. What time is it? Are they there yet? Do you know?"

"They made it to the airfield an hour ago." Dot swallowed and moved her hands just a bit, enough to reveal the rosary beads clutched within them. "I'm handing in my resignation today."

"What?" Margot swung her legs, tangled in a blanket, off the couch. "Dot, no."

"I can't do it anymore, Margot. I had to stop twice on the way here — I couldn't breathe, my vision was spotty. . . . I can't be here now. I need to go home. It's time to go home."

"Dot." She scooted forward, toward the chair where her friend sat. "You're shaken. Last night was horrible. But the fear will pass. Just stick it out —"

"I don't want to stick it out!" Dot sprang to her feet, chest heaving. Breath rasping. "And I don't *have* to. Red and I are going to get married. Soon. I don't have to work

507

here anymore. I don't have to go out every day and —"

"You can't just resign your position and marry him!" Margot tried to stand, too, though the blanket sent her back to the cushions. She pulled it off, tossed it to the end of the couch, and tried again. "Yesterday you were wondering if he even meant to propose and saying how quickly it had all happened — and *resigning*? You've worked hard to learn the job, and you're good at it."

Dot backed up a step. "I'm not like you, Margot. I don't *want* to work. I just want to get married, have a family. Maybe that makes me stupid in your mind, but —"

"I have never thought that of you. Never." She held out a hand, wondering why it seemed to repulse her friend like the wrong side of a magnet and send her another step toward the door. "I know you want to get married. I'm not saying you shouldn't —"

"Just that I shouldn't give up my position? Is that it? Will I be less in your eyes if I decide to stay at home and take care of my husband?" With a shaky laugh, she slashed a hand through the air, her rosary beads whipping around her wrist. "Will I be wasting my life, is that what you think? Because heaven knows you seem to think you'll be wasting *yours* if you dare to let my brother be a part of it."

Maybe it was the sleep still clouding her mind, but that did not seem like the next logical step in the argument. "Why are we talking about Drake?"

Dot stared at her. Glared at her. "Honestly? You ask that? Don't you know how he feels about you, or are you too wrapped up in your own little world of numbers to even care?"

Margot gripped the edge of the admiral's desk. "Of course I know how he feels."

"It means nothing to you, then? Because it doesn't fit into the plans you had mapped out for your life?" Dot shook her head. "Go back to sleep, Margot. Get up and solve your puzzles, write out your numbers. I'm going to go home and plan my wedding. Don't feel obligated to drop in, it would only bore you."

Margot opened her mouth, but she didn't know which thing to rebut first. The spoken accusations, or the unspoken one? Dot had obviously never entertained the notion that Margot *did* love Drake. That was apparently unfathomable. Oblivion or scoffing, those seemed to be the options her best friend had considered for her.

Dot had her hand on the doorknob, and

enough panicked energy probably fired her veins to carry her out and home without a moment's thought.

And Margot didn't know what to say. None of the answers she could give would mean a thing to her friend just now.

But maybe a question would. "Dot."

She paused with the door open, glaring over her shoulder. Furious. Hurting. Scared.

Drake had been right. Having courage didn't mean the fear wasn't always there, ready to pounce. She swallowed. "Will you want to marry him any less tomorrow? Must you make a decision today?"

The door slammed behind her.

Margot sighed and sank back onto the couch. Wrong question, apparently. She buried her fingers in her already-mussed hair and knotted them there. Why was she so miserable at this? She hadn't had such troubles with Claudette when they were girls. She got on fine with Willa and her sisters. She'd thought she and Dot had established a solid friendship too. The kind that could stand a few tests and trials. The kind that would be there through the storms. The kind that tried to understand, not to judge.

"It means nothing to you." She drew a breath in, let it out. *He* knew. Drake knew it

meant something. He'd understood last night that the tangle of feelings inside her couldn't be put into regular language. He'd known what she meant. That *Eighteen* was *I love you.*

Why couldn't Dot understand it too? Had Margot been such a bad friend, shown so little of herself? She thought she'd been honest. Showed her who she really was and been accepted. Maybe she'd been wrong.

Eighteen.

Memory? A fresh command? She rose and moved to DID's window, where she could look out across the parade grounds. Folding her arms across her middle, clasping her opposite elbows, she tried. She *tried.*

God . . .

Her chest hurt. And her hair felt wrong. And the windowpane, when she rested her forehead against it, was so very cold.

Father . . .

Drake was out there, somewhere in France, searching through burned-out rubble for a codebook. Who knew which side of enemy lines it was on, or how safe he'd be. Whether he'd come back.

Lord . . .

What if he didn't come back? What if the Sopwith was shot down, or enemy soldiers were guarding the wreck? What if he died and he never came home and Dot refused to speak to her again? What if that man who wasn't Williams followed him or was lying in wait when he got back or planted a bomb in the plane?

What if he, too, looked at her one day like his sister had just done and decided she couldn't possibly love him?

"Eighteen." She whispered it to the glass and watched her breath make a patch of fog that expanded, halted, and contracted again so slowly. "Eighteen." She lifted a finger and pressed it to the glass. To the fog. Drew a one. Then an eight.

It vanished, of course, as the fog receded. But her finger had left its oils on the glass. It would come back if she breathed on it again. Faintly, but visible. It was there. A prayer. A declaration.

She pushed away from the window and trudged toward the door. The admiral would need his office. And she had work to do.

"Why did I let you talk me into this?" Camden pushed aside another pine bough and ducked under it, holding it out of the way for Drake too.

He checked his compass again and smiled. "Because you were tired of sitting in an office all day."

"There's that. But if we were going to steal an airplane, we could have gone somewhere more pleasant." Hands on his hips, Camden surveyed the forest around them as if the mere power of his scowl could make any zeppelin debris rise from the undergrowth.

"We didn't steal the airplane." Drake angled back to the northeast and slid the compass back into his pocket. They'd gotten a bit off course when they had to bypass that stream. "We'll be within the five-mile radius of the crash site in another minute or two, I should think."

Margot would know it by the second. She could probably chart it all out in her head and keep them on course without even looking at the landscape around her. A compass, a watch, a gauge of their speed.

He glanced around. "You're sure there are no enemy soldiers about?"

"Our reconnaissance said the area is clear." Camden brushed a stray pine needle from his jodhpurs and struck out. "And the RNAS didn't know I was the one flying it. If they had, they wouldn't have let Hall requisition it. Ergo, I flew it without permission, which is, if I'm not mistaken, stealing." Half his mouth tilted up in his usual mischievous smile. "Look at that. Another offense for which they can court-martial me."

"You're welcome." Drake kept pace with ease. And paused to thank the Lord for it. His side didn't hurt anymore, and he really wasn't any slower now than he'd been before. Or if so, not by much. All that training on the stairs had paid off.

They both came to a halt when there was a break in the trees, a winter-brown meadow stretching out ahead of them.

"This must be it," Camden said. "The place the pilots spotted on their descent."

Drake nodded and looked at the treetops on the opposite side of the meadow for any sign of debris. "Assuming they told the truth."

"They didn't seem in a state of mind to lie well." Camden turned in a circle, his neck craned up as well. "I've never seen anything like their disorientation."

Drake squinted at something glinting across the way, in a branch halfway down one of the tall pines. He couldn't make out what it was, but something man-made, surely, to shine like that. He pointed at it. "I didn't realize zeppelins could fly high enough to produce altitude sickness."

"They shouldn't." Camden squinted, too, at where he indicated and nodded. They started off across the meadow. "They must have gotten caught in an updraft. From what I could glean, it was their panic from the sickness that caused the crash, not the weather itself."

They'd survived though and were now in Allied custody. Drake prayed with every step that it would work out to their benefit. That they'd find the codebook, the one they needed. That somewhere in those slips of yellow in the book about Go, there would be answers.

"Will you stop that?"

Drake angled a look at his friend. "Stop what?"

"Praying. I can tell you are, and it's blighted annoying. Reminds me of my brother."

Drake chuckled and looked forward again. Camden had always adored his younger brother — not that he'd ever admit it aloud, but woe to anyone who harassed the younger Camden at school. "I'll stop praying when you stop trying to pick a fight with everyone you see."

Camden pursed his lips. "It's an embarrassment, having to claim a clergyman for a brother. I don't need a pious friend too."

"Apparently you do. Because so far as I've seen, you don't have many others just now."

"Fine by me. I'm not interested —"

"In making friends. Yes, I've heard your new mantra. How fortunate for us both that I didn't need to be made." He craned his head back again as they drew near the tree. Though of course, from this angle he couldn't see anything flashing. "This is the one, isn't it?"

"Yeah. Here, hold this." Camden whipped off his hat, shoved it at Drake's chest, and clapped his hands together. Then leapt up to the nearest branch.

"You don't have to be the one to climb. I'm perfectly capable —"

"You were shot recently, Elton. Last thing we need is you pulling something open halfway up a tree. I don't much fancy carrying you back to the airstrip." He pulled himself up to a standing position on that branch and jumped for another. "Besides, it takes me back to our school days. I passed many a happy hour in those trees."

"Mm. When you should have been in Latin, you mean." Drake backed up a few paces to get a better view. "Try to angle toward me when you can. I think I see it, though I can't tell what it is." Not a codebook, certainly. That wouldn't be glinting in the sunlight. But if they could place it as being *something* from the zeppelin, then they'd know they were on the right track.

"Right. Working on it." Grunting with the effort, Camden continued to scale the limbs, coming round the tree bit by bit as the branches allowed.

"Almost there. Two more, I should think." Camden reached for the next branch. "You know, I've changed my mind about that favor. I didn't owe you. Which means you now owe me."

"Uh-huh." He lifted a hand to his eyes to shield them from the midmorning sun. "Well?"

Camden made a snatch for something, and apparently he hooked it, given his laugh. "Got it!"

"What is it?"

"A canteen."

An odd thing to find fifty feet up a tree, to be sure. Obviously dropped from above, which boded well for them. "German?"

"Well, it sure isn't English — we have more sense than to give ours a round bottom that you can't actually sit on a table."

Drake was still smiling when Camden's feet hit the forest floor again. "Seems like zeppelin debris to me."

Camden was grinning too. "Onward."

They walked another ten minutes before spotting a German hat on the ground.

Another five and they found a mess kit. And then the mother lode, which made Drake's pulse really kick up. Papers.

They were strewn all throughout the forest, some still caught in branches, most littering the ground. He caught up a few at first and then gave that up — they'd be here for a week if they gathered them all.

"Navigation charts." Camden held up a book and then tossed it down. "The codebook would have been stored in the same place, I'd think."

"Then it's here." It was *here*. Somewhere. "What do these codebooks look like?"

Camden took off for something that caught his eye to Drake's right. "Bound, but not like a normal book. Paper binding. Soft, flexible. The ones they have in the OB already are green. Pages are tabbed, marking different sections. And you'll certainly know it when you see it — they'll have pages filled with charts of numbers. Zero to nine across, zero to nine down. Then pages with words."

Drake grinned as he turned to look for something flexible and green. Though just now he rather wished they'd chosen orange or red. "You're a codebreaker. Ever stop and think how odd that is?"

"Every blighted day, mate." Camden

strode toward a bare-limbed oak tree.

Drake chuckled. "Ready to admit that it's better than prison?"

"No. But I haven't punched you again, have I?" He bent down, snatched up a book, and then tossed it away again after a quick glance.

"I just assumed you were afraid of Red Holmes." Drake aimed himself toward a patch of green that didn't quite match the pine needles.

"Careful, Elton. I'm your ride home, you know."

It was paper he'd seen, that much was sure. A book, he decided as he drew closer. And it wasn't sitting stiffly against the tree roots like a typical one would be. It bent a bit in the middle. He hurried over the last few steps and reached down for it.

The paper was damp from its days on the ground, the edges beginning to curl. But the binding had held and all the pages seemed to be intact. He flipped it open. And his heart positively sang when he saw the chart. Zero to nine across. Zero to nine down. "Cam, I found one!"

Camden jogged over to his side and looked over his shoulder. Then slapped a hand to his back. "That you did."

"Is it the right one, though?"

At that, his friend snorted. "If you wanted someone who could tell you that in a glance, you should have brought De Wilde along."

"Then who would have flown the stolen plane?" And this wasn't Margot's world. She'd made no indication that she wanted to tromp around the forest searching for the codebook herself — and he was glad of that. It was one thing to volunteer his old friend to take him into the battlefield. Quite another to volunteer the woman he loved for such a mission. She might be able to take down a mugger, for which he was eternally grateful. But the mugger had only a knife. Enemies they found out here would have guns, and Margot hadn't been trained to dodge them.

Camden took the codebook from his hands and flipped through it. "It's not like the ones I've used, anyway. I say we scour the rest of this debris field and then turn back. That could well be our book. And if it isn't, the right one's either here in this area or it's not here at all."

"Good plan." Another hour of searching, an hour back to the plane, the flight home. They'd be back in London by nightfall.

30

Das Gespenst covered his cough with a handkerchief and stared out at the falling twilight. London's streets were going rose and gold, soon to be overtaken by purple and grey. And then, finally, the brown-black night of the city.

One more night in this godforsaken place. And then he'd either be dead or on his way back to Germany.

"That cough doesn't sound so good."

He didn't spare Elton's sister a glance. Her wrists were firmly bound, as firmly as her ankles. His breathing might be troubled just now, but his knot-tying skills weren't. And up here, in the attic of a building abandoned after one of the zeppelin raids left it flaming, there was no one to hear her if she screamed for help.

She'd already discovered that, hours ago. *This,* at least, had gone according to plan.

Das Gespenst tucked his handkerchief

back into his pocket and looked out, across the river, toward where it would all end tonight. "Do not concern yourself for me, Dorothea." He called her by name simply because it made her wince.

His argument wasn't with her. He didn't mean to make her last day one of terror — but she must be reminded of who was in control.

He turned from the window and checked his pocket watch. Another hour and he'd give her a drink laced with laudanum. She would probably try to refuse it, of course. But if so, a rag soaked in chloroform would render her more pliant. Then he'd slip out. One last play in Go. One last stop at the telegraph office. And if the High Command assured him the air raid was set, that would leave only a few last steps in the game. A boat. A cab. Woolwich.

This time tomorrow, it would be over.

She shifted against the beam he'd tied her to. "I don't suppose I could stand for a while."

Das Gespenst forced his lips to curve into a smile. "Of course. Allow me to assist you." He moved to do so from behind, giving her feet a wide berth. So far as he could tell, she hadn't been trained in how to take a man down even when bound . . . but then, he hadn't thought Margot De Wilde had been trained in how to disarm one. A mistake that had left him limping.

Safely out of kicking range, he gripped her arms and helped her stand. "There we are. Better?"

"Yes. Thank you."

He had to give her credit. Though she'd been a wreck when she'd first come flying out of the Old Admiralty Building — crying, shaking, heaving — she'd actually been rather calm since she awoke from the first dousing of chloroform. It seemed she was stronger under duress than she was under the *anxiety* of duress.

He moved back around to her front and took a seat on the rickety chair he'd found. "You remind me of my brother's wife." Ilse, too, had always shown the greatest distress over the *thought* of something evil befalling her family.

And yet when her little one died of fever last year, she had stood strong. When news of Heinrich's death had reached her, he had no doubt she had done the same. Lifted her chin. Straightened her spine.

His fingers dug into his leg. She shouldn't have had to. She shouldn't have been stripped of her husband, when their second child was still a few months from being born. She shouldn't have had to walk to that grave marker with his mother and see Heinrich's name etched upon it, even though Heinrich's body wasn't buried beneath the grass.

He was sorry for that too. But there had been no way to get his brother's corpse home. He had wasted an entire day trying to determine how to do so, but the High Command had been unsympathetic.

Heinrich had died a spy's death. He had received a spy's burial, secret and alone. But he would be sung as a hero in every story they told of him at home. Das Gespenst had at least made certain of that. Made certain they knew how honorably he had served Germany. His eyes slid shut. They never should have accepted these positions in intelligence. It had seemed a boon at the time, a lark, a . . . a game. *"Think of the stories we will have to tell,"* Heinrich had said.

But they'd never tell these stories. Even if his brother had lived, they wouldn't. They couldn't. They'd lived these last few years like he'd died — secret and alone.

Dorothea Elton stretched against the beam, rolling her head from side to side. "Where are you from?"

Das Gespenst looked to the window again.

The purple had come. Not long now. "A little town called Bamberg."

"What's it like?"

"Beautiful. It is in Bavaria, and its architecture is unparalleled."

Dorothea studied him. Calm now. No shaking. Only her hair, tumbling about her shoulders half out of its pins, told the tale of her graceless arrival in this burned-out attic. "Are you going to kill me?"

"Me? No." He glanced up at the sky. It was clear. That could change in an instant here in England, he knew, but for now it boded well. The *Luftstreitkräfte* needed to be able to reach them. Zeppelins or Gothas. Either would do, and he didn't know which they would send. Perhaps both.

"Why not? You tried last night."

"I was not going to kill you." He looked back, met her gaze. "I am sorry, Dorothea. I have no argument with you, but you have unfortunate alliances. It is because of them that you must die, and I do regret that. You are a pleasant young woman."

Her nostrils flared, and there was the brief trembling of her jaw, but she fought for composure, and she found it. "You just said you wouldn't kill me."

"*I* will not. But you will not live to see your wedding to the impressively loyal Mr.

Holmes. I apologize for that. Every girl should live to see her wedding, and you have been twice robbed." Mother would cluck at him, if she knew.

Until she realized it was necessary, that is. For Heinrich.

"Then let me go. Just . . . let me go. I'll not tell what you've done. I'll not —"

"It is too late for that." Poor girl. As if she really thought bargaining would save her now.

Her whimper sounded of a cry that was caught, muffled, swallowed. "My brother will find you."

He smiled into the window. "I am counting on it, *Fräulein.*"

"He'll kill you."

"Ah. That is the thing." He lifted a brow her direction. And smiled. "He cannot kill a ghost." And that was all he'd been for far too long. Before Heinrich's death. Before the *Boynton.* It's what he'd become when he first gave up his own name and took another for the sake of his country. He was naught but a specter, like Yūrei had said. That was what war made them all. A generation of ghosts.

Yūrei. Le fantôme. El fantasma.

Das Gespenst.

■ ■ ■ ■

Margot sat on the bottom step, staring at the doors through which Drake always entered. The admiral was pacing. Back and forth, back and forth across the tiled floor. Fifteen steps one direction, a one-eighty, fifteen the other, repeat. Perhaps because he had far more concerns than she did. The *Erri Barro* had met with more delays. The vice admiral, under orders by Jellicoe, would be setting up floodlights tonight to try to catch U-boats slipping by and force them down, away from the lights and into the anti-sub nets. New reports had come in from South America of cereal that they suspected was tainted with anthrax.

Anthrax. Margot didn't pace. She sat. *Too still,* Maman would have said. Not a muscle moving that wasn't required to keep her breathing, so that her mind could tick through it all. Line it up into neat columns and add the numbers.

She had thought too highly of herself. Of her work here. She had thought herself important enough to try to be stopped. She had thought it her fault that her mother had died. Because it *had* been her fault they'd been so hunted in Belgium.

527

But it hadn't been about her. Not this time. If the man who'd stolen Williams's name had targeted her, it wasn't because of her actual abilities — he clearly didn't know her or he wouldn't have tried to mug her in an alleyway. She'd just been one of many possible targets for him — that was all that made sense. And even if he *had* known her real position here . . . Margot was just one of many cryptographers. Part of a machine that would keep on ticking just fine without her. Stopping her wasn't a priority anymore. Maman had simply . . . died. Because everyone did. It hadn't seemed right that she'd died now — but asking *why now* would be the wrong question.

The better one was, when would it have been better? There would never have been a *right* time for her to lose her mother. There would never have been a reason that wouldn't have struck her as *wrong.* A heart attack — too much like her father. A stroke — too much like her grandmother. Involved in some accident — too much a coincidence when there were so many enemies in the world.

She'd heard it said so often that there were no coincidences, and she must have begun to believe it. But there were. Of course there were. The law of large numbers — the certainty that everything would happen, sooner or later, given enough instances. Probability insisted on it. Two spouses could and would die of the same ailment, years and miles apart. Random fact.

Not to say that God didn't factor it all into His plan. He would *use* it. But He didn't cause it. The world caused it, their lives caused it, that inevitable probability caused it. Because He'd set a world of order into motion. A world of cause and effect. Actions and reactions.

Maman had died. But the question of *why* was really two different questions. *Why had it happened?* That was what she had been focusing on — the question that led to theories and suspicions and starting at shadows. Or — *or.* She could ask the other question, *What was its purpose in God's plan?*

A completely different perspective. A ninety-degree shift. A question that looked to the future rather than the past, that forced her to focus not on the "this is my infirmity" of Psalm 77:10 and instead on "but I will remember the years of the right hand of the most High."

Hall checked his pocket watch. "They ought to be here any moment. Let him see you home then, my dear. You needn't spend another night on my couch."

She didn't move. Made no reply. Drake wouldn't consent to her going to her flat alone, she knew. But Dot wouldn't likely want her *there* either. He would have to take her to Lukas's house, she supposed.

Not yet. After. After he handed her the codebook and she'd used it on the slips of yellow that now sat, still and neat, in her lap. After they knew.

At last, there was a hitch in DID's stride and he moved to the door with purpose, obviously having spotted them through the window. He bypassed the ever-present guard and opened the door.

Margot stood, yellow slips of paper clutched in her hand. Her heart rate increased, more than the movement demanded. It was the thought of seeing him. Cause and effect. Increase in pulse, change in respiration, dilation of pupils. He would probably be able to tell just by looking at her how glad she was he was back. How much she feared letting him leave again.

Hall said something into the void left by the door, and voices answered. She couldn't make out the words, but she knew the voice, and it ratcheted up her beats-per-minute a little more.

Then she saw him. Brown hair under his

hat, silver-blue eyes, knotted nose. *Drake.*

She couldn't make herself move. She wanted to, but her muscles were locked into *too still,* making her wonder that she'd even managed to rise. She could only stand there, grasping the papers, and watch as he smiled at the admiral, sidled around him, and then finally, *finally* looked at her.

He grinned, and her respiration rate shifted again. A hitch that would drop it from its usual twelve breaths a minute to eleven. And then a few short heaves that would raise it to fifteen.

He strode toward her, obviously not suffering the same paralysis — but then, he wouldn't be. He was a man of action. And she was glad of it, just now. He pulled her against him, and she went gladly into his arms, not caring that the admiral, the guard, and whoever had entered behind Drake were looking on. She wrapped her arms around him and held on. "You made it back," she said into his coat.

"I did." His voice was a rumble in his chest, beneath her ear.

"I say, do I get one of those?"

The *too still* dissolved into the here and now. She pulled away with a laugh and shot a glare at Camden. "Threat number thirty-two from my list, Camden."

He made a show of wincing. "No thank you, I rather like my eyebrows."

Drake shook his head, rolled his eyes, turned up his lips in amusement. And then he reached into his coat and pulled out one of the most beautiful things she'd ever seen. A soft, green-papered codebook.

She snatched it from his hands as if it were the last cupful of sugar. "You found it!"

"We found *one,* anyway. You'll have to tell me if it's the correct one. Cam wasn't certain."

She sat again, there on the stairs, and flipped it open. A two-second glance assured her it wasn't one they already had. But there was only one way to be sure it was what they needed. She spread the telegrams and codebook out on the next step up, twisting around to use the stair as a desk, and got down to work.

"You know, my dear, you could take that upstairs."

As if she had the patience for that trek. Margot ignored the admiral's advice and pulled a pencil stub from her pocket. She hadn't spare paper to use for her usual lists of numbers, but that was all right. Paper was more for form and habit than necessity. But her head would work just fine for now.

She went from codebook to telegram and

back again, her smile growing a little more with each sentence that made sense. It was the right one. They'd found it. Soon she was slapping the first short decrypt to the side — the plain text scrawled directly onto the telegrams, each word above its encoded counterpart.

Drake snatched it up while she went to work on the next. "Identify targets for plan B3." He paused, probably looking at the admiral. "Do we know what that is?"

"No. Where was that one sent from?"

Margot didn't need to check her notes — she'd already memorized the order of receipt and location. "From Berlin. To here in London. As is the next, if we're looking at them in order of dates received." It being no longer than the original, she even then wrote the last word. "This one says, 'Locate admiralty codebooks.' "

A beat of silence, then Hall snorted. "Well, they've failed in that. We'd know it if our codes had been compromised."

They would, as they had been alerted when the minesweeping code had been. But it could be why this agent had been targeting her. The date on the telegram matched up with when he'd begun appearing.

She went to work on the next message, which was longer. The men chattered on about the mission while she decrypted, until she slid the sheet over toward Drake.

"This one is reporting the death of an Agent Regnitz in the line of duty. Requesting transport of body. . . . Regnitz? I don't recognize that name."

"It's a river," Camden said. "In Bavaria. Aside from that . . . it could be a surname, I suppose. Or a code name. Sir?"

Hall's footsteps sounded, and then there was the rustle of paper exchanging hands. "I don't recall seeing it in any of our other information."

Nor did Margot, though she gave it only a passing thought. Her focus was already on the next telegram. A response to the first, it seemed. "Transport was refused. The recipient was instructed to dispose of the corpse however he saw fit and then implement plan A22." She slapped that paper down too. "This next one is also from Berlin but seems to have been sent to England again, sir."

"Where were the previous two received originally?"

"Madrid."

She heard the hitch in Drake's breath. "I suppose I shouldn't be surprised, since we know it has something to do with Jaeger, and the train was bound for Madrid. I suppose A22 commanded him back here, somehow or another."

"So it would seem. Though I would still like to know how an agent of the Central Powers managed to slip past us without my knowing it." Hall's irritation echoed off the marble stairs.

Margot scratched another word onto the page.

"Or was it two agents, even?" Drake asked. "We know Jaeger is here, given the phone call. He must be working with the man who attacked the girls last night. This bloke seems to have been here for a while — I would bet under the name Niall Walsh originally. Perhaps he helped secret Jaeger in somehow too."

"Without our knowing it?" Hall huffed. "Not possible."

Margot's lips twitched. "The law of large numbers, sir. It's possible someone has evaded your knowledge all this time, however improbable it may seem."

"Statistics that don't particularly help just now. What we need are some hard facts. Margot?" Hall stepped closer.

Her smile had stalled and faded. "This is the last one of those we found in the flat, and it just references another plan by alphanumeric designation. The others were sent to South America. Not to our man, I should think." With a frustrated sigh, she set her pencil down. "Useless. All of it. You two put your lives in danger for nothing."

"I don't believe that." Drake sat beside her and bumped his shoulder into hers. "We needed that codebook. It's given us pieces. Perhaps we're still missing a few others, but we'll find them."

"Tomorrow is soon enough to renew the search." Hall blinked, nodded, and motioned to the door. "Everyone to their beds — that's an order. And Camden?"

The pilot paused with a foot already aimed for the door. "Sir?"

"Well done."

His face didn't exactly soften. The shadows didn't exactly abandon their posts in his eyes. But a bit of light entered there, alongside them. After a moment's pause, he nodded. "Thank you, sir." He strode for the door. Though when he pushed it open, his next words had their usual snarl to them. "Well, look who it is. I didn't know nursemaids made office calls."

"Red?" Drake pushed to his feet, brows drawn.

Holmes was pushing past Camden with a scowl. "I haven't time for your nonsense just now. Elton, you'd better get home."

Margot slipped the two telegrams no one

had picked up into the codebook and stood too. "Dot?" She met Drake's questioning look. "She was properly upset this morning. Handed in her resignation, gave me a dressing-down, and stormed out."

"She won't answer the door." Red motioned toward the general direction of her flat. "And she must have dismissed the guard you'd posted. But that's not why I've come, actually. There's an older Spanish gentleman at your building, Elton, demanding to see his grandchildren and causing a terrible uproar."

Drake actually jerked, as if a bolt of electricity had coursed through him. "Well, it can't be *my* grandfather. He never leaves home."

Red lifted dubious brows. "Then perhaps you can at least come and explain why whoever it is keeps yelling for a dragon. One of your neighbors is convinced he's calling down dark magic or some such rot, and he keeps lapsing into Spanish, which no one else can understand."

Drake jolted again, and Margot gripped his hand. "Dragon?" he muttered.

"That would be you, wouldn't it, Eighteen?" She knew she looked a bit too amused at his expense. But she couldn't recall ever seeing him caught so off guard.

"Looks like your abuelo has a few surprises up his sleeve after all."

31

Suddenly Drake thought he knew how those pilots with altitude sickness had felt. Utterly disoriented, he could only stand in the doorway to the landlord's office, sure he was seeing an apparition. Or an illusion. Or a figment of his own imagination. Something other than what his eyes insisted he saw — Francisco Mendoza de Haro. Here, in England, where he had never once deigned to step.

It was Margot who stepped forward first, hand outstretched, and said, "You must be Señor Mendoza. I'm Margot De Wilde."

Abuelo, ever the gentleman, even when he was only an illusion, took her hand and pressed his lips to it, despite that she'd clearly meant to shake instead. "Ah, my granddaughter's new friend. *Es un placer conocerle.*"

Drake shook himself and stepped forward. "Abuelo. What are you — *why* are you . . . ?"

Abuelo's eyes could sparkle with the best of them. "Rarely have I seen you unable to frame the right question, Dragón." Then his too-dark brows lifted toward his white hair. "Is this how you greet your abuelo?"

"Lo siento." Apology muttered, Drake moved forward to embrace him. "You look well."

"As do you, which is a great relief to me." Now he narrowed his eyes, rebuke in his gaze, and motioned with a hand.

Only then did Drake notice that Eneko stood in the corner, clutching a hat, which he now held out.

Not just *a* hat. *Drake's* hat. He took it, knowing he looked as dazed as he felt. "How did you get this?" It ought still to be tumbling through the Spanish countryside. Or on the head of a farmer who laughed over his find.

"The better question, Dragón, is how did *you* lose it?" Abuelo moved to the rickety chair behind the landlord's scratched desk and sat in it with the same grace and authority he used when taking his own seat in Bilbao. Steepling his fingers, he narrowed his eyes still more. "Imagine my concern when the *policía* knocked on my door two weeks ago, your favorite hat in their hands, saying they discovered it at a suspected murder scene in Madrid and traced the label to the haberdasher you favor there. He so very helpfully checked the number he'd put on the tag against his books and gave them your name. Imagine my concern, Dragón, when they said they were not certain whether it belonged to the victim or the culprit, but that you were a person of interest in this crime."

Drake groped for support — a chair back, a shelf, something to keep him upright. Instead he found Margot's hand in his. Which anchored him far better than furniture could anyway. "I beg your pardon?"

Abuelo shook his head. "I, of course, knew you were well. You had wired me since this mysterious death to tell me you were spending Christmas here. And, of course, you are no murderer. That was never in question. So I told the policía they must have been mistaken. That my grandson was but a lackadaisical university student who could not seem to finish his studies in a reasonable amount of time. And one who further prolonged his graduation by deciding to winter here for some unfathomable reason." His eyes darted to Margot, and his lips slid up just a fraction — not enough to be thought a smile on anyone else, but the equivalent of a grin for him. "Or perhaps not so unfathomable now. Why have you not mentioned your *cariño* in your letters to me, Dragón?"

Drake could only shake his head. "I don't understand. What murder scene?"

"Ah. This was of the utmost interest to me, too, despite my certainty you had nothing to do with it. I had to expend considerable effort and call in many favors to determine this." Abuelo waved his fingers again, and again Eneko stepped forward.

Eneko's expression said more than Abuelo's did. That whatever this was, it was serious. He held out a thin stack of papers clipped together, a photograph on top.

Naturally, Drake's eyes went first to the image. And his head went light at the grainy shot of two men entering a building. Grainy, but good enough to see their faces.

"*El Señor* was providing for us with that photograph, sí? A woman had her camera out, at her window, to try to get a snapshot of her son riding on his bicycle — you see him there in the foreground. She did not realize she had captured anyone else in her image until weeks later, when she received her pictures back. And even then, she only came forward when we put an advertisement in the newspaper, asking for any information to be had on suspicious men seen at that address."

"Suspicious men," Drake echoed, eyes still pasted to the image.

Margot had leaned in, too, and had drawn in a long breath. "It's him. The taller one — that's the man who attacked us. Was he the one following you?"

"Yes." Drake swallowed. "And the other is Maxim Jaeger." Jaeger, clutching at his leg. Jaeger, agony on his face. Jaeger, supported by the man in the grey overcoat, looking as though he wouldn't have been able to walk without said support.

Red, who had been hovering in the doorway behind him, eased forward to study the image. "They look a bit alike, don't they?"

"A bit." He'd thought the mystery man had been familiar, hadn't he? Slightly? But he'd assumed he'd seen his picture. It hadn't occurred to him that he looked familiar because a few of those features Drake had memorized were the same as Jaeger's. The nose. The eyes. That was where the similarity ended, but seeing both faces together now, it was obvious. "They're brothers."

Margot's breath eased out again. "Drake . . . have you ever heard that other man speak?"

He could only shake his head, easily following her train of thought. *She* might have, during their Go game, but she'd certainly never heard Jaeger. But if they were brothers . . . "It could have been him on the telephone. Not Jaeger at all."

"If Jaeger is the name by which you know the injured one," Abuelo chimed in from the desk, "then I can promise you he did not place any telephone calls after the seventh of November. He is deceased. His body was just discovered in a shallow grave outside the city a few days ago. A bullet apparently severed the artery in his leg. We believe he bled out in that building the photograph shows him being led into."

"A bullet." Drake closed his eyes, well remembering the pistol in his hands that day as he climbed the ladder on the train car. Firing wildly, blindly, just trying to keep Jaeger down. But if his opposite number had already stood up . . . His fingers tightened around Margot's. He'd killed him. He hadn't meant to. Hadn't, honestly, *wanted* to. Yes, it was war. Yes, he knew what was expected. But recognizing a man was an enemy didn't mean he wanted to eliminate him entirely. Because he wasn't *just* an enemy. He was a man. A son.

A brother.

But Maxim Jaeger was dead — undeniably. And his brother was here. *"You will pay,"* he'd said. Not for the sugar, not for the anthrax. For Maxim's death.

Margot must have been doing the same arithmetic in her mind. She tugged on his hand, angled toward the door. "Red, you said the guard was gone from the door? And Dot wouldn't answer? Not even for you?"

No. Drake didn't need to be pulled. He surged forward, doing the pulling.

"Dragón." Abuelo had stood, and he must have rushed to get to the door by the time Drake put his foot on the first step. "I do not know if it matters, but Jaeger was not the name I was given when I asked one of my German contacts to discover his identity for me. I was told he was Heinrich Regnitz, a decorated officer before he and his brother, Dieter, were both recruited into intelligence."

Feet itching to launch him up the stairs, Drake still paused long enough to shake his head. "How did you discover all that, Abuelo?"

"I have friends in high places. On both sides of the war." His brows lifted again. "Apparently closer than I knew on the Allied side. I expect a full explanation from you before I go home. I have long known you were not taking more classes, but I would like to know what you *have* been up to."

Eneko appeared behind Abuelo. "I told you he ought to have his wings clipped."

Drake didn't spare the time it would take to roll his eyes. He bounded up the stairs, Margot at his side and Red a step behind them.

"Heinrich Regnitz. The one that telegram was about." Margot had no trouble keeping pace. "And the man we're looking for must be Dieter Regnitz. His brother."

"His brother." Drake's chest went tight. "I killed his brother. I had to fire off a few shots as cover, to give myself a chance to get away. I must have hit him. Just before he hit me. I didn't mean to kill him." He knew well that emotion tightened his voice. Emotion he'd never dare let slip out in the presence of another soldier. But somehow, he thought Margot would understand. "I didn't even mean to *hit* him. Just force him down."

Red's step faltered. "Wait, you were . . . ? Elton, I believe I require the same explanation you owe your grandfather."

"Later, Red." They charged up the final stretch of stairs. First he had to make sure Dieter didn't take his revenge on the most likely candidate.

Drake's sister. Drake's sister for Dieter's brother.

But the corridor yawned frighteningly empty when they gained it. No guard, as Red had said, even though Hall had stationed one there in Camden's place last night. Even though Drake had given the chap strict instructions not to let anyone but Red in, not to let her out alone, and not to leave her *there* alone.

"Dot?" he called through the door even as he inserted his key into the lock and turned. "Dot!"

She didn't answer, and he knew as he opened the door and stepped inside that she wasn't there.

The flat wasn't empty though. Muffled noises came from Drake's bedroom — a thumping and a muted vocalization. "Dot?" He surged forward, praying with every ounce of hope he had that his certainty had been wrong, that she was there. Bound, gagged perhaps, but there.

Red somehow beat him to the doorway, his face in agony. "Dotty, we're coming!" He pushed open the door. It swung free about eight inches, then it stuck, and another muffled yell sounded.

Margot stood frozen a few paces from the

door. Seeing it, but not just it. Seeing her mother's door, too, that terrible morning. When she'd pushed it open, only to find it wouldn't go. That it had stuck against her prone figure on the floor.

Her throat went tight. Even though she knew it was different this time, still her throat went tight. And the fingers that Drake had dropped as he vaulted forward curled toward her palms.

Numbers clamored for release. Prayers that had remained too long unprayed. Supplications. *Thirteen, twenty-six, thirty-nine.* Praises. *Three, nine, twenty-seven, eighty-one.* Pleas for forgiveness. *Eighteen. Eighteen. Eighteen.*

Red had squeezed through the opening and helped the blue-clad legs find purchase on the floor. Drake swung the door wide.

It must have been the guard they'd posted. He was clearly a navy man, and even from here Margot could see the bloodied knot on his head. His hands were bound behind him, his ankles tied tight, and a balled-up rag had been tied into his mouth, the poor chap.

Red and Drake soon had the gag removed, the ropes cut. Margot spun for the kitchen, Maman's voice in her head. *Get the poor lad some water, Margot. Can you not see that he will be parched?*

Maman had always been wise. The man was managing little more than a few hoarse croaks until she handed him the water, which he guzzled greedily. Then he sank onto the end of Drake's bed with an audible "Thanks."

"Tell me what happened, seaman. Where's my sister?"

The lad shook his head. "I was escorting her home from the OB, Lieutenant, as you'd told me to do. We'd just gotten to the door, and your sister was fishing her keys out of her handbag — she was upset and having a time of it, so I was trying to help. Then, the next thing I know, I woke up here, and it was afternoon already."

Red spat out his opinion on the matter, shoved agitated fingers through his hair, and spun toward the window. "Where is she? Where? Do you think — is he going to hurt her?"

"I don't know." Drake, too, spun. Margot, still on the threshold because it felt too odd to go into his room, watched his eyes flit from left to right, up and down, every which way. Searching for answers. Or, lacking those, for questions. Then the color drained from his cheeks as he stared at something she couldn't see from where she stood.

549

"Margot. Come here, please."

Her feet obeyed before her mind even commanded them to do so, and that one step was all it took to remove the wall from her view and replace it with the small desk. On top of which sat a familiar game board, black and white stones arranged just so and a white slip of paper anchored under the corner.

She took in the play first, frowning. It wasn't their game. Countless times he had taken the board down and set it up again, and always each stone was in the proper position. But this was different. Had she made a different play two moves ago, it could have gone this way, but she'd been smarter than that. Because she'd considered this move, she'd guessed at his response, and she knew that if she moved her white stone like that, she'd be trapped. As he showed her now.

She snatched at the paper. Two words this time. *Kikashi.* When one forced an opponent into a move that would ruin their momentum. And under that, *aji keshi.* When one had been outsmarted.

Her fingers convulsed around the paper. "He's not going to outsmart us. He will *not.*"

"No. He won't." Drake moved the board

a bit, peered around it. Checked the desk drawer. Peered underneath it. Spun for the small shelf by the window.

"What are you looking for?" Red asked.

Drake darted a glance at her. "My poetry book. And the notebook I kept with it. They were on my desk when I left. They're always there."

So he could write to her. Those beautiful messages, written in code.

"Why would he take that?" The guard sounded baffled.

"Good question. I think . . . I think he intends to tell us something more. More than he can do through Go."

Three of six. The words, the number exploded in her mind like fireworks, so sweet she nearly gasped from their splendor. They trickled down through her spirit, summer rain on parched soil. A balm. A song. A perfect proposition.

She reached for Drake. "My flat. Now. Three of six."

"What is three of six?" But even as he asked, he took her hand and followed her out.

"Eighteen. My flat. That day, anyway. Because it's — it doesn't matter, just come."

His grandfather and his attendant were in the doorway, blocking it, but they slid aside when they saw the speed of their approach. Shouted a question after them, but Drake shouted back that Red would fill them in and didn't slow.

No more words, not on the stairs. They didn't need them. It was enough that he trusted her. It was enough that God had spoken again in her soul. It was enough to make her hope that there was time, still, to save Dot.

Night had fallen again. It was cold and clear and only days until Christmas, but just now those days mattered not at all compared to the minutes before them now. Fingers still knotted together, they ran down the familiar streets.

Her building looked like it always did these days. All the windows were dark with blinds and curtains, the musty smell close around her when she pushed through the door. She dug out her keys as they ran up the stairs, not counting the steps or the rungs or calculating the change of pitch of the railing. Up to the third floor, down the hallway to her door.

The lights were off in there, of course, as she'd left them yesterday morning. But the light from the corridor was enough to show her the rectangle of white on the floor, where someone must have slid it under her door. She picked it up while Drake switched on the lights, slit it open while he closed the door, pulled out the single sheet of paper while he returned to her side.

Numbers, in a familiar pattern. The simple code Drake had been using, the one that used the poetry book as a key. She moved to the table, where she always kept *Les Heures Claires* set out, waiting for the next day's sweet nothings.

She hated that he'd taken this. Stolen their unspoken secret and used it against them. The first time they acknowledged the notes aloud shouldn't be like this, when it was Dieter Regnitz who had used their book to write her a message instead of Drake. It was like an inkblot on a page of newsprint. A mar on what had been perfect.

Suddenly she recalled the notes that were out of order, that night she'd gone on a whim to Drake's flat and ended up fleeing again. The night she'd apparently collided directly with Regnitz and hadn't even re-alized it. He'd been following her, not just watching Drake. He'd been in here. In her haven, in the place that had always been safe. He'd touched her belongings, and she hadn't even known it. She'd been too focused on those stupid newspapers. Too distracted by the muddle of her own mind.

No, not her mind. Her heart.

Perhaps her disquiet showed on her face, or in her stillness, or in the way she held the letter. Because Drake rested a hand on her back and pressed his lips to the side of her head. "You know, I have two matching volumes of *Don Quixote* in Bilbao. I'll send one to you."

She leaned into him for a moment, gave him a smile. And then moved to her chair at the table. They hadn't the time to waste on regrets and horror now. "I suppose we ought to see what he has to say."

"I'll help." He sat at the chair next to her and slid the book of poetry toward him. "You read the numbers off, I'll find them."

It would probably take a bit longer that way, but no numbers rioted about within her to say that two extra minutes would make a difference, so she nodded. "Two. Five. One."

He flipped to the second page, found the fifth line. Read her the first word in French. *Je.*

She wrote the English translation on the blank sheet of paper awaiting her pen. *I.*

A few minutes later, the short message looked back at them from the expanse of white.

I regret to have to use you lovely ladies for this purpose, but I have my orders. My superiors are in need of your codebooks. Acquire them however you must, if you want to see your friend alive again. Tell her brother to come with them at midnight. Deposit them at the crossroad below, in the rubbish bin at the mouth of the alley. I will signal him, and he may then proceed to the address below to collect his sister.

The final words on the page weren't in code. They were just there at the end of the list of numbers. Two directions to somewhere in Woolwich. An hour's ride on the tube.

Margot felt as though she were breathing for the first time in an hour. "It doesn't sound as though he's hurt her. If he's being truthful." She looked up. "Is he after the codebooks or revenge, though?"

"Both, I daresay, if he can get them. It's a smart plan. Have me drop the codebook in one location. While I'm fetching Dot, he could fetch that and be away before I could then catch him. Assuming he doesn't have some sort of trap planned for *me,* which I'm not willing to assume." Drake checked his watch. "We have plenty of time. I can let Hall know. He can give me an outdated codebook, perhaps —"

"Oh, he'll give you a new one." Her lips turned up in a ghost of a smile. "We've long been prepared for this. In the first days of the war, he had us create a false code to pass along if necessary. I still have the original in my desk here. . . ." Sucking in a breath, she remembered again those letters, out of order.

She never should have taken that original home — why had she? But she'd wanted to improve it, have a second version. And surely the German hadn't found it, or he wouldn't still be demanding it. Right? She dropped to her knees, pulled out the lowest drawer of her desk, and reached up to where she'd hidden it.

Still there. Her fingers brushed the paper, gripped the stack, pulled it out. A relieved sigh shook its way out. "There. We can simply get Hall's permission to use it." She stood again and dropped the false codebook onto the top of her desk.

Drake breathed a laugh. "Always surprising me. Perfect, Margot. I'll find him, we can put a team together. I'll take you back to Abuelo and Red, or to your brother, and —"

"No." She covered his hand with hers. When had it become such an easy move, such a comfortable one? When had his fingers begun to feel as familiar to her as her own?

He frowned at her. "Don't insist on coming, mi alma. Please don't."

"It isn't that. It's that he must know how you'll respond. He must know you won't come alone. We must think differently. We must *act* differently."

His brows were still gathered over the knot in his nose. But his breath eased out. "We should listen to my mother. She always said never to neglect our prayers."

Margot would have liked his mother. She nodded and let her eyes fall closed.

Her spirit still felt a bit raw. The ache of her own mother's absence was no less there. But that waterfall of His voice still filled her. She sought the words to match the numbers in her mind. *I'm sorry, Lord God, for shutting you out. I'm sorry for saying no when you asked me to pray. And I thank you, I thank you so much for preserving him anyway. For bringing him here, so that he could help me to see my own heart. And that it's all right to have one.*

Her fingers tightened around his. *Help us now, Lord God, as only you can. Help us to find the move in this game Dieter Regnitz has set up that will turn the momentum in our favor. That will save Dot. Help us to get her back to Red. Help us, most of all, Father, to find the path that will bring you the most glory. Ten, one hundred, one thousand, ten thousand . . .*

Her words ran dry, but her spirit didn't, and the powers of ten multiplied beautifully in her mind for another long moment, a new zero marching into line each time. A perfect circle. Without beginning. Without end. Eternal, like the One who had come before.

Then all the zeros scattered away like autumn leaves in a windstorm, and only the one remained. It folded, folded again. And one of those stray zeroes settled back into place. *40.*

Her eyes sprang open. Not a number the Lord had ever spoken to her before. But it had only one meaning in her mind. She looked to Drake and said the number aloud.

He was pushing to his feet. "The OB?"

"Room 40."

Together they hurried back into the night.

32

The munitions factory had shut down for the evening. Das Gespenst had watched the workers go, laughing together in twos and threes, not seeming to give any thought to the fact that they'd spent their day producing bullets, shells, and explosives that would continue killing off the generation.

It was possible this very factory had produced the bullet that Elton had loaded into his pistol that day in Spain before he boarded the train. Not guaranteed, of course. But possible.

It didn't matter if it was this exact factory anyway. What mattered was that when the zeppelins or Gothas flew overhead in a few short hours and dropped their loads, a blow would be struck to the enemy. He doubted he could trust whatever codebook Elton and De Wilde would get for him, but he'd have succeeded in at least one part of his directive — locating targets for the Luftstreitkräfte. He'd no doubt have *something* to hand over to the High Command in terms of codes, whether it be useful or not.

And he would succeed in his own mission as well. Elton would pay.

Das Gespenst shifted the limp figure beside him. If she remained unconscious as long as she had earlier, he had an hour to sneak her inside. Bind her again. Gag her this time, since there was a night guardsman patrolling the grounds. He, too, would likely die this night. Collateral damage, like Williams. Though, unlike Yūrei, the guard no doubt wouldn't be begging for the sweet relief of death. But that was none of his concern.

He patted Dorothea's motionless hand. She'd slept through the short ride in the little boat he'd procured to get her from one pier to the other. She'd slept as he'd eased her into the cab he'd already hired to be waiting for them. Perhaps she'd sleep until the bombs fell. That would be a kindness. Yes, he would see that she did. He'd slip a little more laudanum between her lips. Because she reminded him of Ilse, and because Heinrich wouldn't have wanted her to suffer unduly when it was her brother who must pay.

He would come, once he and Margot De

560

Wilde found his note. He would come with a codebook in hand, because he loved his sister. As Das Gespenst had loved his brother. *He* had come, hadn't he, the moment Heinrich had called? He'd left the spot where he'd been sent to rendezvous with him and the sugar, to escort it on its final journey to England, and he'd rushed to the little town outside Madrid that Heinrich had stumbled to from the train, clinging to Elton's discarded hat as if doing so would grant him vengeance. He'd hurried him back to the safe house they'd set up. He'd done all he could — all he could to save him.

But no tourniquet was enough to stop that much blood. Nothing could. His hands still felt red from it.

He'd had to watch the very life drain from his brother's thigh. Watch the light go out of his eyes. He'd had to dig his grave himself, carry him to it. Send word home to their mother, to Ilse, that Heinrich was gone. Their hero had fallen.

Berlin had been no help. None. They'd give Heinrich a medal for his service, he was certain, but there had been no aid. No other agent sent to assist him. Nothing. Just instruction to move on to his next assignment.

Those blighted codes. And this factory. He'd had to map out where it was for them, send them the instructions that would enable the Luftstreitkräfte to find it from the air. And he had. He'd done his duty, and he'd sent the telegram that afternoon as he'd been instructed.

But he'd have his own revenge too. For Heinrich. Because the hero couldn't fall without consequence.

A small beam of light passed by the windows of the ground floor of the factory — the sign he'd been waiting for. By the time he carried Dorothea over to the small side entrance, the guard would be long gone, making his rounds on the other side of the building.

Tossing a coin to the front seat of the cab for the driver to find when he awoke from his own drug-induced sleep — assuming the explosion of the factory didn't take him out — Das Gespenst slid toward the door. Opened it, climbed out, and reached for Dorothea.

He only coughed once, which pleased him. His lips curved up just a bit. Perhaps Margot De Wilde's prayers for him were working.

Margot unbuttoned her coat, shrugged out

of it, and tossed it on her chair even as Drake slid the satchel with the false code-book to the floor under it. "What's come in since I left?" She didn't stop at her usual station but rather hurried to where the pneumatic tubes delivered all the newly intercepted telegrams, Drake a step behind.

De Grey looked up from his spot with an exaggerated frown. "I thought you'd been excused from the night shift since you were here all last night."

"I was. Just couldn't stay away. Has there been anything in the new code?"

"Not that I've seen. Though DID dropped off the recovered codebook not long ago. Excellent work on that, Elton. I hope he promised you a prize."

Drake breathed a laugh. "It never came up."

"What are you looking for?" Culbreth looked up from his work, eyes dazed enough to prove he'd been hard at it. "The new one, did you say? I think I . . . yes, hold on. I saw something. Half an hour ago, perhaps. Haven't had a chance yet to —"

"That's all right, I can take it." With a smile for her friend, she snatched at the paper he pulled from a stack of them and spun for the codebook.

"What can I do to help?" Drake pulled

her chair out for her.

"I don't know yet. Give me a moment." She set everything up as she always did. The cypher, the message, scrap paper, a sheet to write the decrypt on, a pen. "Analysis, perhaps. You've been doing enough of that."

"Will it bother you if I look over your shoulder as you work? The faster to see what appears?"

She shook her head. They often worked as a team in here, looking at the same papers, correcting one another, contradicting one another. "Not a bit."

The message was longer than the others had been. Long enough that it made her chest tighten. How much time did they have? Midnight, he'd said. What happened at midnight? They didn't have but three hours now until they found out.

She got to it. She only paid attention to the first words, enough to be sure they were coherent, proof that she was using the right code. But after that she ignored the actual meanings and focused on the details. Encrypted word to number, number to German word, German word to English word.

"He's describing a location." Drake leaned an elbow onto her desk. " 'Follow the Thames inland . . . when the river turns ninety degrees toward the south, watch for a cluster of church steeples.' Have we a map of London and the surroundings around here anywhere?"

"Hall has one, I believe," de Grey said.

Drake patted her shoulder. "I'll be right back."

"Mm." She kept working while he was gone. And it must have taken him quite a while to find what he was looking for, because she was penning the last word into place when finally he came back into the room, Hall himself a step behind him. Drake spread the map on an unused desk and began tracing a finger along it.

"What comes after the part about the steeples?"

She read it to him, turning on her chair to better face him. " 'This is the northmost apex. Follow the river another seven kilometers —' "

"That would be Woolwich." Drake glanced up, face grave. "Keep reading. But I have a feeling I know where he's leading them."

She finished, up to " 'this is your mark,' " watching his finger trace along the map as she did so. The question already burning her tongue. "Is that where he told you to go? Where he has Dot?"

He nodded toward the decrypt. "Is there anything else?"

There was, and it made her pulse slow to a dull throb. "He says he recommends no fewer than two dozen Gothas set out to ensure that at least five reach the mark."

The admiral stepped forward, blinking rapidly. "A bombing raid. He knew I would send a team with you, yes, and didn't care. The more we send in, the more who would die with you when those bombs fell."

"While I leave the codebook a safe distance away." Drake's lips had gone thin and tight. He motioned to Hall. "I told him about that part, too, of course."

"And I agree that our so-dubbed Emergency Code is the perfect answer. Compromising it is no great thing at all."

Margo had expected nothing else. She stood and moved to look over Drake's shoulder. "What's the target?"

He tapped a finger to the map. "It's the Woolwich munitions factory."

Her muscles went still, frozen for a moment. Even if only a few planes made it, even if only a few bombs fell, that would be catastrophic. It wouldn't take much to turn the factory itself into a bomb, killing not only Dot but innocents by the hundreds. Perhaps the thousands. "No."

Drake pushed away from the table. "It isn't enough to just go in and get Dot out.

We have to *stop* them. Not just him, but *them.* How do we do that?"

Culbreth and de Grey had both given up their own work and had gathered round the map. Culbreth tapped something near the mouth of the Thames. "We alert the RFC and RNAS, for starters. There's no great risk to our operations in telling them — the Germans won't know they've tipped us off, they'll just assume we had a scout in the air who spotted them. Then we can get our own lads up in the air to take out as many as they can and get the antiaircraft guns ready." He lifted his brows in Hall's direction.

DID nodded. "Do it."

Culbreth spun for the door.

De Grey turned that way too. "And we can have them sound the sirens in that part of London. The residents ought to have ample time to get to the underground shelters and out of the city."

Hall was still nodding. These were safe actions, precautionary ones. Actions that, as Culbreth had pointed out, wouldn't alert the German High Command to the fact that they'd broken their codes and thereby inspire them to change them entirely. They would assume the Gothas had been spotted. Room 40's secrecy would be upheld.

Even so. When other squadrons that large had made their way across the Channel, their defenses hadn't succeeded in blocking them *all*. A few always slipped through. And though their bombs hadn't seemed to be aimed at specific targets, with detailed information like what Dieter Regnitz had provided, that would change.

Unless . . . unless the *details* could be changed. She gripped Drake's arm, looking at the admiral. "We can send them a supposed correction, sir, as you've done before. Misinformation — an updated message with a new target." For Drake's benefit, she added, "We write a message in their code and send it, supposedly from Regnitz. We just need a decoy target. Something that won't harm anyone."

Hall gave her a small, tight smile. "The very solution I was going to recommend."

Drake was still staring at the map. "An abandoned building. I know of a few near there. I can write out the directions as he did. You can turn it into code."

"And while I'm doing that," she said, squeezing his arm, "go and get your sister."

"Keep your eyes peeled. He said he'd signal me to proceed after I drop the codebook, so he'll be nearby." Drake jammed Hall's car into Park in a shadowy stretch of road.

Red jumped out of the opposite door, and Camden piled out of the back. They'd used the forty-minute drive toward Woolwich to try to guess at what Regnitz meant to do. To anticipate what would change when the bombs didn't fall on their target. To determine how to find him and apprehend him.

Because he wouldn't be at the factory — not unless he meant to die tonight. And somehow, Drake couldn't imagine that was his goal. But he'd want to be close. Close enough to retrieve the codebook, yes, but he'd also want to see Drake walk into the factory. He'd want to see the building go up in flames. He'd want to make certain he didn't escape.

They had decided to assume he'd be armed, possibly with a long-range rifle, hence why they all stuck to the shadows. Red, who had apparently done a fair bit of scouting in France before he'd been sent home minus a foot, took the lead, motioning them forward with hand signals.

For once, Camden had apparently decided to be civil. He'd simply ignored Red, rather than insulting him, while they drove. And now he fell in without any complaints, without any posturing. A soldier, when it came down to it.

At least for a few minutes. But then he stopped while Red was still advancing and grabbed him by the arm to halt him. Drake, bringing up the rear, halted too. "What is it?" he whispered.

"Planes." Camden set his eyes on the heavens, scanning from horizon to horizon.

Red leaned close. "Ours or theirs? Can you tell?"

It took another moment for Drake to even make out the drone of the engines over the sounds of city life. Certainly he couldn't discern whether they belonged to Camels or Gothas.

But if the curse he bit off was any indication, Camden could. And it was the wrong answer. "Hurry!"

Sirens blared. First from a distance, but that seemed to trigger others, and soon the night was filled with the angry warning sound. From somewhere far off, an unmistakable *boom* shattered the night still more. The antiaircraft guns, stationed around London.

Red took off at a run, and Drake and Camden followed. If the Gothas were here, it meant one of two things — either they hadn't received Margot's revisions to their plan in time and this factory would soon be targeted, or they'd soon be dropping their loads on the abandoned warehouse on the other side of the river, and Regnitz would realize he'd been foiled. Either way, they'd probably be safe from any sniping he might have planned right now . . . but not for long.

They stopped at the first of the two locations the agent had given them, where a metal rubbish bin slouched forlorn in the mouth of an alley. Into this Drake slid the false code. And then straightened, looking about, wondering what sort of signal Regnitz would offer.

He had his answer when a bullet bit off a chunk of brick a foot above his head. It had likely come from across the street, but he didn't have time to investigate. He motioned Red and Camden onward.

No more bullets whizzed by them as they made their way, but the drone of the planes was growing louder now, and the sirens continued to scream. "It isn't midnight yet!" Drake shouted as they gained the side door of the factory and, upon testing it, found it unlocked.

Convenient. And probably thanks to Dieter Regnitz, who wanted them to gain entrance.

Let Dot be here, Lord. Help us find her. Help us get her out. Only by your grace, Father.

"They must have caught a tailwind and

made it across the Channel faster than anticipated — those that made it. Some would have dropped off, they always do." Camden bent in half long enough to suck in a breath. "You definitely owe me now, Elton."

Flying him to France and home in one day and then following him to a known bombing target? He'd owe him for the rest of his life. *Lord, let it be long enough to repay him.* "I'll send you a tin of biscuits."

"I see something, chaps. Over there." Red indicated the corner of the factory floor.

Drake followed his finger to where a figure was slumped — too long to be Dot. Too wide to be Regnitz. "A guard?"

"I'll see." Moving quickly, Red took off.

Drake surveyed the factory floor. This room had no machines, no equipment. Just enormous shells, lined up like rows of wheat, from this wall as far as he could see toward the opposite. Support beams stretched up to the ceiling every few yards, and walkways intersected each other in a grid.

Almost, nearly, like a game board. But where were the players?

Another *boom* sounded from outside. A whole series of them, along with an explosion of a different tenor.

"Bomb. Hurry."

"Dot!" Stealth was no longer really going to prove helpful, so Drake took off down the nearest aisle at a run. Praying with every footfall that none of those bombs crashed through this ceiling. "Dorothea!"

"Dot!"

"Dotty!"

"Over here!" Not Red or Camden — Dot herself, from the far side of the cavernous chamber. "Hurry! He's long gone!"

Drake sprinted down the aisle, dodging a beam, nearly tripping over one of the heavy howitzer shells. He reached her a few seconds after Red, a few before Camden. Red had already pulled her up and given her a quick, fierce embrace by the time Drake skidded to a halt, trying to take stock of her in the moonlight while Red went to work on the ropes at her wrist. Camden crouched down with his knife at the ready to take care of the rope at her ankles.

"Are you injured? Did he hurt you?" Drake gripped her by the shoulders and tilted her face toward the window.

She shook her head. An odd answer, given the spatters of blood he saw on her cheek. "Drugged me, but he didn't hurt me. We have to hurry though. He's injured, but he's been gone for at least twenty minutes."

Waiting for them. He'd have fetched the codebook by now and be on his way out of the neighborhood. "Injured? How?"

Dot's smile was a wisp of a thing. Fragile. Yet victorious. "He thought I was still unconscious there at the end, and I let him. When he removed the gag to give me more laudanum, I kicked him in the shin and sent him sprawling into the shells." She nodded to where a few were indeed knocked over, something dark smearing them. "He was bleeding. Coughing fiercely. And holding his hand. I think one of the shells must have caught it somehow. I expected him to come at me then, but he ran out instead."

"He wasn't going to risk being here." And neither should they. Drake pressed a kiss to her forehead while Red worked through the last of her bonds and then gripped one of her newly freed hands. "We need to get out. Fast." He looked to Red. "The bloke by the door?"

Red shook his head. "Shot in the head."

Dot winced. "He tried to stop him. He had come to sooner than expected, I think."

Drake pressed his lips together. But there was nothing they could do for that man. And still much to do about the one who'd done it. He led the way to the nearest door, knowing Dot would rather have Red's arm around her, leading her out, than his. "Do you know where he went?"

"I don't know. He didn't say. But he had me somewhere near here earlier. I could just make out the roof of the factory from the window. There was empty space between us. Near the river, perhaps? He may have gone back there."

Near the river. Across it? In the section that had already been hit by raids once and left largely abandoned?

The place he'd described when Margot had needed a decoy target.

They pushed their way out the door, into the screaming night, just as one of the Gothas banked overhead.

33

The idiots! Das Gespenst stumbled his way out of the building, coughing until he could barely stand. Smoke billowed out after him, stinging his eyes as it burned his lungs. What had gone wrong this time? Were their pilots so incompetent they didn't know which side of the river to target? Did they not know right from left?

Or had he failed to convince the High Command he was useful? Were they trying — perhaps *again* — to eliminate him? How did they know where he'd be?

He tripped over something he couldn't see through the smoke, fell against the lamppost, and loosed a growl of pain when he landed on his hand. That blighted howitzer shell had crushed it. He had made himself probe it and had counted at least five breaks.

But a broken hand would not kill him. He was still on his feet, still breathing, more or less. He pushed away and turned toward the Thames, waiting to see the flames roar up from the factory.

More Gothas appeared. One, two. Three. Enough to finish the job. Elton would be inside now, trying to free his clever little sister, who had played the innocent so very well. She deserved credit for that last stunt. And he ought to have anticipated it. It was something Ilse would have done.

Even if they got out, they wouldn't get far enough. All those munitions would go up like the largest bomb in the land. There was no way they would escape its blast.

Except the Gothas were off course. They didn't veer left, toward Woolwich. They veered right. Toward him.

Biting off a curse, he forced breath into his lungs and ran.

Margot pulled her coat tighter around her and wished her hat covered her ears. One thing to be said for the crisp December night, though — it woke her up. And after the last thirty hours, she needed the jolt it gave her.

But she couldn't go home to her bed quite yet. That was impossible. She aimed herself instead toward Dot's flat, where they'd agreed, as Drake rushed out, that they would reconvene. She had to know they were safe, all of them. She had to see it with her own eyes. She had to hear them say they'd apprehended Regnitz. Then, perhaps, she could sleep.

She knew that to the east, sirens were likely still blaring. But here, on the opposite end of London, all was quiet. She'd heard a few reports coming in over the wireless before she left the OB. Enough to know that the German raid was over and damage had been minimal.

That meant the munitions factory had been spared. In that at least, they'd won.

Dot and the rest would be back soon, then. Wouldn't they? She had to believe they would be. She *would* believe it, cling to it.

The door to Dot's building opened with its usual squeak, and the dim lights of the entryway greeted her. No one else would be about at this hour.

Except, apparently, for the man sitting on the steps. Looking shorter than he was, hunched over. With a gun at his side pointing straight at her.

Her breath caught, went still inside her, and for the briefest of moments she wondered, *Why? Why didn't you warn me, Lord?*

But that wasn't the right question. That wasn't the question that led to life. That was the question that led to bitterness, to walls between her and her God.

She let the door fall shut behind her and met the eyes of Dieter Regnitz. And prayed He would give her the *right* question.

She didn't know if she'd found it. But she could think of only one thing to say as she looked at his blackened hand. Heard the rasp of his breath. And saw his face, pale as a ghost. She eased a step forward and held out her hands to show she had no weapon. "Why did you alter the game?"

The game. She meant Go, he assumed. The pieces he had put where he needed them. Das Gespenst tried to lift the gun, but his hand shook if he didn't keep his arm anchored to his body. And he wasn't nearly skilled enough at shooting left-handed anyway. He wouldn't be able to work the bolt to load another chamber — he'd have one shot, that was all. As he'd had one in the rifle he used to signal Elton. It had been enough then.

This would be enough now.

"It was necessary to prove my point. Do not move, Miss De Wilde. I will score at least one victory tonight — and this may in fact be the sweetest. It may not help the High Command to take out an Admiralty secretary, but it will provide my revenge. Elton loves you, does he not? It will hurt him more than death to lose you."

Her eyes darted to the left, toward the landlord's office. A ploy, no doubt, to distract him, so she could lunge. But he refused to take his eyes off her. Hands still held out, she dared to ease another step closer. "You're ill. And injured. What happened?"

The itching in his chest made it nearly impossible not to cough, but he couldn't give in to that. Not now. It was the smoke, or the pneumonia. But it wouldn't win. *He* would win. That was what mattered. "Do not pretend you care."

"Why do you assume I don't?" She paused and lifted her brows. "I learned long ago that being on opposite sides of a war didn't make a man my enemy. I don't wish you harm. I just wish you *stopped*."

No, she'd never been his enemy. Just his opponent. A clever one, deserving of respect. But cleverness wasn't enough. And respect didn't mean he could spare her. "You are out of moves. I told you that already. *Aji keshi*."

The corners of her lips actually turned up in a smile. "You had to cheat to be able to say that. It isn't true victory."

"It will have the same result." He had to anchor the gun with his side to be able to cock it.

"No. It won't."

He pulled the trigger, but she was already moving. Lunging to the side. Not away, but toward him. As she'd done on the street, when she'd stolen Der Vampir from him. He tried to yell, but it turned into a cough that made his whole body convulse.

And then the gun wasn't in his hand anymore and spots danced before his eyes, and instead of a knee finding his groin, an arm came around his shoulders.

"Would you get him water?"

He didn't know of whom she asked it, and he couldn't look up to see. The spasm kept his head down, his body curled forward into a useless mockery, his lungs on fire.

"Easy. Breathe, Dieter."

She knew his name. How did she know his name? "I will win." He could barely gasp it between spasms, but it had to be said. It had to *be*.

"You nearly did. And perhaps you could have outsmarted Drake. Outsmarted me — even though I'm *not* a secretary. But you cannot outsmart God."

Was it He who had struck him down? No. It was the damp and the cold and lungs already weakened by pneumonia from his near drowning. It was too many nights waiting in the park for her to make a play at Go and traveling all over the city in search of targets. It was the uncompromising commands of his superiors and his own need to see to retribution above himself.

Would he die? Here, now, of this wracking cough, with his hand black with bruising and his opponent's arm around him?

Had he thought he couldn't die? Or that it wouldn't matter if he did? Perhaps it didn't. He had no one to mourn him, not like they would mourn Heinrich. He had never been the hero in the stories.

If only he'd won, his death wouldn't have mattered. But he'd failed there too.

The hand patted his back, though it did nothing to help. "Drake didn't mean to shoot your brother."

He squeezed his eyes shut against the spots. And all he could see was Heinrich, lying in his arms, no light in his eyes. "Doesn't matter. He's dead." Gone. *Das Gespenst.* Elton had made the hero into a ghost. That never should have been Heinrich's role. His own, but not his brother's. Heinrich had something to live for. The war hadn't killed him already, like it had Dieter's spirit.

"I know he's dead. And I'm sorry."

He tried to look at her. To focus on the dark eyes that regarded him so intently even while a haze fell over his vision. Another cough convulsed him. "He has . . . to pay."

"He has." Her voice sounded distant now. Like an echo. "And he will. Forever. Some men may revel in killing in a war, but not Drake. He'll wrestle with this, with knowing the name and face of someone he killed. Knowing he took a brother and son — perhaps a husband and father? — from this world. He'll learn to live with it, but it will never go away." She paused, her hand steady on his back. "You must learn to live with it too."

No. There could be no life after this, knowing he hadn't saved his brother. There could only be roaming the earth like a ghost. Another spasm struck, another cough wracked him.

"Dear Lord," she whispered, but the words were different now. It took him a long, burning moment to realize why. To realize she was speaking in German. And that she sounded like his mother. "Put your hand on Dieter now. Please touch his lungs where the pneumonia has settled in and break them free. Four, eight, twelve, sixteen, twenty, twenty-four, twenty-eight . . ."

He tried to pull away, but the weight of her arm across his shoulders was too much. He tried to insist that he hadn't really wanted her prayers, but he couldn't force any more words from his throat. He tried to find one last move to steal the momentum.

But she was right. He'd had to cheat to make the last move he'd made — and still he'd lost. Another cough shook him. And the darkness won.

Drake rubbed a hand up the arm of Margot's coat, needing the assurance that she was still standing here, alive and talking, after Dieter Regnitz had passed out on that arm. After she'd held him like a friend until the authorities arrived, apparently. He could hardly believe it. Might not have, if Abuelo hadn't been shouting the same story in Spanish, incredulous, while Margot calmly recited it for the officers who had just hauled the man away. While they'd been driving madly back through London to make sure the villain hadn't escaped and come back here, she'd been holding him. Praying for him.

The police had already asked questions aplenty. But they hadn't asked his. He closed his eyes for a moment while he drew in a long breath. And then he rested his forehead against hers. "What would I have done if I'd lost you?"

Margot sighed. Her arms were folded across her middle. And her gaze was locked on the door that had closed behind the uninvited guest and his new escorts. The door that now had a bullet lodged in it. A bullet meant for her.

"He had no moves left to make. He'd already lost, the moment he fired that gun. He just couldn't see it yet. Couldn't see that he'd backed himself into a corner. *Aji keshi.*" Her eyes wandered back to his. And softened. "I felt sorry for him, Drake. If I were in his place, I may have done the same thing. Tried to fill the hole with vengeance, because it's just so gaping."

Always surprising him, this one. He smiled and pressed a kiss to her hair. "I'm not ashamed to say that all I feel about him right now is relief that he's in custody."

But still Margot frowned. "If they put him in prison, he'll probably die of pneumonia."

It was likely. "He has to go to prison, Margot. Those are the consequences for the actions he took. He killed people." So had Drake though. Was it different, that he hadn't meant to? That it had happened in action, in a time of war?

Dieter Regnitz obviously hadn't thought

that made it excusable. The English government certainly would say it did. There would be no imprisonment for Drake, no legal ramifications for Maxim Jaeger's — no, Heinrich Regnitz's — death. If anything, he'd get a commendation for a job well done.

But it didn't feel well done. He'd robbed a man of his brother, a mother of her child. He'd made holes in their lives, and it put one in his too. The government telling him it was right didn't make it feel so.

Margot touched a finger to his chin, making him look up and realize those dark eyes had been on him, a smile hovering on the corners of her mouth. "What are you most proud of, in how all this played out? What are you most grateful for?"

He knew what she was doing. The same thing he'd done with her, that first day in the corridor outside Hall's office. Asking the question that would get at the heart rather than the circumstances. The question that would reveal who a person was far more than their name ever would.

And the answer here was easy. "You and Dot — to both." He'd always thought, he supposed, that his role was to be the one in the action. Saving them when necessary. Rushing in, defending, dodging the bullets.

But they'd done a rather fine job of seeing to things themselves.

At her name, his sister stood from the chair she'd taken in the landlord's office — where their grandfather had apparently set up his base of operations. She moved to the doorway, where Abuelo stood.

He received her with a proud smile and an arm around her shoulders. "Ah, yes. Our girl is a brave one. I am proud of you, Dorothea."

She offered him a tired smile, but she shook her head. "I still don't understand what you're doing here, Abuelo. In England. Why didn't you just send word of what you'd found? You've never come before, even when Mama died."

Abuelo lifted his dark brows, as if the answer should have been obvious. "Because my coming would have done nothing then. Changed nothing. She was gone already, God rest her soul, and you scarcely knew me then, for my presence to bring any comfort. You had your father, your friends. But now, this — my coming could change everything. Why would I not do it, when it meant life for my grandchildren?"

"Well then." Looking exhausted and disheveled, but steady, Dot offered another weary smile. "Perhaps you'll stay long enough to come to my wedding." Then the smile wobbled and she straightened, shifting a bit until she could look at Margot. "I'm sorry. For what I said earlier. I wasn't —"

"It's forgiven, Dot. Forgotten." Margot held out a hand, and his sister sidled past Abuelo so she could take it in her own. "I'm happy you're getting married. I just didn't want you to do it out of fear."

"I know. But I'm not. Perhaps yesterday I was, but . . . but I'm not. Though it must be asked . . ." Dot looked from Margot to Drake and back again. "If you could argue that I should wait a bit because it wouldn't change my love, isn't the opposite true too? How long do you really have to wait when you know God put you together for a reason?"

A good question, to be sure. But Drake already knew the answer to that one. "As long as it takes."

They smiled at him — Dot with indulgence, Margot with gratitude — and then turned together for the stairs. "You can have Aunt Millie's bed tonight, Margot. Drake will have to go to Abuelo's hotel with him. He won't mind, will you, Drake? And Red can . . ."

Drake shook his head as the two women

588

continued up the stairs without a backward look to make sure he'd agreed with the arrangements.

Red slapped a hand to his shoulder. "I'm off for home, then, I suppose. It was good serving with you today, Elton."

"Agreed. I can think of no one I'd rather have beside me in this war." Well, and Camden. But no need to bring him up just now, since he'd already left after seeing everyone had survived the night.

Red turned then to Abuelo. Shoulders straight, chin up, confidence in his eyes that certainly hadn't been there a few weeks ago. "I look forward to getting to know you better while you're here, sir."

Abuelo shook his hand, not so much as a twitch in his countenance to show any unease at the thought of being away from the home that had long been his fort. "Indeed, young man. The very words I was thinking."

With a lopsided grin, Red nodded and turned toward the door.

Drake waited for it to shut behind him before he turned to his grandfather. He wasn't sure where Eneko had vanished to — probably to the hotel on the next street, where they'd reserved rooms. Where apparently Drake would be sleeping tonight too.

But he was grateful for a few minutes of solitude with Abuelo. He owed him an explanation.

Abuelo was already turning back into the office, knowing well Drake would follow. He sat down in the pathetic little chair behind the desk and looked as proud and regal as he always did in his own.

Drake sat across from him. "I didn't leave the navy, as I told you I did."

"So I gathered." Was that a twitch in his lips? The beginnings of a smile perhaps? "And frankly, I could never fathom that you would. You were never a coward, Dragón. Many things, but never that. You are an intelligence agent now?"

He couldn't admit it to just anyone. But no one knew how to juggle trade secrets quite like Francisco Mendoza de Haro. He nodded.

"That makes infinitely more sense than any other explanation. And I am, of course, happy to continue offering my humble abode as your base of operations. On one condition." He leaned forward, eyes gleaming. "Tell me about this Margot De Wilde, whom you look at as though she is the only young lady in the world."

Drake couldn't have stopped his grin had he wanted to. "I believe you saw her at her finest today, Abuelo. She is without equal. Brave. Brilliant. She views the world as no one else."

"Yes, this I saw for myself. But will she make a good wife to you? Give you strong children to carry on your name?"

The smile faltered a bit. "She . . . is a bit unconventional in that regard. She has dreams. Dreams she's afraid she'll have to forsake if she chooses to marry and have children."

"Nonsense." As if that single word was all the answer that was needed, Abuelo waved a hand. "Unconventional may be just what this world needs to recover from the tragedy that has beset it. And dreams . . . dreams are only worth pursuing when we have the right person by our side, sí? And the right person is the one who encourages. Who chases the dream along with you. As your mother and your father did for each other." Abuelo lowered his hand to the desk with a decisive *thud.* "You will convince her of this. You will take life as it comes, as God wills. And you will be happy together."

Drake's smile grew again. He wasn't sure if it was a prophecy or a command, but either way, he was happy to obey.

EPILOGUE

Margot held the umbrella aloft and ran more than she walked toward her flat. There was snow mixed in with the rain, proving that February had some teeth to it. And after another night shift, she was more than looking forward to a hot cup of tea, her clanking radiator, and maybe a not-warm-enough bath before she went to bed. Later, she'd write to Drake. And perhaps make another trip to the Tower of London to visit Dieter. He never said much — and his health didn't seem to be improving.

But she would visit anyway. She had to think that somewhere in Germany, there was a mother who would be glad of it. Glad to know her son wasn't altogether alone in enemy territory. And in her mind, Maman smiled down on her for it.

She darted into her building while the older gent from 4C held the door open for her on his way out, thanking him with a smile as she lowered her brolly.

"There's a parcel at your door, Margot," he said. "Too big for your box, I suppose. Delivered yesterday afternoon — I've kept an eye on it for you."

"Good of you, Mr. Parsons. Thank you." She gathered the post from her box and jogged up the stairs as she flipped through it. A bill. A postcard from the Cotswolds, where Dot and Holmes had gone for their honeymoon, courtesy of the Duchess of Stafford. And a letter in a script that made her heart race more than the stairs accounted for.

She ripped that one open as she reached her floor. Drake had been writing to her nearly every day since he'd been sent back to Spain, but rarely did the letters reach her one at a time. They tended to arrive in weekly batches, and she'd just had a batch two days ago.

But she wasn't about to complain about an extra. She pulled out the sheet, grinning when she saw the paper wasn't filled with words, but with numbers. Lowering the page, she caught sight of the decidedly book-shaped parcel waiting at her door.

A moment later, she'd juggled the brolly, the book, and her other post through the door and into their respective places. She unpinned her hat, shrugged out of her coat, and smoothed a hand over the cardigan Maman had given her.

Then she unwrapped the package and grinned. *Don Quixote,* as he'd promised.

He probably wouldn't say anything in this coded letter that he didn't say, now, in his normal ones. And she'd rather gotten the hang of writing sweet letters back too. She hoped, anyway. She tried. Perhaps her lines were filled more with mathematics than with poetry, but it was all the same thing in the end, wasn't it?

Though she hadn't yet mustered the courage to say what she knew she would when next she saw him face-to-face. That God had shown her, these last few months, that He could be trusted. Not just with her well-being, but with her dreams. She could trust that He had given her this love for Drake for His own purpose, but that it didn't negate the other gifts He'd breathed into her. Loving him didn't mean losing herself. Marrying him someday, creating a family with him, didn't have to mean forsaking her dreams. Somehow, He could make possible what the world said wasn't. Somehow, he would fill her with the love a family would demand — as He always had, for her parents and Lukas and Willa, for Willa's family and little Zurie.

Deciding that tea and a bath could wait, she grabbed paper and a pencil and then sat down with the book. It didn't take long for the message to take shape. It started out as they usually did, lovely and sure to haunt her. But it was the ending that made her pause and read it again, and then a third time.

I want forever with you. I will wait a year, a decade, a century to make you my wife. But tell me you'll take me someday, my love. Tell me that the promise of forever can begin now.

She let the pencil clatter to the table and leaned back in her chair, holding the page before her.

"Well? I can wait for an answer, too, but I do have this ring my grandfather gave me. . . ."

"Drake!" She shrieked his name, nearly falling out of her chair in her rush to turn and stand all at once.

He'd been standing, apparently, in the doorway to Maman's room, which Lukas had just helped her turn into an office. And he was smiling at her. Looking at her in that way he did. Loving her in that way he did, that never demanded anything.

The way that deserved so much. The too-still took hold of her, held for five seconds, ten. But then she forced it away. Forced motion into her limbs, because he was here. He was here, and she owed him an epiphany. She flew across the space between them until she could wrap him in her arms. "What are you doing here? You're supposed to be in Spain."

"Charles the Bold sent me home with a few sensitive items he didn't trust to regular transport. And perhaps because he knew I'd been missing you." His hand found its place on her cheek. "And Dot had a key to your flat. Mr. Parsons kept an eye on me, though, since I arrived."

She laughed and held him close. All the closer because she knew she'd have to let him go again soon. At least for a while. Until the war was over. "How long are you here?"

"Just two days." He grinned and pressed a quick, teasing kiss to her lips. "So if you mean to answer me before I go . . ."

"I can answer you now." And how perfect, that he had shown up again after she'd wrestled her faith back into line on this question too. "Yes. I'll marry you. Whenever you want me to."

His smile hitched. "Whenever? But you have your dreams."

"I do." She strained up on her toes to steal another kiss. "But as a wise man once said, what's so ridiculous about having someone to support and encourage you through the ups and downs of life? I don't want any dreams that don't include you. And I trust — I trust that God will give us His best."

"Mi alma." His eyes slid shut, and he rested his forehead against hers.

She let hers slide shut, too, and held him tight. "Eighteen."

A NOTE FROM THE AUTHOR

Ever since I began doing research on England during the Great War, I knew I wanted to tell the story of the amazing men and women who made up Room 40, the intelligence hub of the Admiralty. This secretive department revolutionized the intelligence game and laid the groundwork for the better-known agencies of World War II and beyond — Bletchley Park, MI6, and so on. And yet, in many ways, the organization of Room 40 would have been completely unfathomable to people in intelligence today. Built more on complete trust and instinct than compartmentalization, Room 40 was in many ways a family, which is what intrigued me every bit as much as the work they did.

As always, I'd like to take a few minutes to differentiate between fact and fiction in my stories. Many of the plot elements are drawn straight from history, though, of course, I fictionalized the players and attributed them to Drake and Margot rather than the actual historical figures who did them, some of whose names cannot be found now, thanks to documentation being destroyed after the war. For instance, the wolfram really was discovered in the warehouse in Bilbao when an agent claimed he was chasing a guide dog inside. By 1917, Gotha and zeppelin air raids over London had become quite common, and though destruction was minimal by World War II standards, it was nevertheless terrifying for the city's occupants, who were still adjusting to the idea of danger coming from the skies. The raid at the end of my book is fictionalized, but it draws on the documented history of other similar raids. Other incidents like Hall sending a false "all mines have been cleared" message to the German minelayers did happen, though the dates have been tweaked slightly, as were a few others in regards to the *Erri Barro* and the U-boats caught skimming over their anti-sub nets, so as to fit neatly in my narrative. A codebook really was recovered from a zeppelin that crashed when its pilots suffered altitude sickness, though it happened a few months earlier than I said. And Hall truly did have his codebreakers create a fake

"Emergency Code" that he deliberately put into enemy hands — sold it to the enemy, in fact, for five hundred pounds, though he never sent a message in it for them to "intercept." I thought it would be fun to include the code briefly in my story though.

One of the greatest challenges of those who ran Room 40 was finding ways to preserve their secrecy and yet still give their leaders the information they needed to make the war go in their favor. Their decisions were constantly based on whether sharing certain information would reveal their hand to the Germans. And so, though they knew about nearly all attacks and raids before they happened, they couldn't always do anything about it. They had to first have a cover story for how they could have found it out . . . which is why Admiral Hall frequently used the identities of German agents he'd arrested to send misinformation to Germany.

One of *my* big challenges in writing this — aside from a heroine who thinks in numbers when I most assuredly do not — was trying to find specifics for an organization that went to such pains to be shrouded in secrecy. Most original documents were destroyed, including Admiral Hall's autobiography, when the government deemed it too sensitive to be released to the public. Even after the Second World War, German officials still had no idea that there were codebreakers in the 1910s who were reading their every communication. It wasn't until recently, when documents began to be declassified, that historians have begun putting the pieces back together to get a view of the amazing work that Room 40 did during the Great War.

Of course, my method of interpreting history is through the eyes of fictional characters, who allow me to focus on a few facts. Margot and Drake were so much fun to get to know . . . and to lead on a journey to the heart. I hope you enjoyed their story as much as I did! And if you haven't read it yet, you can see how Margot ended up in England in *A Song Unheard,* which is Lukas and Willa's love story.

I'd also like to take a moment to thank the people who come alongside me during the writing process and remind me that, yes, I can do this. Thank you, Stephanie, for reading my early chapters and pointing out that my characters should actually *like* each other (duh). And to my husband, David, for brainstorming Das Gespenst with me and insisting that his ideas were better than mine (which they were!). Thanks to Sascha, my foreign-exchange-student brother, for not only telling me which German word for "the ghost" I should use, but also how to pronounce and hyphenate it. My kids deserve some major kudos for bearing with me through a crazy writing season, and I'm pretty sure I would have wept in frustration more than once if not for my awesome virtual assistant, Rachel Dixon, who keeps the rest of my professional world running smoothly so I can concentrate on writing.

Next, huge thanks to my expert readers who went through the manuscript for me to check for accuracy on certain subjects: Rhonda, who answered all my questions about Catholic traditions and could discuss Margot's actions and reactions with me; Elizabeth, who, as always, read an early version to make sure no Americanisms slip into my English characters; Wendy, for checking my French; and Justin, for checking my Spanish.

And, of course, the amazing team at Bethany House! You guys always leave me in awe of your talent and skill at your jobs!

I hope you'll travel with me into the final year of the war through the rest of THE CODEBREAKERS! Our next story will follow the troubled Phillip Camden into some new adventures and give readers a glimpse of some well-loved characters as well.

DISCUSSION QUESTIONS

1. Margot has a unique way of seeing the world through numbers. What did you think of how she viewed and interpreted everything around her? How she interacted with people? Do you have a way of seeing the world through a unique lens that differs from those closest to you?

2. Drake always knows the right questions to ask. Were there any that struck you as being insightful? Odd? Do you ever have a hard time asking the right questions either to open conversation or lead you to the answers you seek?

3. Margot had dreams and goals that went against cultural norms and were sure to create challenges for her in the future. What did you think of her aspirations and her hesitations toward love and romance? Were her concerns justified? What did you

think of Drake's response?

4. What did you think of our "ghost" characters, Das Gespenst and Yūrei? Though Das Gespenst was the villain, did you understand him and his decisions? Did you anticipate the twist about Jaeger?

5. One of Margot's greatest struggles in the book is what to do when God goes silent. Have you ever been in a place of grief or pain when you couldn't sense the Lord? What did you do and how did you move beyond that?

6. Margot and Drake have a unique bond in that God asked her to pray for him anonymously. Have you ever been asked to pray for either a stranger or someone you don't know well? Did you discover why at a later time?

7. Before reading this book, were you aware of the goings-on of Room 40 during World War I? What do you think of the world of cryptography, the decisions they had to make, and the secrecy that was so important to them? Would you have flourished or floundered there?

8. Many of the secondary characters — Abuelo, Dot, Camden, Red — have "issues." Did you find these compelling or off-putting? Did any one of these characters interest you more than another? Of all characters, main and secondary, who was your favorite and why? Your least favorite?

9. There are two ways to think about the question of "Why did this happen?" when tragedy enters our lives: "Why did God let it happen?" versus "What will God do with it?" What did you think of Margot's epiphany about these two interpretations? Have you ever struggled with shifting your focus between the two?

10. Looking ahead, what do you expect to see and what do you *want* to see in the next book, which features Phillip Camden? Historically, we know that the war ends a year after *The Number of Love*. What do you think life will look like then for Margot and Drake and their friends and family?

ABOUT THE AUTHOR

Roseanna M. White is a bestselling, Christy Award–nominated author who has long claimed that words are the air she breathes. When not writing fiction, she's homeschooling her two kids, designing book covers, editing, and pretending her house will clean itself. Roseanna is the author of a slew of historical novels that span several continents and thousands of years. Spies and war and mayhem always seem to find their way into her books . . . to offset her real life, which is blessedly ordinary. You can learn more about her and her stories at www.roseannamwhite.com.